D0252941

THE ELEMENTIA CHRONICLES

BOOK THREE:
HEROBRINE'S MESSAGE

by SEAN FAY WOLFE

HARPER
An Imprint of HarperCollinsPublishers

To my mentor,
Kyoshi Chick Gavitt
(1967–2015)
With great respect
どもありがとうございました

The Elementia Chronicles Book 3: Herobrine's Message
Copyright © 2016 by Sean Fay Wolfe
All rights reserved. Printed in the United States of America.
No part of this book may be used or reproduced in any manner whatsoever without written
permission except in the case of brief quotations embodied in critical articles and reviews.
For information address HarperCollins Children's Books, a division of HarperCollins Publishers,
195 Broadway, New York, NY 10007.
www.harpercollinschildrens.com

Library of Congress Control Number: 2015955155
ISBN 978 0 06 241636 0

Book design by Victor Joseph Ochoa
15 16 17 18 19 CG/OPM 10 9 8 7 6 5 4 3 2 1
❖
First Edition

"Everyone sees what you appear to be. Few experience what you really are."

—Niccolò Machiavelli

CONTENTS

A faint breeze blew through the Great Wood, rustling the leaves of the blocky trees that ringed a small, unassuming knoll. It had been months since Stan2012, so new to the world of Minecraft, had stood at the precipice of Spawnpoint Hill, in awe of the cubic world around him. By all accounts, very little had changed since then. The trees still stood tall, dark, and ominous. The hill was still dotted with patches of overgrown grass, and the occasional patch of red and yellow flowers. The squared-off brook still trickled lazily down the hill, passing by the opening to a bottomless ravine.

However, the server was now drastically different from when Stan had first entered it. On this day, the sky was a dull gray, and the air was charged with the onset of a storm. A roll of thunder crashed in the distance. A light drizzle of rain began to fall as the gentle gusts of wind shook the boughs of the leaf blocks in the trees. The midday sun was unable to shine through the clouds above, and the sky cast barely enough light to see.

Then, all at once, a figure appeared on top of the hill.

A streak of lightning crackled in the distance, illuminating the figure for a split second. The figure held nothing in his pale, blocky hands. He wore navy-blue pants and dark-brown shoes, while the upper half of his body was covered by a black cloak. The covering extended upward over his head, obscuring his face from view.

This figure was known by many names. One of them was the Black Hood.

The Black Hood took a deep breath, then slowly let it out. He held out his blocky hand and opened it, allowing the rain to cascade over his outstretched palm. He relished the feeling as all his senses slowly came to life and he, once again, felt the sheer wonder of existing in the realm of Minecraft.

Oh, yes, the Black Hood thought, euphoria spreading throughout his entire body. *It has been far too long since I have been in this game. I had forgotten just how it feels. It is so good to be back.*

The Black Hood looked around. Spawnpoint Hill was completely deserted. The Black Hood was relieved as he hastily jogged down the hill and into the forest, taking refuge from the light rain. After all, he was *not* supposed to be here. If anybody found out about him, the Black Hood's life could be compromised.

The Black Hood sighed again, this time with determination. There was a reason that he had come to this server called Elementia. Though he had vowed to never again return to Minecraft after his last experience, the Black Hood knew that this particular server was in a state of horrible unbalance. A great evil had risen here, manifested in a power of untold strength. If this power should win the war now being fought, far more than the server would be destroyed. It might very well pose a danger to the game of Minecraft itself.

The Black Hood knew what he must do. Although this unspeakable evil had spread throughout Elementia, a glimmer of hope still shone. Element City, the stronghold of justice and the spirit of rebellion in the world, was still alive, however weakened it may be. *And as long as Element City remains standing,* the Black Hood mused to himself, *so too was there a chance that the people within may be reunited with the one single player who had the ability to lead them to victory over the great evil once and for all.*

I must move quickly, the Black Hood thought urgently. *Although Element City will never stop fighting the invading forces of the Noctem Alliance, there will inevitably come a time when fighting is futile. And if that time comes before I can reach him* . . . The Black Hood glanced down at his pale, blocky hand. It was imperative that he achieve his goals unseen, which may necessitate that he kill any witnesses he encountered. He would need a weapon to swiftly and inconspicuously dispose of anyone unfortunate enough to cross his path. With all his willpower, the Black Hood concentrated on his hand. He imagined the feeling of a diamond sword clutched tightly in his grasp, equipped with the highest of Sharpness enchantments. In a few seconds, the Black Hood could feel the hilt of a sword clutched in his hands, although it was not yet visible. He continued to concentrate.

Just a bit more . . . he thought. *Almost done . . .*

Then, just as the turquoise sword was materializing, there was a crash of thunder and a bolt of lightning lit up the sky, striking near the Black Hood. The explosion on the ground launched the Black Hood backward, through the air, and he came crashing to the dirt-block ground.

Wincing, the Black Hood opened his eyes. He had lost all concentration, and the diamond sword was nowhere to be seen.

Suddenly, another boom of thunder, louder than the last, screamed above him as the sky broke and rain came pouring down. The Black Hood whipped his head upward.

This can't just be a coincidence, the Black Hood realized frantically. *He must know that I am here.*

This thought was followed by an earsplitting boom of thunder that reverberated through the forest. And in the midst of the sound, the Black Hood heard a very distinct voice ring out, not from anywhere in this world, but from within his own mind.

REMEMBER MY LAST.

The Black Hood lay sprawled on his back on the ground,

petrified. He remained that way for a full minute, heart racing and breathing rapidly. However, when no more thunderclaps sounded throughout the sky, the Black Hood finally allowed himself to take a deep breath. Baffled, he looked up at the sky yet again.

What are you trying to tell me? he thought as hard as he could, deeply troubled and puzzled.

There was no reply, from either within or beyond the Black Hood's mind. The only sound that resonated throughout the area was the constant patter of the downpour.

Hmmm . . . This is most interesting . . . the Black Hood thought, intrigued. *Could it possibly be . . . that I cannot use my true power? Is that what you want?*

The Black Hood waited anxiously for a full minute, hoping for a reply that never came. The Black Hood sighed.

Well, he knows that I am here now. This thought unnerved him quite a bit, as he realized the implications that came with this fact. He was now under the constant surveillance and scrutiny of something that had the ability to destroy him at a moment's notice. The Black Hood was surprised that his presence had even been detected, yet he was even more surprised that he had not been destroyed because of it.

I suppose, the Black Hood thought, *that I am safe . . . for now at least. If he knows that I am here, but hasn't yet destroyed me . . . I wonder what else I can get away with. I shall have to experiment with this more as I continue on my mission. As of now, however . . . it's probably for the best to play it safe.*

The Black Hood glanced longingly at his hand. It would have been so simple if he could create his own diamond sword. However, it appeared that was one of the things he was not allowed to do; he supposed he would have to return to the basics.

The Black Hood pulled himself up off the ground, and walked over to the nearest tree. He drew back his fist and sunk it as hard as he could into the wood-block trunk of the tree. Through the dim light of the rainstorm, the Black Hood noticed a small crack appear in the center of the block, and he continued to throw punch after punch into the block of wood.

Look at me, the Black Hood thought to himself with an amused chuckle. *Gathering wood by hand, just like a new player!*

It wasn't long before the Black Hood had punched enough wood blocks to gather what he needed. It didn't take him long to convert the wooden blocks into planks, and the planks into a crafting table. Minutes later, he pulled a wooden pick-axe off the table.

The Black Hood smiled. This tool would suffice until he found time to invest in the creation of better materials. Now, however, time was short. The longer he waited, the further the Noctem Alliance crept toward victory. And if he failed to act, all would be lost.

And so, pickaxe grasped in hand and a resolve of steel in his mind, the Black Hood turned to the west and began to walk, disappearing into the fog.

1: THE MISSIONS BEGIN

It was high noon in the Far Western Desert. The sun shone bright overhead in the crisp blue sky, beating down on the heat-baked sand blocks. Two- or three-block-high cacti sprouted up from the tan earth and speckled the dusty landscape with green, while a few odd Creepers and Spiders wandered aimlessly across the barren wasteland. The endless dune sea was nearly as vast as the Ender Desert, and was far less traveled in this day and age. At any given time, the Far Western Desert contained just a few players, and they rarely stayed there for long.

The average player on the Minecraft server Elementia would find it foolish to venture into the Far Western Desert at all. There was hardly anything to be gained from it and everything to lose in the hot desert sun. However, if a player were to make the long trek across thousands of blocks of sand, into the very epicenter of the desert, he or she would find a small cluster of buildings. The houses were centered around a gravel network of roads and constructed of wood planks, clearly indicating that, at one point in the distant past, this town with no name had been filled with NPC villagers.

No villagers were left now.

Instead, this hollow shell of a village had been

populated by players, though they were not the type that anyone would want to run into. These players bore various scars across their skins, and would snarl and crack their knuckles menacingly should you be so unfortunate as to catch their eye. This was the type of town where an accusation over stolen iron or diamonds would start a fight that only one would walk away from.

And there were a lot of diamonds and iron to fight over. Countless valuable items passed through this trading post of the desert in exchange for services of the underhanded sort, which the residents of the town were happy to provide. Just like the materials, though, the residents of this town never stayed there for long. This was the place to go if you needed a job done discreetly, so it was not a place where you wanted to be caught.

This particular day started off typically. The sun shined hot, and there had already been various fits of bare-knuckle brawling among the players who were in the town.

When the sun was at its zenith in the sky, a figure appeared on the horizon. As the others went about their daily business, the player slowly approached the town. And as he walked down the dusty gravel road, more and more of the ruffian inhabitants of the village seemed to be giving him a steely glance out of the corner of their eyes. He hardly noticed; he was sure that this desert wasteland had never seen a player as important as he before.

The player was dressed in black pants and a black shirt, with a golden cloak draped over his head, flowing like a shimmering waterfall onto his upper body. His striking skin was hard to ignore as he briskly turned and headed into a large building on the main road.

This building, which had once been the village library, had been gutted, the inside library furnishings replaced by tables and chairs. These were occupied by players laughing and shouting in raucous fashion, gulping bottles of QPO and SloPo as they did so. A long stretch of wood blocks created a counter that ran the length of the building. From behind this wooden strip, the bartender shouted out, asking if the golden-hooded figure would care for a drink. The figure gave no reply, simply waving his hand in rejection. After all, he was about to attend a meeting of the utmost importance to the cause of the Noctem Alliance. His mind could not be clouded by potion.

As the figure looked around for his contact, he was momentarily distracted by the taunts, jeers, and general cacophony of a fight breaking out in the corner of the bar. The figure allowed himself a moment to watch as two thuggish brutes in tattered clothes locked their pickaxes. Soon an explosion of cheers erupted from the corner as one of the players slumped to the ground beside his pickaxe, and the crowd scrambled to collect his dropped items for themselves. The figure was slightly irritated by the noise, but he knew that it was by no means a bad thing—quite the contrary, actually. This was the perfect place to go if you didn't wish to be overheard.

As the rumble of the fight died down, the figure once again looked around the bar for his contact. It took a few passes before he finally locked eyes with a lone player, sitting across from an empty seat at a table amid the ruckus. This player was dressed in a relatively common skin, bearing the same body coloring as a spider. However, of the many eyes on the player's face, only the two largest ones had a distinctly human trait to them.

The golden-hooded figure walked over and sat down across from the player. He wasted no time in speaking.

"I've heard a lot about you. They say you're good at what you do."

The spider-player smiled. "And I heard that you might show your face around here again. Count Drake, I presume?"

The gold-hooded figure faltered for a moment, but only slightly. He was nearly positive that this was the player he was looking for, but he had to be sure without a doubt.

"I go by General Drake now, actually," Drake responded evenly.

The spider-player held her poker face; Drake couldn't

read her in the slightest. He knew that the time had come, and he reached into the folds of his shawl. From there, he produced an item, the head of a Creeper. He only showed it to the spider-player for a moment before immediately returning it to his inventory. Drake then glanced at the spider-player expectantly.

With her face still locked into a steely gaze, the spider-player reached under the table. Drake focused intently on her hand, and watched as she produced her own Creeper head for a moment before returning it to her inventory.

Instantly, the aura of tension at the table relaxed, and both players smiled. The two old friends had each revealed the unique items they had given each other the last time they had met, and both now knew they could talk freely.

"It's good to see you again, Arachnia," Drake said. Then he smirked. "From what I heard, you've been pretty busy since I left."

"You might say that," the spider-player replied, amused. "I have to say, Drake, it's good to see you too. It's been a long time. So, you're a general now, huh?"

"Sure am," Drake said.

"And am I to assume that this is a position you obtained somewhere other than under the command of President Stan?" Arachnia asked with a smirk.

Drake chuckled. "Oh, don't patronize me. You know perfectly well what I think of the *illustrious* Stan2012." His voice was dripping with oily cynicism. "No, I'm now a general of the Noctem Alliance."

"Really," said Arachnia, raising an eyebrow slightly. "You don't mean that little protesters group that somehow managed to take over the entire server?"

"That's the one," Drake replied, nodding. "I assume that you know what has happened in the Elementia mainland over the past month."

"Of course I do, Drake. You of all people should know just how much information passes through this settlement," Arachnia murmured darkly. "Although I have to admit, it never did come to my attention that *you* were the one in charge of leading the Noctem Alliance to victory."

Drake looked humble. "Well, I helped, but to be honest, I was just following orders. All the people who truly led the takeover are dead now, and Lord Tenebris appointed me and a few of my colleagues in their places."

"Lord Tenebris . . . I assume that he's the leader of the Noctem Alliance?" Arachnia asked.

A ray of zealous awe crossed Drake's face at this question, causing Arachnia to raise an eyebrow again as Drake replied.

"Oh, he is *far* more than that, my friend. I would say more, but trust me, you'll know soon enough."

Arachnia laughed. "I'll take your word for it. So, what

brings you out here, Drake? Surely an all-powerful general of the ruling organization of Elementia must have a good reason for trekking out into the middle of nowhere."

"As a matter of fact, I do," replied Drake seriously. The pleasantries were over, and it was time to get down to business. "First, let me ask you this . . . do you still have the other members of ELM together?"

"Yes," Arachnia said with a grin. "And we're still the best bounty hunters in all of Minecraft. Why? Do you need us for something?"

"That I do. Actually, it has to do with the Alliance," whispered Drake. He glanced around, making sure that nobody in the rambunctious bar was listening before he leaned in closer to Arachnia and continued.

"In the midst of our campaign to conquer Elementia, the Noctem Alliance managed to capture President Stan2012, and a few of his councilmen as well . . ."

"NO!" Arachnia burst out, unable to contain herself.

"*Shut up!*" hissed Drake, glancing around at several nearby patrons who had given them a sideways glance. "If you don't keep quiet, then the deal is off!"

"Sorry," replied Arachnia hastily. She knew from Drake's tone that this mission of his, whatever it was, was important. And, in her experience, importance equated to quite a large payment.

"Anyway," continued Drake when he was sure it was safe, "it was my job to oversee their prison. Unfortunately, one of Stan's friends sacrificed himself so that Stan could escape. The Noctem Alliance is well on its way to breaking through the walls of Element City and destroying the last of the republic's armies. However, Lord Tenebris is convinced that if President Stan somehow manages to return to the city, he will rally his citizens and turn the tide of the war back in his favor."

"So . . . what you're saying is . . . ," Arachnia replied slowly, heart racing as she pieced together what Drake was saying, " . . . you want me to hunt down and assassinate the president of Elementia?"

"Not exactly," replied Drake evenly. "For some reason, Lord Tenebris is dead set on killing Stan himself. To be honest, I'm not sure why, but I do trust Lord Tenebris, and I'm sure that he has a perfectly valid reason. Therefore, I'm asking you, Arachnia, to capture President Stan and return him to Lord Tenebris alive."

"Well . . . ," replied Arachnia after a moment, trying to appear uninterested despite the fact that she was in utter awe of what Drake was requesting. "This sounds like it's going to be quite a difficult mission, Drake. If you have no idea where Stan is and no way of finding him, that is . . . and I think that you know as well as I do that no team would be capable of it other than mine."

"That *is* why I came to you," Drake said rather impatiently. He had been expecting her to accept without question.

"And . . . because of that . . . I think you'll understand where I'm coming from when I say that the price of pulling this off will not be small," Arachnia said in a rather sleazy fashion.

Drake didn't hesitate. He reached into the folds of his cloak and pulled out something from his inventory. He revealed it only for a moment before returning it, but it was enough time for Arachnia to see the full stack of sixty-four diamond blocks in Drake's hand.

"I assure you that payment is no problem," Drake said simply.

Arachnia was breathing heavily with excitement now. This was it. She and her team were about to pull off the biggest job in the history of Minecraft, and become rich beyond their wildest dreams.

"General Drake," said Arachnia with a smile, "I'm happy to announce that you now have a team."

Drake grinned deviously. "I knew I could count on you, Arachnia. Now, assemble your team, and head to the mainland as soon as possible. President Stan is likely trekking back toward Element City as we speak, so you must make haste. Take the train line to the western wall of Element City. There, you will find one of the legions of the Noctem Army, which has laid siege to the city. They will give you all the information we have gathered regarding where President Stan may be, and then you may begin your search."

"Whatever you say, Drake," replied Arachnia.

"And remember, Arachnia . . . President Stan is not to be underestimated. Keep in mind that this is the player who bested King Kev in combat. He's an exceptional fighter, very smart and very crafty. The last thing that we need is for him to return and lead his city once again. The fate of the Noctem Alliance may very well rest in the hands of your team, Arachnia."

"Don't worry, Drake," answered Arachnia, her face showing exhilaration and a hint of bloodlust. "Stan is as good as yours."

Drake nodded one final time, and stood up from his chair. Without giving Arachnia one more glance, he pulled his golden hood up over his head, made his way through the rabble of drunken players, and left the bar.

All five players sitting around the dimly lit council table in the stone-brick castle were silent except for the Mechanist, who was in the process of the ceremonial roll call and other formalities. Although Element Castle was a good distance away from the outer walls of Element City, the cacophony of the bombardment of the outer wall could be heard throughout the city, day and night. This council meeting was no exception, as the muffled booms of detonating TNT blocks could be heard even through the stone walls.

These sounds of the Noctem Alliance's barrage of artillery only heightened the tension in the room. Out of the nine council members, three of them—Stan, Charlie, and DZ—had been taken hostage in their raid of the Noctem Alliance's Specialty Base. Another one, Blackraven, had been revealed as a traitor who had been working for the Noctem Alliance the entire time. And yet only four players sat around the council room table now.

They had lost someone else.

As the Mechanist finished with the formalities, he put down his papers and glanced around the table with exhausted eyes. In the faces of Kat, Jayden, and G, there was no sign of sadness or grief, but rather of unkempt and wild hatred, driven by a passion that can only be wrought by the deepest sort of betrayal. Giving a soft and brief sigh, the Mechanist began his speech.

"As you know," the Mechanist said tiredly, his Texas accent slightly slurred with fatigue, "a most tragic and unfortunate event has befallen us in the past twenty-four hours. . . ."

"Huh, unfortunate . . . yeah, *right*."

"Please, Kat," replied the Mechanist, far too spent to deal with her sarcasm at the moment. "Protocol dictates that I, as interim leader of the council in President Stan's absence, recount what happened so that it goes on record."

Nobody protested. They were so furious that they were happy to hear it again to have another opportunity to relish in the cowardice and detestability of what had happened.

"Yesterday afternoon," started the Mechanist, "all members of this council were called by myself, Mecha11, to this council room to report on how the defense of our outer walls was going. Kat, G, Jayden, and I all returned as planned. However, we soon realized that Gobbleguy was missing."

There was a shudder of contempt around the room as the Mechanist spoke that name.

"With the help of the police chiefs, we searched the city, and we weren't able to find him. However, in Gobbleguy's bedroom, Ben discovered a book that he had written. In it,

Gobbleguy said that he was leaving Elementia forever, and going to play Minecraft on other servers. He then proceeded to explain, in probably the most passive and nonconfrontational way I've ever heard, that he couldn't take the pressures of being on the council anymore. He said that it was, and I quote, 'far too much stress and effort to put into a lousy Minecraft server.' Because of his desertion, the police chiefs have charged Gobbleguy with treason, and have a warrant out for his arrest should he ever return to Elementia."

As the Mechanist finished his recap, nobody had anything to say. All they could do was stew in their misery and despise the deserter. It was bad enough that Blackraven had turned out to be a traitor to the council and had been working as a double agent for the Alliance the entire time. It was even worse that his treachery had caused Stan, Charlie, and DZ to be captured, leaving the five of them left on the council to wonder if their three friends were even still alive. And now, as one last kick to the emotional stomach of the council, one of their own members had up and left them for no reason other than his own weakness.

"Good riddance, I say," spat Kat in disgust.

"I agree," replied Jayden, his brow knit in scorn. "If Gobbleguy wants to be a selfish little jerk, then it's for the best that he's gone."

"Yeah. I mean, what did he even do?" said G in a nasty

voice. "He just sat at the meetings, looking like a timid little bunny rabbit, never saying anything, and not even having the guts to speak up for himself. Honestly, what did we lose when he left?"

"Nothing at all!" exclaimed Kat fervently.

"True!" Jayden said in an unusually deep voice. "I say we just forget he ever existed and move on."

There were nods and mumbles of assent around the table. Everybody was privately doing the same thing, and trying to project the feeling that they were happy Gobbleguy was gone. In actuality, however, all four of them were scared senseless by the ramifications of his departure.

Although they would rather die than admit it, the remaining members of the council realized that, when Gobbleguy logged out of Elementia, the Noctem Alliance had claimed him as their victim. Even if Gobbleguy had been useless in the grand scheme of things, the fact remained that he had been driven out by the fear and pressure that the Noctem Alliance was spreading throughout Element City so effectively.

The most frightening fact of all, though, was that the council had reached a startling landmark: of the nine of them who had started the war against the Noctem Alliance, more than half of them were now gone.

"I think that it is fairly safe to say," the Mechanist spoke after a moment of scared silence, "that our city is, as of now, incredibly well protected. Due to various innovations in defensive technology—"

"All of which you created," Kat cut in with a smirk. There was a grim chuckle of agreement around the table. In fact, Kat was right; the Mechanist had been the one who had designed the city's superb outer defenses.

"Well, yes, that's true," replied the Mechanist humbly, "but it is also beside the point. As I was saying, because of the resources that we have put into the defenses of our walls, I think that the Noctem Alliance will have a difficult time getting into our city. We are well equipped to fight off any approach of theirs as of right now, whether it be through stealth or by brute force. However, I think that it is also time that we acknowledge that the Noctem Alliance is, at the very least, equal to us in power."

There were sounds of repugnance around the table. The council still found it difficult to accept that what had started off as a small protesters group had grown into an organization that had pushed them to the brink of annihilation in just a single month. Although they could not bring themselves to disagree with the Mechanist, saying it aloud would mean accepting it, something that Jayden, G, and Kat were not prepared to do.

"Therefore," the Mechanist continued, reaching under

the table and pressing a button as he did so, "I am forced to assume that our current stalemate is temporary. The Noctem Alliance will manage to break through our walls if we are not able to weaken them somehow. For that reason, I've asked Bob to come in here and brief us on what we, as high-ranking members of the city, should do to actively fight the Noctem Alliance."

"Wait a sec," said Kat as she realized what he was saying. "Are you saying that you want us to actually go out into the server and fight the Alliance? Like, in combat?"

The Mechanist nodded. Kat's face lit up, and she looked psyched at the prospect of finally going out into the field and actively doing something to take down the Noctem Alliance.

"Hold on," asked Jayden, a puzzled look crossing his face. "If we're out in the server doing the fighting, then who's going to run the council?"

"That's actually the one thing we need to discuss before Bob gets here," the Mechanist said tiredly. "In my talks with Bob, he suggested that while the rest of the council goes out and undertakes several highly important objectives through-out Elementia, I myself remain here as the sole governor of Element City.

"I was the first to point out," the Mechanist continued quickly, as all three of the other council members looked alarmed, "that this idea would give me sole power over the

entirety of Element City, which is something that our constitution was designed specifically to avoid. After all, if handled
improperly, the idea of a single person leading the city sounds
dangerously similar to the doctrine of King Kev.

"However," the Mechanist said as the others nodded in
agreement, "it does say in the constitution that one person
is allowed to control Elementia by him- or herself in time of
emergency. This can be done if the other council members
are required to take action to resolve the emergency, and
only if the police keep a sharp eye on the single ruler to make
sure that he or she does not turn into a selfish dictator, and
keeps the well-being of the city in mind until such time as
a council may be reestablished. I don't think anybody will
disagree with me when I say that we most assuredly have an
emergency on our hands at the moment."

Nobody at the table even felt the need to say that they
agreed; they all knew that it was true.

"Let us be honest with ourselves, my friends," the Mechanist explained, sounding exhausted. "The four of us, along
with the police chiefs, are the most powerful players in Element City. There are various tasks that need to be done for
the sake of protecting our people and ending this war, and
I believe that we, the council members, should carry them
out. Of the four of us, I think we can all agree . . . and forgive
me if I sound arrogant . . . that I am the best leader."

There was a moment of silence. All the other members gave slow, consensual nods.

"So are we all in agreement?" the Mechanist asked with a definite air of finality about him. "I will stay here and lead Elementia while the three of you complete the missions that Bob has put together for you?"

"Sounds like a plan to me," said Kat with a grin, and G and Jayden both nodded in agreement.

"Well, good. That's settled then," the Mechanist sighed, clearly relieved that none of them had been opposed to this admittedly radical idea. As a matter of fact, the three of them seemed hyped and incredibly excited to finally take action against the Noctem Alliance instead of endlessly plotting out troop movements over the stone brick–block table of the council room .

There was a knock at the door, and all turned to face it.

"Enter," ordered the Mechanist authoritatively.

The wooden door swung open, and in marched Bob. He looked somber, and judging by his appearance, he had clearly just come from the front lines. His scarlet jumpsuit was ripped and torn in various places, and his pale face and blond hair were tarnished with soot from being at the back end of a TNT cannon. He was seated on Ivanhoe, who looked equally war hardened; his once-shiny saddle was now worn down, the color faded, and the pig himself bore the marks of various wounds that had been healed by potions.

"Ah, good to see you, Bob," the Mechanist said quietly. "How are the defenses holding up?"

"We're doing pretty good as of right now," Bob answered wearily. "The Noctems didn't launch any major attacks today, and we were able to repel the usual bombardments. That being said, it was pretty obvious that the Noctems weren't fighting full force either. They didn't even seem to have that many guys there. I have a feeling that they're planning something . . . some sort of stealth mission, maybe."

"You're probably right," the Mechanist said. "I trust that you and your brothers will have all the alarms online soon, should they try to use the Invisibility Potions."

"Of course," Bob replied.

"Good. Now, you've arrived just in time, Bob. The council has just agreed to our plan. I will stay here and run Element City under your supervision while Kat, Jayden, and G head out into the server and carry out your missions. Are you ready to brief them?"

"Yes, sir," Bob responded, nodding and looking over to the enthused council members. As soon as they realized that he was speaking to them, Kat, Jayden, and G sat straight up in their seats, their ears perked as Bob began to speak.

"As of right now, all available forces in our army are being used to defend the outer walls of Element City from penetration by the armies of the Noctem Alliance. However, there is a pressing situation that must be dealt with as soon as possible: the hostages. As of right now, Stan, Charlie, DZ, and Commander Crunch of the navy are being held prisoner on the Greater Mushroom Island. We don't know anything about their status, but we must assume for now that they are all still alive, and the Noctem Alliance will be using them to demand a ransom very soon.

"Also, you'll remember that when the offensive on Nocturia failed and our armies were pushed back to the city, the Noctem Alliance captured around two dozen residents of the Adorian Village. My brothers and I have sent some scouts out, and we've determined that these players are being held hostage in Nocturia. If the Noctem Alliance demands anything in exchange for the safety of those players, then we will have to comply. Even ignoring the fact that it's the right thing to do, if we have the opportunity to help those lower-level players and we don't take advantage of it, the citizens of this city will turn on us like a pack of wolves.

"This is why I need you three," said Bob, sounding official. "One of you is going to have to go with a volunteer to sneak into the prison in the Mushroom Islands and free Stan and the others. The other two are going to have to infiltrate Nocturia and liberate those lower-level players."

The three players around the table were quiet as they

thought about what they had just been asked. The idea of sneaking into Nocturia and the Specialty Base, the Noctem Alliance's two most heavily fortified strongholds . . . it wasn't going to be easy.

Kat in particular found herself quite surprised. She had been expecting Bob to ask them to lead a crazy head-on assault with the Elementia Army to drive the Noctem forces back into the Ender Desert. She wasn't anticipating the request to partake in a stealth mission. Nonetheless, she was eager to participate.

"Sounds like a good plan to me," she said, a wicked grin crossing her face.

"Yeah," agreed Jayden, nodding with a subdued smile.

"I agree with you guys," said G proudly. "That's definitely a job for experienced players like us."

The Mechanist gave a tired yet genuine smile at the enthusiasm of these young, spirited players. "All right then," he said. "Let's start planning. First of all, let's determine who's doing what. Who wants to get Stan and the others out of Nocturia?"

"I do!" came two shouts as both Kat's and G's hands shot up into the air. The two turned to look each other in the eye, and instantly they both looked away awkwardly. There was a moment of uncomfortable silence before Bob spoke.

"So . . . um . . . do you two really want to . . . ?"

"No," Kat said firmly, looking back up at G, this time with a hint of contempt.

"Aw, come on, Kat," said G, sounding mildly irritated. "You don't think that just this once—"

"G, I am not working with you," Kat repeated. The Mechanist gave a sigh, while both Jayden and Bob threw their heads back in exasperation.

"Kat, come on, we have to think about the well-being of Elementia. . . ."

"I *am* thinking of the well-being of Elementia," Kat replied coolly. "If I'm going to sneak into a secret base to try to break Stan, Charlie, and DZ out of jail, I need to be in top form. And I guarantee that if you're with me, it'll be that much harder for both of us."

"Oh, *grow up*, Kat," cried G in irritation. "Can't we please just be mature about this, bury the hatchet, and . . ."

"I said, *No, G!*" Kat bellowed through gritted teeth. She glared across the table, staring daggers at G, who was recoiling in intimidation.

"*Enough*, you two!" bellowed Jayden. He grabbed G by the shoulders and spun him around so the two were facing each other. G looked shocked.

"G, you know as well as she does, and as well as the rest of us do, that it's a bad idea for you two to team up. How about you team up with me, and the two of us go and free the hostages in Nocturia?"

G opened his mouth, then closed it again. His expression was outraged as he looked at Kat, then Jayden, then Kat again, then the Mechanist, and then back at Kat one more time before finally turning to Jayden and sighing.

"Fine," he mumbled. "We can do that."

"Well, that's settled then," said Bob. *Crisis averted,* he thought to himself in relief.

"In that case," the Mechanist said, "Kat, are you willing to team up with a volunteer to go and free the officials trapped in the Mushroom Islands?"

"Definitely," Kat said almost robotically, deliberately staring directly at the Mechanist and avoiding any eye contact with G.

"Okay," Bob said, sighing, glad that was over. "We have to get going. The sooner that these hostages are out, the better. Jayden and G, you come with me. We'll go down to the police station, and you'll get your briefing. After that, you're off. Kat, you just wait until we've found a volunteer to go with you, and then you'll do the same thing."

"So," the Mechanist said as the three council members nodded respectfully to Bob. "If that's all, then I officially adjourn this council meeting. Everybody, go do what you need to do."

And with that, Kat, G, and Jayden stood up. Bob walked

out of the council room toward the corridor, tailed closely by Jayden and G, while Kat took the passage that led to her room. On the way out, G and Kat nearly bumped into each other, but as G was about to open his mouth to say something, Kat turned her back to him and continued walking. G looked crestfallen as he followed Jayden out of the room.

The Mechanist now sat alone in the room. The occasional boom, chatter, and whizz of warfare still droned on outside. The barrage was constant; although the wall was holding up well, the Noctem Armies never relented in their assault on the walls. The Noctem Alliance was definitely planning something. The Mechanist knew it. Although the constant assault on the outside walls was easily repelled, it certainly did keep the Elementia Army busy. And perhaps that distraction was all the Noctem Alliance needed to set their grand plan into motion.

The Mechanist knew that, whoever Lord Tenebris was, he was incredibly cunning. Because of this, the Mechanist was well aware that nothing the Noctem Alliance did was arbitrary. Everything was planned, everything was deliberate, and everything had a point. Element City's defenses may have been holding up splendidly, but the Mechanist knew that it was only a matter of time before the Alliance managed to find some way around them. And until that time inevitably came, the population of Element City was desperate and furious, no longer able to obtain any resources from the outside. They were simply left to try to survive while trapped within the walls.

And now he bore the entire weight of the situation on his own shoulders, and his shoulders alone.

The Mechanist was already feeling overwhelmed, leading the council in these dark times. He had had to put up with G and Kat's bickering, as well as the constant news that all their efforts had barely put a scratch in the Noctem Alliance's offensive. He was well aware of how important it was that the hostages be rescued, but the Mechanist was at the point of having a nervous breakdown when he realized that the fate of this country, which was already teetering on the brim of destruction, was now in his own hands.

He felt so stressed, so anxious, and so panicked. The world was crumbling around him, and he alone was responsible for holding it together. He was doing all he could, yet it was hardly helping in the least. As the gravity of the situation spiraled around the Mechanist, he wished with all his might that somehow, somewhere, there was some way that he might be able to escape from it, just for a little while. . . .

Kat sat in the waiting room of the police station. In front of her, a window stretched from floor to ceiling, revealing a landscape view of the lower-level district of Element City. In the far distance, the gray stone-brick wall of the city stood proud and tall. About twice a minute, there would be a flash of white light at some point along the wall, accompanied a second later by a muffled boom.

Kat gritted her teeth and tried to keep herself together. It tore her apart inside that her people were being forced to suffer within the city, with food and supplies being rationed during the siege. It killed her even more that, because of the persistence of the Noctem Alliance, the Elementia Army was being forced to work day and night to combat the attackers, with more and more innocent civilians being drafted from their homes every day to keep up with the demanding costs of fighting this war. Life in Element City was miserable, and there was nothing she could do about it!

Kat forced herself to take a deep breath, and then let it go. *No, there is something you can do about it,* Kat thought to herself, trying to keep a calm mind. *Just focus on getting Stan and the others back here. That's all you can do right now.*

As she thought this, Kat began to grow more and more irritated. The minutes ticked by, and still nobody had arrived to tell her that the volunteer was ready to join her. Kat began to get angry.

If they weren't ready, then why did they call me down here? she thought bitterly, just as the wooden door swung open. Kat looked up expectantly, and was surprised to see Ben looking extremely uncomfortable.

"*Finally!*" Kat cried, jumping to her feet. "Do you have my partner ready yet?"

"Kat," said Ben, and she was alarmed by how nervous his voice sounded. "Before you find out who your partner is, I need you to realize something. We tried as hard as we could to find somebody else . . . but there was nobody else qualified who wasn't already occupied with something else in the war."

Kat was befuddled. "What are you talking about?"

Ben took a deep breath and let it out in a hefty sigh.

"Come on in," he announced miserably.

Ben stepped out of the doorframe, and another player walked up behind him. Kat's jaw hung open, and her eyes boggled in disbelief. She would recognize that pale skin, those giant red lips, that snow-white leather armor, and that smug expression anywhere.

"Oh, no," Kat breathed in horror.

"Oh . . . yes, I'm afraid," simpered Cassandrix in her patronizing, upper-class accent. "It's good to see you again, Kat, darling."

Stan opened his eyes. He took a deep breath of air and let it out slowly. He tried to move his arm but was only able to move it a few inches before wincing in pain. Reluctant to move again, Stan allowed himself a few more minutes of peace lying in bed.

Stan heard faint voices coming from down the wooden stairwell, and he turned his head to glance around the room. The torchlight gave the wooden attic a faint glow, and he noticed that the closet door was slightly ajar. Stan shrugged it off, figuring that it was nothing, and he closed his eyes once again.

As he lay in bed, nearly incapacitated by wounds and fatigue, Stan reflected on just how extraordinarily lucky he was to still be alive. His body ached all over from his leap into the ocean from the Noctem Alliance's prison at the peak of Mount Fungarus on the Greater Mushroom Island. Filled with anguish over the death of DZ and reckless panic at the Noctem forces quickly closing in on him, Stan hadn't been thinking clearly. Rather, he had simply grabbed DZ's sword and taken a leap of faith—a leap, it turned out, that had hurt quite a lot.

After landing in the ocean and plummeting fast and hard to the ocean floor, Stan had swum as fast as his screaming limbs could carry him away from the island, the sirens wailing from the prison and troops shouting as they mobilized to pursue him. At one point Stan glanced back at the island and saw Mount Fungarus, silhouetted tall and proud against the setting sun, with half its top blown off, and troops scurrying around the various outer levels like ants around an anthill. Desperate to find cover from the incoming troops, Stan dived underwater to the seabed (which was thankfully quite shallow around the islands) and, by a stroke of incredible luck, he had found a bubble of air sitting on the ocean floor, a two-blocks-square cube. Far too relieved to question what the glitch was doing there, Stan had instead dived straight into it, lying on the ground and taking a huge breath of fresh air.

Inside that air bubble, Stan lay still for hours, exhausted from his desperate and narrow escape. Throughout that day, he broke down on and off over the death of DZ and the thought that Charlie and Commander Crunch were being tortured mercilessly as he lay there, unable to do a thing about it.

When he wasn't crying or sleeping, Stan spent the rest of that day looking outside the air bubble. Squids would jet by Stan in schools, their rectangular black bodies propelled forward by a set of eight tentacles, with a rather frightening spiked mouth at the center. The surface of the ocean was illuminated with sunlight, and he could see the bottoms of dozens of wooden boats drifting to and fro across the water, undoubtedly searching for him.

Eventually, the day slowly darkened into night, and the watery world around Stan had become black. His stomach was growling, demanding that food be supplied soon, lest his health start to fade like the setting sun. After scouting out the surface to ensure no boats were directly above him, Stan had jumped out of the top of the air bubble and, kicking as hard as he could, propelled his way back to the surface.

As Stan looked around, he saw no ships anywhere near him, but he did notice the bright lights and strident sound that the Lesser Mushroom Island was emitting. Slowly but surely, Stan paddled his way toward the island, which held the promise of food and a temporary shelter. He had to duck underwater hastily, sometimes for minutes at a time, when a Noctem patrol boat had passed by, but in the end, Stan was able to make it onto the island undetected.

Footsteps echoing up the stairwell startled Stan out of his train of thought. He glanced over at the opening in the floor, and slowly the head, torso, and then legs of a player emerged. She wore black leather pants, silver metallic gloves, and a zipped-up navy-blue hoodie, out of which emerged a streak of magenta hair that fell over her deep brown eyes.

"How you doin'?" she asked in a quiet, rather harsh

voice. Stan shook her tone off; he had realized that her tone was not to be taken personally.

"A bit better," Stan replied, propping himself up on his elbows, despite the aches flaring up again.

"Well, that's good," the player replied, pulling a piece of bread from her inventory and tossing it in Stan's direction, followed immediately by a Potion of Healing. Stan caught the two items, and stared at the bottle of red liquid in disbelief.

"Olea!" he breathed in disbelief. "Where did you . . ."

"It don't matter where I got it," Olea replied brusquely as she started to head back down the stairs. "A Noctem soldier just came and told me that we gotta meet in the central plaza in five minutes. I don't know what they're planning, but I gotta hunch it'll destroy whatever safety you have here, President Stan."

"I understand," Stan replied, nodding grimly. "I'll get out of here as soon as possible."

Olea nodded, and walked down the stairs again. As he poured the red potion down his throat and watched her go, he thought about how fortunate he had been to encounter her. When Stan had pulled himself out of the water and onto the shore of the Lesser Mushroom Island less than twenty-four hours ago, he had been shocked to find that it was overrun with Noctem troops. He had ducked from alley to alley, moving with great agility despite his wounds, careful to avoid detection.

It was only when he had passed by the back door of a shop called GoddessOlea's Boat Rentals that he had been pulled into a building from behind by an unseen pair of hands. When he came to his senses, Stan found himself being interrogated by a player who he later found out was called GoddessOlea, or just Olea for short. When she discovered who he was, she wasted no time in bringing him up to her attic and beginning to heal him. The process of healing had been slow, as resources had been incredibly scarce on the Lesser Mushroom Island since it had been invaded by the Noctem armies. The troops had pillaged all stores that sold potions, golden apples, and other healing supplies, meaning that Stan's recovery, which should have taken just a few minutes, had been ongoing for a full day now.

Somehow, though, Olea had managed to get her hands on a Potion of Healing. Now that the red miracle liquid was in Stan's body, he felt all his aches disappear. Stan was sure that this particular potion had been brewed with glowstone; it was particularly strong. Stan leaped out of the bed and onto the wood-plank floor.

He knew that now that he was healed, he had to get off the island as soon as possible. The innocent people of the Lesser Mushroom Island were already suffering enough just because the Noctem Alliance was present there. He knew it was only a matter of time before the Alliance realized that he must be on the island, and when they did, Stan could only imagine what would happen. And if the Noctems found out that Olea had been harboring him . . .

As soon as Stan had finished cramming the last of the bread into his mouth, he jogged over to the chest in the corner of the room and flung it open. It was totally empty, save one item: a diamond sword, clearly old and well worn, with a violent enchantment glimmering dangerously on the blade. Stan reached into the container and clutched the handle of the sword. He had asked Olea if there was a place that he might be able to acquire an axe, but she had told him that, as long as the Noctem troops remained on the island, it would be impossible. So as of now, DZ's diamond sword, endowed with a Knockback enchantment, was his only means of defense against the world.

Stan made his way over to the stairs but halted at the top. He realized that it might be wise to glance out the window and check the conditions on the street before going downstairs. Stan walked over to the wood-plank wall and ducked down beneath the open window before peeking his head up to look outside. He cursed under his breath but was quite glad that he had looked outside first, since the entire street was lined with Noctem troops. Stan sighed, accepting that he would have to wait until this big announcement was over to make his escape.

Then Stan did a double take out the window and realized that he could see the entire congregation of citizens in the central plaza of the city. Stan realized it was risky to stay near the open window, but his curiosity got the better of him and he watched the meeting commence.

The players of the city were gathered in a gravel plaza around a giant brown mushroom, which had been decorated with red mushroom blocks and turned into a water fountain. The crowd seemed confused, and unsure of why they were there. Then, suddenly, there was a collective gasp as two dark forms emerged onto the top of the brown mushroom.

The player farther toward the back looked identical to Stan, though slightly darker in overall tone and covered head to toe in dark spores. Stan clenched his fist in hatred as he realized that he was looking at the chief of the Greater Mushroom Tribe, who had betrayed him and his friends to the Noctem Alliance in their raid of the Specialty Base. Slightly in front of him stood another form that Stan did not recognize. He was wearing the black leather armor of the Noctem Alliance over a camo-colored army uniform and an assault vest.

"Greetings, people of the Lesser Mushroom Island." The camo figure spoke in a voice that Stan was shocked to find that he recognized. "My name is Spyro, general of the Noctem Alliance."

Stan's fist clenched even tighter as he heard that name.

The last time he had seen Spyro, the Noctem soldier had turned Oob and his family into Zombies and recruited them into the Noctem Alliance. Stan shook with rage as he realized that this was probably why Spyro had been promoted to general. Although he knew that he couldn't be reckless, Stan still found himself longing for the day when he could sink a blade into both players standing up on the fountain.

"As you all know," Spyro continued, "tonight marks the start of the third day since the Noctem Alliance established its presence on this island. Therefore, I, the commander of this legion of the Noctem Alliance, believe the time has come to make certain announcements. Firstly, it is my pleasure to announce that the Greater Mushroom Island will, from this day forth, no longer be an independent nation, but rather a province of the Nation of the Noctem Alliance."

Horrified gasps and screams erupted throughout the crowd at this announcement, and intensified as troops began to pour in from the streets leading into the plaza. These soldiers were not clad in black like the Noctem troops, but rather in a light gray.

"The people of the Greater Mushroom Tribe," said Spyro affectionately, gesturing to the troops now encircling the population of the city, "have been instrumental in the agenda of the Noctem Alliance, and we are now amiably considered mutual allies. In repayment for their help, the Chief of the

Greater Mushroom Tribe has requested just one favor for his people. Therefore, in fulfillment of this favor, the Lesser Mushroom Island is now, and forever shall be, under the rule of the Greater Mushroom Tribe."

Although Stan could not see the expressions on the faces of the crowd, he could imagine that they looked absolutely terrified at the implications of this turn of events. Stan felt his heart clench. A conversation came flooding back to him . . . a secret talk between Blackraven and the Chief of the Greater Tribesmen while he himself had been feigning sleep in his jail cell on Mount Fungarus. He had to let the people of the island know of the incredible danger they were in. His mind immediately went into scheming mode as he tried desperately to think of how to warn the Lesser Tribesmen in time.

"The people of the Greater Mushroom Tribe," continued Spyro in an almost casual manner, "feel that you, the people of the Lesser Mushroom Tribe, have betrayed the sacred ideals of the Mushroom Tribe by living in the way that you have for the past six months. Therefore, under the new mandate, the Greater Tribesmen will see that you are put firmly back into your place."

Spyro gave a smug little chuckle, which caused another collective outburst of terrified cries as Stan's stomach flooded with acid. Spyro merely continued, "The second announcement regards a matter of national security. It has come to the attention of the Noctem Alliance that Stan2012, President of the Grand Republic of Elementia and Public Enemy Number One, has escaped Fungarus and is now in hiding on this island."

The crowd was silent. Stan knew they must have been shocked but were far too terrified to speak out.

"As I am sure you are aware," Spyro continued, malice dripping from his voice, "the Noctem Alliance does not take kindly to any who work against us. This island is, as we speak, being surrounded by a heavy blockade by sea. Escape from the island will be impossible. Therefore, if anybody has any information regarding the whereabouts of Stan2012, you are to deliver it to a member of the Noctem Army immediately. Should you carry information regarding the president's location and fail to report it, you will receive a punishment that fits your crime.

"And now I am instating a curfew. All citizens are to return to their dwellings and are not to leave until sunrise."

Immediately, the citizens filed out of the plaza with surprising speed. As a wave of people filed back toward Olea's store and toward their own houses, Stan could practically feel the cloud of dread wafting off them. Stan saw Olea break from the rabble and reenter the front door to her store. Stan turned around as she clambered up the stairs, looking disgruntled.

"How much did you hear?" she demanded.

"All of it," Stan replied. "Olea, I . . ."

"Don't say nothin'," Olea said, speaking quickly and with an urgent look on her face. "You gotta wait for an opening, and then get off this island. It's a hazard to you as well as the people living here the longer you stay."

Stan nodded, his breathing shallow, as he walked back over to the window, looking out the corner. Olea walked over beside him to view the scene on the streets as well, and Stan could almost hear her racing heartbeat, which matched his nearly perfectly.

The roads were now cleared. Not one person could be seen in the streets, illuminated by the redstone lamps even as the sun was vanishing behind the skyline. The only forms of life remaining outdoors came in the form of the mass of gray-armored troops standing in rows in front of the fountain and staring up at the Chief of the Greater Tribesmen.

"The time has come, my brothers and sisters," the voice of the chief rang out over the plaza. "Our evil brethren have desecrated these sacred islands with their heathen ways for the last time. It is time for us to finally rid this server of the barbaric savages once and for all. We have long prepared for this day. You know what to do."

The Greater Tribesmen cheered and pumped their fists into the air, some empty and some clutching bows. Then they dashed out of the plaza, flooding the streets. What happened next made Stan's stomach drop in horror.

Half the Greater Tribesmen were sprinting down the streets, throwing small black objects into the windows of some of the street-side stores. The objects shattered the windows and were immediately followed by a burst of fire and light from within the store. As the blaze from the fire charges intensified, players burst out of the doors of their burning houses and into the streets. There they instantly fell dead to the ground, with arrows sticking out of them courtesy of the Greater Tribesmen, who were armed with bows.

Stan whipped around to face Olea. "What in the . . . what the . . . ," he sputtered, his mind unable to grasp what he was seeing.

"It's the Great Purge," Olea breathed, glancing in awe at the fires now erupting all around them, and the countless civilians being shot to death in the streets. "They talked about it for months . . . but I never thought it'd actually happen. . . ."

"What are you talking about?" Stan demanded.

"The Greater Tribesmen are killing all the Lesser Tribesmen," Olea said, her voice quavering with fury. "They talked about it before, called it the 'Great Purge.' We've always known that the Greater Tribesmen hated the Lesser Tribesmen, but we never figured that they'd go through with something like this. . . ."

"We have to stop them!" cried Stan, looking around frantically at the carnage in the streets and drawing his sword.

"Put that away," growled Olea, grabbing Stan's sword out of his hand and tossing it to the floor. "There's nothin' you can do to stop this, and you know it."

"But . . . I have to . . . ," Stan stammered, unable to accept the truth of what she was saying.

"Whatcha gonna do?" spat Olea cynically. "March out there by yourself and fight the entire Noctem Army? Listen, Stan. I hate what's going on out there just as much as you do, but I know there's nothin' I can do to stop it."

"Well . . . well, what about you?" Stan shouted, trying to get her to see reason. "Won't they come after you, too?"

"No," Olea replied bitterly. "They only attack the places where the Lesser Tribesmen live. They're ignorin' the citizens of the mainland and lettin' 'em be. Though if they want to destroy this city in the first place, I'm not sure what the point of that is. . . ."

"I know why," answered Stan as the conversation in the jail cell rushed back to his head. "The Greater Tribesmen made an agreement with the Noctem Alliance. They're going to take the republic citizens as hostages and then destroy all the buildings on the island."

Olea's eyes widened and then glazed over for a moment, and Stan could see the gears whirring behind them. Then she pulled herself together and looked at Stan.

"Stan, you gotta get out, undetected and fast," Olea said quickly, glancing nervously out the window. "You gotta get back to Elementia if we're gonna win this war, and save not only your people but us here on the Mushroom Islands, too."

Stan nodded, trying to ignore the boiling feeling in his stomach. He knew that, as abhorrent as the massacre outside his window was, he would have to ignore it for the time being, however painful it may be for him. He was about to thank Olea for all that she had done for him when suddenly a sharp knock came from below.

Stan and Olea held each other's glance for an instant. Then Olea, an unnerved look on her face, hissed *"Hide!"* under her breath as she walked over to the stairwell, clearly trying to remain calm. Stan, meanwhile, felt his heart skip a beat as he clutched DZ's sword and ducked into the closet, closing the door quickly yet silently behind him.

The closet was tiny, with barely enough room for Stan to stand in. He was surrounded by chests, stacked wall-to-ceiling, on all sides. Stan spun around to face the door, feeling incredibly claustrophobic in addition to his terror of whatever had come knocking at the door. Stan tried to calm his frantic breathing so that he could hear the voices arguing downstairs.

"Whaddaya want?" Olea's brutal voice demanded.

"We're looking for President Stan," a second voice replied aggressively. "We got a tip that he might be hiding out in here."

Stan nearly gave a squeal of panic, but managed to suppress it. How did anybody know that he was here? He had made sure he wasn't followed!

"Well, whoever told you that was a no-good liar!" retorted Olea, her voice confident and bearing no hint that she was misleading them. "I know better than to risk my life by protectin' that fugitive, even against you cretins."

"Well, then how do you explain the fact that your neighbor saw two heads looking out your window? We know that you live alone."

"Who told you somethin' as ridiculous as that?" Olea inquired, sounding outraged, as a fist of ice clenched Stan's heart. "And how do *you* know that I live alone?"

"Well, let's just say that if your best friend's house is engulfed in flames, and you're talking to a man with a fire charge in his hand, you're willing to hand over information a bit easier."

"You are the *lowest* of the low . . . ," seethed Olea. Stan could envision the almost inhuman snarl of disgust on her face.

"Oh, how wrong you are, little girl." The guard snickered. "If you want to see the lowest of the low, just take a look at who your good friend President Stan has pledged his life to defending. Come on, search the house."

"Whaddaya think you're doing?" shouted Olea, and Stan could hear the scuffle downstairs as the soldiers ransacked her shop. "If you don't stop right now, I will *kill* you!"

"He's not here," the second voice grunted. "Search upstairs."

"Stop that right now!" bellowed Olea, as Stan heard the clomping of footsteps growing rapidly louder. "This is breakin' and enterin'! What are you . . . this is my bedroom! I demand that you leave right now! What the . . . ? Oh, no, don't you dare open that . . ."

Stan was prepared. Just as the wooden door in front of him was flung open, flooding his eyes with light, Stan surged forward with a battle cry, thrusting DZ's sword forward and directly into the stomach of the soldier. The Greater Tribesman gave a yell of anguish as the diamond sword tore through his gray leather armor and came out his back.

Olea whipped out a diamond sword of her own and slashed into the soldier nearest her as the Knockback enchantment on DZ's sword took effect, sending Stan's soldier flying across the room and into the wood-plank wall, his items bursting into a ring around him as he landed. Olea quickly gained the upper hand on the second soldier as the third and final soldier in the room rushed into Stan.

Stan was able to repel the soldier reasonably well, countering the blows and jabs of his opponent, but Stan's skill with a sword was only rudimentary, and he found himself unable to connect a blow of his own. One well-placed hit later, and Stan found DZ's diamond sword spiraling across the attic and landing in a corner with a clattering sound. Stan frantically dived to avoid the following strike from the soldier's iron sword and landed flat on his face. He rolled onto his back and tried to scuttle over and retrieve his sword.

Right as he reached the weapon, the soldier was upon him, leaving no time to arm himself. The soldier's sword didn't hit, however. Before the soldier could deliver a blow, two diamond swords poked point-first out of his stomach, and the soldier collapsed at Stan's feet, a ring of items bursting from around him. Stan looked up and saw Olea, pulling her two swords out of the soldier's back and latching them onto her hips.

"You okay?" Olea asked, not breathing heavily in the slightest as she reached a hand down to pull Stan to his feet.

"Yeah, I'm fine," Stan panted in response. He was too shell-shocked to think and just grasped Olea's hand and let her pull him to his feet.

"I swear . . . when I find out which of those disgustin' vermin ratted us out . . . ," hissed Olea under her breath, but she stopped when she noticed Stan. He was staring at the floor, where the items of one of the three dead players lay—namely, the player who had died at Stan's hand. He stared, almost uncomprehendingly, at those items.

Stan found himself unable to speak. For the first time in his life, Stan2012 had killed another player.

"Hey, don't dwell on it," Olea said, walking up beside Stan and turning her blocky head to face him. "You didn't have a choice. It was either him or you."

Stan sighed. "Yeah, I know," he replied, his voice sounding almost meek. "It's just . . ."

"Just nothin'," Olea replied firmly. "It had to be done, and you know it, so it's not worth thinkin' about no more. You can't waste no more time, Stan."

"Yeah, you're right," Stan said, looking at Olea and a bit disturbed with himself as he found that, despite the fact that he had just ended another life for the first time since he had joined Elementia, he was able to put the conflict within him aside relatively easily. "Okay, I'll head out now."

"Good," Olea replied, "You can slip out the back door."

Stan grabbed his sword, took a deep breath, and marched downstairs. Stan was totally floored to see the complete devastation of the shop that the soldiers had managed in just a few seconds. It looked like they had checked around the few pieces of furniture in the most destructive way possible.

Various picture frames sat on the floor, which was

sprinkled with shattered glass from the busted-out windows. The glass dust was twinkling with radiant red light, and Stan looked out at the blaze now engulfing the city. The fire was spreading to the houses of the other citizens as well, and the streets were flooded with people desperately trying to extinguish the fires and protect their livelihoods from being lost in the inferno.

Stan could hardly take in what he was seeing. He remembered, just days ago, when he had stood in the center of this great city, on tour with a guide named Danny, and was blown away by the brilliant displays of lights and lively players bustling through the streets like blood through the veins of a magnificent living being. At the rate the flames were spreading, the city would all be gone by morning.

What Stan did next was without thinking. It was without logic. It was without any form of common sense whatsoever. Stan burst out of the front door of Olea's shop and into the streets. He was acting on raw, unbridled emotion, wanting to do everything he could to draw the Noctem Alliance, these harbingers of destruction and pain, as far away from this city as possible. Stan raised his arms, still clutching DZ's sword and, with a vein pulsing in his forehead, he opened his mouth and gave a mighty roar.

"HEY! SPYRO! COME AND GET ME!"

Immediately, hundreds of heads, civilian and military,

whipped toward him. There was a moment when time seemed to freeze as the entire populace of the burning metropolis locked their eyes simultaneously on to Stan. Then chaos reigned.

From all across the streets, dozens of soldiers, clad in black and gray, started charging toward him, some releasing a battle cry and some firing off arrows. Stan spun around and sprinted as fast as he could through the alleyway of the city and onto the mycelium shoreline, barely noticing the shower of arrows falling just short of him. He only glanced over his shoulder once, and his eyes locked not on the wave of troops pouring after him, but on Olea poking her head out the back door of her shop. The look on her face was a mix of surprise, fury, gratitude, and trying to comprehend what in the world he was thinking.

Stan didn't look for long, though. He sprinted down the mycelium-covered hill that led to the water's edge, where he noticed a patrol boat quite close to the shore. The black-suited pilot of the dinghy barely had time to turn his head when Stan sent him careening into the ocean via a shock-wave of Knockback energy from DZ's sword. Stan landed haphazardly in the boat, and by the time he had seated himself properly, the Noctem soldiers were already splashing into the bay, just blocks away from him. Before the troops could destroy his boat with their weapons, however, Stan had desperately willed the boat to fly forward like a rocket, leaving the Noctem soldiers in a trail of bubbles behind him.

Stan quickly glanced up at the white rectangle that was the nearly full moon and aligned himself to face east, toward Element City. As he turned the boat, Stan noticed something black poking out from under the boat's seat. He investigated further, and found a black leather tunic and cap, presumably one that the piloting Noctem soldier had had as a backup. Stan gratefully pulled them on; a little extra protection never hurt.

Finally, Stan gave one last glance behind him. He saw no other boats following him, and he noticed a swarm of dark forms scuffling around the shoreline, preparing to follow him. Though he knew that he ought to be thankful that the Noctem troops hadn't been fully organized and ready to pursue him yet, Stan hardly noticed this in comparison to the city. From this distance, the tallest skyscrapers of the Lesser Mushroom Island still stood proud and tall, even amid the scarlet blaze that illuminated the night from beneath them.

As Stan stared in awe at the downfall of this great city, a single tear rolled down his cheek. Stan's mind began to flood with the memory of all the death, slaughter, and betrayal that he had witnessed in the city, but he forced himself to tune it out. All he had to remember, he told himself, was that it was all because of the Noctem Alliance. And the only way that he stood even the slightest chance of taking them down, once and for all, was to return to Element City.

So, with new resolve and a heavy heart, President Stan2012 turned his back to the Lesser Mushroom Island and willed his boat to accelerate at top speed toward Element City.

I still can't believe just how immature she's being," G muttered under his breath to Jayden. Jayden took a deep breath, counting to ten in his head. He could barely comprehend that, even though the two of them were sitting in a military camp and preparing to sneak into the camps of the Noctem Alliance, G was still ranting about Kat.

"G, for the last time," said Jayden slowly, trying to keep his composure despite his frustration, "we kind of have other things to be focusing on. Like . . . you know . . . *a war*?"

"I just really expected more from Kat," G said, throwing back his head in exasperation. "She's a smart, reasonable person, so why can't she just let bygones be bygones like I have? We could have worked together fine. We still make a great team! Yet she continues to harp on it and hate me for it, totally refusing to let it go. . . ."

"Do you even realize what you're saying?" spat Jayden, his tolerance finally snapping. "G, *you're* the one who's refusing to let it go! You haven't shut up about Kat this entire time. *You're* the one who's turning this entire situation into a giant thing, and, frankly, none of us want or have time to hear it."

"Oh . . . that's just great," grunted G, glaring at

Jayden. "Now my best friend won't even take my side."

"I'm not taking anybody's side!" yelled Jayden, his eyebrow twitching in irritation. "I don't know everything that happened, so it's not my place to judge. But what I *do* know is that now is the worst possible time to talk about it! You want to work out your issues with Kat? Fine, go ahead and give it a shot. But wait until after we've destroyed the people who have been trying to kill us nonstop for the past month, please!"

G opened his mouth, then closed it again, glancing at the floor. Although he knew that Jayden was right, he didn't really care, and was so infuriated by the whole situation with Kat that he wanted to rant and rave about it for as long as possible. However, an explosion directly outside the wall they were next to snapped him out of his thoughts. Realizing that they would be entering combat soon, G pushed his anger with Kat to the back of his mind, and made himself promise it would stay dormant until his mission was over.

G noticed Jayden glancing upward, and he followed suit. The army encampment where the two of them were gearing up was located right at the base of the outer wall of Element City, on the east side. The explosion from above had been fired from the outside, and a considerable chunk of the upper wall had been blown apart by the blast. The two councilmen watched in fascination as, through the power of the soldiers standing at the ready, the mighty stone wall seemed to repair itself, like some great animal regenerating its tissue. Meanwhile, other soldiers could be heard yelling from atop the massive wall, accompanied by the high-pitched whistling of fireballs streaking down and into the outside woods, surely targeting the Noctem Troops waging war below them.

"These people," Jayden muttered, more to himself than anyone else. "They're putting so much on the line to defend our city . . . to keep freedom alive on this server . . . I wonder . . ." And Jayden's voiced trailed off into nothing. There was a moment of silence, punctuated only by the yells and other sounds of the ongoing war.

"What?" G finally asked.

"It's just . . . ," Jayden said, clearly in a quite pensive state. "Well . . . it's the Mechanist. I know that he's a fantastic leader and all, and if anybody should take over the city while we're gone, it's him. But . . . all these people are fighting for justice and equality, and now that the council is spread out all over the server, the entire city is under the control of just one person. And I know that we have the police watching the Mechanist and all, and I trust him. But . . . what do you think the citizens will think?"

G was about to respond when suddenly a door opened in the wall, and a soldier dressed in a full Elementia Army uniform appeared.

"Councilman Jayden, Councilman Goldman," the soldier said, addressing them respectfully but with a tone of urgency. "The target group of Noctem soldiers is massed in the woods directly outside the wall. Our intelligence suggests that they won't be there for long. If we are to make our move, we must do it now."

"Okay," Jayden replied, leaping to his feet alongside G. The two of them drew their diamond weapons, all thoughts of the previous conversations wiped clear from their minds. It was time to take action.

"Follow me," the soldier replied, and he marched through the iron door and into the wall, with Jayden and G close in tow.

Neither of them had seen the inside of Element City's outer walls before, but they were totally blown away by just how much was going on. What from the outside appeared to be a ten-block-thick wall of solid stone bricks was actually hollow, filled with various staircases and ladders that led to stone-brick platforms at various levels of the massive height. Soldiers scurried to and fro inside the wall, manning various battlements on the outside, and preparing fireball launchers and TNT cannons. G heard a rush of noise directly above his head, and looked up to see a mine cart rushing across a powered rail above, surely delivering vital materials to a point even further down the wall.

The two players hardly had time to marvel at the pinnacle

of Minecraft defensive technology that was the Element City outer wall. The soldier led them over to a battalion of players, bearing weapons and dressed in an amalgamation of diamond, iron, and leather armor. They all stood in front of a series of pistons that were set up against the outermost side of the inner wall.

"Okay, men," the soldier announced in a booming voice, walking to the front of the group of players. "You know the drill. When the blast doors open, make a charge across no-man's-land into the woods, and engage the Noctem soldiers. They outnumber us by a reasonable degree, so we will only engage them briefly . . . just enough to buy time for Councilmen Jayden and Goldman to execute their mission."

There was a shuffling in the crowd as all heads turned to face Jayden and G. The looks on the faces of the soldiers unnerved them a bit. These were players who had been entrenched in the rage of war for longer than they had ever expected, and their expressions seemed to demand that the two councilmen not blow their one chance to take a huge step in ending the conflict.

"Corporal!" came a shout from somewhere within the highest reaches of the wall, where Jayden and G couldn't see. The soldier leading the charge glanced upward.

"You have to go now!" the voice rang out again. "They're preparing to move out!"

"Okay," the soldier said to his troops, turning to face the wall. "It's time to go. *Open the blast doors!*"

At the soldier's command, Jayden and G heard a series of clicks and whirs as the pistons retracted, pulling the stone bricks with them and opening the wall to the world outside Elementia.

There were no words to describe the white shock that overtook Jayden's and G's minds as they saw what lay beyond the outer walls. The last time they had been there, just weeks ago, the area surrounding Element City had been lush and green, with forest growing right up to the wall.

Now there wasn't a tree in sight. The ground had been reduced to a field of dirt piles on a stone field pockmarked with craters. Everywhere their horrified eyes looked, Jayden and G could see fires blazing and the inventories of dead players scattered across the hilly ground. The remaining forest couldn't even be seen from their position directly outside the wall, as the smoke from the fires was too thick, obscuring the world around the outer wall like render fog.

All this ran through the heads of Jayden and G in an instant. Then they found themselves barreling forward, into the valleys and craters created by the TNT cannons, following the command of the captain who had yelled *"CHARGE!"*

The group of around thirty soldiers, with Jayden and G in the middle, was sprinting as fast as they could, but it was difficult to progress. The uneven terrain underfoot made for a lot of stumbling as they pressed onward, staying together as a group. Then, as the edge of the forest finally came into view, the arrows started to fly.

It was a desperate struggle as the squad of soldiers fought their way out of the craters and toward the forest while dozens of black-clad soldiers rained arrows down on them. Jayden heard the clinking sounds of arrows bouncing off the solid armor of the warriors, along with the occasional cry of anguish indicating that a hit had been scored.

As the soldiers finally managed to reach the top of the hill, a rain of fireballs started flying in from behind them. G glanced over his shoulder and saw lit blocks of TNT, flying far over their heads and landing in the forest with a massive blast. The turrets and battlements on the walls, he knew, were backing them up from afar.

As the soldiers poured forward into the forest, it seemed that the majority of the Noctem soldiers were still scrambling for their gear and weapons. It had been fairly obvious that they hadn't been expecting the attack. Jayden and G hardly noticed this, though. They were sprinting to the side, ducking into a small copse of trees, out of the Noctems' line of sight.

As soon as they were safely hidden within the vegetation, the two councilmen stripped off their armor as fast as possible. They then proceeded to yank black leather caps and tunics out of their inventories and pulled them on. As soon as they had both adorned themselves in the enemy's uniform, Jayden and G made a roundabout back into the trees and emerged behind the Noctem fighters.

It was mayhem on the battlefield. Arrows whizzed through the air, some lit on fire via enchantments, while a steady rain of fire and explosions fell from the smoky skies of the Elementia side. The soldiers were engaged in full-on combat, swinging swords, axes, and pickaxes at a rapid pace, while the vapors of dozens of potions drifted up and into the air.

Jayden rushed forward into the combat right as a Noctem soldier faded into Invisibility right beside him. He whipped out his diamond axe, ignoring all combatants on either side until he found who he was looking for. The corporal leading the attack was fighting a Noctem soldier with a diamond sword that glowed with a red luster. Jayden rushed in to meet the corporal just as he finished off the Noctem soldier. The corporal was about to strike Jayden when the two locked eyes. The corporal realized who it was, and a flash of relief crossed his face. The plan had succeeded. Jayden and G were now in the enemy camp.

"Retreat!" the corporal bellowed, giving Jayden a nod before turning and sprinting back down into the valley. "All forces retreat!"

Within the next few seconds, the Elementia troops were

disengaged from the combat and heading back down into the valley of haze as the rain of fireballs and mortars stopped falling. Although a few Noctem soldiers continued to fire arrows into the crowd of fleeing Elementia troops, the majority just looked confused, wondering what had happened.

"Where did that come from, General?" Jayden heard a voice ask from somewhere in the crowd.

"I'm not sure," a female voice responded slowly. "That attack came out of nowhere . . . and it was over awfully fast. . . ."

"Maybe they just underestimated our numbers," the first voice replied.

"You're right," responded the general, who Jayden still couldn't see. "That's probably what happened."

"So, back with the mobilization?"

"Yep," the general said, before yelling at the top of her lungs, "All right, everybody! It's time to move out! We have to hurry. That attack set us back, and they need us back in Nocturia as soon as possible!"

As the mass of black leather started to march, Jayden glanced around wildly, trying to find G. Before long, his eye caught the eye of a player with green eyes and bronze-textured skin under the leather armor. Jayden nearly began to panic, wondering why this random soldier was keeping eye contact with him, before he remembered that this was G's new skin.

Jayden sighed in relief. He was so used to seeing G in his old skin that he had forgotten the change, which was necessary so that no Noctem troops would recognize his extremely distinct appearance.

The two friends and councilmen gave each other a quick nod and returned to marching. Jayden shivered in excitement. This was it. The plan had worked, and now the two of them were marching their way toward Nocturia, with the Noctem Alliance none the wiser.

"Do you *honestly* need to be so loud?"

Kat halted in her tracks, her foot falling to the ground with a loud squishing noise. She clenched her teeth even tighter than they had been, to the point where she imagined that they were near shattering.

"Cassandrix," she said, trying to keep her head on straight, "this is a *swamp*. Because we are in a *swamp*, the ground is very *soggy*. Therefore, it is difficult for me to walk on it *quietly*. Do you understand?"

"Well, *I* seem to be managing just fine," Cassandrix trilled in reply. "And, of course, considering that we are attempting a *sneak attack* here, well, *I* think that we should practice being as quiet as possible. But if you're not capable of handling that, Kat, I understand . . . I'm not surprised, but I understand."

Kat clenched her fists. She wanted to kill the arrogant,

stuck-up player who trudged through the swamp in front of her. However, she held herself back. As annoying as Cassandrix was, Kat knew that she had to be the bigger person and deal with it. They were on a mission that might decide the fate of her best friends, and Kat knew that she had to stay focused.

Nonetheless, she resented the fact that the two of them were being forced to bushwhack their way through miles and miles of swampland instead of simply sneaking a pair of boats out of Diamond Bay Naval Harbor. That was how Stan and the others had gotten to the Mushroom Islands in the first place, and, despite the fact that the Noctem Alliance now had control over the Northwestern Ocean, Kat saw no reason that she and Cassandrix couldn't do the same thing. However, the police chiefs had overridden them and demanded that the rescue mission stay a secret. Therefore, Kat and Cassandrix had been forced to take a different route, which involved trekking down a long peninsula of uncharted swampland and then sailing to the Mushroom Islands from the north.

Honestly, it wasn't the prospect of the uncomfortable trek through the swampland that bothered Kat, though. Quite the contrary, she was thrilled at the potential for danger and excitement that the swamp held—it was a far cry from the boring council meetings and debates that had consumed the last few months of her life. Rather, Kat had been turned off to the adventure because of the prospect of dealing with the constant stream of whininess and unbelievable snootiness that would surely be pouring out of Cassandrix's mouth the entire way.

And sure enough, the trip thus far had lived up to her expectations. The night before, Kat had gotten the opportunity to fight off skeletons, spiders, Creepers, and an endless horde of Zombies (she suspected that the Zombies in particular had gotten smarter and stronger during the recent update to Minecraft) with Rex the dog by her side, defending Cassandrix as they set up their shelter for the night. It was great fun, and Kat relished the adrenaline rush of the fight; it felt just like old times again. On the other hand, the entire rest of that night had been nothing but Cassandrix yelling at Kat for letting a Zombie or two reach her and complaining about how gross it was to be spending the night in the soggy and putrid swamp, while Kat had been demanding that she just shut her mouth.

Still fuming, neither one of them had had anything to say to the other all day. Occasionally, Cassandrix had made a snide remark to Kat, which Kat answered with stoic silence, but beyond that they had kept largely quiet. The two simply walked single file, stopping occasionally for a silent meal of bread, as the hours slowly ticked by.

Now the sun was finally beginning to set. The two players continued to trek onward through the saturated grass and occasional pools of water, but it was becoming more and more difficult to see. Kat was about to suggest that they make camp when she heard a voice from not too far away.

"Ey, guys! Dat spot looks kinda dry! We should camp dere!"

"Shut up!" a second voice hissed, barely audible over the natural ambiance of the swamp.

Cassandrix whipped around and looked at Kat. They locked eyes, saw the panic in each other's face, and glanced around the swamp, trying to locate a place to hide. As the arguing voices grew closer and closer, Kat's gaze fell on a stone hole in the moist ground. She drew an Ender Pearl from her inventory and pitched it toward the mine. Kat reached over and grabbed Cassandrix's arm, and before she could question what was happening, the two girls warped to the inside of the cave.

Cassandrix glanced around wildly, trying to piece together what was going on as Kat waited desperately for Rex. By the time he magically warped beside her, Cassandrix had realized what Kat had done. The two of them scurried downward into the cave, tailed by Rex, and halted where they were no longer visible from the cave entrance. Hearts pounding, the two girls listened as hard as they could, trying to catch the conversation that was going on above them.

"Why do you *always* have to talk so loud?" an enraged male voice sounded out from above. "Are you familiar with the term 'stealth'?"

"Ey, don't you yell at me!" a stupid-sounding male voice continued loudly on. "I don't have da control ober how loud by boise is!"

"*Shut up!*" the angry voice hissed again. Kat was taken aback by the sheer level of harshness in the voice. "Good Lord, you're useless. . . ."

"Cut it out," a third voice ordered, this one female, sounding slightly annoyed, yet still deadly serious. "Lay into him all you want later, but right now we have to find a place to stay for tonight."

"Omigosh, Arachnia, I am, like, *so* not sleeping in this disgusting suh-*wamp*!" a fourth, ditzy-sounding female voice replied. "It's all, like, soggy and stuff, and the Slimes out here leave these, like, icky puddles of goo all over the place! Ew! It's, like, totally guh-*ross*."

"Oh, get over yourself," spat the third voice, apparently named Arachnia. "Hmm . . . you're right about one thing, though . . . we shouldn't camp up here—it's way too out in the open. Come on, guys, let's head down into that mine over there. . . . That should keep us hidden."

And, to her horror, Kat heard a symphony of footsteps

slogging their way through the grass above and getting louder and louder. Kat realized that Cassandrix had already taken off, running deeper into the mine, and Kat turned on her heel and sprinted in pursuit, Rex hot on her tail. Kat barreled down the natural stone steps of the mine like a cart on powered rails, sending a few bats flying out of her way in surprise. As the footsteps above suddenly turned into the sharp echoes of feet against stone, Kat dashed faster, finally catching up to Cassandrix, who was standing directly in front of a pool of lava. The cave had led them to a dead end.

Immediately, Kat whipped out her sword and sank into a fighting stance, praying that, whoever these people were, they were peaceful, or at the very least bad fighters. As the footsteps grew louder, another sound registered in Kat's ears—a rhythmic tapping directly behind her. She glanced over her shoulder and realized that Cassandrix was swinging an iron pickaxe and digging a hole in the wall, just tall and wide enough for them to escape through. Feeling a combination of stupidity for forgetting this option and hope that their escape would go without a hitch, Kat glanced forward again.

"This spot looks good." Arachnia's voice echoed down into the cavern as the footsteps came to a halt. "Creeper Khan, would you mind making the area a bit more . . . spacious?"

"It would be my pleasure," the enraged voice, apparently

named Creeper Khan, growled back in return. Even now, when he sounded thrilled at whatever it was he was about to do, he sounded remarkably angry.

Suddenly, without warning, the booming blast of an explosion sounded throughout the cavern, deafening Kat's unprepared ears. Another blast followed, followed by a series of rapid-fire detonations that shook the mine. Kat sprinted backward into the tiny hole that Cassandrix had created, terrified by what could be causing this horrific effect. Were these players detonating TNT? Had they run into a horde of Creepers? Or . . . and Kat shuddered as she imagined the implications . . . was it something else the player was doing?

Then, suddenly, the explosions stopped. There was no damage to any part of the cavern that Kat could see, but she wasn't planning to stick around to find out what was really going on. She just wished that Cassandrix would dig faster.

"Omigosh, Arachnia, this is, like, *so* much better," the unfocused, flighty female voice said again. "I mean, it's still, like, totally dark and underground-y and stuff, but at least it's not, like, the suh-*wamp*, or anything. . . ."

"You're welcome," spat out Creeper Khan in disgust.

"Okay, team," Arachnia announced, "Let's set up, and try to get some sleep. Tomorrow, the real hunt for President Stan begins!"

Kat, who was walking through the tunnel and nearly out

of earshot of these players, spun around. Did she really just hear that? Intrigued, Kat dashed down to the end of the tunnel, poked her head out, and continued to listen.

"Hey, Arachnia, I hab a question!" the stupid-sounding voice rang out again, sounding particularly loud as it echoed around the chamber. "Ow do you know dat da President hasn'd already godden dis far?"

"Zomboy," seethed Creeper Khan, *"just SHUUUT UP!"*

A small explosion rang out not too far from Kat, but she didn't care. She was suddenly far too desperate to hear what these people had to say. Were they saying that . . . somehow . . . Stan had escaped?

"Khan, calm down!" exclaimed Arachnia in irritation. "We can't have you lose control in here, not in such close quarters! And besides, it was a decent question. Zomboy, President Stan escaped just a few days ago. He's probably still out in the Northwestern Ocean, hopping from island to island."

"Oh," Zomboy replied. "Dat bakes sense."

"I swear," Creeper Khan growled, glaring at Arachnia, "if you don't find some way to make him less annoying, then I am going to use my Final Nova on all of you!"

"Don't even joke about that!" Arachnia gasped. "I don't want you to use it by accident. . . ."

"Oh, relax." Creeper Khan laughed darkly. "You do realize

that my Final Nova is powerful enough to level an entire city, right? Trust me, I'm not gonna use that attack unless I really, *really* have to."

Suddenly, Kat felt a hand grab her shoulder and whip her around. Kat was totally caught off guard, and her hand immediately went for her sword. However, she saw that it was simply Cassandrix, staring her in the face with an incredulous expression.

"What do you think you're doing?" Cassandrix hissed, as quietly yet incredibly urgently as possible. "We have to get out of here!"

"Shut up, I'm listening," Kat hissed back, pushing Cassandrix to the side and trying to hear what they were saying again. However, before anything could register, Kat found herself being dragged back into the tunnel.

"Are you really that stupid?" Cassandrix whispered, her face showing pure disbelief. "They're distracted. We have to leave now!"

Kat didn't have time to deal with her. These players, whoever they were, were discussing vital information about Stan, and Kat had to hear it. Hoping it would buy her a few seconds, Kat gave Cassandrix a full-on shove, sending her tumbling back into the hole. Kat stuck her head back out to hear Creeper Khan's voice.

" . . . still can't believe that Stan managed to get out of

that prison. It was so well guarded . . . or at least, that's what I heard. What was it, didn't some friend of his blow himself up in order to get Stan out?"

"Yeah," Arachnia replied. "I think his name was DieZombie97 or something, one of the council members . . . killed himself by setting off the bomb that let Stan escape."

After that, the two players continued to talk, but Kat didn't care. She couldn't hear them anymore. All she could hear was that one phrase, resonating in her mind over and over again . . . *DieZombie97 killed himself, DieZombie97 killed himself, DieZombie97 killed himself. . . .*

Stan had broken out of the prison. And DZ was dead.

Kat was having trouble processing, trouble comprehending what was being said . . . DZ, her friend who had been with them for months, for as long as they had been in Elementia . . . could he really be . . .

A hand struck Kat hard across the face, and she felt a flash of pain; her vision went white for a moment before refocusing to see Cassandrix, her face almost inhuman with fury.

"You *dare* to shove me, you obnoxious little brat!" Cassandrix seethed, her nostrils flaring. "I swear, if you *ever* do that again, I will not hesitate to . . . Oh, stop crying, you deserved it and you know it!"

"He's dead . . . he's dead . . . ," Kat managed to get out between shallow, raspy breaths, tears running silently down her face. "Cassandrix . . . he's dead. . . ."

"What are you talking about?" Cassandrix demanded, looking up into the cave in horror; Kat may have been having her breakdown quietly, but they were still in the presence of these hooligans.

"They said . . . ," Kat managed to get out between forcing her snorts of sorrow and fury to stay in her chest, "that DZ . . . is dead. . . ."

"Kat, that doesn't matter!" Cassandrix hissed, her eyes bulging. "We have to get out of here now."

Kat looked up to face Cassandrix. She could not believe what she had just heard. Her eyebrows knitted, and her eyes blazed with fire as she snarled in outrage. Had Cassandrix *really* just had the *audacity* to claim that DZ's death *didn't matter*?

Cassandrix had crossed the line. Kat drew out her diamond sword and prepared to let out a bellow of rage. She knew nothing but an all-consuming desire to destroy Cassandrix. Kat raised her sword and was about to bear down on Cassandrix with all her fury when, all of a sudden, she felt a dull blow to the side of her neck.

Kat fell to the ground, suddenly no longer angry at Cassandrix, or sad about DZ for that matter. In fact, she wasn't able to feel anything aside from a strange feeling of calmness spreading from her neck across her entire body. She was vaguely aware of Cassandrix falling to the ground beside her. As the world around her started to blur, Kat's fading eyes caught the image of a player dressed as a Spider drawing back a glowing hand right before she finally passed out.

The white rectangle that was the moon shone bright in the sky, casting a cool glow down onto the ocean below. The vast expanse of water stretched out as far as the eye could see, only being dotted by a few lonely islands far off in the distance. At the surface, the ocean was totally flat, except for one living being swimming forward, creating a slight rippling around him.

Leonidas was totally exhausted. He had been swimming for days on end, through the seemingly endless brine. The few islands that he had found to rest on throughout his journey had been barren. They held no trees with which he could construct a boat, and only one of them had any food on it, a single cow that Leonidas had killed with his bare hands, desperate and starving for food (he had been so delirious with hunger that he had forgotten that he still had an iron sword on hand). The little bit of rations that he'd had when he'd left Fungarus had nearly depleted, and Leonidas had no idea when his next meal would come.

There was one particular food item, though, that Leonidas had held on to since he had left Nocturia more than a week ago. Although he knew that the golden apple would fill him, and make him feel much better as well, he refused to eat it. He was saving it for . . . a very particular occasion. It was so important that Leonidas's mind had stopped classifying it as food, and rather as a tool. As food swam to the forefront of his mind now, he didn't pay the golden apple in his inventory a lick of thought.

Leonidas was so exhausted, and so miserable, that he had half a mind to simply stop, to allow himself to sink underwater, and wait until his oxygen ran out and he drowned to death. However, Leonidas knew that he couldn't do that. He had been working for the forces of evil for far too long in Elementia to leave now. He had to redeem himself before he could leave Elementia with any degree of integrity. And so, Leonidas forced himself to paddle onward, closer and closer to the Elementia mainland, praying that it would come into sight soon.

Leonidas wondered what was happening within the Noctem Alliance right now. He knew that, with Caesar dead and he himself deserting, the Noctem Alliance was short a chancellor and a general. If Leonidas had to guess, he would say that since Blackraven had officially revealed himself as a traitor to Elementia, he would take over Caesar's role as chancellor. As for the general . . . Leonidas clenched his teeth as he realized that Drake had almost certainly taken over his position. He couldn't wait for the day when he would finally get to face that self-righteous little brat again.

Leonidas paused for a moment to catch his breath,

treading water and focusing as hard as he could on conserving energy. There was still no island in sight, and he would likely be swimming through the night until he found one. After he had caught his breath, Leonidas was about to continue swimming when he heard a faint noise behind him. He soon realized with a start that it was the sound of a wooden boat cutting through water, and it was growing louder and louder.

Leonidas glanced behind him and saw, far off in the distance, a lone boat sailing straight toward him. As he squinted at it, Leonidas could barely make out a figure, unidentifiable at this distance, clad entirely in black leather armor.

A grin crossed Leonidas's face. It was a Noctem Alliance boat, surely out in the ocean to try to find him. Leonidas hastily took a deep breath and ducked his head underwater. He hoped that the Noctem soldier hadn't seen him or, if they had, they would assume that he was just a squid, poking up above the water as they occasionally do.

Leonidas allowed himself to sink down to the seabed. Thankfully, it was shallow here, a mere ten blocks or so below the surface. Leonidas crouched down on the clay basin of the ocean, ready to launch himself upward. Leonidas reached into his inventory and drew out his iron sword. In this situation, he figured that it would be a better choice than his bow.

Leonidas stood absolutely silent, watching the boat,

silhouetted against the moonlit surface, come closer and closer to where he was. Then, just as the boat was above him, Leonidas kicked off the clay blocks, rocketing upward toward the surface, sword outstretched in his hand. Leonidas broke the surface of the ocean and felt himself launched into the air. The player in the boat had hardly comprehended what was happening before Leonidas's sword had struck him across the black leather chestplate, cutting it open and sending the player tumbling out of the boat and into the water.

Leonidas fell back down into the ocean with a splash and saw the player haphazardly trying to gain his bearings and figure out what was going on. Leonidas let out a breath that turned into a swarm of bubbles, realizing that he should probably kill this player. As much as he wanted to abstain from killing, he knew that leaving this Noctem soldier alive was far more dangerous than it was worth.

Leonidas returned his sword to his inventory and drew out his bow and an arrow along with it, taking aim at the player. By now, the player had gained his bearings and was staring back at Leonidas, glowing diamond sword in hand. Leonidas saw that underneath the ripped tunic, a turquoise shirt was visible, and the player's face was pale and shocked. However, only when Leonidas looked the player in the eyes did he come to the realization of who he had just attacked. The eyes, which held the same type of gleam that was unique to every player, were horribly familiar. . . . They were the eyes of Stan2012.

Leonidas couldn't comprehend what had just happened. This Noctem soldier he had just attacked . . . was President Stan? How was that possible? Stan had escaped? He was on his way home? And Leonidas had just attacked him?

Oh, no, thought Leonidas, his mind refusing to accept what had just happened. *What did I just do?*

Leonidas didn't have too much time to think about it though. He instinctively raised his bow in a feeble block as Stan sent an axe blow directly at Leonidas's head, sending them both careening away from each other. Leonidas was totally stuck. He knew that he couldn't fight back against Stan, and he also knew that Stan wouldn't be particularly keen on listening to his explanations, not that they could even speak in this underwater environment.

Leonidas felt a dull blow to his stomach as Stan's sword connected with his black leather chestplate. Leonidas had been thinking so hard about how to avoid fighting Stan that he had forgotten that, eventually, Stan was going to counter-attack. As Leonidas sunk down to the ocean floor, he noticed a trench right beside him. Desperately, he swam downward into it, well aware that Stan was following him in hot pursuit.

As Leonidas plunged deeper and deeper into the trench, he found it near impossible to see. That was the least of his worries, however; his oxygen supply had nearly run out. Leonidas aimed a punch forward, and, by some miracle, his hand struck dirt. As fast as he could, Leonidas threw punch after punch at the wall, hoping to create a tiny safe haven to utilize. Just as his breath was about to give out, Leonidas punched away the second dirt block, creating a small compartment just large enough to stand in, which Leonidas quickly dived into.

Leonidas took a deep breath and felt the air rush back into his head, his bearings quickly returning to his body. Thanking Notch for Minecraft's broken water physics, Leonidas continued to punch into the dirt wall, eventually creating a room large enough for two people to stand and walk around in. Hopefully, if Stan was planning on making his way down to the trench to finish him off, Leonidas would be able to explain what was going on.

However, Stan didn't come down. After a while, Leonidas gave a deep breath and a sigh. He was furious with himself for making such a crucial mistake; he would have a much harder time convincing Stan that he was planning to join the Elementia Army now. Leonidas gave the wall a lurid punch of frustration before slipping out of his air pocket and rising back toward the surface, planning how he could fix the damage caused by this monumental error.

Stan was barely managing to keep himself afloat. The cut across his chest by Leonidas's sword had torn through his armor, leaving a light cut in the center of his chest. This wouldn't have been so bad if it weren't for the fact that he had then tumbled directly into the ocean, ramping up his pain to excruciating levels as the salt water seeped into the open wound. Add that to the fact that Stan had accidentally swallowed a mouthful of seawater during his plunge, and he had become so weak that it had been a struggle to pull himself back into the boat.

And that was back when he still had the boat. The struggle against Leonidas had done substantial damage to the craft, to the point where it barely floated anymore, and he couldn't control it. He had half a mind to just leave it there in the middle of the ocean, but he knew that there was a chance Leonidas might find it and somehow use the wrecked dinghy to his advantage, so he had destroyed it. Stan now held three wood-plank blocks and two sticks in his inventory, the only remnants of the boat.

Stan quivered with fury. He couldn't believe that Leonidas had followed him all the way out here just to ambush him. Actually, now that Stan thought about it, he realized that he shouldn't be surprised at all. He knew that out of all the Noctem Alliance's forces, Leonidas was the most savage, alongside Minotaurus. Leonidas had probably volunteered to hunt him down, Stan thought in disgust.

The one thing that Stan was slightly confused by was how he had managed to escape Leonidas. But, the more Stan thought, the more he realized that it was probably because Leonidas had let his blind bloodlust take over his common sense. He probably hadn't meant to knock Stan into the water. Leonidas most likely was a terrible underwater fighter, and had fled to avoid fighting Stan while he had that disadvantage.

That being said, Stan knew that Leonidas couldn't be far behind him. He was probably just trying to heal up from his underwater melee with Stan, and would be in hot pursuit in no time. Stan was in no condition to repel the Noctem archer now, and he had no place to rest up. *If only,* thought Stan as he gritted his teeth, *somewhere, in this entire ocean, there was . . .*

Stan's heart leaped for joy as finally, on the far horizon, he could see a dark mass of blocks expanding up from the surface of the ocean. *Finally,* Stan thought as he gave a sigh of relief.

As Stan paddled closer and closer to the island, his enthusiasm grew less and less. This island had barely anything on it. There were no trees, no animals, and not much of anything else. It was just a small mound of dirt expanding out from the ocean. At the very least, though, there didn't appear to be any Noctem forces anywhere near it.

Stan finally reached the shoreline and dragged himself up onto the dirt-block shore. Stan collapsed face-down on the ground. He didn't care that he was completely exposed and out in the open. He didn't care about the potential monsters roaming this dark island. All Stan cared about was finally being back on dry land. At that moment, fatigued beyond comprehension from the ordeals of the last few days, all Stan wanted to do was sleep, and escape from his cares in the world.

If Leonidas wants me, thought Stan as he drifted off into sleep, *let him find me.*

"Stan?"

Huh? Stan thought stupidly.

"Stan? Stan, is that you?"

That's funny, thought Stan vaguely, through the cloud of exhaustion in his mind. *I could have sworn I heard a voice. . . .*

"Stan! It is you! Oh, fantastic, I've been trying to contact you for ages . . . come on, wake up, noob!"

"Wait, wha . . . *ow*!" Stan exclaimed, sitting up quick as a bolt and feeling a massive rush of blood from his head because of it. "Ugh . . . Sally, is that you?"

"Yeah, it's me," Sally's voice replied out of the ether, crackling and punctuated by static. "Listen Stan . . . I've got way too much to tell you . . . and not enough time . . . I need you to follow my instructions and fast, okay?"

"Yeah, of course," Stan replied, trying to force himself to

wake up in the midst of his reconnection with Sally.

"Okay," Sally continued, her voice fluctuating greatly in volume as she spoke through the terrible audio. "Here's what you *need* to do, Stan . . . . I need you to *leave* Elementia and join the server that I am about to invite you into."

"Did . . . did I just hear you right?" Stan asked, bewildered. "You're asking me to leave Elementia?"

"Just for . . . little while . . . ," Sally replied, her voice now a consistent volume but barely audible over the outside interference. "You'll . . . able to get back . . . into Elementia . . ." The static was getting worse and worse. "Trust . . . I'll explain . . . when we . . . to meet . . . other in . . . my server . . . called . . . SalAcademy . . . See . . . soon . . ."

And then, with a loud static crackle, Sally's voice disappeared.

Stan was stunned. He had been beginning to doubt that he would ever hear Sally's voice again, and now, here she was asking him to leave Elementia and join her in a different server. Stan didn't even know if it would be possible. He didn't know much about Minecraft servers, but he did know that Elementia still had mods that King Kev had put in place. He didn't know what these mods were—in fact, nobody really did—but Stan knew that they made going in and out of Elementia a risky business.

There were two things that Stan was sure of, however. One

of these things was that Sally knew much more about computers than he did. It took skill to bypass King Kev's leftover defenses against hackers, as well as the efforts against her by whatever tech junkies the Noctem Alliance had on their side. The second thing was that he trusted Sally. She had never led him wrong before and, with her superior knowledge in the subject area, Stan was sure that he wouldn't regret listening to her now.

And so, Stan sat down cross-legged on the dirt beach of the island, took a deep breath, and focused hard on his desire to leave Elementia. For a moment, nothing happened, and Stan began to wonder if he was doing this right. Then all at once, a question appeared in his mind, written out as clearly as if it were actually visible.

DISCONNECT FROM SERVER?

And with a deep breath, and a sense of disbelief that he was actually doing this, Stan answered out loud.

"Yes."

And with that, Stan2012 disappeared.

From his place treading water in the ocean that surrounded the dirt-block island, Leonidas's jaw was slack, his mouth hanging open. What did he just see?

Leonidas was surprised that he had managed to catch up to Stan at all. For starters, Leonidas had given him a pretty good head start. After Leonidas had resurfaced from his underwater hideaway, he had immediately begun to swim toward the Elementia mainland, sure that Stan was headed in that direction.

And now that he finally had Stan, what happened? Stan started talking to himself, pacing around, and then he had left Elementia? Leonidas started to panic . . . He knew that the Noctem Alliance was gaining more strength by the day, and Element City was losing just as much. How could Stan just abandon them like that? Leonidas was almost ready to give a shout of fury at Stan for abandoning his people in the midst of this crisis.

Then Leonidas took a deep breath, and tried to clear his mind. If he himself was to return to Element City, he would have to try to keep as levelheaded as possible. And as Leonidas released his breath, he realized that Stan would never abandon Elementia. He had probably just gone to a different server for a while . . . or maybe he had homework to do . . . or maybe had had to pee or something. In any case, Leonidas assured himself that Stan would be fine, and that he'd probably be returning any moment.

Suddenly, it struck Leonidas what an interesting position he was in. Stan had temporarily left Elementia . . . but he would return eventually. And when he returned, he would be in the exact same spot where he had left. And if he were to return right now, he would see Leonidas standing right in front of him.

Leonidas sat down on the dirt-block mound and squinted his eye, trying to figure out what to do. On the one hand, he had been looking for the perfect time to tell Stan that he had abandoned the Noctem Alliance. Maybe here, on this island, with the two of them and nobody else, was the perfect place for him to do it. In any case, Leonidas didn't imagine that a better time would be coming anytime soon.

On the other hand, though . . . their last meeting had not gone particularly well. After that little fiasco, Leonidas had no idea how he was going to convince Stan that they were on the same side . . .

Suddenly, Leonidas whipped his head up, the debate in his mind instantly vanishing. He could hear something. Ringing out of the dark sea, far beyond sight, was a song that he couldn't quite make out. It sounded like a Minecraft song he had heard on the Internet a long time ago . . . and it was growing louder and louder. Leonidas ducked down behind a pile of dirt blocks. He peeked his head over the top, gazing far into the distance. Out in the sea, emerging from the render fog, Leonidas could see a small fleet of ships. He couldn't make out the exact numbers, he guessed about six . . . but what he could make out quite clearly were the black tunics that each of the players was wearing.

Leonidas glanced around in a panic, looking for a place to hide should soldiers happen to land on the island. His gaze locked on a small cave, not too far away, which led into the center of the dirt mound. With great grace and agility, Leonidas dive-rolled out from behind the dirt pile and into the mouth of the cavern. He peeked his head out the side, praying that the soldiers didn't see him. Thankfully, they hadn't seemed to notice. While they continued to head toward the island, there was no hint of recognition in their voices, just the continuing ring of the sea shanty.

Leonidas sighed in relief. He could hide deep in the mine, and win through ambush if any of the troops should find him. He was about to turn back and begin his trek down into the cavity of rock when an alarming realization slammed into Leonidas like a train.

Leonidas stuck his head out of the cave again, and glanced at the spot where Stan had despawned. He glanced back out at the ships and realized, with a wrench to his gut, that Spyro was at the head of this fleet of six boats. They had stopped their singing. All of them were on course to land on the island, right at the spot where Stan had sat just a few minutes ago.

Stan would return to Elementia. Leonidas didn't know when, but he didn't imagine Stan would be gone for long. And when Stan did despawn, he would find himself right in the middle of the squadron of Noctem troops, totally caught off guard and unprepared to defend himself.

The Noctem troops had gotten out of their boats. The six of them had all manner of weapons drawn, from bows and arrows to diamond swords and axes. Spyro walked over directly to the spot where Stan had been and turned his back to Leonidas, facing his men.

"Okay, men," Spyro said gruffly. Leonidas was floored that he sounded so much older and more weary. "You know the drill. Search every nook, cranny, and crevice of this island. Your target is President Stan. Should you find anybody else, bring them to me."

"Yes, sir, General Spyro!" the other five soldiers yelled in unison.

And with that the troop dashed around the island, starting to inspect every block for a sign of a hidden player. And right as Leonidas ducked his head into the mine to avoid detection, he realized that Spyro was not moving. In fact, he was standing in the same place where he had addressed his men, surveying their progress, and staring directly at where Stan was eventually bound to reappear.

Leonidas ducked back into the cave in a panic. His heart was racing, and the fact that Spyro had somehow jumped up quite a few ranks from corporal to general was barely registering in his mind. All he knew was that these Noctem troops would comb every nook of the island, and eventually they would find him. But even more horrifying was that Stan could reappear in Elementia at any minute. And when he did, he would appear right in the midst of the enemy soldiers.

As Leonidas heard footsteps approaching him, he hastily ducked further down into the cave, his mind racing as he tried to work out what to do next.

Stan opened his eyes. He glanced around, bewildered. All he could see was an expanse of flat, green grass, stretching as far as the eye could see. There were no structures, no landscapes . . . no anything. Nothing but a never-ending expanse of grass.

Stan was puzzled. He was sure that he had picked the right server . . . he had distinctly heard Sally say the words SalAcademy, and when he looked at the list of servers available to join, there it was. He was positive that this had to be the place. But then where was . . .

Suddenly, Stan became aware of a presence behind him. He whipped around, his hand going to his axe, as he had forgotten that his inventory was now empty. Feeling defenseless, Stan glanced around wildly. Then, slowly, his gaze shifted upward.

Levitating in front of him was a player, who slowly started to descend from the sky. As Stan watched in awe, more and more of her features came into view. She was wearing black pants and a black biker jacket, with a purple X across the front of it. Her jet-black hair was no longer in a braid but now hung down, half covering her face, and a streak of neon orange ran through it. However, as Stan looked into her totally unchanged pale face and single exposed green eye, he knew that, although her skin had changed, he was looking at the same person.

"Welcome to the Academy, noob," Sally smirked as her feet finally touched the ground.

The Mechanist's head snapped upward, and he grunted in confusion. Slowly, his sense returned as he remembered where he was. The council room was deserted aside from himself, and all was silent except for the omnipresent sounds of the bombardment on the city walls. The Mechanist rubbed his eyes. He realized that he had been sleeping for a while, though he was unsure of exactly how long.

He looked around the empty room. He was puzzled. What was he doing in here? Why did he remember so little about the time before he had passed out? Why had he passed out in the first . . . ?

And then, in a rush, the Mechanist remembered.

He had been sitting in the council room, poring over battle strategies submitted for his approval, when Bill had burst into the room. He had been frantic and had tears in his eyes. The Mechanist had demanded to know what was wrong. And Bill managed to get out between his choked-back sobs that the Noctem Alliance had sent them a message, and their military had managed to confirm it—that DZ had been killed in an accident at the prison.

The news had slammed into the Mechanist like a truck. He had demanded that Bill leave him be, that he had to be alone. And then . . . what? The Mechanist could barely remember what had happened after that. He vaguely remembered a feeling of overwhelming grief, but besides that . . .

A glint of light from the floor caught the Mechanist's eye. He ducked down under the table and examined the empty glass potion bottle lying on the floor. Intrigued, the Mechanist examined the bottle more closely. There, sitting at the bottom of the container, sat a single remaining drop of the blue-gray potion.

The Mechanist gave a sigh of understanding. Now that he thought about it, he did have a faint recollection of when he had been sobbing over the death of his fellow councilman. He had only experienced grief like that once before in his life, when King Kev had banished him into the town of Blackstone as a laborer. To this day, the Mechanist still couldn't hear the words that the King had spoken to him without the psychological scars of that day floating to the surface.

So when the news of DZ's demise had come to light, the Mechanist had tried to remember what he had done to overcome the trauma of his banishment. The answer was quite simple: he had turned to SloPo. And it looked like in the death of one of his closest friends, the Mechanist had turned to SloPo yet again . . . though for the life of him he couldn't remember where he had gotten it.

The Mechanist shook his head in disgust. He remembered

what Gobbleguy used to tell him back in Blackstone, about how he was when he was on SloPo. He never had any recollections of how he acted, but he knew that he definitely wasn't in the mindset to lead a nation when he drank it.

The Mechanist picked up the glass bottle and shoved it firmly into the deepest depths of his inventory. With a knitted brow, he vowed to never drink the potion again, regardless of how stressed out he may be, as he turned his eyes back down to his work.

Jayden and G were both trying very hard to keep their breathing steady, to keep their bodies from shaking in anticipation. They were standing in the middle of a group of twenty upper-level players, standing in a five-by-four player line, in the center of the Capitol rotunda in the heart of Nocturia.

Both players were relieved that they had managed to merge into the Noctem forces so easily without arousing suspicion. They had spent the last day and a half marching through the forest, jungle, and desert until they reached the tundra where the Noctem capital of Nocturia was situated (they had overheard the higher-ups saying that the fast-travel highway through the Nether was still under construction).

As they marched across the countryside, Jayden and G had been horrified to see the evidence of Noctem occupation of the region. Scattered across all the biomes were Noctem bases constructed out of cobblestone, with black figures swarming around them. Once, they had walked by a community of players living at the edge of the jungle, and they had seen the players living there forced to go underground with no armor by Noctem soldiers armed with diamond weapons. G had found it difficult to keep himself from breaking free of the group and liberating the village.

Finally, after the endless trek through the tundra, they had arrived at Nocturia. The two councilmen found the city to be beyond impressive. In the middle of the endless expanse of snow-white hills and frigid blizzard, the Capitol Building of Nocturia stuck out like an ornate, gothic, and eerie thumb. Beyond the ornate and intimidating design of the stone-brick structure, what most stuck out about the outside design were the pillars of light. These thin rays of iridescence flashed out of the top of Nocturia and protruded high into the dark sky of the eternal snowstorm. G had later informed Jayden that these were Beacons, blocks that omitted light rays and were constructed of very rare materials added into the game a few updates back.

Surrounding the Capitol Building were dozens of other structures. These small stone-brick enclosures with gravel paths running between them were hardly impressive, but the two councilmen knew that within each of those small buildings were more Noctem troops, more soldiers ready to add to the bombardment of the Element City walls.

It had been late last night when G and Jayden had finally made their way into the Capitol Building with the other troops, amazed that they had managed to make it all the way to Nocturia undetected. As they had entered the building, Jayden and G had split from the group as soon as possible, and had, without much searching, found what they were looking for: a wooden sign on the stone-brick wall that read TRAINING AREA with an arrow pointing in their direction.

After following more signs, the duo had reached the training room, and, as their military intelligence had led them to believe, a new group of new recruits to the Noctem Alliance were waiting in the room. The two had waited outside the room until a figure appeared to escort the trainees to their quarters, and when the rabble of new recruits had passed, Jayden and G subtly shed their black armor and mixed into the crowd.

In the large stone-brick quarters lined with two dozen beds, the group of twenty recruits had been loud and raucous, in the process of meeting their new friends. Jayden and G had taken part, trying to look as casual as possible. When the redstone lamps lighting the room finally turned off, signaling curfew, Jayden and G had taken adjacent beds and drifted off to sleep, still not believing how smoothly their plan had run so far.

Now, the next day had come. It was early in the morning, and most of the recruits were groggy, having had to drag themselves out of bed to get their first-ever briefing by one of the generals of the Noctem Alliance. Not G and Jayden, though; the two councilmen were totally awake, well aware that at any point, they might pick up on a tidbit of information that would allow them to locate and rescue the hostages of the Adorian Village.

Suddenly, the entire crowd snapped to full attention, as a player walked onto the elevated platform above the rotunda floor. This player's upper body was covered in black leather armor, but the pink face and white ponytail down her back clearly distinguished this player as female. She had a no-nonsense look in her eye as she stared down the rows of new recruits.

"Greetings, my brothers and sisters," the player spoke in a voice that was neither overly hard nor overly cheery. Immediately, it rang in G's and Jayden's ears as the general who had led them from the battlegrounds of Element City back to Nocturia.

"My name is General Tess," she continued. "I am one of the three leaders of the armies of the Noctem Alliance, subservient only to the illustrious Lord Tenebris."

At the sound of the name, a shudder of excitement rippled through the crowd. They had all heard tales of the great

Lord Tenebris, and were thrilled to finally be serving under him. Jayden and G, meanwhile, gave a shiver of dread as they imagined what the leader of the Noctem Alliance was like.

General Tess smiled. "I can tell that you are all excited at the prospect of meeting the glorious Lord Tenebris. Let me tell you right now that your wish probably won't come true. The exalted supreme commander of the Noctem Alliance will only address his generals, myself included. Furthermore, he is a being shrouded in great mystery. I have never before seen his face, only heard his voice. None but the founders of our great Alliance have ever laid eyes on the magnificent Lord Tenebris . . . and lived to tell the tale."

This time, the wave of fear that passed through the new recruits was not just limited to Jayden and G.

"Nonetheless, in coming here, you have put your fate in the hands of Lord Tenebris and the Noctem Alliance. In doing so, you have already joined the ranks of those who seek truth, and shall therefore be saved. The magnificent Lord Tenebris has already led his armies to nearly conquer the uncivilized, lazy barbarians led by President Stan2012."

At the mention of Stan's name, there were hisses and grunts of disgust throughout the crowd.

"The Noctem Alliance has not yet been able to take back Element City, the greatest bunker of Stan's resistance. This is because those rallying behind Stan won't give up without a fight. They have unwavering faith in their belief that lower-level players of this server deserve to be pampered and babied. They believe that we, the hardworking upper-level players of Elementia, should go out of our way to help the lower-level players rise to equal our strength.

"What they forget," continued Tess, staying calm yet raising her voice to be heard above the angry grunts and roars of outrage from the crowd, "is that we, too, were once lower-level players. And we had nobody holding our hands as we endured the countless hardships, cruelties, and struggles that accompanied our rise to where we are now. But in the end, it was worth it, my friends! Elementia has transformed from nothing into the greatest server in the history of Minecraft! And the server has only us, the Golden Age Players, to thank for it!"

A cheer burst forth from the crowd of new recruits.

"King Kev understood this," Tess went on, her voice dripping with earnest passion. "He realized that, as payment for our work, all we desired was the ability to live our lives happily, reaping the rewards of what we had worked so hard to build. So naturally, when the spineless new players whined that the game was too hard and that they wanted their cut of the wealth, King Kev wouldn't hear it. The world is cruel, however, and King Kev was taken from us by the scum known as Stan2012. Just like that, the upper-level players of Elementia lost a great leader, who died with no crimes besides defending his righteous and honest beliefs. My friends, let us take a moment of silence to honor our fallen hero, King Kev."

Tess bowed her pink head to look at the ground, as did all the other recruits, including Jayden and G. While the two councilmen were clenching their fists to keep calm, the other new recruits around them seemed legitimately solemn. They even heard an occasional sob escape from the crowd.

"The Noctem Alliance," Tess continued after a moment, "was founded out of fate. It was by fate that our founding fathers survived the Battle for Elementia. It was by fate that the glorious Lord Tenebris appeared to them, offering them the guidance and wisdom to destroy Stan2012 once and for all. And it was by fate that all our meticulous planning was carried out flawlessly. The Noctem Alliance has managed to take back nearly all of what was stolen from us by President Stan. And yet, the great Element City, which we built, which we were forced to fight for, and which contains our houses, is still occupied by Stan.

"Many of you have left your homes in Element City to join the Noctem Alliance. Perhaps your realization of the vile nature of lower-level players is new, or perhaps you are just now willing to put your faith into the Noctem Alliance. For whatever reason, you have joined the Noctem Alliance quite late in the game, in the final stages of our operations.

Regardless of this, you have done the right thing. Better late than never, as I always say."

There was an awkward pause before the crowd realized that they were supposed to find this funny. They then burst into gales of laughter. G and Jayden rolled their eyes as Tess smiled at the soldiers' indulgence.

"The road ahead of you won't be easy," Tess continued after the strikingly artificial mirth had faded. "It's my job to transform you all from players into something more. The upcoming weeks of your training will not be pleasant. They will not be comfortable. I will treat you like the warriors you are expected to be, and mercy will *not* be tolerated. However, you'll leave this program as soldiers, ready to storm the battlefields of Elementia and take back what rightfully belongs to you, your brothers, and your sisters!"

Tess pumped her fist into the air. All the recruits followed suit, giving an animalistic roar of power and excitement as they did so.

"And now, my brothers and sisters, the time has come for you to, once and for all, affirm yourself as a true member of the Noctem Alliance! Are you all ready?"

"Yes, ma'am, General Tess," all the soldiers responded in unison. G and Jayden shut their mouths in horror; they had been about to give another shout of agreement, yet that clearly wasn't the right thing to do.

Tess nodded. "Now repeat after me: *I vow to fight for my rightful place in Elementia.*"

"*I VOW TO FIGHT FOR MY RIGHTFUL PLACE IN ELEMENTIA,*" the crowd responded almost robotically.

"*I vow to do all in my power to further the cause of the Noctem Alliance.*"

"*I VOW TO DO ALL IN MY POWER TO FURTHER THE CAUSE OF THE NOCTEM ALLIANCE.*"

"*I vow to submit to every command of the illustrious Lord Tenebris.*"

"*I VOW TO SUBMIT TO EVERY COMMAND OF THE ILLUSTRIOUS LORD TENEBRIS.*"

"*I hereby denounce President Stan2012, all his teachings, and all his followers.*"

As the group of players repeated the last lines back, G shuddered as he spoke the words. Although he himself didn't mean a word of it, he couldn't help but be terrified by the zealous fervor instilled in the crowd of players as they said this one particular line.

"*And I hereby surrender myself to the Noctem Alliance.*"

"*AND I HEREBY SURRENDER MYSELF TO THE NOCTEM ALLIANCE.*"

"*Long live Lord Tenebris!*"

"*LONG LIVE LORD TENEBRIS!*"

"*Long live the Noctem Alliance!*"

"LONG LIVE THE NOCTEM ALLIANCE!"

"Viva la Noctem!"

G grimaced. He had been wondering when he would be forced to say that hateful phrase, the slogan that he had despised since he had first heard it at the Noctem rally more than a month ago. He took a deep breath, swallowed his pride, and belted out the motto of the Noctem Alliance alongside Jayden and all the Noctem recruits.

"VIVA LA NOCTEM!"

Kat's eyes fluttered. Her head felt heavy and clunky. She recognized this feeling from many months ago, when she had been attacked by a horde of poisonous spiders in an abandoned mine shaft. Luckily, Stan and Charlie had been there to fight off the Spiders and heal her then. . . . Now, though, Kat could only guess at how long she'd been knocked out.

She took a deep breath, and realized that she was sitting in a tiny, cramped cobblestone cell with an iron door in front of her. Kat grimaced as she forced herself to sit up straight, and realized what had woken her up. The shrill, irritating, upper-class accented voice of Cassandrix echoed through the space outside her cell. Kat pulled herself to her feet and put her ear to the door, listening to the conversation.

" . . . will have you know that I am a high-ranking member of the hierarchy of Element City!" Cassandrix squealed.

"If you don't release me this instant, Element City will bear down on you with all its might!"

Kat banged her head against the door in frustration. Did Cassandrix honestly think that she was in any position to make demands?

"Ha!" a deep female voice replied from the outside hall, sounding amused. "Do you honestly think you're in any position to make demands?" (Kat slapped her forehead with her blocky hand as she heard this.) "We know exactly who you and your little friend are, and believe me, General Spyro has some business with the two of you."

"I won't tell you *anything* unless you set me free!" bellowed Cassandrix.

The guard gave a chuckle. "Oh, we'll see about that. You'll find that we here at Mount Fungarus can be . . . well . . . rather *convincing*, shall we say."

Kat's ears perked up. *Well,* she thought glumly, *at least they had made it to Mount Fungarus in one piece.*

"What are you talking about?" demanded Cassandrix.

"Well, allow me to put it this way," the guard continued, clearly enjoying hearing Cassandrix sound so desperate. "When the esteemed Councilman Charlie first arrived at this prison, he wasn't willing to talk either. But now . . . well, let's just say that not only have we retrieved some very interesting information from that brilliant mind of his, but he also will probably never be able to walk properly again."

Cassandrix let out an audible gasp of horror as the guard chuckled yet again. Kat shuddered, trying to convince herself that the guard was lying, and that they weren't too late. As Kat heard the footsteps of the guard walking away, she knew that they had to get out of their cells as quickly as possible. If the guard was telling the truth, and Charlie was being tortured to the point of becoming crippled, then they didn't have a single second to spare.

"Hey, Cassandrix," Kat said, trying to be as loud as possible without attracting attention.

"Oh . . . *you're* here . . . ," Cassandrix sighed from somewhere down the hall.

Kat gave a grunt of frustration. "It's good to see you, too. How long have you been up?"

"Oh, I awoke as soon as the guard came, darling . . . what, did you just wake up? Well to be frank, I'm not surprised. What with your low intelligence and strength, it only stands to reason that I would be able to shake off the poison first . . ."

Kat gave a roar of anger and punched the stone wall in frustration. "You're infuriating, you know that? We get captured and thrown in jail, and still you can't stop being so stuck-up!"

"Well, pardon me, darling," Cassandrix replied, sounding

offhanded yet also angry, "but I seem to recall that it was your impudence that got us into this situation in the first place, so pardon me if I find it difficult to suppress my indignation!"

"Oh, I'm sorry," Kat spat in response, "pardon *me* if I actually tried to listen in to find out valuable information from those bounty hunters, and then didn't take it lying down when you said that DZ's death didn't matter!"

"Oh, stop being such a baby." Cassandrix seethed in exasperation. "Honestly, you young players are all the same . . . thinking that you know what's best, barreling headfirst into dangerous situations, letting your emotions get the best of your common sense . . ."

"Excuse me," replied Kat, deeply offended and disturbed, "but you're starting to sound like a member of the Noctem Alliance."

"How *dare* you!" screamed Cassandrix. "I resent the implication that I am on the same level as those evil lunatics! I mean, do I resent the fact that since Stan took over, our city has devoted itself to pampering the younger, lower-level players into wealth and fortune with next to no work on their part? Of course I do! But never in a thousand lifetimes would I dream of discriminating against them or attacking them! It would be like attacking a toddler!"

"WHAT?" shouted Kat. "You think that the new players

have it *easy*? I'm sorry, but I seem to recall that my first few weeks in Elementia were spent fighting an evil dictator who was trying to kill me because of my *level*!"

"Oh, but you succeeded, didn't you?" Cassandrix shot back. "In a matter of weeks, you were able to upgrade your skills and materials until you were able to go toe to toe with the leaders of King Kev's army, players who had been training and gathering materials for years! Do you think that *I* had an Adorian Village to teach me when I first joined Elementia? Do you think that Element City or the Adorian Village would exist today if the people of my level hadn't struggled and toiled to raise it from the ground? And don't get me started on the Spleef tournament . . ."

"What does Spleef have to do with anything?" Kat demanded.

"Oh, don't make me laugh, darling," Cassandrix replied with a bitter, forced chuckle. "I'm referring to players like *you*, Kat."

"What are you—"

"I have worked for as long as I've been in Minecraft to become the best Spleef athlete in the world," Cassandrix spat, an almost imperceptible catch in her voice. "And all throughout King Kev's reign, I was never able to achieve any success. I was the best player in the league, but despite my hard work, it never amounted to anything. When Spleef returned after the fall of King Kev, I realized that, finally, I would have my chance in the spotlight and become the undisputed best Spleef player in the world. At long last, my hard work would pay off.

"And yet, all around me, I saw that new players, who had only been in Elementia for weeks, were playing Spleef along-side the best of us. While I was still the best Spleef player in the league, I was still barely ahead of these spoiled newer players, whose lives have been so easy that that they've been able to pick up the art of Spleef almost effortlessly. And right at the forefront was you, Kat . . . fighting alongside Ben and DZ, two older players who had put in just as much effort as I had. And yet, despite all your inexperience, you still equaled them in skill, while surpassing them handily in arrogance.

"So, yes, Kat, I *do* have a few problems with lower-level players. I hope that you can forgive me from up there on your high horse." Cassandrix sighed bitterly.

Ordinarily, Kat would have jumped on the opportunity to scorn Cassandrix for her insults, but now, she felt no such desire. In fact, Kat wasn't sure what she was feeling. Obviously, she knew that many of the things that Cassandrix had just spouted out were wrong and misguided, but . . . there also seemed to be very real elements of truth to them. And furthermore, Kat suddenly found herself in the inexplicable position of feeling sorry for Cassandrix. Kat hadn't realized just how much Cassandrix had been keeping bottled up, nor how unprepared she had been to see it erupt.

Suddenly, Kat heard footsteps coming from down the hall, and she snapped out of it. This wasn't the time to be thinking about such things. Their only priority had to be freeing themselves, and then finding Charlie and Commander Crunch.

Kat glanced out the tiny window of the steel door and saw the guard, totally obscured by a mask and her black armor, stop outside the door to Cassandrix's cell. Her hand went down to a lever outside the door.

"You in there," she grunted in Cassandrix's direction. "Back to the wall. You're coming with me to see General Spyro. If you cooperate, you won't be hurt."

Kat's heart skipped a beat. They were coming for them already? It had been less than five minutes! Kat's mind raced wildly, trying to formulate a plan.

"And don't even think about trying anything funny," continued the soldier, drawing an iron pickaxe from her inventory, "or I'll lodge this pickaxe into your back."

Suddenly, a thought struck Kat. Quickly, she glanced down the hallway. It was narrow but she was pretty sure that he'd be able to make it, wherever he was.

The soldier pulled the lever, and Cassandrix stepped out into the hallway. Kat saw that, although her white and golden flowing clothes were stunning, Cassandrix's white face was downcast and depressed. Kat only hoped that Cassandrix would take advantage of the opportunity that Kat was about to give her.

"Walk forward," the soldier commanded.

Kat took a deep breath, and gave a two-note whistle. Instantly, Rex appeared in the middle of the hallway. The soldier whipped around just as the wolf's eyes locked onto her.

"Sic 'em, boy!" Kat shouted.

Instantly, Rex's eyes glowed red, and he barreled down the hallway toward the soldier, snarling and barking like mad. She gave a shout of surprise before dropping into a fighting stance, and raising her pickaxe to strike. Rex leaped through the air toward her, and before the soldier could deliver the blow, Cassandrix body-checked her from the back, sending her smashing into the wall and tumbling to the floor.

The pickaxe went flying through the air and landed in Cassandrix's hand as Rex landed on top of the soldier, pinning her to the ground. Cassandrix brought the pickaxe above her head and drove it directly into the center of the soldier's leather armor. Immediately, a ring of items burst out from around her, signifying her demise.

"Good boy, Rex!" Kat shouted out from her cell as Cassandrix picked up the soldier's dropped items. Rex pounced over to the door of Kat's cell and began pawing at the steel barrier, whimpering. Cassandrix walked over to a second lever on the wall and pulled it down, allowing the door to swing open. Rex tackled Kat to the ground, licking her face.

"It's good to see you, too, boy!" Kat laughed, as she scratched the dog under his red collar, causing his tail to wag harder than ever. Cassandrix walked over to them.

"If you two are done," Cassandrix said in a determined voice, "we've still got to find Charlie and Crunch. And I'm sure the guards will be sending some reinforcements up soon. That attack wasn't exactly silent, you know."

Kat opened her mouth, ready to acknowledge in the most sarcastic way possible that Cassandrix hadn't even thanked her for saving her life, but she realized that Cassandrix was right. They had a mission to finish.

"You're right," Kat replied, nodding. "Let's go."

Sally!" cried Stan as the two players ran toward each other, and met in a tight embrace. "Oh, it's so good to see you again! In person, I mean."

Sally chuckled as she let him go. "Haha, yeah, I missed you, too, noob. I mean, being your omnipresent spirit mentor is nice and fun and all, but it's so much more hilarious when I can mess with ya in person."

Stan smiled. "Man, you just don't change, do you? Even after all this craziness, you're still exactly the same person that I met in the Adorian Village all those months ago . . ."

"Oh, don't go getting sentimental on me, noob," Sally scoffed, crossing her arms. "We've got a lot of work to do, and not nearly enough time to do it, so we can't waste any more words."

"Oh . . . okay," said Stan, feeling slightly awkward. *Yep,* he thought to himself. *Nothing's changed at all . . .*

"Anyway, I'm guessing that you want to know why you're here, noob."

"Well," replied Stan, slightly taken aback, "I, uh . . . assumed it was because you just wanted to see me again."

"Oh, Stan, Stan, Stan," Sally chuckled, closing her eyes and shaking her head in amusement. "You know what they say, noob . . . When you *assume,* you make an . . ."

"Hey!" exclaimed Stan, cutting her off. "If assuming things is so bad, then why did you assume that I wanted to know what I'm doing here?"

Sally opened her mouth, then closed it again. She scratched her head for a second, looking confused, and then nodded reasonably.

"Good point, noob," Sally replied agreeably. "Well, regardless, the important thing is that we both ended up looking stupid."

"Okay, fair enough," Stan replied. "So, why do you want me here, anyway?"

"Well, there are actually two reasons," Sally said. "The first reason is that I wanted us to be able to establish a place where we can meet up and talk without any problems. As of now, I've been spending only half my time spying on the Noctem Alliance, and the other half has been spent trying to contact you to tell you about it. Now that I have this server up and running, we can meet here if I have anything to tell you. It'll be much easier to find you for a minute and tell you to meet me here rather than to try to tell you the entire report in Elementia."

"Okay, fair enough," Stan replied, nodding his head. "So I'll still hear your voice in Elementia, and when I do, it means come onto this server?"

"Yes," Sally answered.

"Okay, good thinking," said Stan. "So, do you have any news to report to me?"

"Nothing yet," Sally replied. "I don't know who the Noctems have got doing their tech work, but they're clearly doing their job exceptionally well. I've never seen anything as difficult to hack in my life as Elementia is right now. And the worst part is, even if they're killed in Elementia, they'll still be able to keep working from beyond the server, like I am."

"Well, that's unfortunate," Stan said bitterly. "But I guess that it's a given, and we have to work with it. Anyway, you said you had two reasons for getting me to come over here."

"That I do, noob," Sally said nodding her head, a wild gleam of excitement shining in her eyes. "I'm gonna cut straight to the chase with you, Stan: I'm gonna try to get you operating powers in Elementia."

"Wait, what?" Stan asked, bewildered. He wasn't sure what he was expecting her to say, but it certainly wasn't that.

"You heard me," Sally replied.

"But . . . how . . ."

"Because I think I've figured out how," Sally said. "I was trying to work out how I could rejoin Elementia, but I found out that it wasn't possible. I did figure out that I should be able to give you operating powers, though. And if you had operating powers, then defeating the Noctem Alliance would be cake."

"So . . . hold on . . . questions . . . ," Stan sputtered as he tried to put together what Sally was saying. "Let me ask you this first . . . I've heard a lot about operating powers since I've been in Elementia . . . I know that King Kev and Avery used to have them, but then King Kev gave them up, and now nobody has them . . . but I'm still not entirely sure what operating powers are. I mean, what can you do with them, exactly?"

A devious grin crossed Sally's face. "Weeeellll . . . ," she said.

Then, without warning, Sally jumped off the ground, propelling herself into the air . . . and didn't come back down. She rocketed higher and higher into the sky, and then dipped downward. She bolted around the air like a superhero, performing loops and U-turns, all before returning. She flew suspended in the air directly above Stan, who stood motionless, and entranced.

"Well, you can fly, for one," she shouted from the air, her voice giddy.

Sally closed her eyes for a moment and then, without warning, a diamond sword popped out of midair and landed in her left hand. She stretched out her left hand toward the ground a distance away, took a deep breath and, with a rumbling sound, a tower of brick blocks began to construct itself, reaching high into the sky in a matter of seconds.

"You can also create items and blocks using your mind."

Sally rocketed off directly toward the brick tower, her fist outstretched. Stan watched in awe as she barreled directly through the center of the tower, leaving a gaping hole behind her. She circled backward and cut through the tower at six other points of various heights before finally flying back. Sally punched her fist through the air toward the tower, and immediately, an explosion rang out, taking a chunk of the tower with it. Sally aimed a blitz of quick jabs from the ground to the sky, destroying the tower from the bottom to the top.

"And you can also destroy blocks, either by hitting them with one punch or by creating explosions."

After the explosions had ceased, Sally flew back down to the ground, stopping just above Stan.

"So, yeah, those are a few things you can do with operating powers. There are a bunch more, too, but for now, there's really only one more that I want to show you."

Sally tossed her sword into the air, and stretched out her left hand toward it. The sword stood still in midair. As Sally moved her hand from side to side, the sword moved along with it, slicing through the open space. Sally clenched her fist, and the sword began to spin around in circles, like a midair top. As Sally released her fist and the sword hovered still once more, she directed her right hand down at the ground, toward Stan.

Instantly, Stan found himself unable to move. His arms and legs stiffened, as did his neck, and he began to levitate into the sky. All at once, Stan wasn't feeling blown away by these wonderful powers; quite the contrary, he felt terrified. He wasn't prepared to totally lose control of his body, especially when he was off the ground.

"Okay, Sally, you've made your point," Stan said firmly, trying not to hide the fear that was welling up in his body. "You can stop now."

But Sally didn't stop. Rather, at his request, a psychotic grin crossed Sally's face as she jerked her right hand upward. Stan let out a squeak of terror as he felt himself rocket into the air, jerking to a stop high above the grassy ground below. Sally's left hand moved a little, and the sword spun to face Stan.

"Sally . . . what're you doing?" asked Stan in horror.

"Teaching!" Sally replied, her eyes flashing with madness as she clapped her hands together in front of her. All at once, Stan felt himself fly forward at breakneck speeds, right toward the flying diamond sword.

Stan barely had time to comprehend what was happening before the sword had pierced him through the stomach and shot out his back. Stan felt an instant of pain, followed by a vacuum of light and sound until everything went black and silent.

Then, all at once, Stan found himself on a field of grass. His heart was racing. He glanced around wildly. He was sitting in the middle of the endless expanse of grass, and Sally was still levitating in the air next to her diamond sword. Immediately, Stan's hand went to his stomach . . . and found no wound. There wasn't even a rip in his shirt. And as Stan realized this, he also found that he wasn't in any pain. Confused out of his mind, he glanced up at Sally as she landed next to him.

"What did . . . how . . . are you insa . . . but I was de . . . *WHAT JUST HAPPENED?*" Stan demanded in fury.

Sally chuckled. "Oh, I just thought I'd kill two Creepers with one arrow. You know, demonstrate what my operating powers can do and show you that you can't die on this server at the same time. You know, you—"

"Okay, back up," Stan managed to get out, his head spinning. "First of all . . . why exactly am I not dead?"

"Oh, you poor sap," Sally replied, shaking her head and clicking her tongue in mock sympathy. "You've played on Elementia your whole life, and you're so ignorant to the rest of the Minecraft world."

"Wha . . . ?"

"Elementia isn't like other Minecraft worlds, noob," Sally said wisely. "On most Minecraft servers, after you die, you just appear back in the last bed you slept in . . . or at the spawnpoint, if your bed was destroyed or you haven't slept yet. Elementia is different because King Kev locked the server into Hardcore PVP mode. That means that the difficulty of the monsters is permanently on the hardest setting, players can hurt each other, and if you die you're banished from the server forever."

"So . . . ," Stan said slowly, trying to put things together in his head. "This server . . . SalAcademy . . . isn't like that?"

"Nope," replied Sally. "It's just a normal PVP server. Which means we can hurt each other, but we can also respawn, and operators like me can change the game mode."

"Okay, well, that leads into my other question, actually," said Stan. "How did you manage to get operating powers on this server?"

"You automatically get operating powers if you start a server," Sally answered, as if it were obvious. "Besides that, the only way to get operating powers is if somebody who already has operating powers gives them to you . . . like I'm about to do for you, in fact."

"Wait," exclaimed Stan, jumping to his feet and looking Sally in the eye. "You're gonna give me operating powers? I'm gonna be able to do all that stuff you just did?"

"After I train you," Sally replied, nodding with a smile.

"And once I get my powers," Stan said quickly, becoming more excited by the second as he realized the possibilities this development held, "I'll be able to use them anywhere? Both here and in Elementia?"

"No," Sally replied, shaking her head. "You'll only be able to use operating powers here, in SalAcademy."

"Well, then . . . what's the point?" Stan asked, crestfallen.

"The point is that, here, I'll be able to teach you how to use them," Sally said. "It takes a lot of training and practice to master the use of operating powers. It's not nearly as easy as I just made it look. I'm going to try to illegally hack the powers onto you in Elementia, but before I do, you need to learn how to use them. Once the Noctem Alliance realizes that I'm going to try this, they'll try to stop me, so I'll only have one shot at giving the powers to you without getting blocked. I want to make sure that you know how to use your powers when I take that shot."

"Well then, what're we waiting for?" Stan asked eagerly. "Give me my powers, and let's get training!"

"Haha, okay, noob," Sally replied as Stan bounced around like a puppy about to get a treat. "Stand still and calm down. And close your eyes."

Stan took a deep breath and stood still. He let the breath out and closed his eyes. After a moment, he felt a hand touch his forehead. An instant later, he felt like his entire body was going numb from an electric current. The sensation lasted for an instant . . . and then it stopped. Stan opened his eyes, and saw Sally drawing her right hand back.

"How do you feel?" Sally asked quizzically.

"Well, I felt something for a second . . . I don't feel much different now, though," Stan replied, confused.

"Well, there's only one way to find out for sure if it worked," replied Sally, stepping back and cracking her knuckles. Then she paused.

"Well," she continued, "actually, there are a few other ways we could check—we could check the file systems and such—but this way is a lot more fun!"

Sally stared at the ground in front of Stan. She took a deep breath and pushed her open-palm hand forward. Instantly, a three-block-high pillar appeared in front of Stan. These weren't blocks that Stan had seen before. They were dark stone blocks, streaked across the surface with the colors gray, black, and white.

"This is bedrock," Sally said, her eyebrows knit into a serious face. "It's the hardest block in Minecraft, it makes up the bottom layer of the world, and it's impossible to mine through. If you are a true operator, noob, you'll be able to destroy it in one punch."

"Okay," Stan replied. He stared at the pillar, fists balled

up under his chin. He bounced back and forth on the balls of his feet. He started mumbling to himself under his breath.

"All right . . . come on, Mr. Block . . . you're going down . . . what, you made outta bedrock? I'll tell you what else is made of bedrock . . . my *fist*! Well actually . . . not really . . . but it's as hard as bedrock . . . well, not really, but metaphorically I mean . . . and metaphorically, it's just as tough, too . . . and I'll tell you what else, metaphorically . . ."

"Just throw the stupid punch!" Sally shouted in irritation, snapping Stan out of it. He shook his head and focused in on the block. Then, in one graceful motion, he pulled back his fist and sunk it as hard as he could into the bedrock block.

"Daaaugh!" Stan shouted, clenching his teeth as he grabbed his throbbing fist. He shot an irritated look up at the bedrock block, still sitting there, obnoxiously solid.

"Try again," sighed Sally in a bored voice.

"All right," grunted Stan, "let's *go . . . argh*!"

Once again, he shook his fist in pain. Angry now, he threw punch after punch into the bedrock block, all accompanied by grunts, and all resulting in nothing more than an awful lot of agony in his fists.

"You're doing it all wrong, noob," Sally spoke after a moment. "You're punching the block with all your strength, which is the totally wrong way of going about it. You know that you have the ability to destroy the block . . . but you're still going about it as if you didn't have the powers. You're punching the outside of the block. Don't stop at the surface, Stan . . . I want you to punch straight through!"

And with that, Sally leaped into the air, and threw a punch directly through the highest block in the tower. Stan watched her fist, and saw that she was right: she didn't stop the punch at the surface of the block. Her first plowed directly through the center, causing the block to disappear in the process.

Stan took a deep breath and focused on the block directly in front of him. He looked at the gray-streaked surface and drew back his fist. Then, with all his might, Stan drove his fist into the block. His fist shot through the center of the bedrock block, and it disappeared into thin air. Stan's aching fist didn't feel a thing.

Stan drew back his hand, and looked at his fist in wonder.

"Congratulations, noob," said Sally with a smirk, clapping her hands together. "You're an operator now."

Stan grinned and looked back at Sally, overcome with jubilation.

"And all it took was a little advice from good ol' Sally," she continued with a laugh.

"You know," Stan said, looking at her in an adoringly accusatory way, "perhaps you could've brought up that insignificant little tidbit of advice *before* I nearly broke all my knuckles."

"Yeah, I suppose I could've . . . but that wouldn't have been *nearly* as funny, would it?" Sally responded with a chuckle. "Now come on, noob!" she continued as Stan glared at her in exasperation. "You've got to get back to Elementia soon, but there are a few things I want to show you first!"

Leonidas was beginning to worry. The search had been going on forever now, and every second that he sat holed up in the cave, the chances increased that Stan would return and find himself in the midst of a quintet of heavily armed Noctem fighters. Leonidas had managed to silently take out one of the soldiers who had wandered down the cave to search. He was able to replenish his supply of arrows from the archer. All the others were still scuttling around the tiny dirt island like ants on an anthill. Leonidas was just pondering how much more there was to search when he heard a shout from above.

"All troops, fall in!" Spyro's voice rang out.

Leonidas heard footfalls on the ground above his head, and he crept his way up the cave to spy on them, careful not to alert any bats in the process. He poked his head out of the side of the cave and saw the four black-clad players circled around Spyro, whose face was illuminated by the moonlight.

"Okay, first and foremost," said Spyro, glancing around his men, "where's ShadowNinja?"

"I'm not sure," one of the players replied. Leonidas

recognized the distinct, high-pitched squeaky voice as Commander Squid, an old private of his. "He must still be out searching."

"Hmm . . . he can't be far . . . this is a pretty small island . . . ," Spyro said to himself. "Anyway, not important, we'll find him in a minute. For now, let's set up camp."

Leonidas's heart dropped out of his stomach. They were staying the night? He watched in horror as the Noctem soldiers pulled beds, furnaces, and anvils from their inventories, setting them up all around the spot where Stan would no doubt be reentering Elementia soon.

I have to kill them all, Leonidas thought desperately, *or at least severely weaken them. There's no way that Stan'll be able to handle that many guys if he comes back . . . he'll be totally blindsided! What should I do . . .*

Leonidas knew that he had no time whatsoever to think his plan out further; he would simply have to go for broke. Leonidas poked his head out from around the wall of the cave and drew his bow. He notched an arrow in the string, pulled it back, took aim, and, after he had a clear shot, he let it fly, ducking back into the cave immediately after he did so.

Leonidas heard the cry of anguish that accompanied his arrow and knew that he had hit the mark. He heard the shouts of surprise and terror from the ring of Noctem troops, and Spyro's voice bellowed out, "WHO'S THERE? SHOW YOURSELF!"

Heart pounding out of his chest, Leonidas readied another arrow, and took another shot at the circle, this time aiming for the closest soldier. Again, the shout of pain, and the renewed round of terrified confusion.

"What's going on here?"

"Who's shooting at us?"

"Look, over there! I saw someone in the mine!"

"Argh," Leonidas grunted to himself as he sprinted out into the open. He saw the three remaining soldiers glare at him, but he sprinted away before they could catch his eye.

"It's ShadowNinja! He betrayed us!" bellowed Spyro in fury.

For a moment, Leonidas was confused, but then he realized what had happened. The player he had killed in the mine—ShadowNinja, apparently—had also been an archer. They must have assumed that, with his black leather armor, he was their comrade gone renegade. In any case, thought Leonidas to himself, none of them would live to realize the truth.

Leonidas sprinted his way up to the top of the dirt mound that was the island, and when he was at the peak, he glanced down. Commander Squid was making his way up the island, eyes blazing in fury and iron axe in hand. Another figure who Leonidas didn't recognize was taking aim at him with a bow from the beach below. Leonidas had no idea where Spyro was, but he had more pressing matters to deal with at the moment.

Leonidas sidestepped the arrow fired his way from the beach, and stood back up to find that Commander Squid was upon him. He launched a powerful axe strike at Leonidas's head, which he simply ducked under, sending Squid tumbling back down the slope with a body check.

Having dealt with that problem for the time being, Leonidas then focused his attention on the archer on the beach. He had to duck two back-to-back arrows before he finally managed to get a clear shot on the archer. As fast as possible, Leonidas fired an arrow to the left of the archer, then directly at him, and then a ways to the right. The plan worked; the archer hopped right to avoid the first two arrows, directly into the path of the third. Leonidas sent another well-placed arrow down to finish him, and the ring of items bursting from the beached archer indicated Leonidas's victory.

Leonidas hardly had time to celebrate, however, as Commander Squid was nearly back upon him. Almost effortlessly, Leonidas managed to stay out of the range of Squid's frantic axe swipes, and sunk three arrows into him in a matter of seconds. Leonidas took a deep breath and glanced around the island below him, hoping to locate where Spyro went.

Then, without warning, Leonidas sensed something behind him. He lunged as hard as he could out of the way of the diamond sword that had stabbed at him from behind. Leonidas fell off the top of the hill and landed on the ground with a crash, tumbling painfully down the hill until he landed with a thud on the beach below.

Aching but not badly hurt, Leonidas kicked up onto his feet, loading his bow and standing perfectly still, trying to control his breathing, in the hopes that he might feel the invisible player moving around him.

Before long, Leonidas sensed a presence coming directly toward him. He shot his arrow forward to no avail, and was about to fire another when an invisible fist sunk hard into Leonidas's stomach, knocking the wind out of him. This was quickly followed by an uppercut under his chin that sent him flying backward, leaving him sprawled out on the ground. Dazed, Leonidas focused hard on staying conscious. When a sword appeared from nowhere above him, Leonidas suddenly felt wide awake as he rolled to the side. The sword drove deep into the ground, and Leonidas sent another arrow flying toward the weapon.

There was a grunt of agony as the arrow found its mark, and Leonidas saw the pained body of General Spyro flash into view for a moment before it disappeared again. However, the arrow in his arm remained, revealing where he was. Then,

Leonidas watched in horror as a Potion of Healing poured onto the wound. The arrow popped out of the invisible arm and onto the sand.

"Well, well, well," the invisible Spyro laughed to himself as he picked up the arrow from the ground and snapped it in half. "If it isn't Leonidas . . . the once-great general of the Noctem Alliance."

Leonidas was too exhausted to answer. He chose to devote his energy to coming up with an attack plan during this moment of rest rather than responding.

"I'm gonna get another promotion for this kill," Spyro laughed to himself. "They'll have to invent a rank above general!" And with that, the levitating diamond sword barreled forward, straight toward Leonidas.

Having not established a surefire plan yet, Leonidas raised his bow to fire again, but Spyro's sword cleaved it in half, the tension of the weapon sending the two halves flying into the distance. In the following instant, Leonidas considered drawing the bow he had gotten from ShadowNinja, but instead chose to draw his iron sword and engage Spyro in combat.

The effort, however, was futile. Spyro outclassed Leonidas in sword fighting by a remarkable degree, and it wasn't long before Leonidas's sword spiraled high in the air, landing with a splash in the nearby ocean. Leonidas took off sprinting, though from what, he did not know. He now realized that his efforts were futile and, eventually, Spyro was going to catch him.

Suddenly, Leonidas came across a block-high drop on the sand beach and, not expecting it, he tripped and tumbled across the sand. He landed face-up, and he became aware that Spyro's diamond sword was just blocks away from him.

This is it, thought Leonidas as the diamond sword rose above him. He closed his eyes.

Then, Leonidas heard a clash of two blades, and a grunt of pain. A moment later, he heard the sound of a player landing on the dirt, and Spyro's voice yelling out, "What the . . ."

Leonidas opened his eyes, and painfully propped himself up on his arm before glancing up. Standing there, his back to Leonidas, was a player. In the faint moonlight, Leonidas could just make out dark-colored pants and shoes. A black cloak obscured the top half of his body, blowing faintly in the ocean breeze. In his pale left hand he held a diamond sword, pointed at the ground.

Leonidas saw Spyro a distance away. He was sitting on the sand and flashing in and out of sight as his Potion of Invisibility began to wear off. Spyro glanced up at the mysterious hooded figure standing between him and Leonidas and looked shocked, infuriated, and scared.

"Who are you? Where did you come from?" Spyro demanded.

The figure didn't answer. He simply stood there, not moving a muscle.

"That player is a wanted criminal. In the name of the Noctem Alliance and Lord Tenebris, I order you to stand down!" bellowed Spyro, raising his diamond sword into an attack stance.

Again, the figure didn't respond. But he did raise his right arm, crossing his sword over the front of his body in what was clearly a defensive stance.

"All right, if that's the way it is!" hissed Spyro as he charged the hooded figure. The Noctem general launched countless high-power sword strikes at the figure. The speed and technique was very impressive, yet the figure was able to block every attack without moving a muscle except for his right hand.

After a minute of fighting, the figure executed a twist-block maneuver, sending Spyro's sword flying, and he sunk his left fist hard into Spyro's stomach. Spyro fell to the ground with a thud, cringing in pain. The figure didn't continue the attack; rather, he simply moved his sword back into a defensive stance.

Grimacing, Spyro looked back up at the figure, tears in his eyes.

"Who . . . what . . . are you?" he managed to get out, fear manifested in his voice.

The figure, once again, said nothing. Spyro gazed into the face of the figure for a full minute. And then . . .

"You're gonna get it," Spyro spat, and he whipped a boat out of his inventory and hopped in the water, moving as fast as possible back in the general direction of the Mushroom Islands.

Leonidas looked up at the figure, wondering what to say. He had no idea who this player was, or where he came from, but he had just saved Leonidas's life.

The robed figure turned to face Leonidas. As Leonidas glanced up, he realized that he could not see the figure's face. The black cloak covered the upper body, and the hood obscured the upper half of the player's face, revealing only a pale mouth. And although the figure still said nothing, Leonidas somehow knew the figure's name, despite having no idea who he was.

"Thank you, Black Hood," Leonidas whispered.

The Black Hood turned to face the ocean. Then, in an instant, he dived into the water and disappeared into the murky depths. Leonidas forced his aching body to stand up and glance down, hoping to catch any indication of where the player had gone. And yet there was nothing. When the ripples of the splash finally disappeared, it was as if nobody had ever been there.

Leonidas was perplexed, and was about to start pondering

what had just happened when he heard a noise across the island. Quietly, Leonidas crept back to the top of the island and glanced over the peak. The view of the ocean expanded forever up here, and Leonidas could see Spyro's ship going farther and farther into the distance. And on the bottom beach of the island, Leonidas could see Stan, pulling a bed from his inventory and walking over to the cave.

Leonidas realized just how tired he was. Stan had the right idea; it was late. Leonidas was far too exhausted to think about Spyro, now delivering his whereabouts to Lord Tenebris, or to figure out just who it was who had just saved his life. All Leonidas wanted to do was find the softest pile of dirt he could and go to sleep.

As G and Jayden walked down the hallway toward the Training Center Gymnasium, neither of them spoke. They both knew that, to keep their cover, they should have been chatting like the other trainees around them, eager to partake in the sparring tournament that was only moments away. However, they had given themselves a pass, as they had both been plagued with nightmares last night after yesterday's tour.

Not that the tour hadn't been extremely helpful, because it had. The walk around the Capitol Building had been crucial to figuring out where the Adorian hostages might be held. There had been areas where the tour wasn't allowed to go, and they had pegged those as various places where the hostages might be. The tour of the training facility had been equally helpful, as the layout would have to be memorized if they wanted to be able to make an impromptu escape.

However, toward the end of the tour, the two boys had seen a sight that would haunt them forever. From a glass room overlooking a dark, stone pen, they had finally gotten a glimpse of Stull and Mella. The two Zombie villagers were disgusting, letting out moaning noises and occasionally garbled rambles that resembled speech. Jayden and G had watched in horror as unconscious Elementia soldiers had been dropped into the pen, immobile prey to the Zombie villagers.

It was all that the boys could do to stop from getting sick, and they weren't the only ones. While a few of the recruits either watched in amazement or cheered for the Zombies, the majority of the players just looked really uncomfortable. None could feel the effects more profoundly than Jayden and G, though. Those villagers had visited them in Elementia a good few times, and the sight of them eating Elementia soldiers haunted them even the next day as they went into the area.

"Welcome," said Tess as the recruits filed into rows, the early-morning sunlight blinding them from the glass roof above. "Today is your Aptitude Tournament. You will be called up by me, and two players will fight each other until one is unable to continue. Killing and permanent crippling is not allowed, but all else is. The winner will advance to the next round, and so on. Based on your performance during your fights, I will determine your base rankings during your training. Now, everyone stand at the sidelines. The first fight will be between MasterBronze and LemonKipper."

G took a deep breath and stood up; MasterBronze was his cover name. He stood in the center of the ring, and another player stepped into the arena across from him. Although he was now covered in black leather armor, G recognized this player. He had the skin of a merman, and was cocky to a fault.

A black foot soldier stepped forward from behind Tess and walked over to the two of them. "What is your weapon of choice?" he asked G.

"Pickaxe," G grunted in response, and the soldier reached into his inventory, pulled out a stone pickaxe, and handed it to G. *Well,* he thought, turning it over in his hand, *it's not diamond, but it'll have to do.*

"What is your weapon of choice?" the soldier asked, turning to face Kipper.

"Sword," Kipper replied in a Welsh accent, snatching the stone sword that the soldier had pulled from his inventory.

"Okay," Tess announced as the soldier backed away. "Ready? And . . . Fight!"

G raised his pickaxe in a defensive stance, allowing Kipper to make the first move. He gladly obliged, holding his sword in an attack stance and bouncing on the balls of his feet.

"You're going down, kid," Kipper hissed as he tried for an overhand strike at G's head. In one motion, G sidestepped the attack, caught the sword in his pickaxe, and twisted the weapon out of Kipper's grip. Then G dropped to the floor and swept Kipper's leg, sending him tumbling to the ground. While his foe was dazed, G grabbed the stone point of his pickaxe and clubbed Kipper over the head with the wooden end, knocking him out.

"We have a winner!" Tess announced, and all the recruits clapped. G didn't feel like it was much of an accomplishment. Kipper obviously wasn't a very skilled fighter. He took his place back in line, and received an encouraging nod from Jayden.

A series of fights followed the first one, ranging from two totally equally matched fighters, to two cowards running away from each other, to one player totally dominating the other. G found the fights to be rather tedious, and only really paid attention when it was Jayden's turn.

Jayden's fight was against an archer, and he initially played defensive, blocking every arrow shot with his stone axe. Eventually, though, he found an opening, and managed to use a carefully placed axe throw to deliver a leg wound, causing him to win so the wound could be healed with potion.

The next round of the top eight fighters wasn't very interesting either. Both Jayden and G outmatched their opponents by a considerable degree, and managed to take them out without much effort. The other matches were slightly more interesting to watch at least, ranging from an intense sword fight to two archers sniping at each other.

After the top eight were narrowed to the top four, a series of matches ensued that were a bit more interesting.

Jayden locked swords with an impressive pickaxe fighter, who used the weapon more as a projectile than a melee weapon, dodging Jayden's axe swipes while trying to hit him from afar. Eventually, though, Jayden was able to land a solid blow on her, and he won.

G went into combat with one of the archers, who actually gave him a rough time. The pickaxe was much harder to block arrows with than the axe, and the archer actually managed to land a couple of shots. It wasn't long, though, before G managed to force an approach, and he won his battle with a blow to the stomach not long afterward.

"Okay," announced Tess as the last cringing recruit pulled himself off the field. "We're down to the final round. It's MasterBronze versus Drayden!"

Taking a deep breath, G walked back into the ring. As he looked Jayden in the eye, it occurred to him that he really didn't know who would win this match. Although he and Jayden were both easily better than the rest of the recruits, mostly upper-level players who had lived their whole lives in luxury, he and Jayden were both a bit out of practice. They hadn't sparred at all since before King Kev had fallen, when they were still working in the Adorian Village together. And even back then, they were very evenly matched.

"Ready . . . and . . . FIGHT!" announced Tess.

G caught Jayden's eye, and he knew they were both

thinking the same thing. The two of them had the same fighting style, where they played defensive until they found an opening, and then broke into a ruthless, all-out attack. But if both of them played off counterattacking, then how were either of them going to win?

G sunk into an offensive stance. *It doesn't really matter who wins,* he thought to himself, a*s long as we both get high scores so we can work our way into the higher ranks of the army faster. So I guess I'll give Jayden an opening.*

G rushed in, pickaxe blazing, as Jayden sunk back, ready to counter. Just as he was about to strike, though, he cut left, dodging Jayden's axe jab and knocking the axe out of his hand with a stray strike. G lunged in to follow up with a pickaxe blow, but Jayden rolled out of the way, landing by his axe. Jayden snatched his weapon off the ground and sent it spiraling through the air toward his opponent. G feinted out of the way, but the handle of the flying axe caught his hand, sending his pickaxe into the air. Jayden and G watched as their weapons clattered to the ground beside each other.

The two friends caught each other's eyes for a moment, and then rushed as quickly as possible to retrieve their weapons. G had the head start, but Jayden was faster, and they grabbed them at the exact same time. The two players pressed into each other's blades as hard as they could, struggling for an advantage. Then, right as G was thinking that he couldn't keep up the fight much longer, the two stone blades shattered into a thousand pieces, sending the two players reeling back away from each other.

G turned around to glance at Tess, unsure of whether or not he was in trouble. She just looked at him expectantly, waiting for him to finish. A lightbulb going on in his head, G sprinted toward the recovering Jayden. As the two locked eyes, G, with his back to the others, winked at Jayden and made a face as if he were knocked out before drawing back a punch.

Jayden got the message. G threw the punch at Jayden's head, missing him by a millimeter, but Jayden still went tumbling backward through the air. He landed on the ground with a thud, seemingly unconscious.

"Well done, MasterBronze," Tess said with a smile as a soldier went over to Jayden and poured a Potion of Healing in his mouth. Jayden's eyes fluttered, then opened as he pulled himself to his feet. Though he was rubbing his face where he got punched, he still walked over to G and shook his hand. As the other recruits cheered for them, Jayden shot G a smile and a wink, which he happily returned.

Kat took a deep breath as she caught sight of a Noctem soldier walking down the hallway. She forced herself not to look, and instead to focus on the unarmored back of Cassandrix, and the pickaxe she was holding up to it.

As the duo passed the soldier, he gave a polite nod in Kat's direction. She returned the gesture, and continued walking down the hallway, until he was out of sight.

Kat released the breath she had been holding in. It was a relief to know that the armor that Cassandrix had looted from the Noctem guard disguised her so well. She told herself that it was all fine, and that even if she was captured, she could always just call Rex back out of hiding to help her.

"Seen anything yet?" Kat hissed to Cassandrix as they turned left down a hallway, past a new row of jail cells.

"If I had seen either of them, darling," Cassandrix whispered back in irritation, "don't you think I would have said something?"

Kat bit her tongue to hold back her retort, and forced herself to keep walking. It hurt her to see that, while most of the jail cells were empty, some of them housed players who were clearly not even soldiers. She could only assume they were civilians from the Mushroom Islands. As much as she wanted to, Kat knew that she couldn't break those players out. They just had to find Charlie and Commander Crunch as quickly as possible and be on their way.

The two rounded another corner and checked another row of jail cells, lining both sides of a hallway that led to an iron door. None of these cells held Charlie or Crunch either;

in fact, they were all vacant. Kat snorted in irritation, and was just about to make a left turn at the iron door when a soldier stepped around the corner and into her way.

"What do you think you're doing here, soldier?" the player demanded. He had the skin of an extremely muscular Mexican wrestler.

"I'm just moving this prisoner to a holding block for interrogation," replied Kat somberly, hoping that her prison jargon was believable.

"Do you have clearance to come this way?" the guard interrogated further.

"No," replied Kat, gears whirring in her head. "I wasn't aware that this area was blocked off."

"Lord Tenebris is operating dangerous procedures behind that door, kid," the soldier grunted.

Kat's eyebrows shot up. "He is?"

The guard eyed Kat suspiciously. "Of course . . . and you should know that. Weren't you at the meeting this morning, soldier?"

"Well, I . . . uh . . ."

"You're an imposter!" the guard exclaimed. "*Secu—* ugh . . ."

The guard's shout was cut off as Cassandrix launched forward and wrapped her arms around the guard's neck in a chokehold. Before he could shake her off, Kat slammed the pickaxe into the guard's forehead, knocking him out, and finished him off with a powerful blow to the stomach. A ring of items, mainly food, burst from the player and onto the ground.

"Hey! What's going on over there?" a voice rang out from down the hall, and Kat heard the stomping of footsteps running toward them. Kat raised her pickaxe and dropped into a defensive stance, and was just about to panic when a pair of hands whipped her around. Cassandrix was looking back at her, clad head to toe in the dead soldier's black armor.

"Stay calm," Cassandrix murmured, "and follow my lead."

And with that, Cassandrix bent down and began to pick through the items lying on the ground as the soldier's body disappeared. Kat did the same, praying that Cassandrix did indeed have a plan.

Moments later, a group of six players, armed with bows and fire charges, burst around the corner and aimed directly at the two girls.

"What happened here, soldiers?" the player at the front of the group demanded.

"It was an escape attempt," Cassandrix replied solemnly. "We were transporting a prisoner to interrogation, and she tried to overwhelm us. We were forced to kill her . . . and judging by the inventory she dropped, she's been planning this escape for a while, hoarding her food and everything."

"Which prisoner was it?" the head guard asked. "And what cell did she come from?"

"Well, I know that the prisoner's name was Cassandrix," Cassandrix continued, giving Kat a glare of steel when her eyes widened, "but I'm not sure what cell she was from. The two of us received her a few hallways back from another pair of soldiers whom I didn't recognize."

"Well, if that's the case, I'm going to have to ask the two of you to come with me," the head guard ordered as his soldiers lowered their bows. "General Spyro will be returning from the island raids soon, and you'll present all your findings to him."

"I'm sorry, but that's not possible at the moment," Cassandrix replied, not missing a beat. "The two of us were meant to escort the prisoner to this point, and then hand her off to yet another pair of guards. You see, we were ordered to stop here to guard this door . . . as I'm sure you know, the illustrious Lord Tenebris is operating dangerous procedures in there."

"Very well then," the guard replied. "Who was supposed to pick up the prisoner from the two of you?"

"Again, I'm not sure," Cassandrix replied. "My apologies, but my partner and I are new transfers to Mount Fungarus. We still don't know everybody yet. . . . But as soon as we're done standing guard for the glorious Lord Tenebris, I promise you that we'll be able to show you who the players are if you line up the guards in front of us."

The head guard nodded. "All right, soldier. I trust that you and your partner will report back to the common area as soon as your duties here are completed."

"Please," Cassandrix replied with a snide chuckle. "We stopped an escape on our second day here! Don't think for a moment that we won't want to personally take credit for that."

"Right," the guard said with an amused smile. "At ease, soldiers." And with that, he turned and marched away, followed by the rest of his archers.

Kat looked at Cassandrix in admiration. "That was amazing!" she exclaimed.

"Well, you know, I'm quite good on my feet, darling," Cassandrix simpered. "One would think that after all your experience against me in the Spleef arena, you would realize that."

Always has to kill the moment, doesn't she, thought Kat bitterly. Then again, with the way Cassandrix had managed to save them just then, Kat was willing to let it slide.

The two players turned to face the iron door. Kat reached for the stone button on the wall, but Cassandrix slapped her hand down.

"What do you think you're doing?" Cassandrix demanded.

"Lord Tenebris is behind that door!" Kat whispered urgently. "This might be our only chance to see him . . . or maybe even to take a shot at him."

"Are you insane?" Cassandrix hissed. "Now is neither the time nor place to pull a vigilante stunt. We have a mission, Kat, and even with your abnormally lacking attention span, I'd think you'd be able to remember that."

"I didn't forget," Kat growled, "but this might be our only chance."

"You already said that, Kat," Cassandrix cut in, "and frankly, it's not worth it. You're willing to risk what might be your one chance to save your friends just so you *might* have a *tiny chance* to take down Lord Tenebris?"

"Well . . ."

"Kat, we might never be in this situation again! The guards think that we're with them, and we have plenty of time before they realize that we've escaped! And further-more . . . GET BACK HERE RIGHT NOW!"

Cassandrix sprinted forward to grab Kat, who had jammed the button on the wall and was already through the iron door. Cassandrix pulled on Kat's tunic as hard as she could, but Kat was too strong, and Cassandrix tumbled for-ward through the passage just as the iron door slammed shut behind them.

The two girls were now standing in a room made entirely of stone. Redstone lamps kept the areas light enough to keep mobs from spawning, but even then it was quite dark. The room had a very high ceiling, with stone pillars that stretched from the floor to the top. Across from them, standing against the other wall, was a Nether Portal, glowing purple with luminescence and spewing purple particles into the room. Between the two pillars farthest away sat a throne made entirely of obsidian.

Cassandrix looked around wildly, trying to find another button on this side of the wall. She was shocked, however, to find none. Except for the indentation of the door, the wall on this side was totally flat.

"Oh, for heaven's sake," whined Cassandrix, "who designs a door that automatically locks from the outside?"

"Uh, I don't know," replied Kat, shrugging her shoulders. "Admittedly, that doesn't seem like a very practical design choice . . ."

Cassandrix wheeled around to face her partner. Her face was alight with fury.

"Look what you did, you little brat!" she hissed. "We're trapped in here with no way to get back . . . wait a second!" Cassandrix's eyes drifted slowly to the pickaxe Kat was holding. Before she could respond, Cassandrix had snatched the iron tool from her hand.

"What are you doing?" Kat demanded as Cassandrix fervently rushed her way back over to the stone wall.

"I'm getting us back to the safe side of the wall!" she said, her eyes almost glowing with lunatic fervor as she drove the iron pickaxe as hard as she could into the stone wall.

The effect was immediate. The iron pickaxe snapped off its handle, and landed on the floor with a clang.

For a moment, Cassandrix stared blankly at the wooden handle of the tool. Then, without warning, she sunk to her knees, clutching her head in exasperation, and bemoaning the fact that not only were they now trapped, but they had lost one of the only weapons that they had. As Cassandrix lay crippled on the floor, mumbling to herself, Kat picked up the two parts of the weapon and examined them, fascinated.

"This pickaxe . . . ," she said slowly, glancing at the two halves. "It looks like . . . it looks as if this thing has never been used before. The blade is shiny, and there aren't any dents on it. . . . If I didn't know better, I'd say that this pickaxe has never seen mining or combat before. I mean, it certainly wasn't close to being used up when you tried to use it . . ."

Kat glanced incredulously up at the stone wall. "What kind of stone is this?" she asked quizzically.

As Cassandrix glanced up at the wall, she suddenly forgot to act distraught. She was intrigued, and also a bit unnerved, by this wall. The stone that made up the wall wasn't cobblestone, nor any variety of it. These were dark stone blocks, streaked across the surface with the colors gray, black, and white.

"Kat, I recognize this," Cassandrix said slowly. "This room . . . it's made out of bedrock."

"I'm not familiar," Kat said, glancing at the wall. "It must be pretty hard, though. Is this . . . bedrock . . . harder to mine through than obsidian?"

"It's not just hard to mine through. It's *impossible* to mine through," Cassandrix whispered. "Nothing in all of Minecraft can put a dent in this stuff, not even a charged Creeper blast. Usually it makes up the bottom of the world, and indicates the absolute lowest point that you can mine."

"So . . . if it can't be mined . . . what's it doing up here?" Kat asked.

"There's only one explanation," Cassandrix replied, and she turned to look Kat directly in the eye. "This bedrock must have been put here by someone . . . or something . . . incredibly powerful."

Just at that moment, the two girls heard a whooshing sound and saw a flash of purple light. Somebody was entering through the Nether Portal. Thinking fast, the two of them ducked behind the nearest pillar.

Peeking around the sides, Kat and Cassandrix watched with racing hearts as a player walked into the center of the area, right before the obsidian throne. The player was dressed in black pants and a black shirt, and a golden cloak was draped over his shoulders, the hood pulled back. He turned his head, and Kat recognized the face of Count Drake.

A twinge of resentment struck Kat. She had vivid memories of her past encounters with Drake, from his escape from Brimstone up to his attack on the Spleef World Finals. She pulled a bow and arrow that she had looted from the dead guard and drew it back. She was starting to take aim when suddenly, Drake knelt down before the obsidian throne and spoke.

"Oh great and powerful Lord Tenebris," Drake chanted, "I have returned!"

There was a sound, the same sound an Enderman made upon teleporting. And then, all at once, a player appeared on the throne.

This player had dark brown hair and shoes, a turquoise shirt, and navy-blue pants. His eyes were closed, and his fingers were pressed together in front of him in a businesslike manner.

Kat felt the need to slap herself, because she couldn't believe that what she was seeing was real. Could that . . . could it really be . . .

"Oh, exalted one," Drake replied from his position on

his knees, "I have acquired the materials that you have requested."

"You have done well, General Drake," the figure replied in a deep, booming voice as he opened his eyes.

Kat sighed in relief. Now she knew for sure that it wasn't Stan. She knew for a fact that Stan didn't have that deep, booming voice, nor did he have white eyes.

Kat was a little bit surprised. She didn't know exactly what she was expecting of Lord Tenebris, the founder and supreme commander of the Noctem Alliance, but it certainly wasn't this. This player didn't look at all like he would be the most evil person in Elementia since King Kev. In fact, except for his eyes, he looked exactly identical to Stan.

Those eyes, though . . . there was something incredibly disturbing about those eyes. As Kat looked at them, she tried to see if there were any traces of familiarity. However, she could only look into them for a few seconds before she had to look away in discomfort.

Kat turned to Cassandrix to see what she thought, expecting her to be equally confused. What she didn't expect to see was Cassandrix staring slack-jawed at Lord Tenebris, eyes bulging, expression as terrified as if she had laid eyes on a ghost. Kat assumed that she was just petrified that she was staring face to face with the leader of the Noctem Alliance, but she still couldn't help but feel as if Cassandrix had just realized something about Lord Tenebris that she herself hadn't.

"Thank you, sir, your praise means the world to me," Drake spoke on. "And I assure you, the collection of these materials was not easy."

"And why is that?" Lord Tenebris asked, raising an eyebrow. "You had all you needed to obtain the materials in a timely manner."

"Oh, no, sir," Drake replied quickly, his voice shaky. "I found the patch of Soul Sand without difficulty. However, in terms of the Wither Skeletons, they required . . . how should I put this . . . a bit more thought to handle."

"Go on," inquired Lord Tenebris, tapping his fingers together.

"Well," continued Drake, "as of now, I thought that it might be . . . shall we say . . . prudent to not anger the Wither Skeletons. Our forces have nearly broken through the walls of Element City, and when they do, I have a feeling that we'll need all the security in Brimstone that we can get our hands on."

"I suppose," Lord Tenebris replied, sounding bored, while chills went down Kat's spine. She couldn't help but worry about just how truthful Drake was being, and just how close the walls of Element City really were to cracking.

"In any case, I peacefully requested that they supply their Skulls to me, for the sake of appeasing you, Your Benevolence. They were able to give me two skulls of their fallen brethren after long negotiations, and then volunteers offered to sacrifice themselves for the sake of providing their own skulls.

"It was a tedious process, Your Highness, and many

Wither Skeletons lost their lives—or, rather, afterlives. You see, even with a level-three Looting enchantment, the Wither Skeletons have only slightly over a five percent chance—"

"I'm well aware, Drake," Lord Tenebris cut in irritably.

"Oh, I apologize, great leader," Drake sputtered hastily, sinking into a deep bow. "By no means was I trying to imply that you were in any way—"

"Silence," Lord Tenebris hissed, cutting off Drake's babbling. "It doesn't matter. Did you complete your task?"

"Yes, sir," Drake replied, reaching into his inventory and laying several items on the ground before him. "Four blocks of Soul Sand and three Wither Skulls, all natural and obtained from the Nether, as requested."

"Excellent," Lord Tenebris replied, talking to himself under his breath. "This is most ideal. . . . When they're made with natural materials, they're so much easier to control than synthetic ones. . . . Oh, and one more thing," he said, now addressing his general directly.

"Yes, o glorious one?" Drake replied meekly.

"Your judgment in this scenario was good. Preserving the Wither Skeletons was indeed a wise decision. However," Lord Tenebris continued with a dark look on his face, "I must advise you to never again disobey my orders."

"Oh, my lord . . . I am so sorry!" cried out Drake, tears streaming down his face.

"Don't fret, Drake, I won't punish you this time," Lord Tenebris replied lazily. "However, watch yourself in the future. I must be sure that all my subjects are unwaveringly loyal to me. If they're not, then they are a threat to the Alliance and must be destroyed. And you know that I will not hesitate, Drake. Just look at what happened to Minotaurus and Blackraven if you need more proof."

As Lord Tenebris gave an evil laugh and Drake cowered in fear, Kat felt a whiplash of shock hit her. What *had* happened to Blackraven and Minotaurus? Were they . . . did that mean . . . that they had betrayed the Noctem Alliance? Had Lord Tenebris killed them?

"Leave me now, Drake," Lord Tenebris commanded. "Await my next command outside. And send the villager in."

Drake stood up and, with his head still bowed, he backed out of the room through a door next to the Nether Portal that Kat hadn't noticed before. Moments later, another figure stepped out of the door, and Kat gasped. Into the center of the room walked Oob, his skin sickly green with red eyes and tattered brown robes. The Zombie villager walked to the front of Lord Tenebris's throne.

"Villager," Lord Tenebris said calmly to Oob. "Whatever I say, I am going to need you to repeat in your vernacular. Do you understand, villager?"

"Oob . . . udder . . . stand . . . ," Oob croaked out.

Kat's head was spinning. Oob was there! He was still alive! And . . . he was working with Lord Tenebris?

All Kat could do was watch in horror as Lord Tenebris stepped down from his throne and gathered the materials that Drake had left on the ground. Lord Tenebris assembled the dark-brown blocks—Drake had called them Soul Sand—into a T shape. Kat glanced at Cassandrix. Although her partner's face still showed absolute terror at the mere sight of Lord Tenebris, Kat also detected a slight element of confusion; she didn't know what was happening either.

The two girls watched as Lord Tenebris placed each of the tiny gray Wither Skeleton skulls on top of the Soul Sand formation. After he fastened the last one in place, Lord Tenebris took a step back and stood directly in front of his throne. Kat watched with bated breath as the eyes of the skulls glowed white, getting brighter and brighter, until finally a flash of light illuminated the room. In the moment of blindness, a horrible suction sound filled the room, like a demon taking its first breath. When Kat's vision returned, she saw a sight that made her heart drop into her stomach.

A mob stood in front of Lord Tenebris, but it wasn't just any mob. It was huge, almost the size of a Ghast. Its body consisted of nothing but a black spine, trailing off into a tail and wrapped in the center by a dusky black rib cage. Atop this skeletal body were three heads, perched on a wide, bony structure. The heads were black skulls, and they all looked around in different directions. The skulls all had empty white eyes and mouths, and they were taking deep, husky breaths. The creature was the most terrifying thing that Kat had ever seen.

"Behold, villager," Lord Tenebris spoke out, a half smile flashing across his face as he gazed adoringly at the newborn demon. "The Wither."

Suddenly, the creature began to flash blue and white. Cassandrix and Kat were transfixed on the beast in horror, wondering what this monster, the Wither, was going to do next. Kat started to perceive a change around her. She couldn't quite put her finger on what it was, but it was almost as if all the light, warmth, and energy in the room were being sucked out, and were condensing toward the Wither. Kat saw Lord Tenebris take a deep breath and raise a hand in front of him, and suddenly, she guessed what was about to happen. As the Wither gave another ghastly moan, Kat ducked totally behind the pillar, pulling Cassandrix along with her, and covered her eyes and ears.

"What are you . . . ," Cassandrix hissed, before she was cut off by the explosion.

A thousand megatons of light and sound bombarded the area around Kat and Cassandrix, only missing them because of the indestructible bedrock pillar in front of them.

Kat could feel the incredible rush of energy that engulfed the area around them. It felt like she was standing inches away from a passing bullet train. Only when the light and sound had completely died down did Kat dare peek her head back around the side of the pillar.

The monster was now floating in midair. The three heads glanced freely around the room, taking in all that was around it. As the heads of the Wither basked in their newfound existence, Kat couldn't help but feel as if she were looking at the very faces of evil itself, which sucked all that was good in the world into a void of darkness.

Suddenly, six eyes of the Wither focused on Lord Tenebris, still standing in the open alongside Oob, both of them somehow totally unharmed by the blast. He smiled.

"My name is Lord Tenebris," he said smoothly. "I am your creator, and I am your master."

Oob let out a loud Zombie roar, and the Wither Skeleton glanced at him, seeming to understand. The three heads looked back and forth between one another, and then back at Lord Tenebris. Then, all of a sudden, the mouth of the middle and largest Wither head opened and expelled a small black projectile, which sped at rocket speed toward Lord Tenebris.

The Noctem Leader didn't move. He simply stretched out his hand, and when the projectile made contact, it exploded, engulfing him in smoke. Moments later, the smoke cleared, showing Lord Tenebris totally unharmed.

Kat couldn't process what she had just seen. This Wither had just shot an explosive projectile from its mouth at Lord Tenebris. And he hadn't even been hurt by it.

The middle Wither head let out a raspy roar of fury, and spit even more skulls in Lord Tenebris's direction. Again, he simply held out his hand, and the black projectiles, which Kat could now see as tiny skulls, were simply rupturing on contact, leaving no damage whatsoever. Before long, the other two Wither heads joined in as well, sending a constant barrage of three streams of explosive Wither skulls directly at Lord Tenebris. And yet he continued to take the punishment as effortlessly as if they were blowing wind at him.

Kat didn't know what she found the most alarming about what she was witnessing. On the one hand, the Wither was clearly an incredibly powerful mob. She could feel the force of its blasts from behind her pillar. The explosions were far stronger than those of the Creeper, and the Wither was dishing them out like machine-gun fire. And on the other hand, Lord Tenebris, their archenemy, the one they had vowed to destroy, was totally unfazed by this onslaught of destructive power.

Then, without warning, Lord Tenebris raised his right hand and pointed it directly at the Wither. Instantly, the mob stopped firing on Lord Tenebris and gave a shallow moan of pain. Kat looked on, having trouble convincing herself she wasn't in the midst of a nightmare, as Lord Tenebris lowered his left hand. As he did, the Wither floated downward, still squealing in agony, until it was finally forced onto the ground.

A serious frown crossed Lord Tenebris's face. "I said, I am your master. Should you disobey my commands, you will be subjected to this."

Lord Tenebris waited for Oob to finish translating and then he squeezed his fist. Instantly, the Wither gave the highest, loudest, and most ear-piercingly shrill cry of all, as it squirmed on the ground in excruciating pain.

Kat knew that she ought to feel sorry for the killer beast, but she was too busy dealing with overwhelming dread as she watched Lord Tenebris exercise his mysterious powers. She hadn't been prepared to deal with anything like this. Whenever she had imagined Lord Tenebris, she had pictured a master swordfighter, with an army of soldiers at his command. But this . . . Kat knew that no player in all of Elementia could stand a chance against whatever Lord Tenebris was.

After a moment, Lord Tenebris released the Wither. The giant mob floated back into the air, a tangible element of fear now in its six white eyes.

"Do you understand?" Lord Tenebris asked, followed by a grunt by Oob.

Instantly, the middle head of the Wither let out a brief moan while looking at Oob. The Zombie villager turned to Lord Tenebris and spoke.

"It . . . udder . . . stand."

Lord Tenebris smiled. "Good. Now, come here behind me."

At Oob's command, the Wither proceeded to levitate over Lord Tenebris's head and make an about-face until it was floating behind him. Lord Tenebris turned his head to face the door next to the Nether Portal.

"Enter, Drake. And bring the prisoners with you."

The iron door swung open, and Kat's heart lifted. Through the door, and into the main hall of the bedrock room, marched Charlie and Commander Crunch, followed by Drake holding a diamond sword to their backs.

Although Kat had never met Commander Crunch before, he seemed to be holding up relatively well. Even though he did look tired, his uniform torn and his beard unkempt, he still walked with a strong spirit to him. He glanced around the room in a wily manner, as if plotting out the best method of escape.

Charlie, on the other hand, looked absolutely terrible. His face was covered in bruises, his clothes were tattered and worn out, and he limped into the room, barely able to stay up on his own feet. Kat was beside herself with worry the second she laid eyes on him. Clearly, the time in the prison had taken a heavy toll on him, and the torture of the Noctem Alliance had been nothing short of ruthless.

"Argh, 'tis *you* again!" bellowed out Commander Crunch in his gruff voice as he caught sight of Lord Tenebris. "Don't ye know when enough be enough, ye great bloated fool?"

"Oh, you're in no position to be insulting me, Commander," Lord Tenebris said coolly. "You see, I've found a new method of persuading you to tell me the information that you've been withholding from me."

"Sink me, ye mean that thin'?" laughed Crunch, gesturing to the Wither levitating high above the head of Lord Tenebris. "Ye reckon some giant mutant worm wit' th' face o' th' Jolly Roger will intimidate me? Reckon again, ye scallywag! I'll die before I break, I tell ye!"

Although Commander Crunch was laughing like a lunatic, Charlie was a different story. He glanced up at the Wither in a state of total panic. Kat could see him hyperventilating, clearly terrified as he imagined what the three-headed skeletal demon could do to him.

As Commander Crunch cackled on and Lord Tenebris whispered something in Oob's ear, Kat ducked back behind the pillar. She spun Cassandrix, who had been watching the process with a sickened look on her face, to face her.

"We have to do something," Kat whispered urgently. "They're gonna use that thing to torture Charlie and Crunch!

We need a plan, right now! Any ideas?"

"Well . . . it's not much of an idea . . . ," said Cassandrix slowly.

"We can't waste time!" Kat hissed, panic ripe on her face. "If you have even the stupidest idea in the world, tell me now!"

"Okay," said Cassandrix, taking a deep breath, and shaking her head clear of the sickening feeling that had overtaken her since she had first seen Lord Tenebris. "Here's what we do. I noticed that there's a lever on the wall at the far end of the room."

Kat glanced down to the other end of the room, opposite where Charlie and Crunch were being forced to their knees by Drake. Indeed, Cassandrix was right. There was a switch on the far wall, and furthermore, the wall wasn't made out of bedrock like the rest of the room. Rather, it was made out of stone, and Kat could see that multiple pistons were positioned on the top and bottom of the wall itself.

"I think that wall," continued Cassandrix hastily, "might be an opening, like a hangar door, so the Wither will be able to fly out of here. If we can get to that lever and open the door, this place will get filled with sunlight, which will give us a distraction for a second."

"Okay . . . and what do we do with that distraction?" Kat asked eagerly.

"I don't know!" exclaimed Cassandrix. "I told you it wasn't much of an idea . . . more of a notion, really . . ."

"Aaaarrrgh!"

The growl of pain echoed throughout the bedrock chamber. Kat poked her head around the pillar and saw the two prisoners on their knees. Commander Crunch was gnashing his teeth together with his face screwed up, and wispy black smoke rising off his back. Lord Tenebris whispered something to Drake. Then, with one last look at the Wither, Lord Tenebris disappeared, teleporting back to wherever it was he had come from.

Then, Kat watched in horror as the Wither opened its mouth, and a black skull shot out and exploded onto Charlie's back. A scream of pure agony burst forth from Charlie, and he collapsed to the ground, crying and sputtering as the smoke rose from him.

Kat had to do something now. She couldn't allow this to go on. Even if it was suicide, there was no way that she could just stand by idly and watch this happen. She turned back around to face Cassandrix.

"Get down to that switch," she commanded her friend. "I'll distract them." And without waiting for a response, Kat dashed behind the rows of pillars, finally stopping when she was at the pillar closest to the players. Not even ten blocks away, her friends were being physically abused by Drake for more information. She was so close, and yet so far.

Kat checked to see what she had left. Her inventory had been emptied while she was unconscious, so she no longer had any melee weapon. The two soldiers she and Cassandrix had killed hadn't been carrying much besides food, but there were a few important things.

The first of these was a bow and a stack of arrows, which she kept on hand, ready to fire. There was also a compass, which would prove invaluable should they escape. She had also managed to come across one single Ender Pearl. This item was of the utmost importance; all she had to do was get to Charlie and Crunch without being killed by Drake or the Wither, and she could warp the three of them straight to the door. Kat thanked her lucky stars that Lord Tenebris wasn't there anymore. She had no idea where he had warped off to, but as long as she didn't have to deal with him now, she didn't really care.

Kat glanced down at her bow, and suddenly an idea struck her. She didn't know if it would work, and if it didn't then it would only reveal her and result in far more pain to her friends. But then again, it was the only idea she had, and so she decided to go with it. She drew an arrow in her bow, and peeked around the corner of the pillar. She took a deep breath. These next few shots would not only have to be extremely accurate, but they'd have to be fast, too.

In front of the throne, Drake kicked Commander Crunch to the ground and snarled.

"Fine then," he growled. "If you don't want to talk, let's see if my little friend can convince you otherwise. Villager, order another attack, but don't use minimal power this time . . . make it hurt more."

As Oob growled ferociously, a wave of ice chilled Kat's heart as she realized that she would have to leave Oob behind. She wanted nothing more than to cure the little guy, not just for the sake of taking control of the Wither and the other mobs from the Alliance, but also to get her friend back. Kat shook her head of this feeling. With the operation she was about to attempt, it was no time to be getting emotional.

The Wither Skeleton's middle mouth began to glow, and Kat felt an intake of the energy around the room. She let the arrow fly, just as the projectile left the Wither's mouth. The arrow collided with the airborne black skull, and it exploded in a giant burst of light in the center of the Wither's face. The monster screamed as it careened backward from the blast, crashing into the bedrock wall of the room and tumbling to the floor with a thud.

"What is the meaning of this?" Drake bellowed at the stunned monster. "UP! Get UP! Villager, tell this . . . AUGH!"

Drake shouted in pain as an arrow sunk into his right arm. He whipped his head around to see where it had come from, just in time to see Kat flying toward him. Her fist slammed into his jaw like a cannonball, and he reeled backward, cracking his head against the obsidian throne and slumping unconscious to the ground.

Kat would have loved to take the opportunity to take him out for good, but she had a mission. Crunch, who had tightened his muscles in preparation for the Wither's next strike, whipped around to see Kat sprinting toward the two of them.

"Who are ye?" the Commander asked, eyes wide. "Aren't ye that lass from . . ."

"I'm from Element City, yes. I'm here to get you two out," Kat spat out distractedly, digging the Ender Pearl from her inventory as the Wither slowly levitated back upright.

"Oh, aye . . . uh, that's wha' I was about t' say . . . ," Crunch replied awkwardly.

"Kat?" asked Charlie deliriously, his eyes struggling to stay focused on her. "Is that . . . is that really you?"

"Yeah," Kat said, looking over her shoulder to see that Zombie Oob was almost upon them. She stood up and spun around to face him.

"Sorry, buddy," Kat grunted as she punched Oob in the chest as hard as she could. The villager reeled backward before tripping and tumbling to the ground next to Drake. Unlike Drake, though, he immediately started to recover.

"Get ready, boys . . . we're warping out of here," Kat

shouted, and she pitched the Ender Pearl as hard as she could toward the exit before grabbing the two prisoners around the shoulders. Suddenly, Kat heard a raspy groan behind her, and saw that the Wither was airborne yet again, and all three white mouths were glowing and hissing.

"CASSANDRIX, DO IT NOW!" screamed Kat at the top of her lungs, as she desperately looked up at the monster about to blow her to smithereens. An instant later, Kat had to squint her eyes as the pistons whirred and the entire bedrock chamber flooded with daylight. The Wither reeled back, surprised, and three skulls shot from its mouths in random directions, creating massive explosions across the roof of the chamber.

As Kat watched the Wither adjust to the light, she felt the familiar feeling of warping for a split second before tumbling to the ground at the opening. Kat could see Cassandrix standing next to the lever, which had been pulled down. Outside, a short drop down a steep mycelium hillside led to the edge of the ocean.

"What now?" Kat asked, turning to face Cassandrix as she heard an alarm go off somewhere in the distance. "That was as far as I got in my plan!"

"I have two boats that the soldiers dropped in my inventory!" Cassandrix replied, as Commander Crunch pulled himself to his feet and Charlie lay motionless on the ground.

"Okay, sounds good. Everyone, down the hill!" Kat bellowed. As Cassandrix hopped her way down the slope, followed by Crunch, Kat knelt down and shook Charlie, trying to get him to come around. It was no use. He had been totally spent by Drake's torture, and the landing of the teleportation had knocked him out cold. Kat took a deep breath and hoisted Charlie on her back, resigning to carry him down the mountain herself.

As Kat hopped off the smooth bedrock floor of the cave and onto the jagged mycelium cliff side, two black Wither skulls rocketed over her head, her hair blowing in their tailwind. Realizing that the Wither would likely be in hot pursuit of them, Kat shrugged Charlie off her for a moment and knocked the switch of the wall with a well-placed arrow. With no flow of redstone energy, the pistons returned to their off position, closing the hangar door. Even from outside the prison, Kat could still hear the explosions inside. She knew that it wouldn't be long before the Wither blasted its way through the door, so she picked up Charlie once again and hopped her way down the hill.

The trek down the hill was one of the most strenuous things that Kat had ever done. Beyond the fact that she was sprinting as fast as she could down an uneven slope while carrying another unconscious player on her back, Kat's legs still had an ache in them from the teleportation, which only grew worse and worse with each step down the mountain. By the time she reached the final expanse of mycelium leading to the beach, her legs were killing her, while Cassandrix and Crunch had already managed to make it to the shore.

As they set up the boats, Kat suddenly heard a whooshing sound, and an instant later an arrow stuck into the ground beside her. She strained her neck to look over her shoulder and saw to her dismay that the entire outside of Mount Fungarus was now covered with black-clad Noctem troops, all firing at her. Kat looked forward again, and tried as hard as she could to zigzag back and forth, making herself a harder target.

Then, when she was just ten blocks away from the boats, Kat felt a sharp sting on the back of her right thigh, and she knew she'd been hit. Gritting her teeth, Kat hit the spongy mycelium ground hard, flopping face-down while Charlie tumbled off her back and toward the shoreline. Kat forced herself to get back up to her feet as she became aware that Crunch and Cassandrix were dragging Charlie back to the boats.

Then, as Kat finally got up, she heard a sound behind her, like a car coming closer and closer. She looked over her shoulder, and her heart stopped. The Wither had blasted a small hole through the front of the hangar door. Through that hole, a black Wither skull was flying directly toward her, and it was now less than ten blocks away from her.

Kat had no time to dodge. She had no time to duck. There was nothing she could do as the skull sped toward her at breakneck speed. Kat took a deep breath and closed her eyes, preparing for the end.

Kat heard the explosion . . . but she didn't feel any pain. She felt the wave of force knock her to the ground. Lying there on the mycelium ground, Kat knew that, somehow, the Wither skull had exploded before it reached her. And oddest of all . . . she wasn't dead.

She opened her eyes. Sure enough, the cloud of smoke from the explosion hung right there in front of her. She couldn't see anything through the black cloud, not the island, not the mountain above her, not the Wither, not even the sky. The only form that Kat could make out was a black figure, with a cloak draped over his head, vanishing into the cloud of smoke.

For some reason that she could not explain, the name Black Hood entered her mind.

Kat didn't take the time to question what had just happened, though. She sprinted the last few steps across the shore and climbed hastily into her boat, alongside the unconscious Charlie. By the time the smoke of the skull's blast had cleared, the four players were already dozens of blocks from the shoreline, arrows from the island were falling far short of reaching them, and Kat could hear cries of indignation and fury from the prison guards they were leaving in their wake.

It wasn't until the Mushroom Islands had completely vanished from their view that Kat finally allowed herself to breathe. She glanced over at Cassandrix, piloting the boat beside her with Commander Crunch snoring behind her.

"Hey, Cassandrix?" Kat said.

The girl returned her look, and raised her eyebrows in response.

"Good job in there today."

Cassandrix looked across the water at Charlie's unconscious form, then behind her to the sleeping Commander Crunch, and then back to Kat again.

"Thank you, darling," Cassandrix replied, before setting her sights back out to the open ocean.

Kat sighed, but then smiled a little to herself. She supposed it was a bit too much to ask for Cassandrix to return her compliment. She *had* managed to get a thank you out of her, with no snide remarks to accompany it.

At the very least, that was something.

It was plain that neither of them were in the mood to talk after all they had been through, and so Kat focused on piloting the boat yet again. However, as she tried to turn her mind off and allow her brain to slip into autopilot, she found that a certain question couldn't stop nagging her in the back of her brain. Finally, she turned to Cassandrix yet again.

"Hey, I have just one more question," Kat said slowly.

Cassandrix nodded, still looking straight ahead. Kat spoke on.

"When . . . when that Wither skull almost killed me . . . did you . . . or did anybody . . . block it?"

Cassandrix looked puzzled for a moment, and then turned to look at Kat again.

"Of course not, darling," Cassandrix replied, as if it should be obvious. "The Commander and I were pulling Charlie onto the boat, and there was nobody else on the beach. Why? Did you see somebody?"

Kat thought back to that moment, less than an hour ago. The explosion had gone off right in front of her. She was being struck by waves of force, light, and sound, and in the center, she clearly remembered a figure silhouetted in the smoke, wearing a black cloak, with a sword held in a block . . . as if the player was defending her . . .

"No," Kat replied, shaking her head and glancing down at her reflection in the water. "I'm sure it was nothing. . . ."

gotta admit," Jayden mumbled to G as they filed along with the rest of their class of recruits into the rec area, "I'm a bit surprised that I didn't hate that lesson more than I did."

"Agreed," replied G, pulling the door closed behind them. "I mean . . . I know that the stuff they're showing us is being used against Elementia troops," he murmured under his breath, "but still, I think those interrogation techniques might actually turn out to be pretty useful."

Jayden nodded, and he sat down on a wood block on the floor and watched the other players in their group having fun around the rec room. Truth be told, G was finding it difficult to look around the room without squinting, since everything was almost entirely white.

On the most recent update to Minecraft, quartz had been added in veins throughout the cave of the Nether. In order to flaunt their dominance over the dimension, the Noctem Alliance had apparently taken it upon themselves to mine as much quartz as possible and incorporate it into their buildings. In fact, G had heard Tess saying that their group of recruits would be going into the Nether before long to mine quartz. As of now, there was only one small part of the rec room that was still made out of chiseled stone blocks, not having been remodeled yet.

G ignored that, though, determined not to let the white quartz distract him from the game of Spleef being played in the rec room's miniature arena between several of the recruits. After all, Spleef was enjoyable to watch no matter who was playing, and G felt that he and Jayden deserved some downtime after all their hard work.

In just the last few days, they had managed to learn crucial information about the Capitol Building, and where the hostages may be. They had narrowed it down to three hallways in the building, and all they needed now was some way to check them. How they would do that, they had yet to figure out. Still, they were doing good work, and G was looking forward to an afternoon of relaxation.

As the Spleef match was coming to a close, the wooden door of the rec room swung open. Through the doorway walked General Tess, still dressed in full uniform, her pink face as unreadable as ever.

"Good evening, recruits," Tess said, in a voice that wasn't particularly loud, but nonetheless caught the attention of every single player in the rec room. In an instant, every player dropped what they were doing and stood up, including the two remaining Spleef players. They turned to face Tess, and stood at full attention.

"Good evening, General Tess," all the recruits replied in unison.

"At ease, soldiers," Tess said, still not cracking a smile, or showing any emotion for that matter. "I've only come for one of you. MasterBronze, would you come with me, please?"

G's heart skipped a beat. *Me? She wants me? What does she want with me? Does she suspect me?* Despite his racing thoughts, he tried to keep a determinedly calm and respectful demeanor as he marched over to join the general. He shared one last baffled expression with Jayden before the door closed behind him, and he found himself standing alone in the hallway with Tess.

"What may I do for you, ma'am?" G asked, standing at full attention.

"Did you not hear me before, soldier? I said, at ease," Tess repeated, and she watched as Jayden let his hands hang loose by his side. There was a moment of awkward silence before Tess spoke again.

"What level are you, soldier?"

"Um . . . I'm sorry?" G stammered. *She must suspect me . . .*

"I asked you what your level is."

"I'm level sixty-four," G answered, not sure what it had to do with anything. "I would be higher, but these are tough times, and you of all people must know how necessary it is to have enchanted weapons on hand."

"As I suspected," Tess replied and, to G's amazement, she actually smiled. "A master Minecrafter like you? It doesn't shock me at all that you've got a good number of levels under your belt, even for someone in this Alliance."

"I'm sorry?" G replied, not following.

"Soldier . . . actually, let's drop the formalities for now . . . can I call you MasterBronze?"

"I, uh . . . suppose so . . . ," G answered clumsily.

"Soldier, even at ease, I'm still your commanding officer," Tess said, her voice suddenly stern again. "When I ask you a question, you will respond with 'yes, ma'am,' or 'no, ma'am.'"

"My apologies," G said, taking a deep breath to overcome his discomfort. "Yes, ma'am, you may call me that."

"Good," Tess replied, smiling once again. "MasterBronze, ever since you won that Aptitude Tournament a few days back, I've been keeping my eye on you, and I must say, as a soldier I see some real potential in you."

"Oh. Well, thank you, ma'am."

"Besides already being well versed in fighting, I see that you have a drive to you. In every training exercise that we've done so far, you in particular have given all your energy to it. You do this in every area, from your fighting to your skills training."

"Thank you, ma'am."

"And because of that, MasterBronze, I would like to personally appoint you as my apprentice."

"I'm . . . I'm sorry?" replied G, taken aback. "What exactly do you mean?"

"Well, to be honest, it's a bit unorthodox," Tess replied. "No general in the Noctem Alliance has ever handpicked a student to personally train before. However, I've never seen any recruit come through this program with more potential than you, MasterBronze. Therefore, after initial training sessions are completed each day, I would like to train you myself in various high-level tasks.

"None of the other students will have the opportunity to do this, and it is more than likely that you will advance much faster through the ranks of the Noctem Freedom Fighters than any of your fellow recruits. What do you say, MasterBronze? Does that sound like something that you'd be interested in?"

"Of course, ma'am," G replied enthusiastically, a huge smile breaking across his face. *This is fantastic,* he thought to himself. *The faster I can get access to high-level Noctem information, the better!*

Tess smiled even wider. "Excellent. We will begin tomorrow. For now, you may return to the rec room."

And with that, General Tess turned on her heel and

walked back down the hallway. G pumped his fist in ecstasy, and strutted proudly back toward the rec room. He couldn't wait to tell Jayden the great news that he was one step closer to uncovering the Noctem Alliance's deepest, darkest secrets.

"Okay, noob," Sally said, flying high in the sky. "Let's do one more drill, and then we can take a break. All right?"

"Sounds good to me!" Stan shouted from the ground about a hundred blocks away.

"Here's how this goes," said Sally. "I'm going to try to catch up to you. I won't go at full speed, but I won't go slow, either. Your job is to try to keep away from me for as long as possible. You can use anything that you've learned so far to slow me down. For now, I'll come directly at you, which means I won't, like, loop around anything you put up, I'll go through it instead."

"All right!" Stan shouted back.

"Are you ready?" asked Sally, a devious glint in her eye.

"Just a sec," replied Stan. He took a deep breath, focused as hard as he could on feeling weightless, and, with all his might, he launched himself into the air. Stan flew upward until he was at the same eye level as Sally, and then just floated there, looking back at her.

"Okay," he shouted back to her, a diamond axe popping

into his right hand as a manic grin crossed his face. "Come at me."

Sally flew directly toward Stan, a diamond sword appearing in her own hand. Stan stretched out his hand and, through the power of his mind, he summoned a giant wall of bedrock directly in front of Sally. While she was punching through, Stan focused harder, and a flow of lava appeared at the top of the wall. When Sally burst out through the wall of lava, she gave a short scream of pain as she caught on fire.

"Nice one, noob," she chuckled after the shock wore off, and she swigged down Potions of Fire Resistance and Regeneration. "I've gotta admit, I didn't see that coming."

Stan smirked, and he swept his hand through the air, causing a cascade of gravel blocks to appear above Sally and immediately fall back down onto her. Without flinching, Sally dived to the ground but wasn't expecting to see the grid of sand and cacti that Stan had summoned directly beneath her. Sally did a U-turn in midair and barreled back up through the falling gravel, squinting her eyes as she did so, only to get caught headfirst in the mess of gooey cobweb blocks that Stan had summoned directly above her.

"Well, I give you points for resourcefulness, noob," remarked Sally in a muffled voice as she hacked through the mess of cobwebs with her sword.

"I'm not done yet." Stan laughed as he focused all his

energy on a spot right next to Sally. A moment later, with a pop, a Blaze appeared out of nowhere. The spinning inferno of a mob fired off three tiny fireballs, which hit the cobwebs and engulfed Sally in flames.

There was a teleporting sound as Sally warped out of the disordered cobwebs, floating above them instead. She squinted her eyes, clearly focusing hard, and all of a sudden, there was a crash of thunder as the sky turned gray, and heavy rains started to fall from the clouds in waves. The fire of the Blaze was instantly extinguished, and a moment later the mob itself fell dead from the sky, leaving only a single blaze rod to fall to the ground.

As he watched it fall, Stan felt himself clutched in the grasp of an invisible power as Sally stretched out her hand toward him, followed by a mischievous leer. Try as he might, Stan couldn't break free of her hold, and she levitated him toward her until finally they were close enough for her to poke him in the forehead.

"I win," she replied cheekily. With a pointed blink from Sally, the weather instantly turned back into sunshine again. She released Stan from her telekinetic grip, and, totally unprepared, he plummeted toward the ground, flailing for a good few moments before he caught himself in midair.

"Hey, no fair," Stan laughed. "You weren't supposed to use powers I haven't learned yet."

"Noob, if life were fair," replied Sally coolly as the two of them levitated back to the ground, "then my personal online business that sells pants with built-in life preservers would have taken off by now, and I'd be a multibillion-dollar entrepreneur rather than some chick who stays home all day hacking Minecraft servers."

Sally focused on her hand, and instantly two pumpkin pies appeared.

"Eat up, noob," Sally said with a smile, tossing Stan one of the pies, which he caught in his outstretched hand. "You've earned it."

And with that, the two players both conjured up blocks for themselves to sit on—Stan's block being a block of iron, and Sally's being a block of obsidian—as they began to eat. There was a long stretch of silence as the two players stuffed their faces with food, tuckered out by the long work session. After a while, Sally finally spoke.

"So, how're you doing back in Elementia, noob? Has the Alliance been giving you too much trouble?"

"Actually, no," Stan said, his pleasant surprise at this truth reflected in his voice. "I mean, I had a run-in with Leonidas a few days ago, and I thought I was a goner then . . . but I guess I must have hurt him more than I thought I did, because I haven't seen him or any other Noctem troops since then."

"Well that's good," Sally replied. "You managed to make it back to the mainland yet?"

Stan forced the final bite of his pie down in a giant gulp before responding. "No, not yet, although I am making good progress. I found an island with some trees on it yesterday, so I was able to make a boat for myself and that's really sped the travel up. I also killed some monsters, and got some supplies from them. I'm actually camping in the Taiga Archipelago right now, which means I'm getting pretty close to Diamond Bay. Unfortunately, if my hunch is correct, then it won't be safe to go back to the city through there."

"And what is this brilliant hunch of yours, exactly?"

"Well, I've been out of contact with everybody in Elementia for a while now, so I have no way of knowing anything for sure. But one thing I did find out before leaving the Mushroom Islands was that Blackraven was leaking our plans to the Noctem Alliance, so our attacks almost certainly failed. Element City was probably hurt pretty badly in the attack, so I wouldn't be at all surprised if the Noctems managed to take Diamond Bay."

Sally nodded gravely. "Makes enough sense, I suppose. Well, I'd definitely head for the swampland peninsula, if I were you. Better safe than sorry, you know."

"Yeah, that's what I was planning on doing. I mean, I don't know the swamp well or anything, but I figure it's probably better to go somewhere it's easier to hide than to be a sitting duck out in the ocean."

Sally nodded, and spawned a steak from her inventory. Stan was still hungry, but not *that* much, and so he opted to summon an apple for himself. As he bit into the red fruit, an old thought started to float to the front of his mind.

There was a question that had been eating away at Stan for months now, from even before he had defeated King Kev. Since he had become president, he had found that he had become far too busy to give it any thought. However, having been alone for so long over the past few weeks, Stan had finally had the time to think about it, and it occurred to him now that, just maybe, Sally could help him find the answers he was looking for.

"Hey, Sal?"

"Waddup, noob?" Sally managed to get out as she scarfed down the last bits of her steak.

"I've been thinking . . . about some stuff . . ."

"Oh, come on, noob, don't start with me. You know how much I can't stand sentimentality."

"No, no, it's not that!" cried Stan, shaking his head as if he were trying to shake off a bug. "It's just . . . I have a question. About myself. And I was wondering if you could give me your perspective on it."

"Well, sure, I can give you my perspective, noob," replied

Sally, shrugging. "I mean, I can't guarantee it'll be any good, but you can try me."

"Well, okay then. Hmm . . . how do I say this . . . Do you remember right before the Battle for Elementia, how you told me that I was special, and I was on a higher level?"

"Yeah, what about it?"

"Well . . . what exactly did you mean by that?"

Sally paused for a moment, and a pensive look crossed her face. After a while, she spoke. "Well . . . to be honest, I'm not entirely sure, noob. It was just . . . in that moment, I felt like there was something about you. I couldn't put my finger on what it was, but it seemed like, somehow, you were definitely on some sort of higher plane than the rest of us. And then, when you came up with that amazing speech off the top of your head . . . well, at the time that seemed to confirm it."

"But the thing is," continued Stan, talking faster now, "that you weren't the only one who told me that. During my training session in the Adorian Village, Crazy Steve implied that he could sense something like that in me, too. And then later, in the middle of the Ender Desert, Kat told me that she could feel it, too . . . it's like they felt I was some kind of chosen one or something . . . as if I was destined to defeat King Kev and become the president of Elementia. I mean . . . do you think that that's possible? Do you think that I might be some sort of chosen hero or something like that?"

Stan looked at Sally expectantly, waiting for an answer. None came. Sally simply sat on her obsidian block, hand pressed against her forehead. Finally, after a full minute of silence, she responded.

"Well, let me start by saying this, Stan: no. No, I don't think that you're a chosen one, with your destiny written in the stars or any of that crap."

The breath that Stan had been holding in gushed out of him in a wave. He wasn't entirely sure what to say next. Luckily, he didn't have to answer, as Sally wasn't done yet.

"That being said, I still believe that you're something special."

Stan was confused. "But you just said—"

"Stan, let me spell it out for you," Sally said slowly, turning to look him in the eye. "There are a lot of people in the world who are talented. There are a lot of people who are willing to work hard. And there are a lot of people who care about those who can't help themselves, and want to do all they can for those people. Most people have at least one of those qualities, and if you looked a bit, you could find somebody with two of those qualities without too much trouble. But Stan, let me tell you . . . it's extremely rare to find somebody who has all three of those qualities. And you're one of those people."

Stan smiled. "Do you really think so?"

"Of course," replied Sally, as if it were the most obvious thing in the world. "And I think that the thing that so many people see in you, Stan, that makes you stand out even more, is that not only do you have a ton of all three of those traits, but you also have a habit of influencing people around you."

Stan raised his eyebrows. "What do you—"

"Oh, come on, Stan, look at your two best friends!" sighed Sally in exasperation. "When you first met Charlie, he had talent, and he wanted to help other people, but what happened every time he tried?"

"Well," mumbled Stan awkwardly, "usually he would just end up too scared to be much help . . ."

"Exactly!" exclaimed Sally. "And what was it that finally forced him to buck up and fight for what he believed in?"

Stan scratched his head, forcing himself to think back to their quest across the Ender Desert all those months ago. "Well . . . I guess it was in the NPC village . . . when I made him face that Spider Jockey . . ."

"Right, Stan, *you* did that! You saw that he had potential for greatness, and you gave him the little extra shove he needed to turn into the amazing warrior he is today!"

"Well, I guess . . . I mean, I hardly feel like I deserve all, or even most of the—"

"And look at Kat!" Sally cut in. "I'm sure you remember

what she was like when you first met her, right?"

"Well, I seem to recall that she might have tried to kill me a little bit . . ."

"So you met up with this girl. She had the raw talent, and she was a fearless and hard worker, but her priorities were all in the wrong place. She was using all her potential for her own ends, just trying to claw her way up in the world and not caring who got thrown under the bus because of it. And do you know how she realized that she was wrong?"

"No," Stan replied skeptically. "Do you?"

Sally scoffed at him. "Oh, give me some credit, Stan. You don't think that you were the *only* one I talked to during that training week before the Battle for Elementia, right? I talked to Kat and Charlie, too . . . come to think of it, I probably talked to Kat *more* than I talked to you! I was training her in dual sword fighting, remember?"

"I guess you're right," replied Stan. It was amazing how many details of their campaign to take down King Kev he had forgotten during his last five months as president.

"I'll tell you, Stan . . . it was *you.* Do you have any idea just how much Kat respects you, not just as a friend but as a person? By taking her with you on your journey, even after she'd attacked you, changed her life, and you showed her by example how to be a better person who cares about other people.

"That's the reason that you're special, Stan. It's not any kind of prophecy, or destiny, or anything like that. Simply put, you're one of the best all-around people that I've ever met, and it rubs off on the people you know."

As Sally finished her speech, she took a deep breath, let it out, and pulled an apple out of her inventory to eat. The two players sat there for a while in silence. But as the sun set on the infinite expanse of totally flat grass, a single tear of happiness rolled down Stan's cheek. All he had ever tried to do was be the best person he could be, and every once in a while, it was nice to know that he was doing a good job.

As the sun finally sank out of view, Stan stood up from his block.

"Thanks for the advice, Sally," he said with a smile. "It means more to me than you know."

Sally chuckled and looked up at him affectionately. "You know I meant all of it, noob. You gonna head back to Elementia now?"

Stan nodded. "This has been a great day, Sally, both in training and in talking to you. But I have to get back to my server now. My people need me."

Sally smiled. "Do what you have to do. I'll call you back here tomorrow, okay?"

"Deal," Stan replied. And with that, he turned his back to Sally, and looked straight into the eternal expanse of the starry night sky. He took a deep breath, and before long, the words popped into his head yet again.

DISCONNECT FROM SERVER?

"Yes," Stan replied out loud, and with a faint pop, he disappeared from SalAcademy.

Stan felt his body once again as he rejoined Elementia. The frigid air of the taiga was soothing to his skin, far more pleasant than the biting gales of the tundra. Stan opened his eyes.

All around him, the tall spruce trees protruded into the night sky from the snow-covered ground. Small hills of dirt topped with snow were scattered about the island. In the distance, a ring of ice expanded around the shoreline of the island, beyond which the azure ocean stretched forever until it merged with the starry night sky. And right in the center of all this, standing not two blocks away from Stan and looking him straight in the eye, was another player.

"Hello, Stan," said Leonidas with a smile. "Glad to see that you're back."

11: THE DUSK OF HOPE

There was a moment of silence as Stan stared at Leonidas in disbelief. Leonidas looked Stan in the eye, praying that he wouldn't panic.

Then, without warning, Stan gave a shout of fury as he whipped a diamond sword out of his inventory and swung it as hard as he could. Leonidas just barely managed to leap out of the way as he felt a shockwave leave the sword and brush right by his head. He was forced to hop backward twice more to avoid the two follow-up attacks.

"Stop it, Stan!" cried Leonidas, raising his hands over his head. "I ain't gonna fight ya!"

But Stan paid no attention. He thrust the diamond sword forward, directly at Leonidas's stomach. He was forced to lean backward, his stomach just moving out of the range of the sword jab, but the pulse of Knock-back energy that shot off the sword hit him squarely in the stomach, sending him flying backward. Leonidas landed with a thud on the snow-covered dirt right on the shore of the island. He glanced back up and saw Stan, flying through the air with sword overhead, on course to plunge it directly into Leonidas's heart.

As much as he hated to counterattack, Leonidas knew that he had no choice. With great agility, Leonidas rolled onto his back, and when Stan was over him, he kicked his feet into the air and directly into Stan's stomach. Leonidas flew up off his back and landed on his feet, as Stan was launched backward and skidded to a stop on the ice surrounding the island.

"Stan, I refuse to fight ya!" shouted Leonidas again as Stan struggled his way to his feet, battling the slippery ice underfoot. "I just wanna talk to ya."

"Yeah, well I just want to get home without running into any more Noctem troops. Life isn't fair," grunted Stan, no mercy on his face as he sunk to one knee, driving his sword into the ice block he was standing on. The ice shattered with a crack, and Stan sunk down through the ice and into the water below.

Leonidas glanced wildly around the ice field, squinting to try to figure out where Stan had gone. In the faint moonlight, Leonidas saw no indication of where Stan was going to pop up next. Then, all at once, Leonidas noticed a dark figure directly under his feet, getting larger and larger by the second. Leonidas leaped back toward the island in alarm as a glowing diamond sword drove up out of the ice, missing him by inches. He jumped and leaped back and forth in desperation, narrowly avoiding the jabs of the sword that Stan was sending up through the ice.

Leonidas felt the crunch of snow under his feet, and realized that he had reached the island yet again. He glanced at the edge of the ice, where Stan had burst out of the water and landed. Immediately, Stan's steely eyes locked onto Leonidas, and he began to sprint as fast as he could toward Leonidas. Unfortunately, he had forgotten what he was standing on; Stan slipped on the frictionless ice blocks under his feet and tumbled to the ground. Leonidas seized the opportunity to turn around and flee back onto the island.

"Come back and fight, you coward!" bellowed Stan in outrage, but Leonidas sprinted across the snowy dirt of the island, weaving his way through the grove of spruce trees. *I need to talk to Stan,* he thought to himself, his mind shifting into strategy mode. *And if I'm going to do that, I need to get myself somewhere where he can't attack me.*

Leonidas ducked his way behind a particularly wide spruce trunk, and he glanced over his shoulder. Stan was prowling through the forest in his wake, lunging behind every tree in search of Leonidas. Leonidas was relieved. He had a minute to catch his breath and figure out a plan before Stan was upon him. He turned to look straight ahead and found himself staring directly into the eyes of an Enderman.

The monster was standing about fifteen blocks away from Leonidas, but he could feel the creature's purple eyes piercing into him like knives. Leonidas's heart had stopped dead in its tracks at the sight of the dangerous mob, but it now began to race in panic as the Enderman's mouth opened, revealing its jagged black teeth. It began to tremble in preparation for attack. Slowly and calmly, Leonidas notched an arrow in his bow. He knew that if he were to shoot an arrow at the Enderman, it would just teleport out of the way. He had to wait until the monster moved of its own volition, and when it was upon him, fire the arrow at point-blank range.

Leonidas's eyes began to water. He didn't dare look away from the Enderman, or even blink, lest the monster vanish and catch him totally off guard. Leonidas held the eyes of the open-jawed, shuddering Enderman for another half a minute. The monster refused to let up and, finally, he could take it no more. He blinked for a split second, and when he opened his eyes, the Enderman had vanished.

Leonidas cursed under his breath, and he slammed his back against the tree, bow raised. He glanced around in a frenzy, trying to see the entire area around him at once. The Enderman was going to reappear any second now, and he had to prepare for anywhere that it could possibly . . .

Without warning, Leonidas felt a pair of hands wrap around his throat. As he coughed and sputtered in a panic, Leonidas saw two long, spindly black arms out of the corner of his eye, reaching around from behind the tree. Leonidas kicked and struggled to no avail as the black hands pressed harder into his throat, beginning to pull him up the tree trunk by his neck. Leonidas could hardly see nor feel anything anymore, besides an overwhelming feeling of helplessness as the demon choked the life out of him. Then, from somewhere in his collective instinct, Leonidas became aware of the arrow still grasped in his right hand. Without thinking, acting purely on base impulse, he drove the arrow into the Enderman's hand.

The monster gave a shriek of alarm and vanished, dropping Leonidas to the ground with a thump. Leonidas gasped for air, and the world seemed to be going in slow motion as his senses returned to him. Then, all at once, the Enderman was standing above Leonidas, drawing back its black hand, still stuck with the arrow, in preparation for the final blow. Leonidas loaded his bow as fast as the warped lethargic reality around him would allow, and just as the slow-motion punch made contact with Leonidas's left arm, the arrow entered the Enderman's chest.

Although the slender black body fell to the ground and faded to nonexistence, Leonidas had to bite his tongue to refrain from uttering a holler of agony. The Enderman's punch, imbued with the monster's dark magic, had burned a hole in Leonidas's leather armor, and the pulsating pain coursing through his arm was unfathomable. As he clenched his teeth nearly to the point of cracking, Leonidas attempted to move the arm. Only by the highest willpower imaginable did Leonidas not bellow as indescribable pain engulfed his immobile limb.

Taking a deep breath, Leonidas grabbed the tree trunk with his good arm, pulling himself to his feet and wincing as his left arm swung back and forth limply. *Wow,* Leonidas thought to himself, cringing. *I guess they really did make the monsters' AI better on the last update.*

"You've got five seconds to tell me if there're more soldiers with you."

Slowly, Leonidas turned his head to the left, an exhausted look taking to his face. There, pointing his diamond sword directly at Leonidas's heart, stood Stan, his face ugly with hatred.

"Two seconds left," Stan spat out in disgust.

Leonidas sighed. To be honest, he was really sick of finding himself in these situations. No matter where he went, he could never catch a break. Never once had things ever gone his way, and he had always walked in the worst place possible. He was tired of it. Maybe . . . just maybe . . . it would be worth it to just let Stan run him through, and allow all his problems to just end . . .

"Answer me, you monster!"

The shout jolted Leonidas out of his trance. His eyebrows creased, and adrenaline shot through his body. *No. I've come too far. I'm too close to give up now.* Leonidas gave a shout of fury, which Stan clearly wasn't expecting. The distraction allowed Leonidas to raise his good arm and knock the sword to the side. He desperately searched for a plan, when his eye fell upon a turquoise orb lying in the snow.

Finally, Leonidas smirked to himself. *Something goes my way.*

Leonidas snatched the Ender Pearl from the ground, pitching it fastball style toward the limb of a tall spruce tree as Stan recovered. Leonidas closed his eyes, and before Stan's sword could harm him, Leonidas felt himself be sucked through the vacuum of space and land on the cushioned, snow-covered leaves of the tree.

Leonidas paused for a moment to catch his breath as Stan looked around wildly in confusion. In the moment of peace, the adrenaline began to drain from Leonidas, and the stinging pain in his arm became more and more prevalent. Leonidas gritted his teeth and realized that now was as good a time as any to talk to Stan.

"Hey, Stan! I'm up here!"

Stan whipped around to face Leonidas, and their eyes met. Instantly, Stan's befuddled face morphed into a scowl, and, with no words, he drew a bow.

"Don't, Stan!" bellowed Leonidas, his heart skipping a beat. "I already said, I don't wanna fight ya!"

"I'm not interested in anything you have to say, Leonidas!" grunted Stan as he notched an arrow and aimed at Leonidas's heart.

"Well, fine then! Kill me! But I refuse to fight!" shot back Leonidas. Taking a deep breath and praying that it wouldn't come back to bite him, Leonidas extracted his bow from his inventory and, before Stan could react, he pitched it down off the tree. It landed on the snow right in front of Stan's feet. Stan stared at the weapon.

"What're you playing at?" growled Stan, his brow creasing further as he glared back up at Leonidas.

"Nothin'," replied Leonidas, sounding much braver than he really was. With no bow in hand, he felt almost naked, and incredibly helpless. "I just don't want to fight you or your friends ever again."

"What're you talking about?" spat Stan.

"Exactly what it sounds like, Stan. I quit the Noctem Alliance already, and I wanna join you and fight for Element City."

"Ha!" laughed Stan bitterly. "There's no way you're gonna lower my guard by lying . . . where're your other guys? Are they getting ready to ambush me? Are they watching now with Invisibility Potions?" Stan's eyes flickered around the snowy island nervously before returning to the now angry Leonidas.

"No, Stan, I'm bein' serious! I was wrong to ever follow anythin' the Alliance said! They're a bunch of no-good, vile murderers with twisted ideals and horrible methods. I never believed in anythin' they said, and now I've broken free and want to fight for ya!"

"Give me one good reason that I should believe you, and not shoot you right now," Stan spat out in disgust.

"Well, how's this?" Leonidas replied, thankful that at least one good thing had come out of the fight from a few minutes ago. "All the mobs in the game are fightin' for the Alliance now. If I was still with the Alliance and had guys with me, how come I got attacked by the Enderman just now?"

Stan's mouth opened for a moment, then closed. He looked confused, and Leonidas grinned, realizing that he had gotten the point across.

"Well . . . that's . . . ," sputtered Stan, " . . . maybe . . . that was just a rogue Enderman that you just so happened to come across! I mean, come on, Leonidas! You expect me to believe that you realized overnight that you were fighting for the most evil organization in the history of Minecraft?"

"Course not!" cried out Leonidas in indignation. "Stan, I told ya this the last time we met, and I'll tell ya again . . . I didn't *choose* the Alliance, the Alliance chose *me*! The only reason I *ever* joined those evil cretins is 'cause I had to! When I was a noob, they threatened my family and said that if I didn't join . . ."

Suddenly, Leonidas found that he couldn't continue. Although he was sure that he was about to win Stan over, it finally occurred to him who he was talking to. Stan was well known for being very friendly toward, and extremely protective of, the NPC villagers. If anybody would know what Leonidas so desperately needed to, it was him.

"Stan . . . the moment that I quit the Alliance," Leonidas continued slowly, his voice trembling with emotion, "was the moment . . . when they told me they had attacked the NPC Village. I never did hear . . . what the casualties of the attack were, before I left. So . . . I'm so sorry, but I have to ask you . . . did Moganga survive?"

Stan's eyebrows, which had been slightly raised at the sheer levels of poignant sadness in Leonidas's voice, now shot up, and his mouth hung open. How did Leonidas know Moganga by name?

"Um . . . no, she didn't . . ."

"Then what about Ohsow? And Leol? And Vella?" Leonidas was desperate now to hear the news that even one member of his family had survived the raid. "Stan . . . what about Mella and Blerge? What about their sons?"

Stan couldn't believe his ears. Leonidas knew the names of the villagers? How was that possible? And Stan recognized the tone of Leonidas's voice as strikingly . . . sincere. And . . . if that was true . . . could it possibly mean that Leonidas really . . .

Suddenly, Stan flashed back to his fight with Leonidas in

the Jungle Base. During that fight, too, Leonidas had spoken with true emotion in his voice, trying to make it seem like he was an actual human being with feelings . . . right before he had sunk an arrow into Charlie. This was clearly just Leonidas playing another mind game with him. Surely there was some other explanation for how Leonidas knew the villagers' names. Stan was about to release the string of his bow and let the arrow fly when, from the other side of the island, he caught the tone of faint whispering.

Stan whipped his head to face the source of the noise, instinctively sinking to his knees to make himself as inconspicuous as possible. As he glanced through the tall, spruce-wood tree trunks, nearly black in the midst of the night, he didn't see anybody. Then, without warning, a dark figure emerged from behind one of the trees. Without hesitation, Stan drew an Ender Pearl from his inventory, and, praying he wouldn't be seen, he pitched it upward into the boughs of the nearest tree. A second later, Stan found himself comfortably perched in a hollowed-out den of leaves in the top of the tree. He looked up and realized that he could see Leonidas, crouching up in another tree.

Becoming aware that somebody was staring at him, Leonidas whipped his head around, only to realize it was just Stan. The two locked eyes for a moment before Stan hastily looked away. Leonidas didn't care. Although he truly had been emotionally invested in his own speech, he had shifted right back into hiding mode the instant that Stan had realized that there was somebody on the island. Right now, the fate of the village didn't matter to Leonidas as much as ensuring that he and Stan gave this mysterious figure, whoever he was, the slip.

As Leonidas glanced down onto the dark snowy ground, he realized with a start that not one but three figures were walking across the island. The three of them stopped in a clearing in the trees, not too far from where Stan had been just moments ago. In the faint moonlight, Leonidas could make out the bodies of all these players.

One of them had the exact costume of a Spider, and an intrigued look on her face. The second player resembled an Enderman almost perfectly, but she had blue eyes and a black ponytail down her back, her face seeming a bit unfocused. The final player had the body and face of a skeleton, with a mop of white hair, tinted black on top. This player's face looked stony and stoic.

Leonidas's heart dropped. He knew these players. He knew them well. And he knew just then how much trouble he and Stan were in.

Arachnia looked around the clearing, surveying the trees and landscape. Enderchick opened her mouth to say something, but Arachnia raised her hand, and her mouth immediately closed. Arachnia took a deep breath and closed her eyes, focusing intently on something. After a moment of silence, she opened her eyes.

"Somebody's on the island," she whispered, looking to Enderchick and the skeleton-player, who Leonidas knew to be called Lord Marrow. "I can't tell where, exactly . . . but they're not going anywhere."

Leonidas inhaled sharply, praying that Stan wouldn't hear this and take it to mean that he should run. Nothing could be further from the truth; they both had to stay put, lest Arachnia sense them.

Back when Leonidas had been commanding troops in Nocturia, Drake had told him about some old friends of his, bounty hunters who they could hire if they ever needed any extra hands. He had told Leonidas that this team, composed of five players named Arachnia, Enderchick, Lord Marrow, Creeper Khan, and Zomboy, was known as the Elite Legion of Mobhunters, or ELM. A mobhunter, Drake had explained, was a type of hacker who took on the skin of a mob in the game, and used cheats and mods to give themselves all the abilities of the mobs they were disguised as.

Drake had pointed out that Arachnia, for example, was a mobhunter dressed as a Spider. Therefore, she had given herself the ability to poison others on contact, high agility and wall-climbing abilities, and the ability to sense when others were around if she devoted all her focus to it.

At that point, Leonidas told Drake that he'd consider hiring them if need be. Now, Leonidas hated himself for not having Drake go into more detail as to what exactly the other mobhunters of ELM were capable of. Leonidas assumed that Enderchick had some sort of teleportation ability, and Lord Marrow was most likely a skilled archer, but he still couldn't guess exactly what these players could do. And he had no idea where Creeper Khan and Zomboy were . . .

"You know what to do, Enderchick," whispered Arachnia. Leonidas couldn't see Enderchick's face, but she nodded her head and then, in a puff of purple smoke, she was gone. Leonidas's heart sank; she *was* able to teleport.

Leonidas tried to keep his breathing as silent as possible as he heard the sound of teleportation go off every few seconds below him, indicating that Enderchick was clearly scouting out the island. He glanced up at Stan, in the tree directly across from him. Stan appeared to have the right idea and was crouched down, sword in hand and trying to be as inconspicuous as possible. Leonidas sighed in relief, and hoped that Stan would stay that way before the mobhunters managed to find him.

Enderchick appeared back in front of Arachnia in another burst of purple smoke.

"He's, like, not underground or anything, Arachnia," Enderchick chirped softly, a ditzy, Valley girl tone to her voice. "All the blocks on the island still have, like, snow covering them and stuff. Also, just over behind those trees, I found this thingy."

Enderchick reached into her inventory and pulled out a bow. As she handed it to Lord Marrow, Leonidas realized in horror that she was holding his own bow. Beyond being terrified that ELM now had evidence that somebody was indeed on the island, the feeling of helplessness that came with being unarmed crashed over Leonidas once again.

"Lord Marrow, what do you think?" Arachnia asked, as she and Enderchick turned to the skeleton-skinned mobhunter. "Has this bow been used recently?"

There was a moment of silence. Lord Marrow turned the bow over in his hand, and held it up to his eye level, examining it. Then, without a word, he turned to Arachnia, and nodded.

"All right," Arachnia replied, a grin cracking on her face. "He's here. Enderchick, please bring over our little friend."

Enderchick disappeared and reappeared an instant later,

holding another player by the shoulder. As Leonidas looked closer, he realized that she wasn't holding another player; this was a Zombie villager. As he got a closer look, Leonidas wondered in horror if this could be a citizen of the NPC Village he had once called home.

"Villager, give the command," Arachnia ordered. Leonidas was puzzled. What did that mean?

The villager gave a series of short roars, sounding vaguely similar to hacking coughs. There was a moment of silence as the three mobhunters and the Zombie stood there, and Leonidas wondered what was going on. Then, the sounds of Zombie moans, Spider hisses, and rattling bones caught Leonidas's ear as he watched dozens of hostile mobs appear and begin to swarm between the tree trunks, clearly searching for someone.

"I still think that this is, like, a totally suh-*tupid* idea," whined Enderchick, sticking her tongue out in disgust. "We could, like, totally find him ourselves, Arachnia."

"I know that we could," replied Arachnia, "but trust me, the mobs will find them much faster."

Leonidas sighed, and looked down at the leaf blocks he was sitting on. If they were using the mobs to search, then he was probably safe. The only real danger would be if he looked an Enderman in the eye, so if he just kept staring down, he'd more than likely stay undetected. Leonidas gave a quick glance up at Stan, to ensure that he, too, had the same idea. Indeed, Stan was still in the same position, crouched and ready to strike if need be, keeping his gaze fixed on the mobhunters below. Leonidas was about to return to looking down when, out of the corner of his eye, he noticed something.

Crouching on top of another spruce tree, not too far from where Stan was, was another player. Leonidas's heart stopped for an instant, as he feared that he was being surveyed by another mobhunter. Yet, as he got a closer look at the player's features in the faint moonlight, Leonidas realized that this player was quite different.

The figure had dark-colored pants, and his upper body was covered by a black cloak that draped down over his head, obscuring his face. Leonidas could still see a pale mouth.

Leonidas remembered back to days ago, when the same mysterious player had appeared out of nowhere to defend him from Spyro. The Black Hood had returned.

Leonidas had no idea what to do. He had no idea why this player was following him. And he had no idea why the Black Hood continued to stare directly at him. Leonidas raised his eyebrows at the player, eyes wide, as if trying to ask, *Who are you? And what do you want?*

The hooded figure—the Black Hood—said nothing.

Instead, he simply raised his pale hand and pointed directly above Leonidas's head.

Leonidas glanced up behind him and immediately rolled out of the way to dodge the Spider that was dropping down from the leaves above him. The arachnid landed next to Leonidas with a clicking hiss, and Leonidas cringed, as the pain in his arm had flared up yet again from the sudden motion. He had no time to tend to his wound, though. The Spider had already hopped into the air and was about to land on Leonidas, teeth bared. Without flinching, Leonidas drew back his good hand and sunk it as hard as he could into the airborne Spider's stomach.

On contact with Leonidas's fist, the Spider hissed in pain and flew farther into the air. Then, to Leonidas's dismay, the mob fell down off the tree and directly toward the mobhunters down below. Leonidas turned in a panic back to the Black Hood, wondering if the mysterious stranger could help him in any other way. But the Black Hood had vanished. And out of the corner of his eye, Leonidas saw something that made him immobile with alarm.

Stan was still in his same position in the tree, crouched and ready for action. He was staring down at the mobhunters, completely oblivious to the Spider leaping down toward him from above. Leonidas waved his hands around in desperation, trying to catch Stan's attention. He looked up at

Leonidas with a look that questioned Leonidas's sanity, right as the Spider slammed into Stan's back, and he tumbled down out of the tree, landing with a thud on the snow-covered dirt below.

The mobhunters, who had all been preoccupied with the Spider that had fallen on them, now turned on their heels to face this player who had fallen on the ground. Arachnia took a step forward and glanced down at the player in surprise before a wild grin of victory crossed her face. The Spider reared up behind her and prepared to strike, but she cut the beast in half with a diamond sword without even turning around.

"Well, well, well," Arachnia chuckled, elation flowing through her voice. "If it isn't the great and powerful President Stan2012 of Elementia."

Stan, winded from the sudden fall to the ground, struggled to push himself up and look her in the eye, a pained expression on his face.

"Enderchick," Arachnia said, looking to her black-skinned companion. Without hesitation, Enderchick disappeared in a puff of purple smoke and reappeared with her foot on Stan's back and a wild, sadistic look in her eye as she forced him to face-plant back into the snow.

"Try anything funny, Stan," Arachnia spoke softly, as Lord Marrow drew a bow and notched an arrow, which instantly began to swirl with strange, dark magic as he loaded it, "and we won't hesitate to kill you."

Stan gave a tiny grunt but no other response. He seemed totally unable to move as Enderchick ground her foot harder into his back. Arachnia raised her fist and clenched it. Before long, the fist began to swirl with blue-gray smoke. Slowly, Arachnia brought her hand lower and lower, toward the back of Stan's head.

Then there was a roaring sound from out of nowhere. Arachnia barely had time to turn around before Leonidas's right arm struck her across the forehead. As Leonidas landed on the ground, a sickening crunch emanating from his legs, Arachnia fell unconscious to the ground. His limp left arm struck Lord Marrow against the back of the head, sending his bow tumbling to the ground, the dark arrow flying into the night sky. Leonidas gave a scream of agony and fell to the ground as Enderchick, shocked by the sudden attack, warped away from Stan, appearing a few blocks away. As she drew her sword for self-defense, Stan leaped up onto his feet, drawing his diamond sword and surging forward to attack Enderchick.

Leonidas was vaguely aware of Stan and Enderchick beginning to fight, but he was in too much pain to fully comprehend what was going on around him. Beyond the stinging in his legs from jumping off such a tall tree, his left arm, which had struck Lord Marrow across the head, was now in such agony that he found himself unable to move. And as Leonidas gritted his teeth, tears streaming down his face, he realized there was no reason to move. Arachnia and Lord Marrow were both down for the count, and Stan was fighting Enderchick—there was nobody left to harm him.

Then, all at once, Leonidas became aware of the monster directly above, preparing to bear its fangs down into him. His deflating adrenaline levels suddenly pumped up to maximum yet again. Leonidas reached into his inventory and threw the bottle of Potion of Weakness, which he had been saving for weeks now, directly into the face of the Zombie villager. As the monster flinched, Leonidas plunged his hand into his inventory again, and forced the golden apple into the mouth of the Zombie.

As soon as the glimmering fruit disappeared into the mouth of the mob, it stopped trying to attack Leonidas. After a moment of standing still, the Zombie villager fell backward onto the ground, no longer pursuing Leonidas but rather shuddering as the wisps of smoke curled up off its body. Realizing that his job was done, Leonidas flopped back onto the ground, taking in the joy of lying still as he tried to catch his breath.

"You seem like you're having a totally awesome time, Stan!" giggled Enderchick, as she warped around Stan, dodging every strike of his enchanted diamond sword.

Stan panted with exhaustion, a slight growl of frustration escaping his mouth. He had no idea who these people were, and he was baffled as to how this player named Enderchick apparently had gained the ability to teleport at will. The one thing that he did know, however, was that he was beginning to tire, and he hadn't landed one single hit on her yet.

"You know, sweetie, if you just surrendered," simpered Enderchick, "then we could stop all this right now and just, you know, cut to the chase and stuff."

Stan's vein pulsed in his temple as she gloated, and he rushed toward her at top speed. Drawing back his sword, he launched himself into the air and spun around like a blender, trying as hard as he could to emulate the technique that he had invented on his day of axe training in the Adorian Village. Shockwaves shot out of the spinning sword, and one of the Knockback blasts slammed into Enderchick, who had teleported to avoid Stan's attack. Caught unaware, she toppled to the ground, giving Stan a free shot to her right leg before she warped away.

Suddenly, Stan sensed something approaching behind him, and he ducked to avoid the arrow that flew past his head. The glowing projectile stuck into a nearby tree, and the wooden block caught fire. Realizing that the other player must have a bow with Flame on it, Stan spun around to face the archer, who he had heard Arachnia call Lord Marrow. He was loading another arrow, but Stan saw that this one was different. As he squinted at it, he realized that the tip of this arrow had a tiny Creeper head on it. Baffled at what that could mean, Stan found himself forced to sidestep the arrow. It landed not too far from Stan, and there was a massive explosion at the spot where it landed. Stan had to raise his hands up to block the force of the blast, and he turned to face Lord Marrow again.

A horrible realization dawned on Stan. These players must be hackers! And Lord Marrow had several deadly types of arrows in his arsenal.

Frightened by the idea of what these arrows could do, Stan clutched his sword tightly and prepared to approach Lord Marrow. He knew how to approach archers; he had done it before. And if he could just get into close range, he would have the advantage.

Stan rushed forward as Lord Marrow fired another arrow directly at him, this one trailing purple, Enderman-like smoke behind it. Stan ducked under the arrow and it curved downward in midflight, still aiming for his head. The smoking projectile snagged onto Stan's black leather cap, pinning it to the snowy ground behind him.

Stan was too stunned to speak. Did he see that correctly? Did Lord Marrow have homing arrows?

He had no intention of sticking around to find out as Lord

Marrow readied his next shot. Stan ducked behind a tree to avoid another purple-smoked arrow, this one also curving off its path to find him but sticking in the corner of the tree before it could. Stan sprinted between the trees, as arrow after arrow flew after him. Some zigzagged their way through the branches, missing him by inches. Others connected with the trees in a massive explosion, clearing the woods of places for Stan to hide. And still others set the trees on fire, causing entire groves to go up in flames in a matter of seconds.

It wasn't long before Stan was exhausted, and he ducked behind a tree trunk that had avoided the blaze to dodge another homing arrow, this one coming within a centimeter of his foot. Stan glanced up, seeing what type of arrow Lord Marrow was going to fire next—an explosive one. Stan readied himself to dash out of the way, when suddenly, a shout rang out through the burning forest.

"Hey, Lord Marrow! Check out what happened to our little villager pal!" Enderchick screamed, her voice sounding bitter.

Stan's heart skipped a beat, and he peered around the side of the stump, preparing himself for whatever may have happened to the Zombie villager. But to Stan's total shock, the villager, who he didn't recognize, was now completely cured, no longer showing any signs of Zombie-hood. He merely looked around in a confused sort of way, the typical behavior of a villager.

"He's, like, totally useless to us now," Enderchick spat in disappointment. "Hey, Marrow, you should totally take a break from Stan for just a sec . . . take care of that villager for me, will ya?"

And Stan watched in horror as Lord Marrow loaded his bow with another arrow—a new type, this one sparkling with electricity—turned his back to Stan, and took aim at the villager. He let the arrow fly, just as the cry "NOOOO!" escaped from Stan's mouth.

And yet, to Stan's surprise, relief, and alarm, he wasn't the only one to utter this cry. He looked on as Leonidas dived out of the shadows of the forest, flying in front of the oblivious villager right into the path of the arrow, which sunk into his stomach. There was a massive crash of light and sound as, without warning, a bolt of lightning dropped out of the clear night sky through the power of the hacked arrow, striking the dark form of Leonidas. He went through a short fit of spasms in midair before he finally fell lifeless to the ground, smoke curling off his singed black leather armor and sparks dancing around his body.

Stan acted without thinking, moving purely through some primal, animal instinct as he charged into the clearing, a war cry escaping from his mouth. He sliced his sword across the unarmored back of the totally unprepared Lord Marrow. The archer tumbled across the clearing of snow, his pained face illuminated in the light of the burning forest, and he landed with a thud next to Enderchick, who was nursing her leg beside the still-unconscious Arachnia. When she saw Stan rushing toward them, sword raised and eyes blazing with unfathomable hatred, Enderchick, with a shriek of horror, grabbed on to both of her companions and disappeared in a cloud of purple smoke, leaving Stan to sink DZ's sword into nothing but dirt.

Stan didn't care that the players had escaped. He didn't even care right now why they had come in the first place. All that mattered to him was the player lying in the snow, covered in the soot of the lightning blast, the rising and falling of his chest slow and strained. In desperation, Stan pulled off Leonidas's charred chestplate. There was a noticeable wound on his left arm, where Stan assumed the Enderman from earlier that night had probably hit him. His leather chestplate had stopped the arrow from entering his body, and the place where the lightning had struck him bore a scar in the shape of a snowflake-like pattern, directly over his heart.

"Leonidas? Can you hear me?" Stan asked, desperate to hear a response.

"Yeah," Leonidas breathed, with no hesitation, "I . . . can hear ya, Stan."

Stan's heart flooded with relief, and he let out the massive breath he had been holding in.

"Leonidas . . . that was . . ."

"Pretty stupid of me?" Leonidas asked with a faint chuckle, followed by a raspy cough.

"No . . . it was amazing," Stan replied, tears of joy streaming down his face.

Leonidas gave a faint smile, immediately followed by continued coughing and wheezing. Stan reached into his inventory and pulled out a raw pork chop, the only bit of food he had left. He put it into Leonidas's mouth and, slowly but surely, Leonidas began to chew, and eventually the entire piece of meat entered his system. Leonidas sighed in relief.

"Thanks, Stan," said Leonidas softly, though noticeably stronger. "That helped."

"You're welcome. Leonidas, do you think . . . are you gonna . . ."

"I'll be fine, Stan," Leonidas cut him off, his breathing now more even. "I've survived a lot worse than this. Just give me a couple hours to heal up, and I'll be ready to move again."

Stan smiled, not believing that he was feeling so thankful, relieved, and even overjoyed that Leonidas, who he had once called the most savage player in all of Elementia, was going to live. Finally, Stan managed to speak.

"Leonidas . . . did you mean what you said before? Do you really want to help me?"

Leonidas took a deep breath, and let out a heavy cough before responding.

"Stan, I'll tell it to ya one more time . . . I didn't choose the Alliance. The Alliance chose me. But now, it's about time that I start makin' my own choices. And ya know what, Stan? I choose the NPC villagers. I choose Elementia. And . . . I choose you."

With that, a smile crossed Leonidas's face, his head rolled to the side, his chest rising and falling in the peaceful rhythm of sleep.

Stan noticed something lying beside him, and he picked it up. It was Leonidas's bow, the one Lord Marrow had picked up before Leonidas had knocked it out of his hand in the sneak attack. Stan turned the bow over, examining it for a moment, before looking back down at the sleeping player beside him.

Stan reached into his inventory and pulled out an arrow, half-aware of the villager still wandering around aimlessly behind him (he did not recognize the villager but would be sure to point him toward his home in a little while). He notched it in the bow and got into a crouching position, ready to fire. When Leonidas had healed and he finally woke up, Stan would give the bow back to him. Until then, however, Stan stood crouched in the snow in the midst of the burning forest, ready to take down anyone or anything that attempted to harm his new ally while he rested.

Even now, as Bob entered the courtyard of Element Castle, he could hear the sounds of hard labor taking place outside the castle walls. The sounds of toil and ruthless work were occasionally interspersed with cries of suffering as the citizens of Element City worked as hard as they could on their mandated task. These sounds alarmed Bob, and he prompted Ivanhoe to run faster as they entered the main hallway of the castle.

As he steered Ivanhoe up the stairs, Bob thought about what was going on outside. He knew that what was going on was definitely necessary. While the Element City walls were still holding up, all it would take was one breach of the defenses for Element City to fall to the Noctem forces. Should that fateful day arrive, the citizens would need somewhere to stay safe, and the Mechanist's solution was indeed a brilliant one, as his solutions usually were.

For the past few days, under the authorization of the Mechanist and the oversight of Bob and his brothers, all citizens of Element City had been recruited to take up their shovels and pickaxes and construct a defensive bunker underneath the city. While the underground of Element City already held a series of mines from its founding days, the Mechanist had ordered these tunnels to be strengthened, fortified with defenses, and enlarged so that the entire population of Element City could be safe underground.

However, in his messages relayed to the police chiefs from Element Castle via soldiers, the Mechanist's orders had become increasingly demanding. The Mechanist had commanded the citizens to work through the night, constantly digging and building to upgrade the tunnels as quickly as possible. Countless citizens had collapsed from fatigue, unable to work any longer. In the dark mines, dozens of citizens had been wounded by mob attacks, lava flows, and falling gravel, including one player who had died via a TNT blast set off by a miner who was delirious with exhaustion. It was this player's death that had finally made Bob realize that he had to confront the Mechanist.

As he reached the top of the stairs, Bob and Ivanhoe dashed down the stone-brick corridor until they came to a stop at the door to the council room. Bob took a deep breath and gave three sharp knocks on the door. After a moment, a growling, irritated voice rang out.

"Whaddaya want?"

Bob was taken aback; he wouldn't have been surprised if the Mechanist had sounded exhausted, or even hopeless, but he hadn't been expecting any brashness. Tentatively, Bob pushed the door open. The Mechanist was sitting at the table, a mess of papers strewn out haphazardly before him, and, for whatever reason, he no longer seemed irritated. In fact, he was smiling in a goofy way.

"Ah, look who it is!" the Mechanist cried, despite the fact that Bob could hear him perfectly fine. His voice was slurred and giddy, and his Texas accent had all but vanished. "It's always a pleasure to see my favorite little pile of pork . . . oh, and you, too, Ivanhoe!"

The Mechanist burst out laughing, clutching his sides and falling out of his chair as he banged the ground with his fist. Bob looked on, feeling extremely uncomfortable. Was this the same player they had agreed would run their city?

"Okay, okay," the Mechanist slurred after a moment of hysterics, grabbing the stone table and pulling himself to his feet. "All . . . *hic* . . ." A tiny hiccup escaped the Mechanist's mouth before he continued. "All hilarious comedy aside, how're you doing, Bob? Are the front lines holding up okay? And what about the tunnels? How're"—the Mechanist gave a huge, open-mouth yawn—"how're those coming along?"

"Well, uh," Bob said slowly, trying to keep his composure after the display that he had just seen. "Well . . . the front lines are holding up just fine. Our resources are starting to run a little low, but we won't have anything to be concerned about for a while. As for fortifying the old mines . . . well . . . that's actually what I came in here to talk to you about."

"Oh, don't tell me something went wrong!" cried the Mechanist, jumping to his feet, an infuriated look flashing over his face. "We need those mines fortified as fast as possible, we can't afford any setbacks!"

"Calm down!" replied Bob in hasty alarm. He was totally caught off guard by the rapid mood swing. "There hasn't been any setback! As a matter of fact the work on the mines is going at just the speed that you wanted."

"Well, then what's the problem?" spat the Mechanist as he plopped back down in his chair, no longer furious but rather agitated.

"Well, to be honest, I've come to request that you order the work schedule to slow down," said Bob, deciding that it wasn't worth it to beat around the bush. "The citizens are exhausted. They've been working nonstop, and they just need a break. Not to mention that several people have been injured, and a girl actually died earlier today."

"I'm sorry," replied the Mechanist, glaring at Bob and not missing a beat, "but do you realize what we're up against here, Bob? You're the *Chief of Police* . . . you must realize that the Noctems are coming closer and closer to breaking through our walls every day."

"Well, I—"

"And surely you realize that the second the Noctem Alliance breaks through that wall, they're going to try to take as many Elementia citizens hostage as possible. And that underground tunnel is the only place that will be safe—if you designed it the way I told you to, that is," the Mechanist spat.

"Of course I realize—"

"Then you should *also* realize," the Mechanist cut in, sounding more irritated by the second, "that completing those tunnels is incredibly important! Frankly, I don't care if a few people get hurt just so the tunnel gets done faster. If it means that the people of this city have somewhere safe to go when we get overrun by Noctem troops, then it's totally worth it! And I'll thank you to shut up and not question my logic, because I've spent far more time alone in this room thinking about what's best for this city than anybody else around here! Now go down there and get back to work! I'll have the plans for the blast doors done soon, and when I do, I expect them to be installed with no hesitation! *Do you understand?*"

As the Mechanist finished his rant, nostrils flaring and eyes bloodshot, Bob was more than a little disturbed. On the one hand, he knew that the Mechanist had a point; the Noctems could only be held at bay for so long, and it was imperative that they finish the tunnels before the walls failed them. But on the other hand, it frightened him that total control over their city was in the hands of the player who had just screamed at him.

"I understand, sir," Bob finally replied. "I'll tell my brothers, and we'll be ready to go when you finish the plans for those doors." And with that, Bob steered Ivanhoe back to the door and, vowing to keep a closer eye on the Mechanist from now on, he left the council room.

The Mechanist glanced in disgust at the door where Bob had just left. Preposterous it was, the Mechanist thought, that Bob had questioned his authority. He knew what he was doing, and clearly, if the people were demanding that they slow down their schedule, he was the only one with a clear scope of the situation.

Well, I guess what they say is true, the Mechanist thought to himself. *If you want something done right, you've got to do it yourself.*

And with that, the Mechanist extracted a bottle of blue-gray potion from his inventory, took a huge gulp, and wiped his mouth. When he was finished, he put the bottle down and got back to work on the designs for the blast doors.

"LAAAAAAND HOOOOOOOH!"

Kat, who had nodded off in the cramped back of the boat, jolted upright, causing the boat to rock sharply from side to side, prompting Charlie, who was steering, to cry "Watch it!" in irritation.

"Would you all shut up?" hissed Cassandrix, looking at

Charlie and Commander Crunch, who had just shouted in surprise. "I don't know if you people remember, but we still have an entire army of Noctem troops looking for us!"

"Oh, well, pardon me," growled Commander Crunch in irritation. "Ye know, I would 'ave expected that a bunch o' landlubbers like ye would've been more excited by th' prospect o' gettin' off these bloody ships . . ."

"Oh, trust me—we are," replied Kat, staring fondly at the mass of swampland rising up out of the distant ocean. Finally, after days and days of nothing but ocean and scattered, barren islands, they were back to the mainland. Then, suddenly, a thought occurred to her. She glanced up at Charlie sitting in front of her.

"Are you . . . gonna be okay, Charlie?"

"What? Oh, yeah, don't worry about me. I'll be fine," Charlie replied, and although Kat knew he was trying his hardest to sound earnest, there was a noticeable hint of apprehension in his voice. Kat looked at Charlie with sympathy. Although she had asked him once before, he hadn't been able to talk about the exact methods that the Noctem Alliance had used to try to get information about Element City out of him. However, Kat knew that they had targeted his legs. She imagined that he was dreading the prospect of having to walk all the way back to Element City.

It wasn't long before the two boats reached the swampy

land mass that Commander Crunch joyfully identified as the peninsula that would lead them back to Element City. As they exited their boats, Kat took a deep breath and stepped onto the soggy dirt blocks. Rex, who had been paddling beside them, pulled himself out of the water and shook his fur dry. Kat relished in the feeling of finally setting foot on dry land again after so long at sea.

The sensation lasted only for a moment, though, before there was a splash behind her. Charlie had tumbled out of the boat and into the water, and Kat helped him back to his feet, despite his protests. However, as Kat had expected, Charlie moved across the swampland with a limp, and Kat wondered how much of the damage would heal over time . . . and how much was permanent.

Without hesitation, all four players set to work. Kat and Commander Crunch broke down their two boats by hand, Cassandrix pulled out the compass and examined it, and Charlie hobbled his way over to the nearest tree and began harvesting wood. When the four of them had finished their various tasks, they walked over and met each other in a circle.

"Okay," said Cassandrix, pocketing the compass. "By my estimation, we're still a few days' walk from Element City." Charlie let out a small groan. "I think that we should take a rest for now, though. We still have enough food to last us for one more night, and if we go underground then we can get materials to make some new weapons for ourselves. We'll start hiking tomorrow, after we've gotten a good night's sleep."

The four players nodded and Charlie pulled a crafting table out of his inventory. Using the wood that he had collected, he crafted some wood planks and sticks, which were soon turned into a wooden pickaxe. As Cassandrix gathered some more wood for their weapons, Charlie punched the dirt blocks on the ground until he finally hit stone. Drawing out his pickaxe, Charlie brought it down onto the stone with a mighty strike, only to wince in pain as he did so. Kat's eyebrows raised in concern. Clearly, the damage from the torture was more severe than she had expected.

"Let me see that," Kat said kindly, taking the pickaxe from Charlie's hand and intentionally avoiding his crestfallen face. It wasn't long before Kat had tunneled down into ground, and, to her delight, came across a vein of coal ore. She harvested the black lumps, and, after she had Charlie toss a few sticks down to her, she put up torches to illuminate the cube-shaped cave she was carving out. Before long, however, the wooden pickaxe snapped off its handle, having lived out its incredibly short life span.

"Charlie!" Kat yelled. "Can you—"

But before she could finish, she watched as Charlie dropped down the hole and landed on the stone-block floor, stumbling with a grimace and an audible grunt of pain. Kat was alarmed. He shouldn't have taken any fall damage from such a short drop. She was about to go help him when Charlie looked up at her, determination in his eyes.

"Give me some stone, Kat," he grunted, pulling himself back to his feet.

"Charlie, you're hurt. Please, just let me—"

"I said, give it to me, Kat!" Charlie growled, anger coursing through his voice as he pulled the crafting table out of his inventory and slammed it to the ground in a huff. Kat stared at Charlie, taken aback by how aggressive he was all of a sudden. She handed three blocks of cobblestone to him, and he snatched them up. She looked on in shock, having trouble believing that this was the same happy-go-lucky player she was best friends with.

Kat continued to put up torches, still allowing Charlie to widen the space of their underground chamber, despite the clear fact that every stroke of the pickaxe was hurting him. It wasn't long before the chamber was a perfectly rectangular shape, large enough to comfortably hold all of them. Looking around the room, Charlie nodded to himself, drew a cobblestone block from his inventory, and placed it down, sitting on it and wiping his brow.

"All right, guys. We're done!" Kat yelled up the hole as she placed the last of the torches on the wall. "Come on down!"

Cassandrix plopped down the hole, landing gracefully next to Kat and immediately walking over to the crafting table. Then, Kat heard a yell come down from the hole in the roof.

"Ahoy scallywags, guess wha' I found!" Seconds later, Commander Crunch fell through the hole and landed next to Cassandrix and, without hesitation, he tossed a whole mess of wool blocks from his inventory onto the ground. "Thar was a flock o' sheep roamin' through th' swamp! We gonna be sleepin' comfy tonight! Well, I mean, personally, I prefer t' sleep on rigid wood planks . . . but I 'ave a feelin' that ye'll appreciate it!"

Although the prospect of a good night's sleep on a real bed did appeal to Kat immensely, it paled in comparison to the joy she felt when Cassandrix pulled a stone sword off the crafting table and put it into Kat's eagerly awaiting hands. It had been far too long since Kat had felt the wholesome completeness that came with being armed with her weapon of choice. While the bow was definitely a decent second, Kat still felt overjoyed to finally be holding a sword again.

The next couple of hours were spent mainly in silence. While her three friends stayed in the cave and crafted various necessities, Kat climbed back into the swamp and crept her way through it, gathering food for their journey with Rex at her heels, and keeping an eye out for Noctem forces hidden between the trees. As the sun started to set, Kat returned to the hole, leaping her way back in and securing a dirt block above her head before settling into the hideout.

Cassandrix and Commander Crunch were both sitting on beds that had been made from the wool, while Charlie was still sitting on the cobblestone block. All of them looked rather bored. Kat deposited the steaks she had obtained in the furnace and sat down on her own bed, stretching and giving a yawn.

Kat, not being in a particular mood to talk, simply lay down on her bed, closed her eyes, and attempted to drift off to sleep, with Rex curled up at the foot of her bed. However, try as she might, Kat was repeatedly distracted by a rumbling in her stomach. It appeared that eating could not wait until morning.

"Hey, Cassandrix," mumbled Kat to the girl in the bed next to hers. "You wanna reach into the furnace and grab a steak for me?"

After a moment with no reply, Kat continued, "Come on, Cassandrix, you're right next to it, and I really don't feel like getting up."

Still, there was no response.

"Blimey, Cassandrix!" cried out Commander Crunch, his eyebrow knitting as Kat groggily sat upright in her bed and glanced over at Cassandrix. "Th' lass asked ye a question, th' least ye can do be respond."

But suddenly, Kat wasn't interested in the food anymore. Or at least, not for the time being. Rather, she was distracted by Cassandrix, who was sitting upright on her bed, her eyes glazed over and a terrified expression on her face, as if she were in some sort of trance.

"Cassandrix? Come on! Snap out of it!" cried Kat, clapping her hands together in front of her face. Instantly, Cassandrix's head gave a jolt, and she looked around in confusion, clutching her chest, before finally realizing that she was in no danger.

"Did you not hear me?" Kat demanded. "I was asking you a question!"

"Oh, quiet yourself, you impudent twit," growled Cassandrix. "Get it yourself if you're so hungry."

"What's with you?" snapped Kat. She had actually been slowly warming up to Cassandrix over the course of their journey, and she was fully taken aback by this sudden return to her stubbornness.

"Oh, that is just like you, darling . . . so ignorant, so concerned about fairness and avoiding work. Kat, do you have any idea what we're up against?" screeched Cassandrix, her eyes wide and desperate, pure, primal fear ripe in every inch of her face. "Of course you don't! You're just as ignorant as any other young player! You didn't even recognize who Lord Tenebris was, did you?"

Kat opened her mouth, then closed it. She had been about to scold Cassandrix for dwelling on what they had seen Lord Tenebris do, rather than focusing on returning to Element City. On the one hand, Kat knew that, even though they had seen Lord Tenebris demonstrate terrifying and unexplainable powers, they couldn't dwell on that now if they wanted to get back to Element City as fast as possible. On the other hand, now that Kat remembered when the two of them had first laid eyes on Lord Tenebris, Kat had definitely sensed some fearful recognition on Cassandrix's face even before he had demonstrated what he could do.

"No, I didn't recognize him," Kat finally admitted.

"WHAT?" bellowed Commander Crunch, causing them all to jump as he leaped onto his feet in outrage. "Are ye tellin' me that ye looked wit' yer owns eyes into th' most infamous, most powerful, 'n' most evil demon in th' history o' Minecraft, 'n' ye didn' even recognize 'im?"

"What are you talking about?" demanded Charlie. "Of course we recognized him, Crunch . . . it was Lord Tenebris! Anybody with half a brain could figure that out!"

Rather than responding to Charlie, Commander Crunch turned to look at Cassandrix, who in turn stared back at him. Both of the older players held looks of equal disbelief on their faces.

"I don't believe it," whispered Cassandrix.

"Aye," replied Commander Crunch in an uncharacteristically soft voice. "They really don't know. . . ."

"Could you two cut to the chase already?" growled Charlie in irritation.

"Yeah," added Kat, indignant but also a little bit disturbed at her friends' reactions to her and Charlie's ignorance. "Clearly you know something that we don't, so spit it out!"

Cassandrix and Commander Crunch held each other's gaze for a long time, as if both were lost for words. Finally, Cassandrix turned to face Kat and Charlie, who had stood up and walked over next to Kat.

"The head of the Noctem Alliance," Cassandrix said slowly, as if carefully choosing her words, "is actually very well known. He's probably the most famous being in the history of Minecraft. And . . . most of the people who know of Lord Tenebris . . . know him by a different name."

"Aye," replied Crunch, giving a solemn nod. "She speaks th' truth. Have either o' ye two scallywags ever heard o' th' legend o' Herobrine?"

As the last word left Commander Crunch's mouth, Cassandrix gave a shuddery outtake of breath, and the aura of dread about her was palpable. Even Commander Crunch seemed fully absent of his usual upbeat sailor demeanor as he spoke. Charlie and Kat, on the other hand, were just confused; neither of them could recall ever hearing the name in their lives.

"No," Kat replied, quite uneasy but also intrigued. "What do you know about this . . . Herobrine?"

There was a moment of silence in which not a sound was uttered by anybody. Finally, Cassandrix spoke.

"Herobrine," she replied, taking a deep breath and trying to keep her voice stable, "is a demon. The most evil and most powerful entity in the history of Minecraft, which all but the most gullible believe to be simply an urban legend. I used to believe that as well, before I finally set my gaze upon Lord Tenebris myself."

"If it'd help ye," growled Commander Crunch slowly, his stony face flickering in the torchlight, "I jus' so happen t' know th' tale o' Herobrine's origin. 'Tis an ole tale—passed from sailor t' sailor since th' earliest days o' Minecraft—'n' perhaps, I may be able t' shed some light fer ye two on jus' wha' we be dealin' wit' in th' mastermind o' th' Noctem Alliance."

Kat and Charlie glanced at each other, then back at Commander Crunch. After a moment, Kat nodded.

"All right, Commander," Kat said, a tiny seed of fear in her heart as Charlie sat down in his bed to listen to the story. "Tell us the story of Herobrine."

And with that, Commander Crunch pressed his fingers together in front of his mouth and began to speak.

"Nigh-on three years ago, a Minecraft player posted a

message on an online message board. T' this day, nobody can say fer sure who this player was. This was back in th' days when Minecraft was in th' Alpha stage o' development, 'n' prone t' countless bugs, errors, 'n' glitches. Th' post consisted o' a simple thread o' text. Here be wha' it said:

"'I had recently spawned a new world in single-player Minecraft. Everythin' was normal at first, as I began choppin' down trees 'n' craftin' a workbench. I noticed somethin' move amongst th' dense fog . . . I 'ave a mighty slow computer, so I 'ave t' play wit' a wee render distance. I thought 'twas a Cow, so I pursued it, hopin' t' grab some hides fer armor.

"'Aye, but it wasn't a Cow.

"'Lookin' back at me was another character wit' th' default skin, but his eyes were empty, white, and lifeless. I double-checked t' make sure I wasn't in multiplayer mode. He didn' stay long, though . . . he looked at me 'n' quickly ran into th' fog. I perused out o' curiosity, but he was gone.

"'I continued on wit' th' game, nah sure wha' t' reckon. As I expanded t' world I saw thin's that seemed out o' place fer th' random map generator t' make by itself; square tunnels in th' rocks, wee perfect pyramids made o' sand in th' ocean, 'n' groves o' trees wit' all thar leaves cut off. I would constantly reckon I saw th' other player in th' deep fog, but I ne'er got a better look at 'im. I tried increasin' me render distance t' far whenever I thought I saw 'im but t' no avail.

"'I saved th' map 'n' went on th' forums t' see if anyone else had found th' pseudo-player. Thar were none. I created me own topic tellin' o' th' scallywag 'n askin' if anyone had a similar experience. Th' post was deleted within five minutes. I tried again, 'n' th' topic was deleted even faster. I received a private message from username "Herobrine" containin' one word: "Stop."

"'When I went t' look at Herobrine's profile, th' page was gone.

"'I received an email from another forum user. He claimed we were safer usin' email. Th' email claimed that he had seen th' mystery player, too, 'n' had a list o' other users who had seen 'im as well. Thar worlds were littered wit' obviously man-made features as well, 'n' described thar mystery player t' 'ave no pupils.

"'About a month passed till I heard from me informant again. Some o' th' players who had encountered th' mystery scallywag had looked into th' name Herobrine 'n' found that name t' be frequently used by a Swedish gamer. Aft some further information gatherin', 'twas revealed t' be th' brother o' Notch, th' game's developer. I personally emailed Notch 'n' asked 'im if he had a brother. It took 'im a while, but he finally emailed me back a mighty short message.

"'He said: "I did, but he be no longer wit' us."

"'I haven't seen th' mystery scallywag since our first encounter, 'n' I haven't noticed any changes t' th' world other than me own. I was able t' press "print screen" when I first saw 'im. Here's th' only evidence o' his existence.'

"'N' attached t' this player's message," Commander Crunch continued, as Charlie and Kat listened on, intrigued, "was a picture. Th' picture showed a Minecraft world in deep fog, wit' trees, hills, 'n' a chicken. 'N' peekin' out o' th' edge o' th' fog be a player wit' navy-blue pants, a turquoise shirt, 'n' empty, white eyes.

"Naturally, at th' time when this all came out, 'twas ignored, 'n' th' player was called out as a faker," Commander Crunch continued. "However, afore long, this mysterious, dead-eyed player named Herobrine began t' appear in other servers. Everywhere he went, he brought havoc wit' 'im, spawnin' lava in houses, creatin' mysterious structures in the worlds of unsuspectin' players, destroyin' thin's that others had created.

"He would also kill some players, playin' psychological tricks on them by leavin' items behind them when thar backs were turned, makin' bumpin' sounds in the night, makin' them feel as if they were bein' watched, 'n' slowly drivin' them further 'n' further into madness afore finally endin' them, 'n' corruptin' thar entire Minecraft server once 'n' fer all.

"It wasn't till a few famous Minecraft players had Herobrine appear on thar livestreams that scallywags finally began t' share thar tales. Since then, Herobrine has become somethin' o' an icon t' Minecraft. 'N' as soon as he became famous, thousands o' scallywags started t' fake sightin's o' 'im, eager t' get thar fifteen minutes o' fame by convincin' scallywags that they've got th' real proof that Herobrine exists.

"They be a bunch o' no-good leeches, be wha' they be, nah takin' th' demon seriously jus' 'cause they wants a good laugh. They don't care fer th' scallywags who really 'ave lost entire servers full o' players t' th' scourge o' Herobrine.

"Oh, 'n' if ye're feelin' skeptical, 'n' don't believe that Herobrine exists, then I ask that ye look no further than Minecraft itself. Every time a new update gets released, they'll also put out a list o' all o' th' changes t' Minecraft in th' newest version. 'N' at th' end o' every single list, ye'll always find th' same message: 'Removed Herobrine.' They keep on removin' Herobrine from th' game . . . but he keeps comin' back. I rest me case."

"I know that it's incredibly hard to believe," cut in Cassandrix, sounding stressed. "Trust me, I never believed it for a second . . . I always assumed that all Herobrine sightings were hoaxes, and when Mojang said that they'd 'removed Herobrine' from Minecraft, they were just going along with the joke. But when I saw Lord Tenebris sitting on his throne, I knew that he wasn't a player, not even a player who was using mods. There was something about him that was . . . off. Something that seemed . . . inhuman, though I couldn't put my finger on what it was. And seeing him use those powers only confirmed it for me.

"Trust me, you two . . . I'm a grounded person," said Cassandrix, and Kat could sense Cassandrix's heart racing almost as fast as her own. "I'll have trouble believing anything until I see it with my own eyes. And Lord Tenebris . . . he's no player. He's something far worse than that . . . far worse than you can even comprehend."

The four players sat in silence for nearly five full minutes, as Kat and Charlie tried to absorb everything that Crunch and Cassandrix had just said. Finally, Charlie spoke.

"So . . . as far as you know"—he spoke tentatively, and Kat sensed, for the first time in months, a tiny element of his old fear worming its way into his voice—"what exactly *is* Herobrine? And what exactly is the extent of what he can do?"

"That's th' scariest part . . . nobody has an answer t' either o' those riddles," Crunch replied solemnly.

"If I had to venture a guess," Cassandrix replied slowly, "Herobrine is most likely some sort of major coding glitch in Minecraft that managed to grow stronger and stronger the more the people at Mojang tried to fight it. And eventually, it got so strong that it was able to behave and act like some sort of mob."

"Aye, that be one theory," agreed Crunch, nodding his head. "Yet another be that Herobrine be th' agonized spirit o' th' dead brother o' Notch, th' creator o' Minecraft, that managed t' fuse itself wit' th' codin' o' Minecraft itself 'n' become some sort o' half code, half demon monster."

"Oh, please, let's try to stick to rationality here," spat Cassandrix at Crunch arrogantly. "Even if it were somehow possible for a dead person to become part of a game, Notch has gone on record to say that he doesn't really have a dead brother."

"That's jus' wha' he wants us t' think . . . I smell a conspiracy here, I do . . ."

"Anyway," continued Cassandrix, pretending that she couldn't hear Commander Crunch prattling on, "to answer your second question, Charlie . . . nobody really knows exactly what Herobrine is capable of. I think we can all agree that he was obviously born out of some sort of glitch—although we can only guess what that was—and the fact remains that he's already shown himself to have powers that are at least equal to those of an operator. If he can do that . . . well, as to the rest of his abilities, we can only speculate until the day when we get to see more of them firsthand."

"I gotta say, Cassandrix," cut in Commander Crunch in a taunting voice, "fer somebody who claims they ne'er believed in Herobrine till now, ye seem t' 'ave a decent amount o' knowledge about 'im."

"Well, I think you'll find a solid reason for that, Commander," Cassandrix replied coolly. "While I never saw fit to believe something with no evidence behind it at all, I always found it a pleasure to look on at those who did and have a good laugh to myself about it. And yes, I do in fact remember a thing or two of what those gullible saps said."

"Oh yeah?" cut in Kat. For some reason, something in Cassandrix's reply had plucked a nerve in her. "Well, if you're so high and mighty, how does it feel to know that this entire time, you were wrong and those 'gullible saps' were right?"

Cassandrix whipped around to face Kat, and opened her mouth to retort, then abruptly closed it. Kat was shocked; she had never seen Cassandrix rendered speechless before. There was a split moment of silence before finally, Charlie cut in.

"It's late," he grunted. "We've all been at sea for way longer than is good for us. It'll affect your mental state if you stay out there too long—"

"Hey! What're you tryin' to say?" Commander Crunch cut in, outraged.

"And we really need a good night's sleep," finished Charlie

without missing a beat. "Let's just go to bed now. We hit the road for Element City in the morning."

And with that, Charlie flopped down on his bed, turning his back to the others. Seeing no reason to argue, the other three players did the same thing, with Commander Crunch still grumbling softly to himself about Charlie's final comment. Kat hardly noticed, though. Her head was too full of thoughts from the stories she had just heard.

Kat had always fantasized about having operating powers. From the moment that she had heard about them, she had imagined herself wielding their incredible strength, using them to become the most unstoppable force in all of Elementia. And now here she was, preparing to fight against a being that not only had abilities that were apparently quite similar to operating powers, but were even stronger than that.

Long after the snores of the other three players had started up with various degrees of volume, Kat still lay awake in her bed, dreading just what exactly it was that she was preparing to face.

A re you kidding me?"

"Calm down, Khan!" shouted Arachnia, her firelit face tired and stressed. "The situation is bad enough, and getting angry won't help."

"Oh, just shut up!" spat Creeper Khan, his gritted teeth showing as he sunk his hand into a nearby tree in frustration. "Honestly, you have no idea how hard I'm trying to stop myself from blowing up this entire forest . . ."

"Arachnia, I don'd ged id," said Zomboy innocently, looking at her in confusion. "If dere were tree of you—and jusd two of dem—how come you did nod win?"

"Finally, that giant hunk of rotten flesh says something logical!" hissed Creeper Khan as he whipped back around to glare at Arachnia.

Arachnia took a deep breath, then replied, "I told you, they had the element of surprise on their side. I certainly wasn't expecting Leonidas to jump me like that. It's the same reason I was able to take down Kat and that other girl she was with by myself—they didn't see me coming."

"Well, even if you did manage to . . . ugh . . . lose to just two people, then why is it that Enderchick didn't warp Zomboy and me over to you guys?" Creeper Khan demanded. "We weren't doing anything, and if you knew that Stan was on that island, then we definitely weren't going to miss anything by leaving our posts. Why didn't Enderchick just grab us?"

"Ugh . . . right, that . . . ," spat Arachnia in disgust. She still couldn't believe the excuse Enderchick had given her. "Apparently, she was just *too tired* from warping three people at once, and couldn't bring herself to warp again until she rested."

"You cannot be serious!" bellowed Creeper Khan, a vein pulsing in his forehead. "You're telling me we lost the opportunity for the biggest paycheck we've ever gotten just because that little spoiled brat couldn't be bothered to move?"

"Yep," sighed Arachnia in disgust.

"Argh!" Creeper Khan gave a bellow of rage, and not too far away from him, an explosion came from nowhere and blasted all the leaves off the top of a tree, leaving the trunk engulfed in fire.

"Watch it! You'll kill us if you can't control yourself!" cried Arachnia, leaping to her feet before clutching the lump on her head, and forcing herself to sit back down on her tree stump while Zomboy lumbered over to the burning tree and punched the fire out.

"Whatever," shot back Creeper Khan, plopping himself onto the soggy ground with a wet smack, and beginning to punch the dirt in frustration. There was a moment of silence, with nothing but the ambient sounds of the dark, soggy swamp around them as Zomboy lumbered back over to the group and sat down next to Arachnia.

"You know, it's been way too long," grunted Creeper Khan impatiently after a minute. "Why isn't Enderchick back yet?"

"Well, that's a good point, actually," replied Arachnia, as she realized just how long Enderchick had been away. "She should be back. Her talk with Drake shouldn't be this long. Do you think that he might have done something to her once he found out what happened?"

"Doubt it," Creeper Khan said, with a dark snicker. "If there's one thing we know, it's that she'll always be able to warp if it's *her* sorry self on the line. Wouldn't you say, Marrow?"

Lord Marrow, who had been leaning up against a tree a distance from the campfire while looking down at the ground, glanced up to look at Creeper Khan. The player's skeletal face raised an eyebrow and took a tone of indifference for a moment before returning to its original position.

Creeper Khan gave a soft growl. To be honest, he was getting really sick of everybody on his team being so intolerable, what with Arachnia's condescension and Enderchick's ditziness, and the less said about Zomboy, the better. Lord Marrow was the only one who Creeper Khan had really been able to tolerate, and now even his perpetual stoic silence was wearing on him.

"You know, maybe I won't even wait," he spat. "Maybe I'll just use my Final Nova on all of you—"

"I told you not to joke about that!" Arachnia cried, suddenly looking terrified.

Creeper Khan's retort, however, was broken by the sound of teleportation, as Enderchick appeared next to the campfire in a puff of purple smoke.

"Finally!" grunted Creeper Khan in disgust as he whipped around to face her.

Arachnia sat up straight and asked, "What did Drake say, Enderchick?"

"Omigosh, just, like, give me literally two seconds to rest, people," whined Enderchick, sitting down on another tree stump and looking pouty. "Ya know, it's not, like, *easy* to warp from Element City to this stupid suh-*wamp* . . ."

"Cry me a river," cut in Arachnia, as Creeper Kahn sputtered in outrage, "build a bridge . . . and then go jump off it. You were the one who caused us to lose Stan, Enderchick. You're in no position to ask for favors."

"Well ex-*cuuuse* me, princess," huffed Enderchick. "You know, whatever, I'll tell you. Basically, Drake told us that he was, like, super mad at us for losing Stan. Like, I dunno, he said something, like, *'If you don't get Stan to me before he gets to Element City, I will be forced to turn you over to Lord Tene-bris.'* I mean, he's like, so melodramatic . . ."

"Haha . . . melondramatic . . ." Zomboy chuckled, his mouth hanging open and a dopey expression on his face. "Haha . . . I like melons . . ."

Zomboy continued laughing while Enderchick absent-mindedly wiped a spot of mud off her leg. Creeper Khan gave a roar of frustration and glared at Enderchick and Zomboy, then yelled, "You two are nothing but a couple pieces of brainless, incompetent—"

"SHUUUUT UP!"

Arachnia's yell was so loud, so forceful, and so harsh that immediately, all three of her fellow mobhunters whipped around to face her, and were terrified by the wrathful expression on her face as she clutched her diamond sword. Even Lord Marrow glanced up from the ground, his eyes locked on to her.

"Do you people realize," whispered Arachnia with more power than a yell could ever convey, and her face devoid of anger but ripe with fear, "the position that we are in right now? Do you realize what will happen to us if we *don't* have Stan delivered to Drake on a silver platter within the next couple of days?"

The four other members of ELM just stared at her for a moment. They all knew the answer, but Arachnia said it anyway.

"We'll suffer. We'll suffer hard. I don't think that any of you truly comprehend the kind of forces that we're dealing with here. The Noctem Alliance is powerful, but they're also ruthless and merciless. I think that if you'd just put your ridiculous squabbling to the side for a minute, you'd realize that we've got one foot in the grave and another on thin ice right now."

There was yet another moment of silence, but now the truth of Arachnia's words sunk into the other mobhunters. They all remembered the things they had heard about the Noctem Alliance, all the horrible stories that had passed through their small outpost in the middle of the desert about what the Noctem Alliance was capable of. Never had it fully hit them that, should they fail, all that power would be directed on to them. They all knew now that the time had come to fully devote themselves to their work. Even Zomboy waited with bated breath for Arachnia's next order.

"Okay," continued Arachnia, her breathing calm but her tone serious, "Enderchick, did you ask Drake how close they were to breaking into Element City, like I told you to?"

"Yes," Enderchick replied, no longer distracted but fully focused. "He told me that they would be through the wall within a matter of days . . . that something special is headed for Element City, like, right now, and when it gets there, they'll finally be able to get in."

"Okay then, team," replied Arachnia, her mind kicking into hunting mode as she glanced around at her four fellow members of ELM. "Here's the plan . . ."

"You can't be serious!" Stan exclaimed.

"As much as I hate to say it," replied Leonidas, his eyebrows knitted and his expression grim, "it's true, Stan."

"And . . . you're saying . . . ," continued Stan, as he tried to wrap his head around the ramifications of what Leonidas had just told him, "that . . . *that's* the guy who's leading the Noctem Alliance? The guy who can do all *that* stuff?"

Leonidas nodded, his expression dark. As much as he had hated to explain to Stan exactly who Lord Tenebris was, he knew it had to be done. Although Stan was most assuredly terrified out of his wits at the prospect of fighting the most powerful and evil being in Minecraft history, he still had to know as much as possible about what the Noctem leader was capable of. Suddenly, Leonidas realized that he was walking alone. He stopped, and looked behind him to find Stan stopped in his tracks, staring at the ground in foreboding between two particularly large swampland trees.

"Are ya all right, Stan?" Leonidas asked in concern, doubling back to where Stan was.

As he looked up to face Leonidas, Stan's face showed a mixture of confusion and fear. "Not really, no," he replied honestly. "So you're telling me that Lord Tenebris, or . . . how do you pronounce it . . . Hiro . . . Haro . . ."

"It's Herobrine, Stan," Leonidas corrected him, and he sounded it out. "Heh-roh-brine." Leonidas shook his head in disbelief. "Honestly . . . You're a Minecraft fan, you've been on the internet before, but ya still don't know who Herobrine is? How's that possible?"

"I don't know!" exclaimed Stan. "I mean, to be honest, I've just been playing on Elementia for as long as I've been in Minecraft . . . I've never really had to leave for anything, I learned how to play in the Adorian Village, and I've kind of been too busy since then to look around at a lot of other Minecraft-related stuff."

"Well, in that case, lemme make one thing clear to ya, Stan," replied Leonidas, and Stan looked him in the eye.

"All that stuff I just told ya about Herobrine, and what he can do . . . some of it might not be true. Everythin' that I think Herobrine can do is based off what people've spread around. Nobody knows for sure what he can and can't do, 'cause people keep on pullin' off hoaxes and pranks to make their friends think they've seen Herobrine and stuff like that. Matter of fact, the people who made Minecraft've said that Herobrine doesn't really exist. 'Cause of that, your guess is as good as mine what Lord Tenebris, the *real* Herobrine, is capable of."

"Wait . . . hold on," said Stan slowly. "You're saying that people fake sightings of Herobrine all the time? The same way that people fake, like, Loch Ness Monster sightings or Bigfoot sightings?"

"Exactly."

"Well . . . then . . . how do we know that Lord Tenebris is really Herobrine?" Stan asked, his spirit lifting slightly at this idea. "How do we know that the Noctem Alliance isn't just faking it to intimidate us?"

"'Cause I've been face to face with him, Stan," Leonidas replied darkly. "Once, months ago. Right after you and your army beat the King, me, Caesar, and Minotaurus made our way to Spawnpoint Hill, and he appeared in front of us. And he was floatin' in midair, Stan. That's not just somethin' that any old player could do. He was either an operator, which ain't possible, or he was somethin' else.

"And trust me, Stan . . . it wasn't no special type of monster spawned in with mods or nothin'. When I first saw Lord Tenebris, I looked him straight in his dead, white eyes. but I could only hold eye contact for a second. I'm not entirely sure why, and to this day I can't put my finger on it, but there was somethin' in those eyes that was more sinister and evil than I can put into words, maybe because they definitely belonged to somethin' that wasn't human.

"To be totally honest with ya, Stan, I haven't seen Lord

Tenebris since that day. All my communication with him has been through Caesar, and 'cause of that I have no idea what he really is capable of. And maybe that's the scariest part. Besides, even now, months later, those eyes still haunt me . . ."

Leonidas realized how long he had been talking, and he looked up at Stan. The look on his face was concerned, anxious, and unnerved all at the same time. There was a moment of quiet, as neither of them knew what to say. Then, finally, Stan spoke.

"Well, I can tell you one thing, Leonidas. If the prospect of just seeing Lord Tenebris affected you that badly, then I can only imagine how hard it must've been for you to leave the Noctem Alliance and join us." Stan's voice was kind and sympathetic. "I'm glad that you're here with me, Leonidas, and I'm proud to call you my friend."

Leonidas looked up. When he looked into Stan's eyes, there was no fear. There was only simple joy and contentedness.

"Thanks," Leonidas replied with a smile.

Before Stan could reply, though, Leonidas suddenly became aware of a sound, and he held his hand up to silence Stan. A screeching noise vaguely reminiscent of a jet engine was coming from above their heads, and it was growing louder by the second.

"What is that?" Stan asked, looking skyward as Leonidas

glanced around, his eyes finally locking onto a small mine not too far from them. Without hesitation, Leonidas grabbed Stan's arm and yanked him down into the tunnel. The two glanced up through the canopy of leaves above their heads and into the pink glow of the sunset sky as the sound escalated into a deafening roar.

Then, without warning, a massive black form rocketed directly over their heads. The two players couldn't make out what it was through the thick foliage, but the deafening sound and strong tailwind that rustled the leaves forced them to duck their heads even deeper into the mine. They barely had time to comprehend what had happened when another giant black object flew overhead, bringing the same cacophony and strong wind stream with it.

Stan and Leonidas stood with their backs to the wall in the mine, their hearts racing, armed with sword and bow, trying to ready themselves for whatever it was that had just passed them. After a minute, however, nothing happened. The environment had returned to normal, and while Stan could still hear the jet sound, it was getting softer and softer.

"What were those things?" Stan breathed.

"No idea," replied Leonidas, "but I'm gonna find out."

And before Stan could stop him, Leonidas jumped up out of the mine and onto the soggy dirt blocks of the swamp ground. He aimed a few well-placed punches into those dirt blocks, and used them to create a stairway on the side of one of the tall trees they were next to. Leonidas sprinted up the dirt blocks and perched himself on top of the tree.

Above all the rest of the swampland forest, Leonidas could see the landscape stretching out for thousands of blocks. He scanned the darkening pink horizon, and there, far in the distance, he could make out two indistinguishable black forms, flying away. Leonidas glanced at the sun behind him, hardly noticing the gorgeous sunset, and realized that the creatures were headed southeast. As he realized this, Leonidas's heart skipped a beat.

"What did you see?" asked Stan apprehensively as he pulled himself out of the mine.

"I couldn't see what those things were, Stan," Leonidas replied, distraught. "But whatever they are, they're headed straight toward Element City."

"Ah, he lives!" snickered Jayden as G walked over to him. "How're you doing, man? And what've you been up to? You're hardly ever around anymore."

"Well, there's a good reason for that," G sighed, sitting down on a seat next to Jayden in the only other available seat in the packed rec room. "Tess has been working me nonstop. To be totally honest, I'm exhausted."

"Wait, seriously?" asked Jayden, his mouth hanging open

in surprise. "You've been doing stuff with her this whole time? Even during training exercises?"

"She says that she needs me training with her more than I need combat training," G said, reaching into a nearby chest. "What've you guys been doing in combat training, anyway?"

"Well, to be honest, it's actually pretty boring. You should feel glad you're missing it." Jayden sighed. "It's pretty much a rundown of the same sort of advanced combat lessons we used to give in the Adorian Village . . . nothing too exciting."

"Sorry. Although I personally would be happy to take a break and be with you guys. I mean, Tess is nice to me and all, but she just has the constant need to keep training me. She never gives me a break, and I'm getting sick of it."

"Really," replied Jayden. "Do you think she might be into you or something?"

"I don't think so," replied G. The thought had crossed his mind, but he was pretty confident that that wasn't the case. "She might as well be, though. The constant work after training is done is really wearing me out, and I've just about had it with her."

Jayden opened his mouth, one step away from saying something, but he closed it before he could. Now that he finally had a chance to relax, Jayden was sure G wouldn't particularly care to hear what he wanted so badly to say. There'd be time for that later.

"Anyway, I just stopped by to grab my pickaxe," groaned G, pulling his iron tool out of the chest. He had his diamond pickaxe hidden on hand, but he was saving it for an occasion in which he really needed it. "I have to go see Tess again."

"Are you serious?" asked Jayden in disbelief.

"Yep," replied G glumly, standing up and walking away from his friend. "I'll see you later, okay?"

And with a stunned look on his face and an absent-minded waving hand, Jayden watched G walk out the door.

G looked up and saw General Tess, her pink face alert and attentive, standing at the same place in the marble hallway where she always was when they met up after hours.

"Good evening, MasterBronze," Tess greeted him, in the same way that she did every other night.

"Good evening, ma'am," G responded, as if programmed.

"Tonight, I have a very special job for you, soldier," Tess commanded, sounding rather important. "As I'm sure you know, in conquest of the lands surrounding Elementia, we were able to capture and occupy the Adorian Village. In doing so, we have taken several members of the village as captives, who will be used as ransom as soon as the glorious Lord Tenebris sees fit."

"I see, ma'am," replied G, trying as hard as he could to hide the fact that his heart was racing at the mention of these hostages.

"I feel that in the past few days, you, soldier, have proven yourself competent enough in my leadership exercises that I feel comfortable entrusting you with a task on your own."

"Thank you, ma'am," G said, his heart skipping a beat. What exactly did she mean by that?

"Therefore, MasterBronze, I am entrusting you with the checkup on the captives. You will go down into the left chamber of the ground floor, where you will find the Adorian Villagers. You will give them their weekly ration of food, ensure that no escape attempts are in progress, and report back to me."

"Will do, ma'am," said G. His response came out a bit happier than it ought to have been, but he was having trouble keeping himself from dancing with joy. Finally, at long last . . . he had a clear shot to free the prisoners. They were almost being gift-wrapped for him.

"Go ahead now, it shouldn't take you long," Tess commanded lazily, handing G a stack of bread before turning around and walking back down the hallway. "I'll tell the guard to give you clearance."

Wasting no time, G turned on his heel and made his way down the marble hallway, down a flight of stone-brick stairs, and into the central rotunda of the building, a bounce in his step the entire way. He followed the directions that Tess had given him, finally arriving in front of a player holding a diamond axe, dressed in full black leather armor and standing before an indentation in an obsidian wall alongside a lever and an iron door.

"Nobody's allowed in there," the guard grunted.

"My name is MasterBronze," G replied. "I was sent by General Tess to check on the prisoners."

With no hesitation, the guard pulled the lever, and the door scraped open. *Wow!* G thought to himself as he walked through the doorway. *This isn't nearly as difficult as I was expecting it to be!*

The inside of the room was dim. There were a few torches lighting the walls, but they kept the room just bright enough to keep mobs from spawning, and the little light they did cast seemed to be consumed by the blackness of the obsidian that coated the roof, floor, and walls. Huddling over in the far left hand corner was a mass of players, looking malnourished and miserable.

One of the players turned his head around in a jerky manner, and glanced up at G in an equally twitchy way. All at once, G felt himself stop in his tracks.

G knew this player. His skin was identical to Stan's, though lighter overall. G guessed that this was a common skin, and so he looked into the player's eyes to be positive. It was true. G recognized this player from months ago—he would recognize the skin, eyes, and twitchy, spastic mannerisms anywhere.

The strange thing was, though, G also knew this player was dead.

"Sirus?" G asked, as though he were addressing a ghost.

"Wha . . . how . . . how do you know my name?" the player asked, his face shifting from downcast to paranoid.

"Dude, look into my eyes . . . it's me, G. From the old Adorian Village," G answered with a smile.

Suddenly, comprehension flashed across Sirus's face for a split second, and then he broke out into a tremendous smile.

"Goldman! Oh boy, am I glad to see you, because, you know, it's so dark in here, and I've been stuck with these people for weeks. You know, I mean, no offense to you guys, but it's so nice to see somebody else, somebody I know, somebody who—"

And then, like the flip of a switch, Sirus ceased to be happy, and instead looked baffled.

"Who would never work for the Noctem Alliance in a million billion years, and so what gives, G? Why're you here? Did you have some sort of change of heart or what?"

"I'm here to rescue you guys," replied G hastily, more focused on asking the dozens of other questions exploding in his mind as Sirus's face flipped back to ecstasy. "But I'll get to that in a minute. First of all, how are you still alive?"

"Whaddaya mean?" Sirus asked.

"I mean . . . I . . . you got killed!" cried G. "In the Battle for Elementia! Archie told me that he saw you get killed by one of King Kev's soldiers who was dressed up like a giant zucchini wearing a sombrero! How did you get back into Elementia if you died?"

"Huh . . . oh, yeah, that little thing," Sirus replied with a chuckle, shifting gears from confusion to laughter. "Well, it's kind of a funny story, 'cause you see, after I helped you guys disarm all those redstone contraptions before the battle started, I went into battle with you, and I managed to stay alive for a pretty long time, 'cause, you know, I can never stay in one place, so it's pretty hard to catch me, but then that thing happened where I took an arrow to the knee, and then the zucchini guy hit me with a potion and then killed me and stuff, and the next thing I know, I'm sitting right back on Spawnpoint Hill, and then I—"

"WHAT?" demanded G, so loudly that the other hostages, who had turned their heads in curiosity, jumped with surprise. "You managed to respawn? How is that possible? Elementia's a Hardcore PVP server. You can't respawn after you die!"

"Well, that's what I thought, too," continued Sirus, shrugging. "But it still happened, even though I have absolutely no idea what caused it."

G scratched his head, trying to think of what could possibly have caused this phenomenon. "Well, I guess it could've just been a glitch in the system or something. A lot of people did die in that battle, maybe the blacklist got overloaded or something . . ."

"Yeah, maybe," replied Sirus, still extremely jittery. "Anyway, after I respawned, I saw somebody duck into the woods and I figured that the hill probably wasn't safe, so I decided that I wanted to go out into the middle of the Ender Desert because I thought that could be fun, but then I got hungry and tried to eat part of a cactus, and it kind of caused me to hallucinate to the point where I imagined that I was at a wedding between a cantaloupe and a watermelon whose families disapproved of their union due to the parents' deeply rooted prejudices against fruits that were different from themselves, but then I woke up from the hallucination and found myself in the care of a player in a black uniform who was trying to teach me how to use seashells as toilet paper, and then I realized that the Ender Desert was a weird place and I wanted to go home, so I made my way to Element City, and may have gotten a bit lost on the way, but when I stopped in the Adorian Village for a snack break, the Noctem Alliance captured me and brought me here, and weren't you saying something about an escape plan?"

G, who had tuned out the insane redstone mechanic in the midst of his rambling, was still floored that Sirus was somehow alive. As he realized that Sirus had stopped talking, though, he realized that now was neither the time nor place to question it. He had a rescue to pull off.

"Yeah, I was. Take this," replied G, reaching into his inventory and pulling out his diamond pickaxe, relinquishing it to the deranged-looking yet brilliant player sitting across from him. "And here's your food for the week, too.

"Now I don't have much time," continued G as he removed the bread from his inventory and put it on the ground in front of Sirus. "If I'm in here too much longer, they'll start to suspect something. Here's the plan: Tess told me that they check on you guys once a day. So after three days, I want you to tunnel out of here. The pickaxe will be strong enough to break through the obsidian, and you guys can tunnel your way into the tundra and make your way back to Element City from there. Don't do it any earlier than three days from now, or they'll suspect me of helping you. Got it?"

"Sure do," replied Sirus, glancing down at the diamond pickaxe he was holding in his hand and feeling elated. "I'll be sure to get all these guys back to Element City safely, Gold-man, don't worry about nothin', you can count on me to—"

Suddenly, he was cut off by the iron door creaking open. Light flooded the obsidian room, and G heard the guard's voice call out, "Hey, is everything going okay in there?"

Without hesitation, G lunged forward and sunk his fist as hard as he could into Sirus's stomach. Sirus let out a tiny choking sound and shock flashed across his face, but he concealed the diamond pickaxe in his inventory all the same as he slammed to the floor, wheezing.

"And you'll get far worse than that if you ever mouth off to me again!" G bellowed harshly. Sirus's shocked eyes suddenly showed comprehension as he realized what G was doing.

"Do you understand, you maggot?"

"I do," croaked Sirus feebly, as he gave G an almost inconspicuous wink. G looked sympathetic for an instant, and mouthed the word "sorry" before turning his back on the prisoners, all of whom were looking at G with bemused expressions.

"Don't worry about it," G assured the guard, with a confident nod. "He won't be showing any more disrespect to a member of the Noctem Alliance any time soon. I've made sure of that."

The guard nodded, showing no signs of suspicion whatsoever as he pulled the lever down to close the iron door. As G walked down the hallway and back toward the rec room, he knew that he ought to be thrilled and relieved that their plan had gone off flawlessly, and the hostages would escape from Nocturia within the next few days. However, this was not at the forefront of his mind.

He couldn't wait to get back to Jayden and discuss the

fact that Sirus was still alive. That meant that somehow, something had gone wrong in the coding of Elementia, allowing Sirius to respawn after he'd been killed. And if it had happened once, G realized that it was possible that it could happen again. . . .

Stan?"

"Hold up!" Stan cried out, holding up his hand and stopping dead in his tracks. Leonidas, who had been walking alongside Stan, stopped abruptly and turned in alarm. "Stan? Can you . . . hear me?"

"Yeah, I can," Stan replied, raising his hand to silence a perplexed Leonidas.

"Come to . . . SalAcademy. I have something . . . to tell you . . ."

"I'm on it," Stan replied, and with a pop of static, Sally's voice disappeared.

"What *was* that?" Leonidas inquired, sounding confused.

"That girl Sally just contacted me," Stan replied.

"Again?" Leonidas groaned. This had happened quite a few times before, and it always slowed their progress.

"Afraid so," replied Stan, and with that he sat down on the ground, taking a deep breath and preparing to disconnect from Elementia.

"Now wait just a sec, Stan!" Leonidas interjected, grabbing him by the shoulder and pulling him back to his feet. "Do ya *really* have to go see her right *now*? Do ya realize just how close we are to Element City? If we traveled all day, we'd be there by nightfall, get a good night's sleep, and we could spend the entire day tomorrow figuring out how to get past the Noctem forces outside the city walls."

"I know that, Leonidas, but I still really have to do this," Stan replied firmly. "I seriously do have important business to take care of. The fate of Elementia may depend on it!"

"I still don't understand why ya can't just tell me what this incredibly important *stuff* you have to do is," mumbled Leonidas bitterly.

"Trust me, if I told you, you'd think I'm crazy."

"I think you're crazy now," retorted Leonidas as Stan made his way to sit down again. "At the very least, though, could you join this other server in a more hidden spot? You realize I'm gonna have to defend the place you left while you're gone."

Stan nodded, and immediately, the two of them scouted the swampland around them until they came across a cave. They walked down into it and found a pool of molten lava, providing a nice, inconspicuous source of light at the bottom. Leonidas noticed a rectangular indentation in the wall, as if somebody had tried to dig through but hadn't gotten very far.

Stan sat down next to the pool of molten lava as Leonidas drew his bow. Leonidas looked on as Stan took a deep breath, and a moment later, he disappeared. Leonidas took his position looking up at the cave mouth. He was a little annoyed at Stan for forcing him to do this, but at the same time, he was intrigued by what this mystery task could possibly be.

Stan opened his eyes and once again gazed over the familiar sight of the midday sun peaked in the blue sky over the endless field of green grass. Intent on locating Sally, Stan turned his head to the right, only to find himself face to face with a Creeper.

"*Augh!*" bellowed Stan as he summoned a diamond axe into his hand with the power of his mind and sunk it as hard as he could into the creature standing beside him. As it fell over, Stan was shocked to see Sally's body fall to the ground with a smack, a tiny Creeper Head and a diamond sword bursting out of her inventory as she did so. Seconds later, there was a pop as Sally reappeared next to Stan, giving him an accusatory glare.

"What was that for?" she demanded. "I was just trying to have some fun!"

"I'm sorry, you scared me!"

"Ugh . . . I forgot who I was dealing with," spat Sally, walking over to her items and retrieving them from the ground. "The great Stan2012 . . . the guy who's gonna save Elementia from descending into chaos, and also has a spaz attack the second a Creeper looks at him funny. Don't worry, noob, next time I'll play a slightly more tame prank on you. Hmm . . . I know! How about I replace Element Castle's doorbell with a farting sound? You think you could handle that without freaking out?"

"Well, you're forgetting one thing," retorted Stan, flustered with embarrassment. "In order for that to work, you'd kind of have to be *in* Elementia, Sal."

"Ouch," she replied, her eyebrows raising. "To be honest, I didn't think you'd go there so easily. Oh, and speaking of which, thank you for killing me by sinking a diamond axe into my chest, Stan. That didn't give me any horrific flashbacks of the Battle for Elementia at all."

"Ooh," cringed Stan. He had almost forgotten that. "Sorry . . ."

"Eh, whatever, I don't really care. Just watch what you say to people, noob. Anyway, there are a few really important things we've gotta discuss," Sally said solemnly, and immediately, Stan wondered what could have made Sally suddenly so serious.

"First, though, let's do a little review. You know, just to be sure you retained everything from the last time we met up."

"Sounds like a plan to me," Stan replied.

"All right, noob . . . Take care of this for me." And Sally closed her eyes and stretched out her hand, instantly causing a wall made out of wood to appear.

Stan took a deep breath and stretched out his hand. He focused hard on a feeling of warmth building up inside of him and then, with all his mind, he pictured a Ghast. All at once, a fireball shot out of Stan's hand, rocketing forward until it hit the wooden wall in a burst of flames. With a grin, Stan proceeded to launch a volley of fireballs at the wood until finally, it all burned away.

"Okay, then . . . try this one!" cried Sally, and a solid stone wall appeared in place of the wooden one. Stan focused all his power into his fist, imagining the explosive power contained within a lightning-charged Creeper as he did so. Stan launched a punch in the direction of the wall, and he felt a pulse of invisible energy leave his fist. An instant later, there was a powerful rupture in the center of the wall, which formed a circular hole. Stan fired off a blitz of continuous punches at the wall until, finally, the last stone block had disappeared.

"Not bad at all," replied Sally with a smirk. "But now, here's the real challenge!" Sally stretched out her hand, and concentrated as hard as she possibly could on a patch of ground in front of Stan. Then, all at once, a swarm of about ten Blazes encircled Stan, taking deep metallic breaths and preparing to fire.

"Don't use a weapon, Stan," ordered Sally with a leering grin, "and get out of this one."

With only an instant to think, Stan realized what he had to do. He leaped into the air, narrowly dodging the storm of fireballs flying in his direction. The Blaze's projectiles all hit one another, yet they took no damage from the resulting fire bursts. The smoking mobs made of yellow rods rose up toward Stan, ready to pursue him, but Stan was prepared.

He took a deep breath, stretched out his hand, and after a moment, an arrow appeared from nowhere at the tip of his hand and flew directly into the skull of one of the blazes. With a laugh, Stan proceeded to fire a rapid chain of arrows as fast as a machine gun, which mowed down the entire row of mobs in a matter of seconds.

Sally clapped her hands together as a shower of Blaze Rods showered down onto her, and Stan landed gracefully on the ground a moment later. "Well done, noob," she said with a kind smile. "I've taught you well."

Stan gave a dark chuckle of reply. "Yeah, you have . . . although I hope it doesn't end up being useless. What's the status on getting me those powers in Elementia?"

"I'm glad you brought that up, actually," replied Sally, summoning herself a chair of leaf blocks to sit on, raising her feet on an ottoman made of a sponge block and crossing her legs at the knee. "We have to talk about that."

"Oh, boy," replied Stan, conjuring up a similar chair for himself out of wool blocks. "In my experience, 'we have to talk about this' means that I'm gonna walk away from this conversation unhappy."

"Well, unfortunately, you're right," Sally replied, and Stan gave a preemptive sigh of disappointment as Sally continued.

"I've been doing a lot of digging into Elementia's coding, trying to find a good access point to try to hack operating powers onto you. What I've found, though, is security has been increased big time. I'm not sure why, because I've been covering my tracks pretty well, so nobody can tell that I've been looking in there. And for some reason, most of the security seems to have been added to the player files—in other words, the place I have to hack into in order to give you operating powers."

"Well, that's just wonderful," sighed Stan in exasperation. "Why do you think that is?"

"I was about to ask you the same question, noob. I can't think of any reason they would beef up the firewalls and safeguards of the player files . . . unless, of course, you've told anybody about our plan?"

"I promise you, I haven't," replied Stan quickly, raising his hands into the air. "I'm not going to tell anybody about the plan, no matter what, not even Kat or Charlie when I finally get to see them again. I haven't even told Leonidas, and he's the only player besides you I've been able to talk to for weeks."

"Hmm," murmured Sally, a disapproving look on her face. "Stan, I know that I've brought this up before, but . . . that player you're traveling with has committed some pretty horrendous crimes. What makes you so convinced that he's really on your side?"

"Believe me, Sally," answered Stan with no hesitation, "I believe him. He nearly sacrificed himself to save an NPC villager. And he was raised by Oob's family. The Noctem Alliance lost him the second they attacked Oob's NPC village. He's a changed player now."

"Okay, okay, I trust your judgment," sighed Sally, nodding. "Just . . . promise me you won't tell anybody . . . especially him."

"I promise," repeated Stan.

"Okay, good. Unfortunately, though, noob, the increased security isn't the only bit of bad news."

"Ugh . . . what else is new?" spat Stan in disgust.

"You see," continued Sally, "when I was looking through the server's coding, I came across a few very interesting things. As it turns out, Elementia isn't like other Minecraft servers. It has a few unique tics to it that make it . . . different. And not in a good way."

"Example, please?" asked Stan, despite not really wanting to know.

"I was getting to that," growled Sally irritably. "One of the biggest things I noticed is that, even though I thought there were no mods on the Elementia server itself, just on a few of the players, there actually *is* one."

"Really?" Stan inquired, floored by this news. "But everybody tells me that, besides the whole you-can-only-die-once thing, Elementia is the same as every other Minecraft server!"

"Well, actually, noob, the mod I'm talking about ties into the . . . ahem . . . 'you-can-only-die-once thing,' as you so eloquently put it. The mod in Elementia is called the Modelock Mod. I'd be here forever if I explained to you everything that this mod is doing. To put it simply, the Modelock Mod makes it so that not only can operators die and get banned like everybody else, which is another something that isn't like other Minecraft servers—usually the operators are unkillable—but operators also can't change the game mode."

"Um, what do you mean exactly, when you say 'game mode'?" asked Stan, puzzled.

"Well, basically, game mode controls the settings for how difficulty in Minecraft servers works. Like, Elementia is a Hardcore PVP server, which means that you get banned if you die, you regenerate health really slowly, and the monsters are locked on the hardest setting. But in a normal server, an operator could change Elementia into a Regular PVP server, which lets players respawn when they die and makes the monsters easier to kill."

"So, are you saying that if King Kev hadn't installed that mod, and I got operating powers in Elementia, I could have made it so that people could respawn after they were killed here?" Stan asked, mortified.

"That's correct," replied Sally grimly. "Because of the Modelock Mod, the only person in Elementia able to change the server's game mode was King Kev, and only back when he still had operating powers. And because he died and got banned from his own server, now it's impossible for Elementia's game mode to ever be changed again."

"And . . . the only reason that King Kev isn't able to get back into Elementia . . . is because of that same mod?"

Sally nodded.

"Well, if that's the case, then King Kev is an idiot!" shouted Stan, leaping to his feet and punching his chair in frustration. "Why would he install a mod that could do that?"

"Well, I'll tell you at least one good reason," replied Sally glumly. "I looked up the Modelock Mod, and apparently it's one of the highest-quality mods ever made. It would take somebody way more talented than me to hack it now that it's set up. Once it's installed, it's not ever getting uninstalled. I don't think King Kev himself could undo it if he wanted to. Elementia's game mode is permanently locked onto Hardcore mode, and it's totally impossible for anybody to hack their way back in—all because of this one mod."

"Well," sighed Stan, "as much as I hate to say it, it's probably best that we don't even try to get rid of it. The last thing we need is for King Kev to make his way back into Elementia."

Sally nodded in agreement, but suddenly, her face looked even more distressed.

"Stan, to be honest, I really wish I could say that that was the worst news I have to tell you but . . . I can't."

Stan stared blankly at Sally. What else could she possibly have found out? She didn't wait for his response before continuing.

"When I was looking through all these files, there was one other thing that I noticed besides the new security and the Modelock Mod. And that was that the normal programs were . . . I'm not sure how else to put this . . . starting to fade."

"What are you talking about? What does that mean?"

"Well, to put it simply, the normal program files that run vanilla Minecraft—you know, the original code, with no mods, that allows regular Minecraft to run the way it does—they need power in order to run. Normally, when a Minecraft server is run, power is given equally to all the different parts that need it. But for some reason, in Elementia, power is being drained out of the programs that make the world run, and it's being sucked into something else."

"How is that possible?" demanded Stan. "And what does that do? Will it have effects on the server? Does it mean that the world of Elementia is going to start fading away or something?"

"To be totally honest, Stan . . . I have no idea. I've never heard of anything like this before, and your guess is as good as mine what the effects will be like in the world. But I can tell you one thing for sure: The Noctem Alliance is the cause of it. As I tried to find out what the power was being diverted to, I had to make my way around firewalls, and all of them were the same type used by the Noctem Alliance, telling me to go away or face the consequences."

"So . . . you're telling me that the Noctem Alliance is actually stealing energy . . . *from the server of Elementia itself*?" Stan managed to get out as he started to panic. "And you have no idea how, or why? Are you saying that the power they're stealing could be used to make their players more powerful? And, if they're taking power away from Elementia, then there's a chance that Elementia could be destroyed for good?"

Sally, who had begun to breathe heavily, nodded, took a deep breath, let it out, and looked Stan directly in the eye.

"Stan . . . as much as I hate to say it . . . it gets worse than that."

Stan's jaw dropped. "But . . . how?"

"The Noctem Alliance isn't just diverting power from Elementia. They're also taking power from other Minecraft servers, too, using the internet. I don't know how they're doing it, or why, but somehow, the Alliance is drawing in and stealing power from every other Minecraft server in the world, and putting it toward something."

Stan's mind couldn't comprehend what Sally was saying. She had said that there was a chance that, by drawing in power from Elementia, the server itself could be corrupted, and maybe even destroyed. So . . . if the Noctem Alliance was also drawing in power from other Minecraft servers using the internet . . . then . . . that meant . . .

"Stan, the situation is dire now," Sally told him. "You have to get back to Element City as quickly as you can. You have to lead your citizens to take down the Noctem Alliance. As soon as I figure out how to get around the Modelock Mod and get operating powers to you, you have to defeat Lord Tenebris immediately. We have no time to waste. Every second is precious. Stan, the fate of not just Elementia . . . but of the game of Minecraft itself . . . is in your hands."

"Bill! Yo, Bill!"

Bill, who had been surveying the depths of the tunnel with increasing anxiety, whipped his head around. His eyes locked onto Ben, standing at the mouth of the tunnel. Bill had to squint to block out sunlight from above, which was jarring after the dark of the cave he had been working in.

"What is it?" Bill hollered back up to Ben, struggling to make himself heard over the sounds of hundreds of laborers and the construction from deep within the bunker.

"I want to go see how Bob is doing, but I can't. I'm too busy up here!" Ben yelled. "Could you go do if for me, please?"

"Sure!" Bill responded, and he began to make his way back up the mines, running parallel to a rail track that led up into the street. To be honest, he had been totally wrapped up in leading the digging of the bunker, which still wasn't large enough to hold the entire population of the city if the Noctems launched an attack. He had nearly forgotten about Bob, who had been out of commission since earlier that morning, when Ivanhoe had tumbled down an uneven patch of rock and injured his leg.

With no Potions of Healing in the city to spare anymore, Bob had been forced to use other foods to try to heal Ivanhoe as quickly as possible. Bill desperately hoped that Bob would be back on Ivanhoe soon—they were in need of all the help they could get. A group of laborers pushing a mine cart with a chest approached Bill, and he helped them push it over the last stretch of upward track until they finally made it out of the mine and back onto the street.

The laborers immediately emptied all the stone from their inventories into one of the scrap fires scattered around the street. Bill, figuring that he might as well help them finish, proceeded to help empty the chest in the mine cart into the fire as well. He only threw out the stone, leaving the coal and various ores that had been excavated in the chest. With the lack of supply lines from the outside, this mine was presently one of the only sources of materials for the people of Element City, and they weren't going to waste it. As soon as they had finished, the laborers gave Bill an appreciative nod of thanks, and brought the mine cart back down for another load as Bill proceeded to jog down the street.

Bill continued to walk until he reached an unassuming storefront a distance away from the entrance to the mine, where the ruckus of the excavation could barely be heard. The building was made of wood-plank blocks. It was clearly old and altogether plain and featureless, save a worn-out sign spelling out the word **APOTHECARY** above the door. Bill gave three sharp raps on the wooden door, and it opened. On the other side was a player dressed in an indigo robe emblazoned with golden stars, and a long white beard.

"Hello, Chief," the old player greeted him wearily, a smile spreading across his face.

"Hey, TrumpetBlaster. How's he doing?"

"Quite well, you'll be happy to know," TrumpetBlaster

replied. "I suspect that Ivanhoe will be ready to return to work by the day's end. He's already walking about by himself perfectly fine, and with a few more hours of healing he'll be able to carry Bob again."

"Excellent," Bill said, his heart lifting. "You're a genius, you know. Not just anybody could heal a pig up that fast using just stale bread and carrots. You have no idea how much we appreciate it."

TrumpetBlaster gave a wise chuckle. "Don't mention it, my dear boy. I'm always happy to assist any friends of the Apothecary. Thank him, if you're going to thank anyone. He taught me all I know. I only wish there were more in this city like me, who are able to appreciate the art of healing without the assistance of—"

"Bill? Is that you?" a shout from within the house cut in.

"Yeah, it is," Bill shouted in reply, giving the old player a look of apology, to which he gave an understanding smile.

"Bro . . . you need to see this."

Instantly, Bill was seized with dread; he hadn't heard Bob sound that scared in a long, long time. Ignoring Trumpetblaster's raised eyebrows of confusion, Bill ran into the house. The inside was bare, containing only a few chests, and a staircase, next to which Ivanhoe was lying down. On the wall directly opposite the door was a bed, on which Bob was sitting, staring out the window, unmoving.

Bill sat down on the bed next to his brother, and followed his gaze out the window. What he saw made his heart stop.

They could see the entire city. Hundreds of houses and buildings stretched out for thousands of blocks, finally culminating at the Element City wall, which was raised high above the tallest buildings of the outer ring of the city. And far beyond the wall, outside the city and up in the sky, were two black forms, growing closer and closer by the second. As they drew nearer, the sky outside Element City darkened. As Bill focused intently on them, he could make out two mobs as large as Ghasts, with skeletal black bodies and three skulls sitting atop of each of them.

Leonidas's head popped up out of the hole as fast as lightning, his hand instantly going to his bow. Before he could draw an arrow, though, Leonidas's gaze fell onto a chicken, wandering in and out of the trunks of the dense grove. Leonidas released his breath and let out a sigh, shaking his head. This wasn't the first time an animal had spooked him, and he had a feeling it wasn't going to be the last.

Ugh, I am gonna kill Stan when he gets back, Leonidas thought to himself bitterly, as he sunk back down into the stone basin of the cave in which he was sitting. *Why is he takin' so long? He knows that we've gotta get back to the city!*

What could he possibly be doin' that's more important than savin' Elementia?

Leonidas took a deep breath and sighed to himself. He supposed that he had signed himself up for this. After all that the Noctem Alliance had put Stan and his people through, Leonidas hardly felt that it was his place to be complaining, especially considering that Stan had forgiven him. It was still frustrating, though. Although Leonidas had faith in Stan and was sure that he had a plan, it was infuriating to be left in the dark.

With a sigh of acceptance, Leonidas glanced down into his inventory and checked his supplies. They were nearly out of food again. Perhaps he could go do some hunting before Stan got back. Leonidas drew his bow, glanced back up, and froze.

Four players were standing on the dirt above Leonidas, encircling him from all sides of the cave entrance. Turning his head slowly, Leonidas realized he recognized two of them. Kat had a stone sword clutched in her right hand and was giving Leonidas a steely glance, her wolf beside her, snarling. Charlie looked ferocious, as if he were barely keeping himself from diving into the mine and tearing Leonidas apart with the stone pickaxe clutched firmly in his right hand. The other two players Leonidas didn't recognize. One had an Elementia soldier uniform and a scruffy beard, while the other was wearing a dirty white robe and had gigantic red lips. Both were staring Leonidas down with equal contempt.

"Make one wrong move and we attack," growled Kat.

Stay calm, Leonidas, he told himself, taking deep breaths, glancing around nervously and suddenly becoming aware that his weapon was still clutched in his hand.

"Where is Stan?" the girl in white asked, an upper-class accent in her voice.

"He's gone for now," Leonidas answered calmly. "But I'm—"

"What do you mean?" Charlie barked, causing everyone to jump. "Where's Stan? What did you do to him?"

"Boy, if ye so much as laid one single finger on 'im," the bearded soldier growled, "I'll 'ave yer head!"

"That's not what I mean!" Leonidas replied, a note of panic creeping into his voice now as he scolded himself for his choice of words. "Stan's alive, he's just . . ."

"Are you torturing him somewhere?" the big-lipped player squealed, sounding abhorred.

"No!" Leonidas shouted desperately. "Stan's totally fine!"

"Then where is he? Show him to us!" demanded Charlie, a passionate rage emanating from him that shocked Leonidas. The last time he had fought Charlie, he had come across as a cowardly wimp.

"I . . . I can't!" Leonidas sputtered as he tried to explain himself. "He's just . . . he went to . . ."

"If you don't tell us *exactly* where Stan is *right now,* then we are going to kill you, Leonidas," Kat said, jabbing her sword in his direction.

"That's what I'm tryin' to tell you guys! Stan is . . . well, he left . . . he's not here, so . . ."

"Charge!" bellowed Commander Crunch, and in one motion, all four players and the wolf leaped down into the cave, weapons ready and flying directly toward Leonidas.

For a moment, Bill and Bob could only sit frozen, transfixed as the two giant, evil mobs flew closer to the city. With every passing second, they could see more details of the charred skeletal structure and empty eyes. And as the two mobs neared the outer wall, an alarming realization struck Bill.

"This is what they've been holding out for," he breathed, still staring out the window as his brother turned to look at him. "This is the Noctem Alliance's trump card. They've managed to create and tame a pair of Withers, and they're going to blast their way into the city by force."

Bill turned to face Bob. For a moment, the two of them stared at each other in silence as the reality of what was happening dawned on them. Then all at once, the aura of tension and panic in the tiny room of the shop broke.

"One of us needs to go down and help out the army," said Bob, his eyes wide with intensity.

"I'll do that," replied Bill, turning around to face TrumpetBlaster, who was standing in the doorway of the house with a concerned, confused look on his face.

"TrumpetBlaster," Bill ordered, "I need you to get Bob and Ivanhoe back to the bunker. Take as much medicine as you can with you. I have a feeling you're going to be needed down there."

"Understood," TrumpetBlaster replied. He darted over to his two chests and began filling his inventory with remedial medical supplies. Bill turned back to face his brother.

"I'll get all the workers down into the bunker, and tell Ben to round up the rest of the citizens," Bob said. "I can't move by myself right now, but I can still help organize from the bunker's entrance."

"You've got to do it fast, though," continued Bill, foreseeing a great danger and determined to prevent it immediately. "Once the Withers break through the wall, they'll probably start attacking the city next. The Noctems still don't know where the bunker is, but if the Withers see everybody rushing into it, then they'll know where we are. That means that you have to get everybody in the city down into the mine before the Withers get here. That should only be, like, a minute or so after they break through the wall."

Bob's jaw dropped. "But . . . but . . . there're no way that we can possibly get everybody in the city down into the bunker in time! And even if we could, it's not nearly big enough to hold everybody yet—"

"Then just get as many in there as you can!" cried Bill in desperation. "We can make runs back into the city later to get more people. For now, we just have to get as many people down into that mine as possible. Now stop wasting time and go!"

And without waiting for a response, Bill leaped up off the bed and sprinted out the door, leaving his brother, the pig, and the disgruntled pharmacist in the tiny shop behind him.

Bill looked around, and in a second his eyes locked on to what he was looking for—a stone-brick pillar, a support beam for the monorail track that ran above the rooftops of Element City. Bill sprinted down the street and before long, he reached the base of the pillar, and leaped up to grab the bottom rung of the attached wooden ladder. With a grunt, he pulled himself up on to the ladder in full, and proceeded to climb until he had reached the top of the pillar. Bill now stood on a flat brick surface, on top of which were two side-by-side train tracks, glowing red and gold with redstone power.

Reaching into his inventory, Bill set a tiny mine cart onto the tracks that, upon touching the rails, expanded into a full-size mine cart. Thankful that he always carried one of these around with him (one never knew when a crime might take place on the railroad), Bill leaped into the cart and drew out his fishing pole. He drove the wooden rod into the ground and gave an almighty push, setting the cart in motion.

The redstone-powered rails accelerated the mine cart at an astounding rate until Bill was rocketing full speed down the rail tracks in the direction of the outer wall of Element

City. There was nothing to do now but wait to arrive at his destination, so Bill watched in awe at the scene unfolding over the wall.

The two Withers were still approaching, getting closer to the top of the wall itself. Despite the fact that it was midday and the sun still shone overhead, the sky above the two Withers was eerie and dark, a deep purple fog blocking out the light. It was like the onset of some ancient evil. Then, when they were just outside the wall, the two Withers stopped. They simply hovered in midair, each of their heads looking down at the scene below them, as if they were scouting out the situation. Even from halfway across the city, with the rumbling *clickity-clack* of the rails singing beneath him, Bill could make out the cacophony of yelling soldiers in the wall, barely audible at such a distance but still clearly shocked, panicked, and terrified.

Suddenly, a ghastly sound fell over Element City, as if some evil, metallic skeleton were taking a dying breath. The middle head of one of the two Withers began to glow, and two black projectiles shot from their mouths. They flew almost faster than Bill's eyes could track, and they ruptured with thunderous blasts on the wall, leaving two sizable holes.

The response was immediate. Bill could make out what appeared to be a flock of birds rising from the wall, but which he knew to be hundreds of arrows flying up toward the two Withers. The giant mobs were forced to double back to avoid the rain of attacks from the Elementia soldiers, and the workmen inside the walls repaired them in an instant, regenerating the walls as though its cells were growing back.

The moment of victory, however, was just that—a moment. The Withers began to glow again, this time not just the two middle heads but all six of the black skeletal heads. A rapid-fire, machine-gun spray of black bombs flew from the Withers' mouths, causing a destructive flashing over the walls more intense than the fireworks at a Fourth of July finale. The constant barrage of skulls tore into the wall, shrinking it faster than the soldiers within could put it back together.

The soldiers weren't going to go down without a fight, though. All throughout the barrage of explosive attacks from the Withers, the soldiers were firing back. Arrows thickened the air, and the constant sound of high-pitched fire charge attacks gave Bill goose bumps. At one point, Bill was amazed to see a block of TNT fly up into the sky and make contact with one of the Withers, sending it careening backward.

However, throughout the attacks on the Withers, the monsters kept firing, and Bill realized that they were becoming surrounded in some sort of dark energy. Streams of purple smoke seemed to be rising out of the walls of Element City and wafting back up to the Withers, and, despite the fact that the monsters were clearly raking in a few hits from the counterattacks, they continued to fire on the wall.

It was then that Bob realized, with a terror-stricken start, what was happening. In their police academy training, he and his brothers had learned about the Wither, alongside all other hostile mobs in the game. What he was witnessing before him was proof of the Wither's most terrifying attribute, which made it arguably harder to kill than the infamous Ender Dragon. Every living mob that the Wither hit with its blasts was inflicted with the toxic Wither effect, the same type of deadly poison that a Wither Skeleton could give a player. However, unlike the Wither Skeletons, the Wither was healed by all the health that it stole from its victims.

The Withers had to be poisoning dozens of Elementia soldiers by the second. And as long as they kept doing that, the Withers would keep healing. There was no way they were ever going to die.

The attacks from the wall were starting to die down. The soldiers below were running out of arrows, or retreating to avoid the onslaught, or . . . Bill realized with a clench of his heart that they might all be dead. The two Withers continued to fire, the barrage of explosions never slowing down, until finally, the two monsters ceased their attack.

The outer wall of Element City, which had once stood so tall and proud, and defended the city from the attacks of the Noctem Alliance, now had a giant hole right in the center. A huge expanse of the wall had been totally destroyed, leaving Element City, the only safe haven from the Noctem Alliance left on the server, completely vulnerable. From his elevated perch on the rail tracks, Bill could see hundreds of black-clad Noctem soldiers rushing across the ravaged landscape and into the streets of the city.

Bill reached into his inventory and drew an iron sword. Usually he only held it as an alternative to his fishing rod, but he was glad he had it now. He grabbed the hilt of the sword with both hands and jammed the tip of the blade into the stone ground below him. Sparks flew out from the iron blade, showering the rails and, slowly but surely, bringing the mine cart to a screeching halt.

Now that the wall had fallen, there was no point in going there anymore, Bill thought gravely. He had told his men what to do when this inevitable day finally came. As he sat there in the mine cart, his men were falling back, preparing to fortify secondary defensive positions within the outer merchant district of the city. With any luck, they would be able to hold the Noctem Alliance at bay for a while, allowing the citizens time to retreat into the bunker.

When he and his brothers had made those plans, though, they hadn't accounted for Withers. . . .

In any case, Bill knew where he was most needed. He used the sword to give himself a solid push back in the direction he'd come from. It wasn't long before the mine cart was barreling down the tracks yet again, carrying the steel-hearted police chief back to his two brothers to help get as many citizens into the mines as possible.

Bill turned around and glanced behind him at what the Withers were doing. They appeared to have set off in opposite directions, using their machine-gun-fire explosions to rip the now undefended wall to shreds. Bill was perplexed. That didn't make any sense . . . surely, the Noctem Alliance would want to keep the walls as intact as possible, right? He imagined they would want to keep the defensive measures around the city, so that the city wouldn't be defenseless when they won the war.

Suddenly, Bill realized the errors in his thinking. *If,* he told himself sternly. *If they win the war. Which they won't. Because we're going to beat them.*

Before long, Bill reached the stone pillar where he had first boarded the train. He hopped out of the moving cart and landed gracefully on the tracks. He slid down the ladder and landed on the ground, just as the redstone lamps around the city started to go on. The darkness of the Withers had spread over the city, and it was now dim as night. Bill sprinted down the street, and eventually reached the entrance to the mine.

It was pandemonium. Everywhere the eye could see, players were rushing around desperately, all clambering toward the entrance to the mine in a massive wave. Bill saw one player, with a red skin and a purple sash, trip as he made his way to the entrance, and the rush didn't slow down or even acknowledge him. He struggled to get up, constantly being forced back to the ground by the people trampling over him. It wasn't until Bill drew his sword and stepped into the midst of the crowd, creating a disruption in the flow, that the player was finally able to get up and continue his way into the bunker, giving Bill a look of thanks as he did so.

"Ben!" shouted Bill, locating his brother and running up to him. The black-haired police chief was leading a group of volunteers, assisting them in pulling up the rail tracks that led out of the mine, erasing any evidence that the bunker had ever been there. When he heard his name, he looked up and jogged over to meet his brother.

"Are they almost all in?" Bill yelled, struggling to be heard over the panic around him.

"Yeah, almost," Ben shouted back. "Bob's down in the mine, getting people organized. I say we close up the bunker door in a couple minutes. We can organize missions from inside the bunker to get the people who we had to lock out."

"Fine," Bill grunted, sadness gripping his heart as he thought of the hundreds of people who would be left exposed in the city.

"How's the wall holding up?"

"Not good, bro," Bill sighed. "The Withers tore through it entirely, and the Noctems are in the city now. The soldiers are going to their secondary positions, but they won't be able to hold them for long. The Noctems will reach Element Castle within the next ten minutes, I'd say."

A look of despair crossed Ben's face at the news, but then, all of a sudden, he looked mortified, like he had just realized something.

"Oh, no . . . ," he breathed. "Element Castle . . ."

"Yeah? What about it?" Bill yelled, the noise still deafening. "We can't worry about it now, I'm sure we'll be able to take it back eventually—"

"No, it's the Mechanist!" Ben shouted, looking his brother in the eye. "The rest of the staff of the castle came by a few minutes ago . . . but not him! He's still up there, and I have no idea why!"

Bill glanced up at Element Castle, with its proud stone spires silhouetted against the ominous black sky. If the Mechanist was still in there by the time the Noctems arrived . . .

"Go to the castle now, bro," ordered Bill, gripping his brother's shoulders. "I'll tell Bob what's going on."

Ben nodded and sprinted as fast as he could toward Element Castle as Bill turned around and ran down through the throng of players and into the bunker.

Leonidas's senses tingled, and he dive-rolled to the side as the big-lipped player, who Kat had called Cassandrix, swung her sword around the side of the tree he was hiding behind. As her stone blade wedged into the tree, Leonidas simply got to his feet and ran. Try as he might to explain what had happened to Stan, he had never been able to get more than two words out before another one of the four players had been on top of him, thirsty for his blood.

Leonidas doubled back yet again as the bearded soldier, apparently named Commander Crunch, leaped out and jabbed his sword directly at Leonidas's head.

"Stand 'n' fight, ye lily-livered swine!" the Commander bellowed, following up his initial strike with a series of swipes. Leonidas ducked and weaved through them all, just as he sensed another player coming up behind him. Thinking fast, Leonidas sprawled to the ground, dodging Charlie's pickaxe. The two fighters, who had both been aiming for Leonidas, locked their blades together, and he used their recovery period to draw an Ender Pearl from his inventory and pitch it up to the top of a nearby tree, warping there an instant later.

Leonidas took a deep breath, relishing the brief moment of peace. As good as he was at evading attacks, even he couldn't deal with the constant onslaught for too much longer. For the past five minutes, every turn he had made had seen one of the four players ready to bear into him with the full force of their weapons. It was a miracle that Leonidas hadn't been hit yet.

"Get down here right now, Leonidas!"

As he heard Charlie's voice screaming from below him, Leonidas glanced up from the leaf blocks he was lying on and looked down at the clearing, only to immediately duck to avoid the arrow flying at his shoulder. Leonidas popped back up, outraged. The four players were standing in the clearing, eyeing Leonidas with the utmost contempt, as Kat loaded another arrow into her bow.

"Get down here!" Cassandrix screeched up at him yet again.

"I'll come down only if y'all promise to stop tryin' to kill me!" Leonidas bellowed back. He was beyond enraged that these players, who were supposed to be the representatives of goodness and justice in Elementia, couldn't stop attacking him long enough for him to explain.

"If you don't come down right now, Leonidas," Kat growled, looking at him through the sights of her bow, "then I'll make you come down myself."

Leonidas gave a harsh laugh. "Oh, and how're ya gonna do that, eh, Kat? Ya gonna shoot me or somethin'?"

Kat put her hand up to her mouth, and let out a two-note whistle.

Leonidas heard a rustling in the tree behind him. He barely had time to turn around before Kat's wolf barreled into him, head-butting him out of the tree and crashing them both to the soggy ground with a thud. Leonidas cringed, the wind knocked out of him. He was barely aware of Kat calling the wolf back to her side.

Slowly, Leonidas forced himself up onto his elbows and then his knees, only to realize that two stone swords, a stone pickaxe, and a bow were all aimed directly at him.

"Put yer hands in th' air, ye dirty rotten villain," Commander Crunch spat at him.

Slowly, trying to be as cooperative as possible despite the anger boiling in his stomach, Leonidas obliged.

"Tell us where Stan is right now," Kat continued, her voice monotone and her face steely as she continued to train her bow on him.

"I told ya," Leonidas replied desperately, "he ain't here . . . in Elementia, I mean . . . he left . . ."

"So Stan was killed?" Cassandrix demanded, her already pale face now nearly colorless.

"No, he ain't dead . . . I'm helpin' him now, I swear . . ."

"Cut the crap! Where is he?" Charlie bellowed, his face radiating with supreme hatred. *"Answer me!"* He dashed forward, a noticeable limp in his step, with pickaxe drawn, and shoved it up under Leonidas's chin until they were nearly face to face. *"What did you do to my best friend?"*

"I . . . uh . . . he . . . ," Leonidas sputtered, panicking as he stared directly into Charlie's wrathful eyes. "I mean . . . he left . . . to go to . . . another . . ."

"That's it!" Charlie screamed, and he raised his pickaxe high over his head.

There were shouts behind him. "Charlie!" from Cassandrix. "Charlie, no!" from Kat. "Control yerself, lad!" from Commander Crunch. But it was too late. Charlie's pickaxe fell fast and hard toward Leonidas's skull. There was no time to react. Leonidas simply closed his eyes and winced, waiting for the blow to connect.

Then, with no warning, there was a powerful gust of wind in front of Leonidas, followed by a sharp clang of weapons colliding and the grunt of Charlie falling backward to the ground. Amazed, yet perplexed, Leonidas opened his eyes. What he saw made his heart skip a beat.

Directly in front of Leonidas, between him and Charlie, was a cloud of purple smoke, the by-products of an Ender Pearl. As the smoke particles cleared away, the form of another player became visible. Leonidas would recognize the navy pants and dark shoes, flowing black cape, and head covering anywhere. The Black Hood turned around and looked at Leonidas. He still couldn't make out the upper half of the face, but the player's pale mouth was curled up into a reassuring smile. Leonidas could nearly hear the words ringing in his head—*It's going to be all right*.

The Black Hood turned back around, diamond sword still raised in front of him in a block, to face the four players and the wolf before him. Rex looked curiously up at the strange player, while Cassandrix, Commander Crunch, and especially Charlie, who was still lying on the ground, looked terrified at this mysterious stranger, who had appeared from nowhere to aid Leonidas.

Kat, on the other hand, stepped forward, hardly daring to believe her eyes. She looked into the hidden face of the Black Hood, and suddenly recognized him.

"It's you," she whispered, staring in awe. "From the Mushroom Islands."

The Black Hood turned his head to look at her, and gave a subtle, yet very distinct, nod.

"Then . . . why are you protecting Leonidas?"

The Black Hood cocked his head to the side for a moment, and then turned to look down at Leonidas again. He proceeded to give a small smile, before again turning back to Kat. She looked at him, and suddenly, an overwhelming feeling came over her. Inexplicably, she knew what the Black Hood was trying to tell her.

"Are you . . . trying to tell me . . . ," Kat managed to get out, hardly believing what she was saying, "that . . . Leonidas is telling the truth? That he *is* helping Stan?"

As her three friends glanced at Kat as if she had gone insane, the Black Hood said nothing. Instead, he turned on his heel and proceeded to sprint toward the cave opening where Leonidas had been hiding. When he had reached the mouth of the cave, the Black Hood jumped into the air, and an instant later, was consumed by a cloud of purple smoke. When the smoke cleared, the Black Hood was nowhere to be seen.

All five players stared at the smoke, transfixed. They continued to stare until the purple smoke had dissipated completely, and even then they still found themselves unable to move as they tried to comprehend what had just happened.

Then, all of a sudden, the players heard footsteps echoing up out of the cave. They looked on expectantly, waiting to see the mysterious player emerge from the ground. And yet, the Black Hood was not the one who emerged.

Instead, Stan2012 emerged from the cave, staring down at the ground, his face heavy and troubled, as if he had found out that the weight of the entire world was resting squarely on his shoulders. As he set foot on the soggy ground again, Stan suddenly realized that he was being watched. He glanced up, and immediately did a double take, not willing to believe his eyes.

"Guys?" he let out, barely breathing.

"Stan?" Charlie whispered, afraid that if he spoke too loud, he might scare Stan away.

There was a moment of silence as Stan stared into the eyes of his friends, and they all stared back. Then, all at once and without warning, Kat rushed forward, tears streaming down her face with Rex hot on her heels, and embraced Stan, hugging him hard and long, as if she was never going to let go.

"Kat . . . I can't believe it . . . ," Stan managed to get out as he choked back his sobs of joy. "It's so . . . I mean, it's just . . ."

"I know, Stan," Kat managed to get out as she buried her face into Stan's shoulder. "I know."

Stan became aware of the sound of uneven footsteps, and he glanced up to see Charlie, clearly on a damaged foot, moving as fast as he could directly toward Stan. Immediately unaware of anything else, Stan let go of Kat and ran toward Charlie. The two best friends met in the center of the clearing and threw their arms around each other, squeezing as hard as they could. Neither of them could say anything. There were no words. They just continued to hold each other in an embrace. Nobody spoke as these two players who had come so far since their first day in Elementia and grown closer than brothers were finally reunited.

"I missed you so much, man," Charlie sobbed, not even

trying to hide the fact that he was crying.

"Me, too," Stan choked out in return. "I'm . . . just . . . *so* glad you're okay . . . you . . . you have no idea."

The two players finally broke apart and were immediately pulled back together as Kat threw herself back into the circle, and the cycle started all over again. The three players, companions since the beginning, couldn't leave one another now that, after months of separation, they were finally together once more. Leonidas, Cassandrix, and Commander Crunch could only look on with joyous tears in their eyes as Rex jumped up against the trio of players and began to lick Stan's hand.

The wolf's presence finally caused Stan to remember that the others were there, and he let go of his friends to face the others.

"Guys, I just . . . I can't believe . . ." Stan still seemed to be overjoyed, and at a total loss for words. "How . . . how did you manage to find me? Was it you, Leonidas? Did you find them?"

All at once, Charlie, Kat, Cassandrix, and Commander Crunch all turned to stare at Leonidas. Even Kat, who had understood what the Black Hood had been trying to say, was completely floored by this. "Nah," Leonidas chuckled, looking back at Stan. "It was just a bit of dumb luck is all. Although I gotta say, it's lucky ya turned up when ya did."

"Aye, Leonidas," Commander Crunch suddenly burst out, his voice sounding deeply remorseful, "we be so sorry fer wha' we did." The other three players stared at Leonidas with equally mortified and repentant looks on their faces. "We should've listened t' ye . . . we didn' realize that . . ."

"Don't worry 'bout it," Leonidas replied with a smile. "Frankly, I don't really blame ya . . . after all the stuff I've put ya through in the past, I'd call ya stupid if ya trusted me up front. Tell ya what, let's make a deal. If y'all can find it in your hearts to forgive me for all the terrible things I did, then we can just let bygones be bygones."

Without hesitation, all the other players nodded and gave their assurances of agreement. All, that is, except Charlie. Try as he might, he couldn't find it in himself to say the words out loud, and couldn't help but feel an uncomfortable pit open in his stomach the more he looked at Leonidas, smiling and being initiated into their group.

Thankfully, he thought to himself as he forced a joyful look onto his face, *nobody noticed.* And as Charlie turned to Stan, his best friend in all of Minecraft, finally standing next to him once more after all this time, he found that he didn't need to force himself to smile in the least.

Bill stood attentive at the base of the stone staircase with an iron sword drawn. *What is taking Ben so long?* he thought in desperation. *What if he wasn't up there? Or what if somebody else was up there? A Noctem soldier? Or what if . . .*

Suddenly, footsteps echoed from the top of the stairs, and Bill caught a glimpse of a player coming down the stairs. As he grew closer, Bill realized with a start that it was Ben, hauling the unconscious Mechanist on his shoulder. Bill sprinted up the stairs to meet his brother, helping to lift the limp form of the Mechanist.

"Thanks," Ben grunted as they continued down the stairs.

"Don't mention it. What happened? Why is he unconscious? Did somebody attack you guys?"

"No," Ben grunted in disgust. "He was passed out on top of his papers, and a half-empty potion bottle was on the table next to him. He's been hitting the SloPo again."

"What?" Bill asked, shocked at this revelation. "I didn't know he used that stuff!"

"He told me about it once," Ben grunted as he readjusted the unconscious Mechanist on his shoulder. "Apparently he started when King Kev banished him to the desert. It made it easier for him to forget his guilt over helping the King with his redstone contraptions. He told me that he hadn't done it again since he had joined Stan's army."

"Well," Bill replied, "either he was lying or he started again."

"Clearly," Ben agreed. "I tried everything to wake him

up—water, food, hitting him, everything I had on me—and I couldn't find any milk to clear the potion effects, so I figured it was best to just bring him down the way he is."

"Well, we can worry about that later," Bill said as they reached the doorway to the castle courtyard. "Okay, the entrance to the bunker isn't too far outside the courtyard. We should just be able to make a run for it without anything happening."

"Sounds good," Ben agreed. "Let's move!"

And with that, the two brothers sprinted out of the castle and into the open. Bill felt incredibly exposed as he dashed past the lava moat and across the wide-open courtyard, nothing above his head, and nothing to duck and cover behind should an attack come. By the time they had finally reached the castle gates and found an arch to hide them, Bill's heart was nearly beating out of his chest.

"There's the entrance!" Ben cried, pointing. Indeed, he was right. Just a block down the street, the gates of the mine opened into what appeared to be just a hill. They could barely make out Bob sitting at the mouth of the bunker, looking wildly around, presumably for them, his hand on a lever. Bill knew that, when Bob pulled the lever, as he would be forced to do if the Noctems appeared, the entire face of the hill would close up. The bunker door would blend into the hillside completely, creating a totally natural-looking stronghold that was invisible to anyone who didn't know where it was.

Bill and Ben, still carrying the Mechanist between them, made a mad dash down the cobblestone street toward the entrance to the bunker. Bob finally noticed them and gestured for them to move faster—it was only because of them that the bunker hadn't yet been sealed.

Just as the two police chiefs and the Mechanist were less than twenty blocks away from the mouth of the bunker, a giant, dark form rose from behind the hill. For an instant, the two brothers froze, locking eyes with the Wither. Bill grabbed his brother's shoulder and steered the three of them to the right.

"What're you doing?" screamed Ben as they sprinted forward, the skull-like projectiles the Wither was shooting tearing up the street behind them.

"We can't go in there now!" bellowed Bill in reply. "The Wither will know where the entrance is! There, go into that house over there!"

They continued to sprint, and finally ducked their way into a two-story mansion, made almost entirely from gold and lapis lazuli blocks. Bill and Ben collapsed onto the blue and gold wool-block carpet in the entrance. They were so exhausted from running to escape the Wither while simultaneously dragging the Mechanist between them that they could barely move. However, as soon as the explosions began to rock the house around them, both brothers found themselves racing with adrenaline.

"What do we do now?" asked Ben desperately, as the explosions continued from above. "The Wither will blast its way in here in the next minute. And if it sees us going into that bunker, then the entire city is dead. What do we do?"

Bill glanced around for a minute before his eyes locked on a window on the other side of the house. He took a deep breath, let it out, and then turned to face his brother.

"Get the Mechanist to the bunker," he said pensively. "You'll know when to go. Don't worry about me, whatever you do."

Before Ben had a chance to ask what that meant, Bill leaped to his feet and sprinted at full speed toward the window before punching through it and disappearing outside.

Ben stared at the window, trying to comprehend what had just happened. What was it that his brother had just done? And *why*? A giant blast from above jarred all the questions from his mind. He ducked down and threw himself over the unconscious Mechanist, covering his head as a rain of rubble fell onto them. When the dust cleared, Ben glanced up, and his heart stopped.

The Wither was levitating directly over the mansion. It had blasted its way through the upper story, and now it had a clear shot at Ben. As the three mouths of the Wither began to glow, Ben didn't even bother to try to run. Instead, he merely threw his body over the Mechanist, hoping that he could at least save him, and then maybe Bill could get him to safety in the mine. Ben stared the Wither's middle head directly in the face, determined to leave Elementia in a dignified way.

Then, without warning, the entire Wither jerked backward and careened sideways, as if it had lost its balance. The three black projectiles shot off in random directions—two flew into the sky, while a third fell with a blast onto the street outside. Ben looked up in confusion, and as the Wither attempted to restabilize, he noticed a tiny white object lodged in the back of the Wither's main head, and a string leading off it and down onto the street.

Ben knew what this meant. This was the diversion. It was time to go.

He hoisted the Mechanist onto his shoulder and sprinted as hard as he ever had sprinted in his life out the door and toward the entrance to the bunker. The Wither didn't even notice him. It was too focused on trying to shake off Bill, who had latched a fishing line onto it and was now yanking and pulling, doing all he could to unbalance the evil beast. The Wither fired off a volley of blasts at Bill, but they were all uneven and untargeted, so he was able to jump out of their way.

Ben barreled headfirst into the bunker, and the Mechanist

flew off his shoulder and into the arms of two soldiers waiting on standby. Ben stood by Bob, still standing with his hand on the lever and ready to pull it. The two of them watched the battle on the street, eyes wide, breath bated, and hearts racing.

Slowly but surely, the Wither was regaining its focus. Despite the fact that Bill was still disorienting it, its shots were getting closer and closer to him, and Ben knew that it was only a matter of time before Bill would be hit. He glanced around wildly at Bob, who showed an equal look of horrified confusion, and then at a soldier standing next to him.

"You have to do something to help him!" Ben bellowed at the soldier.

"What can we do, sir?" the soldier asked desperately. "If we do anything, we'll reveal the location of the bunker. In fact, if Bill even lets the Wither turn around, it'll see the location of the bunker. Sir, I'm sorry, but we need to close the blast doors now."

Ben's response was cut off by the anguished cry from outside.

He watched but didn't comprehend, as Bill flew through the air, wisps of black smoke trailing off him, and landed with a thud onto the cobblestone pavement below, his fishing pole still gripped tightly in his hand. With monumental effort, Bill raised his head and caught the tear-stained, anguished eye of his brothers. "PULL THE LEVER!" Bill yelled at the top of his voice as the three black projectiles flew down from the sky above him and hit him in a tremendous explosion.

Ben could only stand there, unmoving, and watch the scene unfold, while Bob pulled down almost robotically on the lever, as if he were a machine that had been voice activated by Bill's final yell. The redstone machinery in the bunker door roared to life, and the hilltop above them seemed to slide down toward the ground. All the soldiers backed away from the bunker door as the pistons did their work.

Ben and Bob didn't move. Their eyes stayed locked in sheer disbelief on the body of their red-haired brother, items scattered in a ring around him on the cobblestone street, and charred fishing pole still clutched tightly in his hand, until the bunker door finally shut, closing them into the mines.

PART

THE ULTIMATUM

There was silence in the Capitol rotunda, save the sound of hundreds of pairs of feet marching. Row by row, the black-clad troops filed into lines. Jayden and G glanced around the room nervously at the dozens of dark figures positioned in the upper balcony, all of whom had loaded bows aiming down into the giant mass of soldiers.

G took a deep breath and let it out. He knew what was going on. Four days had passed since he had left Sirus alone in that obsidian chamber with a diamond pickaxe in his hand, and now Tess had ordered that all soldiers meet in the rotunda for an emergency.

Sure enough, Tess emerged on the highest, most ornate, and most pronounced balcony of the rotunda, made from chiseled quartz blocks. There was no hint of joy on her face. There was only a scowl as she looked down on all the soldiers. Gazing back up at her and cowering under her intimidating leer, they were all silent. Finally, Tess spoke.

"Last night," Tess announced, "our hostages from the Adorian Village escaped captivity."

A collective gasp rolled across the soldiers as they realized what that meant.

"To escape, the hostages tunneled through a five-block-thick wall of solid obsidian," continued Tess.

"This is a feat that would take at least two full days to complete if done by anything other than a diamond pickaxe. And seeing as no guards saw any sign of an escape in progress during their checkups, this can only mean that somebody in this room managed to sneak a diamond pickaxe to the hostages."

A collective burst of panic rose off the crowd, and though nobody dared to speak, the tension in the room could be cut with a sword.

"I know that someone among us is the traitor," Tess said slowly as her eyes swept over the soldiers below her. "If you step forward and reveal yourself to me now, then you shall simply be executed by firing squad, quickly and painlessly. However, if you don't, then I shall be forced to begin interrogations, and when I discover who it is, you will be tortured without mercy before you become food for the Zombie villagers. If anybody would like to speak out, you may do so now."

G, who was struggling to keep his own heart from exploding with panic, heard Jayden beside him take a deep breath, let it out, and then raise his hand.

"I confess," Jayden said, a slight warble in his voice. "I did it."

G's mind went blank, refusing to comprehend what was happening. He turned to stare at Jayden in utter shock, totally blindsided and utterly bewildered by what his best friend had just said.

"Is that so?" asked Tess, a hint of surprise in her voice as all the soldiers around Jayden backed away from him in abhorrence. G followed suit, convinced that he had gone totally insane. "How did you do it, Drayden? And what was your motivation?"

"My name is *Jayden*!" he exclaimed, pulling off his black leather cap, throwing it to the ground, and stomping on it. "I am a member of the governing council of Element City, and a friend of President Stan2012. I have been living undercover among you for these past weeks, working to free the hostages you have taken from us. Now, my work here is done." A manic smile crossed Jayden's face as he pumped his fist into the air and, with patriotic fervor, he bellowed, "LONG LIVE THE REPUBLIC! LONG LIVE PRESIDENT STAN!"

G's mind was still reeling from what was going on. He was hardly able to comprehend that Jayden had just revealed himself for no good reason, and that soldiers were drawing their bows and taking aim at him. Suddenly, a lightbulb clicked on in G's head. There was at least one good thing that could come from this turn of insanity. G leaped forward and into the ring, letting the overwhelming despair that was boiling inside him burst from his mouth.

"How could you do this?" G shouted, tears streaming

down his face as he let all the white shock he was feeling burst through his voice. "You were my friend! I trusted you! How could you work for that evil president?"

Jayden glanced back at G, and caught his eye. For an instant, he looked miserable, as if all he wanted was to be able to say "sorry." However, the look soon vanished, to be replaced by nothing but zeal.

"I'd never lower myself to the level of calling myself the friend of a Noctem!" Jayden spat in disgust.

There were so many things that G longed to say but knew he couldn't. He was forced to simply stand still, quiet and motionless. It was all the same, though. Words could not describe the agony that wrenched his heart as two soldiers pinned Jayden to the ground, and a third raised a bow to his head. G looked away, preparing for the arrow to fly.

"Hold your fire!" Tess's voice rang out from the balcony above.

G looked up, hardly daring to believe his ears. The collective group of soldiers, including those who were restraining Jayden, seemed to follow suit as their eyes locked on Tess. She was staring back and forth between Jayden and G, an intrigued look on her face. G's heart skipped a beat. Did she suspect something?

"Executioner, stop," Tess said again, holding up her hand. "I have a better idea. All troops, move out. Leave this rotunda.

Guard and MasterBronze, stay put."

G was petrified as the troops began to move out around him, giving him uncomfortable glances as they flooded through the doors. The executioner put his bow away and drew a glowing diamond sword, jabbing it up against Jayden's back and grunting, "Hands in the air, dirtbag." Jayden complied, and his eyes darted to the side and met G's. He could tell they were both thinking the same thing.

Tess knows, G thought in a panic. *She's got to know. Why else would she have singled me out? All the recruits probably realize that Jayden and I have been talking this entire time. And why did Jayden reveal himself anyway? She might not have ever guessed it was me. He didn't need to sacrifice himself!*

The sounds of footsteps on the stone-brick floor echoed throughout the cavernous rotunda as Tess made her way to the center. G and the executioner snapped to full attention as Jayden scowled at her.

"General Tess," the guard asked in disbelief, "why did you tell me not to execute this spy?"

"Trust me," Tess replied, a devious grin creeping across her face, "I know what I'm doing. Guard, you are dismissed now."

The guard stared at Tess with a total lack of comprehension, and then turned around and made his way to the door, grumbling the whole way. Jayden watched as he went, hands still raised, and Tess drew a glowing diamond sword from her own inventory, pointing it at Jayden.

"MasterBronze," Tess said slowly, turning to face G, "I understand that you are friends with this traitor. Is this correct?"

"I thought I was," G grunted, trying to sound hurt and betrayed, and not let his true dread be too obvious. "He always seemed like such a nice guy, I can't believe that he's been working for President Stan this entire time."

"Well, I hope that you can bring yourself to believe it," Tess chuckled, "because you're going to be the one who kills him."

G heard, but he didn't understand. "I'm . . . sorry . . . ?" he finally croaked.

"For the past few weeks, I have been training you as my apprentice, MasterBronze," Tess continued matter-of-factly. "I must say that, so far, I am quite impressed by your progress in combat and skills training. However, if you are truly going to become a great leader of the Noctem Alliance, you must learn to make sacrifices for the sake of our cause . . . even if it means stabbing your best friend in the back. And besides, if your loyalties are in the right place, then you should be able to get over it quickly."

G stared blankly at Tess, still not understanding what he was being asked. Then, out of the corner of his eye, G saw

Jayden staring at him with wide, fearful eyes, and finally snapped back to his senses.

"Um, well . . . ," G sputtered, trying to think fast. "I mean . . . General Tess, ma'am . . . can I at least kill him in private? It's . . . going to be difficult enough without you watching."

Tess sighed and rolled her eyes. "Whatever. We'll go to the holding chamber. Move it, you worthless piece of trash!"

Tess poked the diamond sword into Jayden's back and he began to walk forward, hands still raised above him. G followed Tess down the hallway. He realized that they were headed toward the room where Sirus and the others had been imprisoned. G glared with contempt at the back of the general who was walking in front of him, and his hand started to crawl toward his pickaxe before he stopped himself. As easy and satisfying as it would have been to strike Tess down right then and there, he knew that he couldn't do that. They were the only ones in the room, and Jayden was unarmed, so the rest of the Alliance would know that he had done it. And regardless of what happened, he still had to cure Mella and Stull, something that would be much easier if the Noctem Alliance trusted him.

It wasn't long before they reached the obsidian room. At Tess's command, G pressed the button to open the iron door. Once it had swung all the way around, Tess gave Jayden a kick in the back, sending him tumbling. He face-planted on the floor of the now vacant obsidian chamber. G glared at Tess with burning hatred but forced himself to curb his anger as she turned to face him.

"I'm coming back shortly," Tess decreed sternly. "And I will expect you to bring me his weapon."

And with that, she stepped back into the hallway and pressed the stone button again, swinging the iron door shut.

"What were you thinking?" bellowed G, spinning around to face Jayden the second the door closed.

"Don't yell at me!" Jayden retorted, crossing his arms over his chest. "Do you have any idea what I just did for you?"

"You almost left me without a best friend?" spat G. "You made Tess expect me to kill you? You put me into an incredibly difficult position? Take your pick, they're all true!"

"Oh, open your eyes, man!" cried Jayden. "It was only a matter of time before Tess realized that *you* let those prisoners go. Since I took the fall for you, you can stay in Nocturia for as long as you want! You can free the villagers, you can find out so much information, do so much damage to the Alliance. For the first time since we started fighting this war, Element City has eyes on the inside of the Noctem Alliance, and that's not something worth giving up, even if it means I have to die. Actually, the fact that Tess ordered you to kill me makes all of this so much better!"

"How do you figure that?" exclaimed G incredulously.

"Because now she's going to have total faith in you!" Jayden said, sounding as if this should be incredibly obvious. "She's already rearing you up to be her little lackey. If you do this, then she's going to trust you with anything and think that you're totally devoted to the Noctem Alliance, and to her."

"Oh, my apologies. You're right, Jayden!" G replied, a mock cheerful tone in his voice. "I mean, gee whiz, why didn't we do this in the first place? Oh, yeah, that's right! Because in order for this plan to work, it still required *me killing you!*"

"Oh, don't be so sure," Jayden replied with a smile. And with that, he reached into his inventory and pulled out a bottle. The potion within it was transparent, almost clear, but it had a definite gray tint to it. G gasped.

"Jayden. Where did you get that?"

"I swiped it," he replied, taking the bottle and tipping it down his throat in one giant gulp. "Yesterday, we went to the Brewing Plant in the Nether while you were surveying the grounds with Tess. Here, catch!"

Jayden's hand plunged into his inventory for a second time and out came his diamond axe, which he tossed through the air toward G, who caught it. "Just wait until the potion takes effect, then show the axe to Tess, and I'll slip out through the door, invisible, and make my way back to Element City!"

"Wha . . . wait," G said, as he put together what Jayden was saying. "You're . . . you're leaving me?"

"Well, the alternative is that you kill me, and I think that option is considerably less appealing to everyone," Jayden replied, sounding a little annoyed.

"But . . . you can't leave!" cried G. "I need you here! Tess has been working me into the ground, never leaving me alone, making me be with her all the time, taking me away from everyone else so she can train me. The fact that she's so nice to me isn't even cool anymore—it's just uncomfortable! I can't lose the only person that I can still talk to!"

Jayden simply stared at him for a moment in disbelief. Finally, he managed to get out, "Dude . . . do you . . . realize what you're saying? Do you see *any* hint of irony at all in *anything* you just said?"

G stared back, looking confused. Then, without warning, Jayden began to fade away, becoming dimmer and dimmer by the second.

"The potion's taking effect!" exclaimed Jayden, pulling off his armor and frantically reaching into his inventory and tossing random items to the ground, making it look like a player had died. "G, go open the door now, and hurry! I don't have much time before the potion wears off, and I have to get all the way into the tundra. I'll say hi to Kat and the others for you when I see them . . . bye!"

And with that, Jayden disappeared.

G stared at the place where his best friend now stood, invisible, and then down at the diamond axe in his hand. He knew that Jayden was right. He forced himself to walk to the iron door. He gave three sharp knocks on the iron face, and seconds later the door swung open. G stepped out and felt a rush of wind behind him, indicating that Jayden had silently taken off down the hallway.

"Did you finish the job?" Tess asked.

G took a deep breath, reached into his inventory, and pulled out Jayden's diamond axe. He handed it to Tess, who took it, looking thrilled.

"Well done, MasterBronze!" Tess exclaimed, patting him on the shoulder, which made his skin crawl. "In honor of your loyalty to the Noctem Alliance and to me, I am promoting you to the rank of Corporal. You will, from now on, have the duty of being my assistant commander in the training program."

"Thank you, ma'am," G replied. He knew he ought to be thrilled at this promotion, which would allow him access to even more high-level secrets, but he still couldn't shake the feeling of total isolation now that Jayden was gone, and he was stuck with this Tess, this player who had total control over his life.

"Now, come with me, Corporal MasterBronze," Tess continued, a grin crossing her face. "It's time to go and see your fellow trainees, and present their new second-in-command to them."

G's stomach churned as he followed Tess down the hallway. She was talking to him so affectionately, like he were her prized show dog instead of another person. It made him feel powerless, degraded, and humiliated. G shuddered and wished that somehow, he still had Jayden to talk to.

"Charlie, please . . . let me take a turn, I can see how bad you're hurtin' . . ."

"Leonidas, for the last time, I am *fine*!" Charlie bellowed, whipping around to face him. "Stop interrupting me or we're never gonna get to Element City!"

"Okay, fine, calm down, man!" Leonidas cried out, raising his blocky hands defensively.

Charlie shot one last steely glare at him before turning back around, and continuing to hack away at the solid cave wall with his stone pickaxe. Leonidas stared at Charlie's back, illuminated by torchlight. He had been baffled by the hostility Charlie had been showing toward him. Since they had joined up with him and Stan, Leonidas had been pleasantly surprised by how quickly everybody had warmed up to him. Everybody, that was, except Charlie. And even as

Leonidas watched Charlie mining, it was clear that he was hurting. Every swing of the pickaxe brought another grunt of discomfort, and every step he took through the newly mined cave saw another limp.

Leonidas was the only one who even noticed Charlie's outburst, however. Commander Crunch was busy tunneling forward alongside Charlie, while Stan, Kat, and Cassandrix walked behind, talking among themselves. Stan put torches on the wall as they walked, and Rex trailed lazily behind Kat.

"I still can't believe that we're being forced to sneak into our own city," Kat spat in disgust.

"Oh, I'm sorry, dear. Allow me to play you a sad song on the world's smallest violin," Cassandrix replied, sticking her bloated lip out in mock sadness before reverting back to a scowl. "Kat, we're all down here together. There's no need to whine about what we're all feeling!"

"Shut up!" cried Kat, so loudly, that Stan cringed and raised his hands to his ears. "There's no need to be so obnoxious about it!"

"I'm sorry, what's that, Commander?" Cassandrix said loudly, looking over at Crunch, who was still firmly fixated on his digging. "I'm sorry, I can't hear you. There appears to be an infant who's crying because her feelings are hurt. I do wish the parents would take care of her."

Kat turned red as a beet, and was about to retort when Stan forced his way between the two of them.

"Enough, you two!" he cried, indignantly glancing back and forth between them. "We're all stressed enough as it is in this stupid tunnel. We don't need your bickering making things worse!"

"She started it," Kat mumbled, causing Cassandrix to roll her eyes and shrug with an arrogant sigh.

"I don't care *who* started it, I'm finishing it," said Stan firmly, as he continued to walk forward between Kat and Cassandrix. *Man, I'm so glad to be back with everyone,* Stan thought to himself, trying to think as optimistically as possible. *I missed talking with everybody so much . . .*

"Hey, Charlie!" Kat hollered right next to Stan's ear, causing him to cringe again. "Are we past the wall yet?"

"If my calculations are correct," Charlie replied, trying to keep his breathing steady as he winced with the effort of mining, "we passed underneath the wall a little while ago, and we should be underneath the Merchants District of Element City by now."

"Hey, did you hear that, everybody?" Stan asked, looking around the mine at all his friends. "We're back in Element City! Welcome home, guys!"

There were lackluster murmurs of assent around the mine as Charlie and Commander Crunch tunneled into a sizable natural cave. Stan sighed. He knew that they had to get to Element City as quickly as possible, and the fate of all of Minecraft might lie in their hands. But that didn't change the fact that they had been walking for three straight days with no sleep, and everybody was worn out.

"Okay," he said, finally letting his inner exhaustion come forward. "Maybe we should take a break for a little while and rest."

As soon as Stan said this, the entire group collapsed onto the ground, letting the fatigue of weeks of trekking with almost no rest finally hit them. Stan lay down as well, not even caring that the stone-block floor below him was uncomfortable. Rex curled up at his feet, and Stan was just about to doze off when he suddenly had a startling realization.

"Hey, guys, we can't all go to sleep yet," he mumbled, forcing himself to sit up. "Somebody has to stand guard."

"I'll take care of it," Leonidas said, grabbing a ledge on the cave wall and pulling himself to his feet.

"NO!" Charlie cried, causing everybody to snap up right as Charlie jumped, wincing as his bad leg hit the ground. "Get back to sleep, Leonidas. I'm standing guard."

"Come on, Charlie!" exclaimed Leonidas, looking concerned. "You've been mining all day. You really ought to take a rest!"

"What's that supposed to mean, huh?" Charlie demanded

accusatorily. "Are you saying you don't think I can do it?"

"No, I . . ."

"Then shut up and sit back down!" Charlie spat out bitterly. "I don't recall asking for your help!"

Leonidas stared at Charlie, amazed at the harshness in his voice. After a moment, Leonidas lay back down and, with an uncomfortable glance at Charlie, rolled over to face the wall. Stan was outraged, and was about to chastise Charlie for his harshness when, without warning, an explosion erupted in the wall beside them, showering the entire group with dust.

Within seconds, all six players and the wolf were on their feet again, weapons drawn, glancing into the misshapen hole in the cave wall. A shadowy form appeared in the smoke, and as the dust settled, a row of figures came into view. The form of Creeper Khan, with Arachnia, Enderchick, Lord Marrow, and Zomboy standing directly behind him.

There was a moment of silence. Stan and his friends stared at the mobhunters, transfixed in horror that they had been discovered. Meanwhile, the members of ELM stared back, their eyes alight with joyous amazement.

"Fancy seeing you here, Stan," Arachnia hissed with a grin, stepping forward to the front of the group.

"How did you find us?" Stan demanded as he uncomfortably forced himself to look into Arachnia's eight red eyes.

"Lucky break, I guess," she replied with a grin. "We were just about to set some traps for you guys down here. We didn't expect you to get back here so quickly."

"We've been walking nonstop," Stan replied slowly, trying to buy time as he wildly thought of how they could escape from these bounty hunters. "We wanted to make it back to Element City as fast as possible."

"Aw, poor tragic you," Arachnia sneered. "You tried so hard, and got so far . . . but in the end, it doesn't even matter."

"Haha! I ged id!" Zomboy shouted. "Because dose are da words to a song! And you used dem in . . ."

"Shut up, Zomboy," Arachnia said offhandedly.

"Okay," he replied meekly, looking to the ground.

"Well, congrats to you," Stan said, still desperate for more time. "You finally managed to catch up to us. Now what?"

"Well, you're going to come with us, Stan," Arachnia replied in a disturbingly sweet-sounding voice that made Stan's skin crawl. "Lord Tenebris is most anxious to see you. And as for your friends, well, they're of no use to anybody anymore, so they will be disposed of."

"Well, I'm sorry, Arachnia," Stan retorted, keeping his voice pleasant and conversational as he realized that there was no escape, and they would have to fight. "But I'm afraid that I can't let you do that."

And before the mobhunter could respond, Stan leaped

forward and locked his axe against the glowing diamond sword that Arachnia had pulled out, and the two of them began to duel. Immediately, the players who had been standing behind the two leaders leaped into action. Kat lunged toward Enderchick with Rex at her heels, Cassandrix and Creeper Khan struck at each other simultaneously, and Commander Crunch rushed in to help Cassandrix. Lord Marrow and Leonidas both released a barrage of arrows at each other, while Zomboy lunged at the nearest target, Charlie.

Charlie feinted backward to avoid the giant stone axe that the oversized player slammed into the ground, leaving cracks in the stone blocks of the cave floor. As he moved, Charlie felt a sharp pain in his foot, and it nearly gave out, but he managed to stay on his feet, cringing in pain. Charlie glanced up at Zomboy, who was raising his axe and preparing for another attack. *He's not very fast,* Charlie noted to himself, and *he's taking way too long between attacks. He must be a heavy fighter.*

Charlie became aware of explosions going off behind Zomboy as Creeper Khan started to use his pyrokinetic powers and Lord Marrow fired off explosive arrows, but Charlie forced himself to focus on his own fight. Zomboy continued to walk toward Charlie, swinging his giant stone axe from side to side, forcing Charlie back down the cave toward the way they had come. Charlie saw multiple openings in the attack that would allow him to counter, but each time he was about to strike, the pain in his leg flared up again, and he was forced to fall back to avoid another attack.

Finally, after a frustrating minute of dodging, Zomboy launched a particularly powerful downward axe strike, which Charlie sidestepped. The axe blade shattered the stone block beneath it in a shower of sparks and became lodged in the ground, forcing Zomboy to struggle to pull it out. Seeing his chance, Charlie launched himself forward off his good leg, and sunk his stone pickaxe directly into Zomboy's chest. The giant mobhunter winced and staggered backward, axe still in hand, before collapsing to the ground with a massive thud.

Charlie took a deep breath, and let it out as he looked down at the massive body of his defeated adversary. He was infuriated with himself. That giant thug was so unskilled that it should have been an effortless kill, but his leg had made it much more difficult than it had to be. A dark thought crossed Charlie's mind. What if he came face to face with a skilled opponent? Not somebody like Leonidas in their fight in the forest . . . someone who actually wanted to hurt him? Charlie shuddered as his mind clouded with these thoughts, and he began to walk back toward the fight, past the body of Zomboy, determined to prove himself.

What Charlie hadn't expected was for Zomboy's axe to fly up off the ground and directly at him.

Charlie managed to pull his backup pickaxe out of his inventory to block the attack, but the impact of the oversized stone axe on his weapon still sent him flying across the cave. He hit the wall with a smack, landing hard on the stone-block floor, right on his bad leg. Charlie let out a holler of pain and clutched his damaged limb in agony, glancing up through his teary eyes to figure out what had just happened.

Zomboy was back on his feet. His stone axe was held firmly in his right hand, Charlie's pickaxe was still lodged in his chest, and he was staring at Charlie with a grin, no sign of pain on his face at all.

Charlie was perplexed, not sure how it was that Zomboy was still alive, until it hit him. Zomboy was part of the assassin team, and, according to what Stan had told him, each member of their team seemed to be modded to have some sort of special ability. Charlie realized that this player must be modded to have extra HP, and be able to take a ton of punishment before he died.

As the giant beast of a player lumbered toward Charlie, he prepared to kick off the wall, and get out of the way of the incoming attack. Zomboy began to raise his axe over his head as Charlie kicked off the wall, only to have his knee buckle under the pressure. Charlie hardly noticed, though; he was too focused on the axe raised over Zomboy's head.

Just as the blow was about to fall, an arrow flew from

deep in the cave and lodged itself into Zomboy's skull, right between his eyes. The giant player gave a yelp of pain, and then proceeded to look down the tunnel toward the source of the arrow, not dead from the blow (somehow) but most certainly angry.

"Hey!" he bellowed down the mine, his eyebrows, with an arrow sticking out between them, knitted in fury. "Wads da big idea?"

Charlie glanced down the cave, and his face lit up in amazement and relief. There, standing in the mouth of the cave, was Sirus, bow raised, and an army of twenty players, all armed with stone weapons, standing behind him.

"Charge!" the crazed redstone mechanic bellowed.

The entire mass of players barreled through the cave, sending arrows and flying weapons at Zomboy. Sensing that he was overwhelmed, the massive mobhunter turned, the attacks simply sinking into his back to no effect. With his axe in hand, he dashed down the cave and back toward his comrades.

As the wave of freed hostages continued to rush past Charlie, Sirus stopped to help him to his feet. "Hey, Charlie, man, long time no see, how're you doing?"

"I'm . . . fine," Charlie replied. He couldn't believe his eyes. From what he had heard, Sirus had perished in the Battle for Elementia. "I . . . I'm *really* glad to see you. But . . . I thought you . . ."

"Oh, I get it, you thought I died," Sirus replied with a short laugh. "Yeah, I thought that, too, but I respawned, and I saw somebody duck into the woods and I figured that the hill probably wasn't safe, so I decided that I wanted to go out into the middle of the Ender Desert because I thought that could be fun, but then I got hungry and tried to eat part of a cactus, and it kind of caused me to hallucinate to the point where I imagined that I was at a wedding between a cantaloupe and—"

"I'm sorry, but do we have to talk about this now?" Charlie cut in urgently, jerking his head toward the blasts and shouts of the ongoing fight down the cave.

"Seriously though, dude," Sirus continued, as he got into position to help Charlie up, "you must have done something pretty bad to that leg of yours, 'cause it's totally busted, gone south, practically useless, comparable to the poop of—"

"Okay, I get it, Sirus," Charlie cut in, irritated. "I'm already frustrated enough without your commentary."

Sirus merely shrugged and pulled Charlie to his feet. Charlie attempted to take a step forward, but his bad foot couldn't take the slightest bit of pressure without him screaming in agony. Sirus noticed his suffering and placed Charlie's arm around his shoulder, slowly helping him follow the horde of Adorian Villagers that had surged down the cave and toward the ongoing fights.

Look at me, Charlie thought to himself bitterly. *I can't even walk by myself. I'm nothing but a cripple now.*

As they reached the end of the cave, Charlie saw that, to his confusion, there was no fighting. Stan, Kat, Charlie, Cassandrix, and Commander Crunch were all standing around, looking exhausted and in various states of injury, but the assassins had vanished.

"Where'd they go?" Charlie inquired to Commander Crunch as Sirus helped him sit down on a loose stone block.

"They warped away, lad," the Commander replied as he nursed a blast wound on his arm. "As soon as Sirus 'n' his scallywags arrived, the other scallywags realized that they were outnumbered, 'n' couldn't win. Th' poppet that goes by th' name o' Enderchick grabbed her mates, 'n' they all warped away. T' where, we can only venture guesses, but I doubt they'll be comin' back anytime soon."

Charlie nodded in understanding and looked around at the scene around them. Sirus and Stan were in deep conversation, Stan's eyes wide, as if he were talking to a ghost. The hostages were wandering around the cave, some of them tending the wounds that had been inflicted during the fight. Suddenly, there was a commotion in the back of the cave, and two of Sirus's followers came forward, holding Leonidas with his arms behind his back.

"Hey, what do ya think you're doin'?" Leonidas demanded,

clearly too tired from the fight to resist them.

"We found another one of them, Sirus," one of the two players said, and Sirus turned to face them. Immediately, his jaw dropped.

"Leonidas of RAT1! Force him down, men!"

And with that, the two players delivered sharp kicks to the back of Leonidas's knees, forcing Leonidas to fall to the ground, a grunt of agony escaping his mouth as Sirus loaded an arrow into his bow.

"I'll take care of this," he announced heroically, and he was about to let the arrow fly when Stan realized what was happening. He knocked the bow out of Sirus's hand, sending the arrow flying down the mine.

"President Stan, what're you doing? This is a dangerous criminal who needs to be executed!" Sirus cried out.

"Sirus, calm down, it's okay! Leonidas is on our side now. He's realized the errors of his ways and he's fighting for Element City."

Sirus looked at Stan incredulously for a moment, and then raised an eyebrow in skepticism.

"President Stan, with all due respect, this player is responsible for tons of terrible things that happened during the rebellion against King Kev, and he's killed more people than you'll ever realize as a part of RAT1, so are you sure you don't want me to kill him?"

"I am positive!" Stan barked in fury. "I'm granting Leonidas a complete presidential pardon for his past actions. He's been traveling with me for weeks, and has proved to me time and time again that he's sorry for what he did under King Kev and the Noctem Alliance. Now, he's willing to give everything that he has to make up for what he did in the past! So I'll thank you for not being rude to him!"

Sirus opened his mouth, and then closed it again. He gave a sideways glance at Leonidas, who had pulled himself to his feet and was shooting a dirty look at Sirus. Finally, Sirus spoke again, his voice still sounding suspicious.

"If you say so, President Stan," Sirus replied slowly, and with that he turned to work on Charlie's bad leg.

"Thanks, man," Leonidas said, smiling at Stan for a moment before going to tend to a burn wound left on him by one of Lord Marrow's attacks.

"Don't mention it," Stan replied offhandedly, barely paying attention as he came to a startling realization.

Within the next day, Stan would be at the underground bunker of Element City, which held his friends and all his citizens. They would surely be overjoyed to see him, along with Charlie, Kat, Cassandrix, and Commander Crunch. However, he had never considered how the citizens of Element City would react to Leonidas.

As clear as it was that Leonidas had had a change of heart

now, Stan still couldn't change the terrible things that Leonidas had done in the past. And as he led his citizens forward in the greatest challenge that Element City had ever faced, Stan wondered just how they would take it when they found out that he had granted a full presidential pardon to one of King Kev's most powerful soldiers.

As the frigid winds of the eternal blizzard tore through the streets of the Nocturia complex, the Noctem Capitol Building stood tall and looming. Throughout the war, the Elementia forces hadn't come close to scratching the capital city of the Nation of the Noctem Alliance, and the Capitol was proof of that. The building was totally untouched, and still the crowning jewel of the Noctem Empire with its gothic stone-brick block design, gold and lapis lazuli block accents, and beacon blocks that shot radiant pillars of light into the sky. The building was also by far the largest and tallest in Nocturia—the highest spire of the building extended out of the base castle and far into the sky.

Atop this spire, a single light could be seen. Torchlight shone from an open window, the only pinpoint of luminescence in the midst of the raging snowstorm. And it was within this one window atop the highest tower of the Noctem Capitol Building that Lord Tenebris sat on his throne of obsidian and quartz, deep in thought.

Lord Tenebris had his eyes closed, yet he could quite clearly see through the eyes of one of the Withers, patrolling the skies over Element City. Lord Tenebris had been experimenting in private, drawing energy from the server itself to bolster his power and discovering more and more new skills by the day. However, this particular new ability that he had discovered had proven to be the most useful by far. On a whim, Lord Tenebris could borrow the eyes of any player or mob, provided, of course, that he knew where they were, and see all that they could see.

In the past few weeks, during the Noctem Alliance's drive to take Element City, this power had been especially helpful. Between clairvoyance and his ability to speak using telepathy, Lord Tenebris had been able to have direct control over the troops on the battlefield through the eyes of General Drake, while still staying hidden away in Nocturia and Fungarus. And he knew that it was for the best that he remain hidden. After all, though the Noctem Alliance now had the upper hand in the war, fear was still by far their greatest asset.

To be honest, Lord Tenebris quite enjoyed the feeling of commanding the troops from far off and tactically maneuvering them to ensure total domination over a region. Furthermore, he was also well aware of how necessary this step was if he truly wanted control over the server. Lord Tenebris knew that, if he wanted to, he could destroy all the Elementia forces in a matter of minutes using just his own abilities. However, he fancied himself a wise leader, and he was well aware of the vast difference between destroying all the enemy forces and winning the war.

Lord Tenebris saw through the eyes of the Wither that soldiers, clad in black, with bows, weapons, and potions at the ready, patrolled the streets of Element City, securing them in the name of the Noctem Alliance. He gave a sigh of satisfaction. Finally, after all these months, Element City was back in the hands of the players who had earned it, those who had toiled and struggled to raise the city after starting from nothing but a meadow.

At long last, they had done it. The Noctem Alliance had conquered Elementia.

One thing still tainted Lord Tenebris's perfect victory, however. Although the Noctem Alliance now had military control over the entire server, they had yet to capture Stan2012. Lord Tenebris actually found it rather surprising. Drake knew exactly what Lord Tenebris was going to do to him should Stan return to Element City. If there was one thing that was certain, it was that Drake would go to any lengths to save his own neck. When added to the fact that Drake had hired a group of trained assassins to track Stan down, Lord Tenebris found it difficult to believe that Drake hadn't delivered Stan to him yet.

Lord Tenebris stood up from his throne and stopped using his clairvoyance, looking once again into the plain stone brick–block room, flickering in the light of the torch.

The time had come, he decided. The military offensive was now over, and the Noctem Alliance had a strong foothold in Element City. There was no purpose in his staying in Nocturia any longer. It was time for him to return to the city that he had worked so long and hard to conquer.

Lord Tenebris took a deep breath, focused intently on the Council Room of Element Castle, and vanished in a puff of purple smoke.

G felt disgusted with himself as he dragged himself up the quartz stairs toward Tess's office. He still couldn't get the image out of his mind of the wounded recruit in a blue and green jumpsuit, lying on the ground and clutching the cut on his side. He had stepped in and declared the round of the sparring tournament over, and ordered that the fallen recruit be given medical attention, but the two soldiers overseeing him had cut him off. He could vividly remember the Noctem captain in the metallic Creeper costume staring him in the eye and growling those hateful words.

"If you're a true Noctem corporal, you'll tell him to finish the job right now."

Despite the fact that every fiber of his body was telling him to stand up for the fallen recruit, G found himself unable to speak. Before he could, though, a messenger arrived and told G that Tess was looking for him. As G had left to make his way to the stairs, the two corporals had turned back to the sparring recruits, and right before G turned a corner, he heard one of them say, "All right . . . finish him!"

G still couldn't get the sound of that last shout out of his head. He could only imagine what they were doing to the wounded player now . . . and here he was just walking away. Even if that player was in training for the Noctem Alliance, he didn't deserve the abuse and harassment that G was sure was coming his way. In fact, he had half a mind to turn around and go help that player, but he knew that he couldn't. Jayden had been willing to sacrifice his life to keep G in Nocturia, and there was no way that he was going to risk anything until he cured Mella and Stull, regardless of what the cost may be.

Finally, G reached the top of the staircase, and was standing at the threshold of General Tess's room. The room was beautifully designed. The walls were made out of quartz blocks fashioned into different patterns, the floor was carpeted with blue wool blocks, and the ceiling was covered in glowstone blocks. A fire burning eternally in a Netherrack fireplace projected a warm glow into the room, and picture frames, showing pixel-art paintings, hung on the walls. There were glass windows that revealed the howling storm outside, and behind a cedarwood plank desk sat General Tess, her diamond sword hanging in an item frame behind her.

"Greetings, ma'am," G said automatically, suppressing

his self-loathing for the time being.

"You took a long time," Tess retorted, not bothering to return the greeting. "Please try to be quicker next time, Corporal."

"Yes, ma'am," G replied, his disgust with himself now replaced with irritation at Tess.

"I have a task for you," Tess continued. "I need you to patrol the grounds again."

"Yes, ma'am," G replied, glad that it was only a mundane task that was being asked of him, and he turned back down the stairs to go carry it out.

"Oh, and one more thing, Corporal," Tess continued, sounding almost lazy. G turned around and watched as she reached into a chest next to her desk and pulled out a Potion of Slowness. "Tell Captain Zingster to execute those twenty Elementia prisoners today instead of tomorrow. Now that we've taken Element City, there's really no point in keeping hostages anymore."

G's eyes widened, and he did all that he could to hold back a gasp of horror. Regardless, Tess still raised an eyebrow, setting her glass back down on the table and glaring at him.

"Do you have a problem with that, Corporal?"

"No, ma'am," G replied quickly, the gears in his mind spinning as he tried to work out how he could possibly save these prisoners without arousing Tess's suspicion.

"Well then, get to it," Tess ordered, taking another sip of potion as she reached into her desk a second time. G was about to go down the stairs when he paused for a moment.

All throughout his stay in Nocturia, G had spent hours upon hours with Tess. Because of her constant presence, incredibly high expectations of him, and casual talk as if they were the best of friends, G had felt incredibly awkward and hated every minute of it, but he had forced himself to do it for the sake of Element City. And he had done his job quite well, never letting on to his aversion to Tess, and always letting her feel like they were becoming close friends. And perhaps now would be the perfect time to try to get some payoff for all his hard work for the sake of rescuing those trapped players from Element City.

"Um . . . excuse me, ma'am?"

"Why are you still here, Corporal?" Tess asked in irritation as she glanced up. She had been searching for food in the chest, and hadn't realized that G hadn't left yet.

"Well, because I have a suggestion for you."

"I don't want to hear it, Corporal. You have duties to attend to."

"Please, ma'am, I think that it may be important."

"Fine!" Tess shouted in frustration. "What do you want, Corporal? And make it fast. I have a lot of work to do, and so do you!"

G took a deep breath, and let it out before continuing.

"Well, it occurred to me that the war in Elementia is going to be over soon and it seems like we're on the verge of winning. I think that, if we're going to rule over the citizens in Element City again, perhaps we might be able to get more support from them if we were to be a bit lenient."

"Oh?" Tess asked, her eyebrow raised suspiciously as she eyed G. "And how do you propose we do that, exactly?"

"My suggestion," G replied tentatively, aware of how Tess was probably going to react to his proposal, "is that we don't execute the soldiers just yet. We hold them captive here until—"

"That is a preposterous idea."

There was a moment of silence as Tess glared at G, and G struggled to hold his feelings in. He knew what he had to do, and even though he was aware that he was pushing his luck, he tried to press on.

"Well, the reason I think that is—"

"What are you trying to say, Corporal? That the atrocities that the soldiers of Elementia have committed during the war deserve to go unpunished?"

"No, of course not, but—"

"Then I see no reason why this conversation should continue."

"Please, listen to me!" G exclaimed, something snapping in his head as he felt a surge of anger toward Tess for all the wrong reasons. "I've been following you faithfully since the day I arrived here, and I've devoted my life to you. The least you could do is hear me out!"

Tess's face took on a dangerous look. "You're treading on thin ice, Corporal."

"Please, General," G said again, trying to curb the acid boiling in his stomach. "It would mean a lot to me if you would just allow me to—"

"I am your commanding officer, Corporal MasterBronze," Tess shot back, standing up at her desk and giving him the evil eye, "and I am *this close* to having you executed for insubordination! Stand down right now!"

G stood still, his mouth still slightly open, and found himself unable to speak. As Tess had yelled at him, a startling realization had hit G like a train. He merely stood still for a moment as he flashed back to over a month ago, when he was standing in the hallway of Element Castle, enraged and hurt, and he had yelled . . .

"Get a move on!" Tess barked at him. "Are you just going to stand there all day? You have no idea how lucky you are that I haven't already ordered you out in front of the firing squad!"

G barely heard her. He was making his way down the quartz block stairs, back toward the group of recruits, his mind swimming in a vortex of realizations and guilt.

Since G had entered Nocturia, he had given barely any thought at all to Kat. The two of them were clearly done and over with, and with far more important things going on, the issue had been dormant in G's mind for quite some time. However, the last time he *had* thought about her, he was still under the impression that she was being unreasonable in not getting over their fight, and that she had been stupid to want to break it off in the first place, given how much attention he was lavishing on her.

Now, though, G found it amazing that, given everything General Tess had put him through since he had joined Nocturia, Kat hadn't come to his mind sooner. It hadn't occurred to him for a second, all this time, that the way that he had treated Kat, his former girlfriend and fellow council member, was disturbingly similar to the way that General Tess, the commanding officer of the organization that he had sworn to destroy, had treated him as an underling.

It felt like a void had opened in G's chest as memories came flooding back to him. All that time, he had thought that he had been an amazing boyfriend to Kat, and he was frustrated because he didn't feel like she was putting in as much effort as he was. But now, G could see quite clearly that he had been far too demanding of her, and incredibly disrespectful. She had agreed to go out with him, and continued to make an effort even when things got difficult while still keeping sight of her responsibilities. But he had neglected his duties to the council, only wanting to spend time with her, and was infuriated when she hadn't done the same.

And to top it all off, he had only put up with Tess because he had to. Why Kat had put up with him at all, G could only guess . . .

G sat down on the stairs for a moment, overwhelmed. He had just snapped at Tess for something that he himself had done before. Because he had done that, Tess was now suspicious of him, and his cover would surely be blown soon. And if he was executed as a spy, not only would Mella and Stull never be saved, but G would never get a chance to return to Element City and let Kat know how sorry he was for what he had done to her.

G stood up, his stomach blazing with resolve. He knew what he had to do. It was do-or-die time now, and drastic actions were called for. All at once, an insane plan formulated in G's head, and he knew that he'd have to go through with it. If it worked, then not only would he spare the hostages' lives but free them as well, along with curing the NPC villagers and escaping the nightmarish Noctem Capitol. If the plan failed, then they would all die.

G took a deep breath, let it out, and set off down the stairs to put his plan into motion.

A roar of furious shouting erupted from the base of the cave as Ben walked off the stone brick–block balcony. Even as he walked back inside the command post that had been carved into the cave wall, he could still hear the threats and boos that followed his most recent announcement. He gritted his teeth in frustration. He still couldn't stand the fact that he'd had to cut the food rations *again,* but unfortunately there was nothing else that could be done.

Ben shut the wooden door behind him, yet he could still hear the jeers. Sighing, he walked into the room, which was nothing more than a small cave that had been cleaned up and turned into the head office of the military as long as they were stuck down in the bunker. A few chests sat pressed up against the stone-block wall, and some maps and papers sat on a wood plank–block table, but other than that, the room was barren. Bob was sitting on Ivanhoe, and upon his entry, they both looked up.

"Sounds like it went well," Bob muttered bitterly, glancing at the door, which was doing nothing to block out the noise.

"Well, how did you expect them to react?" asked Ben, a resigned look on his face as he pulled another wood-plank block from his inventory, set it on the ground, and plopped down on it. "I'd be pretty upset, too, if somebody told me that I'd only be getting two slices of bread a day, every day, for the foreseeable future."

Bob gave a grim nod. The two brothers sat in silence for a moment. Both of them knew that they had the same thing on their minds. It had been the only thing on their minds since the incident.

"It's eerie," Bob finally said, his voice sounding almost disconnected as he stared off into space, "to think that it's already been four days."

"Yeah," Ben replied, glancing at the ground. "It's even more eerie that the two of us are still here and talking to each other, like normal, while . . . while Bill is . . ."

Ben couldn't bring himself to finish the sentence. He had finally managed to stop the waves of nauseating depression over the past few days, and he wasn't going to allow them to return. They were still fighting a war, and grief had no place in a war. Ben choked back his sob, letting it out as a raspy sigh. Bob was about to open his mouth to respond when, all of a sudden, there was an earsplitting crash.

Both brothers leaped to their feet, bow and sword drawn, ready to defend themselves as they whipped around to face the source of the sound. What they saw was the door they had just exited through knocked down, window broken, and a brick lying on the ground not too far inside the room. With no door, there was no barrier to protect the two brothers from the raging, hateful taunts from the basin of the cave below them.

Ben let out a growl of fury, which was drowned out by the jumbled chants of protest from outside the door. "This is ridiculous!" he yelled to his brother. "What are they complaining about? Yeah, sure their food supply got cut. Well, you know what? At least they're safe from the Noctem Alliance for now! At least they're not dead!"

Bob sighed in disgust. "And I suppose you want to go out there and tell them that?"

Ben was about to respond when, without warning, the Mechanist hurdled into the room through an entrance in the back wall, pickaxe drawn.

"What's going on?" he demanded. "I thought I heard a . . ."

Suddenly, the Mechanist realized that Ben and Bob were in the room, and he stopped in midsentence. He hadn't spoken to the brothers, except through messengers, since Bill's death.

"Well," the Mechanist said, recovering and attempting to regain his composure. "Is everything all right out here? I thought that I heard a crash."

"Yeah, someone threw a brick through our door," replied Ben forebodingly, gesturing to the wooden door and brick lying in the empty doorframe, through which the boisterous anger of the crowd was still raging. The Mechanist's eyes widened at the sight.

"It would seem," Bob continued for his brother, giving a look to the Mechanist, "that the citizens aren't very happy with us right now. Since we've been holed up in this bunker, they haven't gotten any good news at all. The only thing that we've done for them is cut off their food supply."

"Well, what do they expect?" the Mechanist asked, baffled. "We're doing everything that we can for the citizens. What else do they want us to—"

"Oh, open your eyes!" Ben yelled, the anger that he had barely been holding back since the Mechanist's arrival surging forward. "These people have had their entire lives uprooted! The Noctem Alliance has taken over their city, stolen their homes, and forced them to lock themselves down in this stupid mine! Some of them have friends who are still up there, and the Noctem Alliance is probably abusing them, or worse! They need to hear good news!"

"But . . . I . . . ," the Mechanist sputtered. "What do you expect . . . We don't have anything good to tell them . . ."

"Well, that's your job!" bellowed Ben, marching up to the Mechanist and now yelling directly into his face. "Like it or not, when you volunteered to take over Stan's job, you took on the responsibility of keeping your people happy! And since the beginning, you've stayed holed up in the castle, drinking yourself into a stupor, and running the country without caring what your people think of you.

"Even now, when we're all trapped down here, do you have the nerve to talk to your citizens face to face? *No!* You just locked yourself in your room, feeling sorry for yourself, and had me and Bob take the fall for you! We've been trying as hard as we can to keep the people of Element City from hating us. What have you done to make the situation better? *Nothing!*"

There was a moment of silence, broken only by the ongoing, enraged roar of the crowd, during which the Mechanist stared into Ben's furious eyes, unable to speak. Ben glared back, his anger slowly fading, and grief starting to well up in his face.

"My brother died to save you," Ben spat bitterly. "And so far, I don't think that you're worth it. You'd better prove me wrong."

And with that, Ben shoved the Mechanist away from him and, with tears streaming down his face, he marched out of the room.

For a moment, Bob and the Mechanist just stood there. The Mechanist stared blankly at where Ben had just stood. After a moment, Bob turned around and had Ivanhoe run out the back door and down the hall after Ben, leaving the Mechanist standing alone in the midst of the barren stone room.

Ever since he had woken up and realized that Bill had sacrificed his life so that he could live, the Mechanist had been totally distraught. After he had joined Stan's militia all those months ago, the Mechanist had sworn off SloPo. Yet, in the stresses of running the entire country, the Mechanist hadn't been able to resist the relaxing allure of the potion. If he had had the power to resist, to keep off the potion, Bill would still be alive.

And the more he thought about it, the Mechanist realized, in horror, that Ben was totally right. He hadn't done anything since they had entered the mines, too wrapped up in his own self-loathing, only ordering cuts to the food rations when supplies began to run low. He had abandoned his police chiefs and he had abandoned his country. And now the Mechanist knew what had to be done.

Taking a deep breath, the Mechanist walked out the doorway and onto the stone-block balcony, overlooking the basin of the giant cave, which was swamped with players. The mob of players, which was beginning to become slightly calmer, erupted yet again at the sight of the Mechanist. Now, however, the anger emanating from the crowd was far more potent. This was the first appearance the Mechanist had made before his people since before the construction of the bunker. All the hatred at the overwork and ruthless discipline that the Mechanist had ordered came surging forward.

"Excuse me!" the Mechanist yelled, raising his hand,

struggling to be heard over the tumult of the masses. "I have something I would like to say to you all."

The noise did not die down. Rather, another brick flew up out of the crowd, and straight toward the Mechanist. Acting out of instinct, the Mechanist whipped his pickaxe from his inventory and shattered the brick in midair. Shocked and appalled, he looked down into the crowd and saw soldiers surging into the throng to apprehend the one who had thrown the brick. He forced himself to take another deep breath.

"Anyway," the Mechanist continued, trying as hard as he could to ignore the struggle between the attacking player and the soldiers going on below him, "I would like to personally thank all of you for your continuing cooperation. Being holed up in this cave is difficult for everybody, but it is necessary to—"

"It's not hard for you!" a single voice rang out above the noise. "I bet you've been on SloPo every minute of every day since the war started!"

A fresh round of fury burst forth from the crowd at this accusation. The words stung the Mechanist, and he gave a shudder of disappointment in himself before responding.

"I fully admit that since the departure of my fellow councilmen, I have not always acted as I ought to. I have made many mistakes, and for that, I offer you my sincerest apologies. However, in the present situation—"

"You're nothing but a dictator!" the voice cut back in, from a player somewhere in the center of the crowd who the Mechanist couldn't see. "You've done nothing but lay around and drink while us normal people have been doing all the hard work!"

"Okay, guards, apprehend that player. I can't get a word out!" the Mechanist spat out without really thinking. Had he given it any thought, he would have realized just how big a mistake that it was.

"He's trying to silence me!" the player screamed, sounding disturbed and terrified. "He's gone crazy with power!"

The soldiers, who had just finished detaining the brick thrower, now surged toward the shouting player, who was in the center of the crowd. However, the rest of the citizens began to fight back. They were punching the soldiers, slamming into them, doing all they could to keep them from reaching the center of the crowd where the one player was. The Mechanist watched in total shock as the soldiers drew out their weapons and began to fight against the hundreds of players now pressing into them.

What the Mechanist was witnessing was a revolt.

"Please, calm down!" the Mechanist cried out in desperation. "Guards, I order you to stand down. Return to your positions immediately!"

The guards couldn't hear him. They were too busy

fighting against the citizens, who had drawn their own weapons and were starting to attack the soldiers. As he stared down into the crowd, awestruck, the Mechanist suddenly realized that something else was flying directly at him. He ducked down under the cobblestone-wall railing of the balcony, and watched the arrow fly directly through where his head had been seconds before and stick into the stone-block wall above him.

The Mechanist's heart was pounding out of his chest as the gravity of the situation dawned on him. One of his people had just tried to assassinate him. He would never be able to find out who. The entire population had turned on him. A full-on battle was breaking out among the people of Elementia.

All of a sudden, the Mechanist knew that he wasn't safe anymore. Nobody was. The Noctem Alliance hadn't even found their cave yet.

The Mechanist realized that he had to find Bob and Ben. They, of all people, might be able to fix this dangerous mess. He crawled across the cobblestone balcony and was about to enter the room again when an explosion echoed throughout the cavern.

All concerns for safety flying out the window, the Mechanist leaped to his feet, terrified at the thought that somebody in the crowd below had detonated a TNT block. However, looking down into the throng, he saw no sign of the blast. Rather, all fighting had ceased in an instant, and all eyes were now turned to a giant hole that had been ripped in the upper wall of the cave.

The entire cave watched with bated breath. What was this? Was it some sort of military operation? Was it an accidental TNT detonation? Had the Noctem Alliance finally found them?

Then, one by one, players emerged from the opening, standing on the ledge, and the Mechanist's heart lifted.

He recognized the tattered army uniform and scraggly beard of the navy officer Commander Crunch and the dirty white robes and full red lips of Cassandrix. Kat's orange shirt, pink shorts, and blond hair were still radiantly bright despite their heavy wear and tear, and Rex's head poked out joyfully beside her. Charlie hobbled up next to her, his leg clearly damaged but still in one piece.

And then, from amid a group of people that the Mechanist could see standing behind the four players, another stepped to the front of the pack. His turquoise shirt was stained, his navy pants were torn, there were scratches and bruises pock-marking his face, but it was still completely undeniable as to who this player was.

"People of Elementia!" Stan2012 announced to the stunned mass of hundreds of players. "We . . . are . . . back!"

And with that, Stan pumped his fist into the air in a triumphant gesture as, all at once, the entire population of the cave burst into applause. The Mechanist could only stare, tears of joy in his eyes, as he took in the wonderful, wonderful truth that his friends were home alive.

Ben and Bob rushed out of the door and stood beside the Mechanist.

"What's going on out here?" Ben demanded, astonished by the aura of amazing joy that was now echoing throughout the cave.

The Mechanist said nothing. He simply turned back around and pointed up at the hole in the wall. As soon as the two brothers realized who they were looking at, they erupted into hoots and cheers, hugging each other and jumping around, totally elated.

And there, far up on the ledge, as his friends broke down in tears at the fact that they were finally home, and they hugged each other, and danced, and shouted their love down into the crowd, Stan didn't move. He simply stood still, his fist still raised into the air like a beacon of victory, and looked down into the faces of his people, his heart filled with joy such as he had never known before.

Within minutes, he knew that he would have to meet up with the Mechanist and the three police chiefs. He knew that he would have to reveal the tragic news of DZ's death. He knew that he would have to lead his people. He knew that he would have to plan an attack. He knew that time was of the essence. He knew that the fate of the game of Minecraft may very well be resting on his shoulders.

But Stan still allowed himself, just for a minute, to live in the moment. He had worked so long and hard to return, and he had sacrificed and lost so much, that never, in a million years, could this moment be ruined.

The holding room was nothing but a giant cube, constructed of cobblestone blocks and taking up a sizable space within the Noctem Capitol Building. Torches lit the perimeter of the room, making it light enough to see and prevent other mobs from spawning. Cutting through the solid wall of cobblestone on the upper half of one wall was a row of glass, through which any curious onlookers could see what the two Zombies were doing.

These two Zombies did not resemble typical Zombies. Rather than the square head reminiscent of a player, they had elongated heads, with bloodshot red eyes and giant, droopy green noses hanging down off their faces. These Zombies, one fully grown and the other half the first one's size, had once been two villagers.

They were once mother and son, named Mella and Stull, and they had lived happily together in their village, which was now long gone. Not that they knew it, though. Besides their names, Mella and Stull had no memory of their previous lives. Oh, it was there, hidden somewhere deep within the layers of instinct and bloodlust that had overtaken their already primitive reasoning upon being bitten by a Zombie.

The two of them lumbered around aimlessly. For the past month, this had been their lives. They had spent the majority of their time ambling aimlessly around this room. Occasionally, they had been pulled out by the players who had put them there to serve as a communication bridge between the players and the mobs, and they had soon after been rewarded by unconscious players, who they would devour with pleasure.

It had been quite some time since they had been utilized, however. The Noctem Alliance's mobs had been of great use on the battlefield, but now that the fighting was all but over, they served little to no purpose besides controlling the Withers. In fact, Lord Tenebris had made it clear that no tamed mobs were to be allowed into Element City. Only players who had been members of the Noctem Alliance would be allowed to live freely within the walls. Not that the villagers knew this, though. The only thing they knew was that at some point, the iron door on the ground would open again, and it would be time to feast.

Sure enough, the door did eventually scrape open, and Mella and Stull glanced at it. Through the frame marched a player, a bronze skin showing under his black armor, followed by another black-clad player with a thunderbolt across his red face, and around twenty players in soldier uniforms. The Zombies were beside themselves in anticipation. They had never seen so many players in one place before.

"Are you sure about this?" the lightning-faced player asked, turning to face G.

"Hey, don't look at me," said G, sounding annoyed as he gave a noncommittal shrug. "I'm just following what General Tess told me."

"Yeah, but I heard something totally different," the player replied, sounding confused. "She told me to bring these players to the firing squad, not the Zombie chamber. And it makes more sense to do it that way. I mean, there are way too many players here for the Zombies to eat all of them at once."

"Look, Zingster," G retorted, looking Corporal Zingster directly in the face. "I *just* came down from talking to Tess, and she told me that she wants *me* to knock out these players and let the Zombies have them."

"But—"

"But nothing!" G spat at him. "As of today, I outrank you, Corporal, so you'll do what I say!"

Corporal Zingster stared at G for a moment.

"Yes, sir, Captain MasterBronze," the Corporal replied, giving a respectful salute before backing out of the room, the door closing behind him.

Wasting no time, G started rummaging through his inventory. He knew that it would only be a little while before Corporal Zingster discovered that he wasn't really a captain like he had said. G hated that he'd had to lie to Zingster like that; it was just another complication to be thrown into the plan, but he knew that it was the only way to ensure that Zingster obeyed him without question. In any case, it didn't matter now. If this plan worked out, he would most likely never see Zingster or Tess again until they met on the battle-field.

"Take these!" G said, as the horde of captive soldiers, who had been looking on in terrified silence, now stared at him in surprise. From his inventory, he threw dozens of pick-axes into the crowd, which he had looted from the supply room.

One of the soldiers caught the pickaxe, and looked it over uncomprehendingly before returning his gaze back to G.

"Who are you?" he asked in awe.

"My name is Goldman2," G replied hastily. "I'm a spy for Elementia and a member of the Element City Council of Eight, and we're busting out of here."

Instantly, a ripple of excitement spread throughout the crowd, though, with the discipline of the soldiers they were, they remained quiet. G continued to look through the sup-plies he had stolen until he found what he was looking for. He held a liquid Potion of Weakness in his right hand, and had a golden apple on standby. G turned to face the two zombies, who had been looking at him expectantly since his arrival.

"Come here, Mella and Stull," G called out to them like dogs. "It's time to eat."

Their eyes flashed red with excitement as they lumbered forward toward G. Then, when they were a few blocks away, G launched the Potion of Weakness in their direction. The glass bottle shattered on the ground, enveloping the two villagers in a cloud of fumes. The two forms of the villagers stumbled around in confusion within the cloud for a few seconds before falling to the ground. Without hesitation, G took a deep breath and sprinted into the cloud. He shoved the golden apple down the throat of Mella, and then drew a second golden apple and did the same to Stull. The mother and son sputtered for a minute, before falling unconscious to the ground, golden wisps of smoke curling up off their bodies.

G barreled out of the smoke, and finally allowed himself to breathe in the fresh, nontoxic air. After he had regained his breath, he turned to face the soldiers, who were all looking at him.

"Start digging," G commanded. He pulled a compass from his inventory, glanced at it, and then pointed toward the left wall of the room. "Aim that way. And hurry up, we don't have much time before the Noctems discover that we're gone."

The soldiers nodded and immediately began to tunnel into the ground, creating a sizable staircase down into the underground in a matter of seconds. G called over to a few soldiers to help him carry the shuddering Zombie villagers, who were slowly but surely becoming less and less green.

Two of them hoisted Mella up over their shoulders, while the other scooped up Stull in her arms.

As the last of the soldiers disappeared down into the tunnel, G gave a sigh of relief. He couldn't believe how well his plan had worked, and allowed himself a moment of self-congratulation. Then, he picked up a handful of loose cobblestones on the ground, descended into the tunnel, and placed the blocks back into the floor. The room was now identical to how it had looked just minutes before, save the absence of the two Zombie villagers who were nearly cured and en route back to Element City.

Lord Tenebris looked around the Element Castle council room, upon the stone-brick table of the Council of Operators. He found it odd that when Stan2012 had taken control of Element City, he had not destroyed the throne, which Lord Tenebris now sat on. Perhaps he had kept it as a reminder of King Kev's rule, so that the decisions that they made should never allow a monarch to rule Elementia ever again. In any case, Lord Tenebris couldn't help but feel an innate sense of contentedness sitting on the throne. He had waited so long, and worked so hard for this throne, that, no matter who sat on it, he knew that it would always truly be his.

The feeling of satisfaction only lasted for a moment, however, before Lord Tenebris's dormant rage swelled back up. As relieved as he was that the Noctem Alliance had now conquered the entire server of Elementia, it was still inexcusable that Stan2012 had not been located yet. Furthermore, although the citizen population within the city was locked in their houses under quarantine, it was obvious that not all of them were there. A good number of the Element City citizens had clearly escaped to somewhere.

The five-note doorbell, ringing out through the unseen note blocks, signaled that somebody was at the door. Lord Tenebris reached down to a button on the side of his throne and clicked it. Within seconds the redstone circuit executed its job, and the iron door swung open.

Through the open door frame marched eight figures. The five players dressed as hostile mobs, who Lord Tenebris knew to be called ELM, dropped their jaws in awe. Lord Tenebris was familiar with this reaction. It was typical for players to respond this way upon first laying eyes on him. He hardly cared about them, however. Lord Tenebris was far more focused on his generals, Drake, Tess, and Spyro, as they proceeded past the council table and knelt before him.

"Greetings, my generals," Lord Tenebris said unemotionally as he looked down upon them.

"Greetings, my lord," all three generals responded in unison, still looking down at the ground.

"First and foremost, I would like to congratulate you on

the work you have done," Lord Tenebris continued. "At long last, after months of planning, of struggling, and of toiling, we have done it. The Noctem Alliance has conquered Elementia. The dreams of King Kev have now been realized, and we are on the threshold of creating a perfect server, where those who have earned their place reign supreme, and the weak are in their equally rightful place. I could not have accomplished this vision without your undying loyalty."

"Thank you, my lord," all three generals replied again, their voices full of elation. To be directly praised and thanked by Lord Tenebris himself—it was more wonderful than they could have ever imagined.

"However," Lord Tenebris continued, his voice suddenly full of anger, causing all in the vicinity to look up in alarm, "the fact that we have accomplished so much is irrelevant next to the fact that Stan2012, his military leaders, and his council members are still at large! I will have you know that I blame each of you for this failure."

"My lord," Drake replied submissively, terror in his voice, "I assure you, I have been doing all that I—"

"Silence, Drake," Lord Tenebris hissed, and instantly, Drake stared back at the ground in shame, shaking in horror. "I shall get to you in a moment." First, he turned to face Tess. She had been looking up at him in respect, but now she looked to the side, finding it impossible to meet his empty, white eyes.

"I admit, Tess, that out of the three of you," Lord Tenebris spoke on, "it is you with whom I take the least umbrage. You have done a perfectly respectable job in your rearing of the new recruits, and during your time as a commander on the front lines, you were properly able to keep Element City under lockdown while I prepared the Withers for the final strike."

"Thank you, my lord," Tess replied, trying to sound as humble as possible.

"That does not excuse the fact," Lord Tenebris continued, "that the highway through the Nether has yet to be completed. I'm sure I don't need to reiterate how much easier it would be to find Stan if our soldiers could easily fast-travel all throughout the server."

"I apologize, my lord," Tess replied, sinking into a deep bow, "but it's been very difficult. The more troops that leave Nocturia to join the occupation of Element City, the longer work will be delayed. I've even forced the new recruits to mine for Nether quartz, rather than training them, so that I would have more soldiers available for construction of the highway."

"Do not expect any lenience from me, Tess. It's been over a month now!" Lord Tenebris said, not raising his voice, but still commanding enough power to echo throughout the council room. "Either force your people to work faster or I will make an example of you to inspire their work ethic."

Tess gulped in fear, but still managed to get out, "I understand, my lord. Thank you for your mercy."

"You, Spyro," Lord Tenebris continued, glaring down at Spyro, who shuddered as he forced himself to look up.

"I am extremely disappointed in you. The fact that four prisoners escaped from Fungarus and you were not able to stop them is unforgivable. I would think that after I gave Drake what he deserved for allowing the escape, you would do all in your power to ensure that they were captured."

Drake's face returned to a grotesque wince as he remembered the sheer agony that Lord Tenebris had put him through as punishment for his mistake.

"My lord . . . I apologize most dearly. I did send many of my forces out into the ocean to search for them . . . I would have sent all that I could, if I weren't preoccupied with the revolution on the Lesser Mushroom Island—"

"That is no excuse!" Lord Tenebris replied, glaring down at Spyro. "Your army should have no difficulty in subduing the ruffians of that island, especially after the Great Purge."

"Well, there was no trouble at first!" Spyro replied, his eyes wide with fear. "We kept the republic citizens as hostages, as you requested, while we hunted through the remains of the city for those Lesser Tribesmen who had escaped the Purge. But now, the republic citizens and the surviving Tribesmen have begun to fight back! They've rallied around a leader who calls herself Goddess Olea, and even though we've done all we—"

Spyro cut off in midsentence, and his hands flew to his throat. A small choking sound escaped his mouth, and Drake and Tess, who were watching him in horror, whipped around to face Lord Tenebris, who was leaning forward and glaring intently at Spyro. The white-eyed demon surveyed his prey with emotionless eyes as Spyro began to levitate into the air, his eyes bulging and his legs flailing.

"Perhaps you don't understand me," Lord Tenebris said in a deadpan as Spyro continued to struggle. "The rebellion in the Mushroom Islands *will* be eradicated in a timely manner. Do you understand, General?"

There was a moment of tense silence, broken only by the continued coughing and sputtering of Spyro. Then, a raspy "yes" managed to escape his throat, and Lord Tenebris relaxed his gaze, leaning back in his throne. The Noctem general crashed to the ground, lying still for a moment before finally raising himself onto shaking hands and knees, coughing and taking in deep breaths.

"Thank you . . . my lord . . . ," Spyro croaked, "for your . . . forgiveness . . ."

"Enough of your groveling, Spyro," Lord Tenebris replied lazily. Then, Lord Tenebris turned his head very slowly, until finally, his vacant white eyes landed on Drake, who cowered in dread.

"General Drake," Lord Tenebris said slowly. "I'm sure that you remember what I said, regarding what I would do to you if Stan2012 was not in my custody by the next time we met."

"My lord," Drake stammered, "I can explain—"

"Tread carefully, Drake," Lord Tenebris said, in a voice that was nearly a whisper, which was somehow ten times more terrifying than if he were yelling. "You're one wrong step away from feeling the full extent of my wrath."

"My lord, I beg you to hear me out," Drake pleaded, looking up at Lord Tenebris, forcing himself to look into his eyes, only to glance away a moment later before continuing. "I've been leading your invasion force during the entire campaign against Element City. I've graciously accepted the task of being your eyes and ears on the battlefield, and as a result, the entirety of Elementia is now under your command."

"That does not change the fact that Stan2012 is still at large," Lord Tenebris replied, a slight taunting sound in his voice.

"Please, my lord," Drake simpered on. "I've hired the most renowned assassin team in Elementia to hunt Stan2012 for me. If they've been unable to apprehend him . . . well, then I'm not sure what we're to do."

Lord Tenebris gave a slow nod and looked down at the floor, as if he were debating something in his mind. The entire room, especially Drake, waited with bated breath for him to speak. Finally, Lord Tenebris raised his head.

"You five, back there . . . come forward, please."

The three generals spun around to face the back of the room, and their eyes fell on the five mobhunters of ELM. The jaws of Arachnia, Enderchick, and Creeper Khan dropped to the floor. Lord Marrow's eyebrows raised slightly, while Zomboy's face lit up, like a teacher's pet who had just been called on in school. However, none of them hesitated in walking forward, around the council table, and standing in a line behind the three Noctem generals.

"You are the assassins that General Drake has hired to capture Stan2012?"

"Yes, sir," Arachnia replied, stepping forward and keeping remarkably well poised given how terrified she was to be speaking to this monster. "My name is Arachnia, leader of the Elite Legion of Mobhunters, the most renowned bounty hunters in Elementia."

"Indeed," Lord Tenebris replied, nodding slowly. "And you have encountered Stan2012 multiple times since you have started hunting him, yes?"

"This . . . is true, sir," Arachnia replied, recovering from her horror that Lord Tenebris knew this. "We have encountered Stan2012 twice since we started hunting him. Both times, he was joined by accomplices, and he managed to evade our grasp. As I'm sure you are well aware, sir, Stan and his friends are the highest-caliber fighters in all of Minecraft . . . regardless, we are still hot on the trail of—"

BOOOOM!

The massive explosion knocked Arachnia to the side and into Enderchick, while Creeper Khan tumbled to the ground. Lord Tenebris's hand was still pointed toward the spot where, just seconds before, Zomboy had stood next to Arachnia; there was nothing but a cloud of black smoke there now. Slowly, the smoke wafted away, allowing the seven players on the floor to stare in blank shock at the body of Zomboy lying dead on the stone brick floor, his items in a ring around him.

There was a moment of silence as nobody moved a muscle. The four remaining were unable to process the fact that their teammate, who had been modded to be twenty times as hardy as a normal player, had just been taken out in one shot. Lord Tenebris lowered his hand.

"Your services will no longer be required," Lord Tenebris said coldly. "Leave my presence now if you know what's good for you."

There was no hesitation. Within seconds the room was cleared of the four mobhunters, all of whom glanced down in disbelief at Zomboy's body before exiting through the door. Not a second after Creeper Khan left and closed the door behind him, the body of Zomboy vanished, leaving only his various items on the ground. However, even when the mobhunters were completely gone, the three generals still couldn't help but stare at the ring of items, jaws dropped and traumatized looks on their faces. In front of them, Lord Tenebris gave a satisfied smile.

Perhaps now they will take their work a little bit more seriously, he thought to himself.

"We are changing our tactics," Lord Tenebris announced, causing Tess, Drake, and Spyro to turn back toward him. "It's about time that we ended this war once and for all. Drake!"

"Yes, Your Glory?" Drake replied, bowing to the floor and looking up at him.

"I believe that it's about time that we reunite the people of Element City. You know where Mecha11, the police chiefs, and the rest of the population of Element City are hiding, correct?"

"Yes, indeed, my lord," Drake replied hastily, as if Lord Tenebris would be more impressed the faster he delivered the information. "They're located in a cave they dug below the city, and I know where the entrance is. It's in the side of a hill right outside this castle, as a matter of fact. I've known ever since—"

"Silence," Lord Tenebris ordered, to which Drake looked to the ground in shame. "It's time for action. Drake, prepare the troops in the city to lead an attack on the underground bunker. Spyro, return to the Mushroom Islands, and put down the resistance there within the next week. Tess, return to Nocturia, and order half your troops to march to Element City. Send the two villagers with them, and I'll send the third one your way, with whom I will expect you to start to create a massive army of mobs. You will have the troops here by tomorrow."

"But . . . my lord!" cried out Tess in surprise, as Spyro stared at Lord Tenebris in confusion. "I won't be able to transport all my troops to Nocturia in one day. Even if the highway through the Nether was completed, I couldn't do that! And it will take General Spyro at least three days to make his way to the Mushroom Islands . . ."

Lord Tenebris smiled. "Don't fret, my generals . . . Lord Tenebris would never ask something impossible of his underlings."

And with that, Lord Tenebris stood up from his throne and stretched out his hands: one toward Tess and the other toward Spyro. He closed his eyes, took a deep breath, and tightened his focus. Then, in one instant, his eyes flew open, and he released all the tension in his body. Tess and Spyro's bodies flashed for a moment, and then, in the blink of an eye, they were gone.

Drake glanced around wildly, trying to figure out what had happened. The thought that Lord Tenebris may have just killed his two comrades flashed across his mind, but just as he was about to let out a shout of horror, the sound of Lord Tenebris's voice echoed throughout the room.

"Do not concern yourself with them, Drake. I have merely used my abilities to transfer your two fellow generals to exactly where they needed to be. Tess is now in her office in Nocturia, while Spyro is in the Capitol Building of the Lesser Mushroom Island."

Drake's mind took a moment to comprehend what Lord Tenebris had just said, but as soon as he did, he stared up at him, awed by this incredible display of power. Lord Tenebris allowed Drake a moment of marveling before glaring down at him. The second his piercing white eyes met Drake's, the general cringed yet again.

"Now, go, Drake, and prepare the armies of Elementia for the invasion of the bunker. The end of war is near."

Drake gave a zealous nod of agreement, and with that, he stood up and was out the door of the council room within seconds, the iron door slamming shut behind him.

The stone-block command room was silent as the players filed in. Stan took a seat at the head of the makeshift cobblestone table as Kat, the Mechanist, and Commander Crunch sat down around the other sides. Ben, Leonidas, Cassandrix, and Sirus stood against the stone wall behind them, while

Bob sat beside his brother on Ivanhoe, Rex sitting obediently beside them. Only Charlie, who was getting his leg checked out by a medical team, was missing.

"First off," Stan said, as he looked around the room, meeting the eyes of each individual player, "I would like to say how happy I am to finally be back here with you guys. You're all like family to me, and there's nobody else that I'd rather be defending my home with than you. And even though . . . we've lost . . ."

Stan took a deep breath, and fought to retain his composure. Although this was the first time that he had spoken to this entire group since he returned to the mines, the knowledge of which of their comrades had fallen since they last met had spread through the group rather quickly. The memories of DZ, Bill, and so many more whose fates were unsure still lingered in his memory as he continued his speech.

" . . . and even though we've lost many brave players along the way, it is our duty to ensure that their deaths weren't in vain. Though it's true that during the course of this war, the Noctem Alliance has pushed us to the brink of extinction, one crucial fact remains true: *we're still here.*

"The republic—the *true* government of Elementia, which is willing to fight to the death to defend the principles of equality for all—is still alive and well. My friends, we are that government. And it's our mission to take back our city and once again turn Elementia into the place that its founders intended it to be. We have been hiding, defending, and running from the Noctem Alliance for far too long. The time has come, my friends, to fight back."

There were nods and murmurs of assent around the table, as looks of grim determination took to the faces of all in the vicinity. Everybody knew that what Stan was suggesting wouldn't be easy . . . or perhaps even possible. But they also knew that he was right. They couldn't hide forever, and sooner or later, they would have to retaliate.

"Ben, Bob," Stan said inquisitively, looking at the two police chiefs. "Do you have a prediction on how long it will be before the Noctem Alliance discovers this cave?"

"Well, I doubt that they'll find us anytime soon," Bob replied reasonably. "This bunker is pretty far underground, and it's far away from Element City's active mines. When we closed the bunker, the pistons shifted the dirt blocks to make the hill look totally natural, so they'd never recognize it as a mine entrance. You can thank the Mechanist's redstone designs for that."

Several players gave a nod of congratulations to the Mechanist, who glanced down at the table, as if he were embarrassed. Stan found this odd; the Mechanist had never had any false modesty regarding his redstone creations before (although he had never been excessively braggy either). In any case, it didn't matter. They had a game plan to assemble.

"Okay, I trust your judgment," Stan said to Bob, nodding in approval. "If that's the case, then we've probably got a little bit of time to get a plan together. Now, here's the question: What do we do?"

"Well, where's the best place in the city to strike?" Kat asked. "We have enough manpower down here to take at least part of the city back by force, and then at least we'll be above ground and have access to resources again."

"I don't think that will work," Ben replied gravely. "We've been sending spies out into the city to monitor the Noctem occupation, and it seems like they've formed some sort of impenetrable web across the city. Their military operations run like clockwork; if we try to invade part of the city at dusk, we'll have the entire force of the Noctem Army bearing down on us by morning."

"I have an idea," a voice came from behind the players. They turned around and saw Charlie. He hobbled across the room into his chair.

"What did TrumpetBlaster say about your leg?" Bob asked anxiously, as Ivanhoe gave a grunt from beneath him.

"I didn't go," he replied, a dark look on his face. "I heard that you guys were having a meeting to discuss what to do next, and I figured that I should be there. I'll go see him afterward. Anyway, did I hear you say that you're looking for an idea of how to take back Element City?"

Stan nodded. "What's your idea?"

"Well, what if we at least tried to sneak into the city under the radar?" Charlie asked, his face lighting up. "If we somehow managed to get a bunch of footholds all across the city—you know, like, take over houses in a bunch of different parts of the city—then we could launch an attack from all over the city at once."

"Negatory, sir," Bob said, shaking his head. "The Noctem Alliance would never let an operation like that go undetected. Their surveillance is incredible, and they have invisible troops stationed all over the city, on the lookout for anything suspicious. We can only send out one spy at a time because their security is so tight. We'd never be able to carry out an operation that big without them noticing."

"Now hold on a sec, I think Charlie's idea could still work!" Leonidas replied thoughtfully. "I mean, maybe if we were extra careful, and only let a few of our guys into the city at . . ."

"He said it wouldn't work, Leonidas, so drop it!" Charlie spat, glaring at Leonidas. All eyes in the room turned to Charlie, caught totally off guard by this alarming display of hostility. However, when Charlie looked up, his face showed nothing but crestfallen depression, and there was a collective, unspoken decision around the room to forget that it had happened.

Nonetheless, though the conversation continued, Leonidas found himself staring at Charlie. He had tried to be polite to Charlie, to try to get around whatever it was that he was holding against Leonidas. Clearly it wasn't working, leaving Leonidas to wonder if his efforts to befriend Charlie would ever pan out.

"So what should we do?" Charlie demanded, an urgent tone in his voice. "We need to get out of this stupid cave, and we have to do it fast! The Noctem Alliance is going to bust in here any—"

"Hold on a moment," Cassandrix cut in, her eyes lighting up and a smile crossing her face.

"What is it?" Stan asked, as the entire room turned to look at her.

"Charlie, you seem to be experienced in underground navigation," she said slowly, and Stan could see the gears whirring in her head. "How long do you think it would take to dig a tunnel to the Adorian Village from here?"

"I don't know," Charlie sighed, still looking crestfallen. "A couple days, maybe . . ."

"Then that's what we ought to do!" Cassandrix exclaimed. "We should dig a tunnel and invade the Adorian Village! They'll never be expecting that!"

There was a moment of silence as the idea sank in. Then, Ben spoke up.

"Cassandrix . . . that's brilliant! All of the Noctem Alliance's attention is focused on securing Element City. They'll never be prepared for an attack on the Adorian Village. And once we take control of the village, we can use the resources stored there to launch an assault on Element City!"

"Hold your horses, Ben," Bob cut in, turning to face his brother. "I think that this is a good plan, except for one thing. The citizens that we have down here in the mine aren't all soldiers. Not only that, but being down here for so long has done a number on them. Before we reveal ourselves, we have to be sure that those who aren't able to fight have somewhere safe to go. The second we invade the Adorian Village, it's going to turn into a combat zone."

"Well, why don't we just have them stay in the cave for now?" Kat suggested. "You just got through saying that the cave is probably gonna be safe for a while, Bob,"

"Uh . . . guys?" Charlie said slowly, sounding mortified, as if he were on the verge of divulging classified information. "I . . . um . . . *really* don't think that this cave is safe. I think that we should leave . . . like . . . as soon as physically possible."

"What are you trying to say, Charlie?" Leonidas asked, not sure that he wanted to hear the answer.

He was cut off by an earsplitting explosion.

The blast shook the walls. Seconds later, the sounds of terrified screams started to ring through the air, followed by a second explosion. Stan leaped to his feet and dashed onto the balcony, his friends hot on his tail.

He looked wildly around the basin of the cave and saw people running around panicking but no visible signs of damage. A third explosion rattled the cave, but yet again, Stan could see no damage.

"What's going on?" he yelled to his police chiefs, struggling to make himself heard over the sound of yet another explosion.

The two brothers sputtered in confusion, trying to piece together what was happening. Suddenly, a soldier burst onto the balcony through the door. Ben whipped around to face him.

"Private! What's going on here? What's the meaning of the explosions?"

The private gulped, took a deep breath, and spoke.

"It's the Noctem Alliance, sir. They've found us, and the Wither is blasting its way in."

Although the Wither's assault on the outer walls of Element City was nearly a week in the past, the fires continued to blaze on. There were still piles of loose stone-block rubble scattered around the perimeter of where the proud wall used to stand. The remnants of pistons and mechanisms scattered the ground, forming a barrier of rubble that served as a border to the city in its own right. Although the buildings adjacent to the wall within the city had taken some damage through the invasion and the subsequent fighting between the two armies, the outside of the wall had fared far worse.

A plain of stone and dirt blocks extended around what had once been the outer wall, expanding far out of sight until it finally connected to the untouched forest. This battlefield, blasted far below ground level by TNT cannons, still bore the scars of the fights that had raged at the wall for so long, and the four players who were now trekking through the silent plain had to avoid craters, blazing fires, and arrows stuck in the ground as they continued to hike hastily away from Element City.

The four members of ELM did not speak. Since they had watched Lord Tenebris strike down their comrade and then threaten to do the same to them, they hadn't stopped moving, running through the streets of Element

City until their legs ached. They continued to walk until, at last, they reached the outer wall. Crossing the threshold of the city into the war-torn biome beyond, the four mobhunters saw no reason to stop walking. After all, they had nowhere to go. It wasn't like they were aiming for anywhere in particular.

After trekking across hundreds of blocks of stone, the mobhunters finally reached a steep incline of dirt blocks, atop which sat the forest. Upon reaching the hill, they didn't break stride, opting instead to make their way up the hill using the path of least resistance, occasionally punching dirt blocks out of the way.

Arachnia reached the top first, and she turned around to watch her team scale the incline behind her. One look at their faces and Arachnia knew that it was time to take a rest. She jerked her head over to a clearing a ways into the forest, and without speaking, they walked over and proceeded to pull an assortment of spare blocks from their inventories to set up camp for the night. Creeper Khan placed a Netherrack block in the center of the clearing and stretched his hand out over it. A tiny explosion erupted in midair, just grazing the block enough that it caught fire.

The four players huddled around the makeshift campfire, and Arachnia reached into her inventory, a somber expression on her face that was reflected by the other members of ELM. She extracted four bottles, which were filled with liquid.

She was a bit disappointed that water was all they had, but it was better than nothing. The bottles were distributed around the fire in silence. As soon as everybody had one, Arachnia raised her bottle into the air. The others followed, and she took a deep breath, and let it out.

"To Zomboy," she whispered.

"To Zomboy," Creeper Khan and Enderchick mumbled in response, and Lord Marrow gave a grave nod of the head. The four glass bottles tilted back, and within a moment, all the water had drained. With nothing left in the capsules, the four remaining members of ELM bowed their heads in respect and pitched their bottles into the fire. The items burst into flames and disappeared an instant later, sending a shower of sparks into the sky.

"I still can't believe that he's, like, actually gone," Enderchick sighed, staring into the fire.

"Yeah," Creeper Khan grunted. "I mean, the guy got under my skin like nothing else, but it's hard to think that he's dead."

"Well, it's true," Arachnia replied, and the three other mobhunters looked up at her. "Zomboy *is* dead, and we've officially failed our biggest job ever."

There was a moment of silence as the four mobhunters let those facts sink in, the fire crackling and blazing in the background. Finally, Creeper Khan spoke.

"So . . . what're we gonna do now? We can't stick around here. You couldn't pay me to mess around with someone that powerful. Do we go back out into the desert?"

"Oh please, you can't be serious," Enderchick laughed darkly. "After losing a job that was, like, *this* big? We'd be total losers. There's no way I'm going back to that dump."

"Then there's only one thing to do," Arachnia replied.

"What?"

"We're gonna capture Stan2012 ourselves."

Enderchick and Creeper Khan stared at her, eyes wide, as if she'd gone insane. Even Lord Marrow, who was leaning against a nearby tree and examining his bow, looked up in surprise.

"Uh . . . . *scusi*?" Enderchick asked softly.

"Did I stutter?" Arachnia scoffed, standing up and looking down at her accomplices.

"Oh come on, Arachnia. You can't really—"

"Shut up!" she spat, causing Creeper Khan to growl in anger as she began to rant.

"We have put so much time and effort into finding this player. We've traveled all across the server. We've slept in caves and swamps, we've had to fight against some of the most skilled players in Elementia, and now we've lost Zomboy. Enderchick is right, there's no way that we can show our faces in the desert with any dignity without completing this mission, but it's become more than that. Drake sent us out on a mission, guys . . . and with everything that we've put into it, there's no way that I'm gonna back out now."

Arachnia's eyes were blazing with a fiery passion, and she spoke with such earnest fervor that the other three mobhunters couldn't help but realize that what she was saying was true.

"Now that you mention it . . . I was forced to sleep for, like, an entire week in a disgusting, icky, slimy suh-*wamp*," Enderchick groaned, shuddering in disgust at the memory before standing up alongside her leader. "It would be, like, a total shame if all of that was for, like, nothing. I'm with ya, girl—we've gotta find Stan."

"All right!" bellowed Creeper Khan, leaping onto his feet and pumping his blocky fist. "Let's show Drake who's in charge!"

As the three other mobhunters converged to develop a strategy for finding and capturing Stan, Lord Marrow looked toward them. He surveyed them for a moment, as they schemed away with zealous enthusiasm, bloodlust and vengeance in their voices. Then, he looked at the ground, shook his head in sadness, and went back to inspecting his bow.

"Take *this*!" Stan screamed, launching his fist in Sally's direction.

Quick as a whip, she feinted to the side, causing the

energy blast to hit the dirt blocks below in a massive explosion. Unfazed, Stan started throwing a blitz of rapid jabs, as Sally gracefully dodged the energy shots blasting the ground to rubble below her and started to fly directly toward Stan, weaving between his blows as she did so. Stan realized what she was doing, and summoned an axe to his hand. Sally somersaulted forward through the air, her sword slices turning the space around her into a globe of death as she rammed into Stan. With expert skill, he maneuvered his axe with incredible speed, blocking every sword attack she threw at him. However, he was totally unprepared when she delivered two final uppercuts, which left his stomach exposed and allowed her to combo into a kick.

The force of her foot on his stomach sent Stan tumbling backward, causing him to hit the ground so hard that he loosened the dirt blocks around him. Aware that he was in massive pain, Stan focused all his energy on feeling better. In an instant, he was healed, just in time to see Sally rocketing down toward him, sword outstretched and ready to deliver the final blow.

A split second before Sally's sword could impale him, Stan teleported to the side, causing Sally's diamond sword to plunge deep into the ground. Stan reappeared beside her, and used the brief moment of disorientation to launch a punch into her side. She flew through the air but landed safely on all fours, sliding across the dirt blocks in a trail of dust. Stan took a moment to catch his breath, and watched as her eyes, burning with determination, locked on to him for just a moment before she disappeared in midair.

The back of Stan's neck quivered in anticipation, and he spun around to counter the sword strike that Sally had launched from behind. As the two blades ground together, sparks flying from the point of contact, Stan and Sally both teleported at the same time. The duo warped through the air again and again, each desperately trying to outdo the other, but equally matched and continuously locked together. Before long, both realized that their efforts were futile and, in one motion, they pressed into the other's weapon, sending them flying apart. Stan and Sally teleported backward and simply hovered in midair.

Both players were staring each other down and breathing heavily. They each had a smile on their face that was one part exhilaration, one part frustration, and one part admiration.

"I gotta say, Stan, I'm impressed," Sally panted, giving a quick laugh as she tried to catch her breath. "I've taught you well."

"Well, every good student will one day surpass their master, Sal," Stan said with a devious grin. "And you're about to realize that right . . . *now*!"

And with that, Stan stretched out his hand and sent a

volley of fireballs from his palm toward Sally. *This is his grand finale?* She snickered to herself as she lazily raised her hand, conjuring a wall of bedrock to block the fireballs, which proceeded to hit the blocks and dissipate. However, without warning, Sally found that more and more bedrock blocks were appearing all around her, and before she could react, she found herself totally covered, unable to breathe and nearly unable to move.

Stan lowered his hand, looked at the cube of bedrock floating in the air a ways away from him and laughed out loud. *Ha.* He smirked. *She can't survive in there for long . . . I'll be seeing her respawn on the ground any second now . . .*

"I must admit, Stan," a voice rang out inside Stan's head, "that you managed to catch me off guard. You truly have become an operator worthy of the title. However . . . if I were you . . . I wouldn't count your chickens before they're . . . *hatched*!"

As she shouted, a roar rang out through the server as the sky turned black, an evil, terrifying roar that resembled the cries of the Enderman, elephant, and T-Rex all rolled into one. Stan recognized the roar, and gave an involuntary shudder as he realized what was about to happen. Then, the bedrock cube exploded, blocks flying everywhere as a giant pair of black wings opened wide, propelling a giant dragon, with a black hide and a silver exoskeleton, into the air. As the

Ender Dragon rose higher and higher into the sky with each beat of its mighty wings, Stan could only watch in stunned silence.

Aw, he thought to himself bitterly. *Why didn't I think of that?*

Underneath the rising dragon, Sally floated in midair, her hand pointed up toward the dragon and a wide grin on her face. She turned to face Stan, and their eyes locked for a moment. Then, Sally swung her hand forward, and the dragon took off like a jet plane, rocketing at top speed toward Stan.

Stan warped to the side, only to have the dragon make a tight U-turn and be on him again in seconds. Shocked, Stan warped again, axe raised and ready to assault the dragon, but the great black beast whipped its head to the side quicker than Stan could react, and he just barely managed to avoid a snap of its powerful jaw.

Stan was floored. This Ender Dragon was, for whatever reason, much more aggressive than the one he had fought in The End all those months ago. Stan continued to warp backward and out of range of the dragon's claws and teeth, sending dozens of fireballs from his hands, which peppered the dragon's face with miniature explosions. Nonetheless, the dragon didn't slow down, and Stan knew that it was only a matter of time before the monster landed a hit on him.

Suddenly, Stan had an idea. He warped away from the dragon (seeing Sally enjoying the show from a distance out of the corner of his eye) and, as it proceeded to speed toward him, he focused with all his might until a giant white mob appeared in midair in front of him. Stan warped to the side as the dragon collided with the Ghast in a flurry of shrieks, wails, roars, and explosions. Wasting no time, he proceeded to turn and face Sally, and reach his hand out toward her.

All at once, Sally felt herself unable to move. She focused as hard as she could on warping away, but she couldn't. She looked down in shock as Stan drew his hand slowly toward himself and, without warning, Sally rocketed toward him. A scream of surprise escaped her mouth as Stan dropped his axe to the ground below him and summoned a diamond sword, glowing red with enchanted heat, outstretched in his hand. Sally flew toward him, unable to do a thing about it as she collided with his sword, the blade impaling her through the chest and her body disappearing the instant the blade stuck through her back.

With his sparring match now over, Stan turned to face the dragon. The great monster was still recovering from its run-in with the Ghast, and it seemed out of sorts. Formulating a plan instantly, Stan proceeded to fly at top speed toward the dragon, sword outstretched beside him. As he flew past the dragon, the sword grazed the black hide, leaving a flaming cut on the monster's side, causing it to cry in agony. Not checking his speed at all, Stan proceeded to warp again, right next to the dragon, and landed another blow.

Stan rocketed around the dragon like a bug, repeatedly warping around it and dragging his sword across until the Ender Dragon was completely covered in trails of flame. Sensing that the Dragon was weak enough to finish, Stan proceeded to teleport directly under the monster and, aiming skyward, he stretched his sword out in front of him and burst through the dragon's neck swordfirst, leaving a large, gaping hole.

He took a deep breath and looked down at the dragon. The monster was frozen in midair. Stan watched as rays of light erupted from within the Ender Dragon until, finally, the monster exploded in a beautiful burst of light.

"Well done, noob," Sally smirked, applauding Stan as he levitated downward and landed next to Sally with the crunch of dirt block underfoot. "I admit it, I got too cocky. You fully deserve that victory."

"Well, you're not wrong," Stan replied smugly, a self-indulgent smile wide on his face. "That was a good warm-up. What've you got to show me today?"

Sally smiled and shook her head. "There's nothing else to show you, noob. Your training is complete."

Stan did a double take, and then stared at Sally, mouth

hanging slightly open. "Are you . . . are you serious?"

"Come on, noob, when am I not?" Sally replied again, conjuring a wool block beneath her and plopping down on it. "We've been working at it for weeks now, and I've finally shown you everything that I know. Ha . . . You know, I remember back when you really were just a noob . . . walking into the Adorian Village, training with me and the guys, and heading off to Element City for the first time. And look at you now. You're an *operator*, Stan."

An overwhelming feeling crashed over Stan. He didn't know how to describe it—it wasn't sad, but it certainly wasn't happy, either. It was as if, in that moment, the entire weight of how far he'd come crashed down on him like an avalanche. He remembered all that he'd learned . . . all the people he'd come to know . . . all those he'd lost . . . and all that he had left to do.

"Sally," Stan said, turning around to look at his teacher. "Do you . . . do you really think that I'm going to be able to beat Lord Tenebris?"

"You know, Stan, that's something that's really bothered me," Sally spat out in annoyance. "You know *who* Lord Tenebris really is. And you know what he's doing to Elementia, and thousands of other Minecraft servers, as we speak. He's the most evil and destructive force that Minecraft has ever faced, so the least you can do is call him by his real name."

Stan shuddered. It was true. He, along with the rest of his friends, had avoided calling Lord Tenebris by his true name. It just seemed that if they didn't say it, they wouldn't have to face it. They wouldn't have to face the reality of what they were going up against, what they had to destroy. Stan took a deep breath and spoke again.

"Fine. Sally, do you think that I'm going to be able to defeat Herobrine?"

Sally looked at the grass-block ground for a moment, and then looked up at him, an earnest look in her eyes.

"Stan, do you want my one-hundred-percent honest answer?"

"Yes."

"I don't know. I have no idea whether or not you're going to be able to beat Herobrine. I mean . . . something that has the ability to steal energy from the game of Minecraft itself . . . to put thousands of servers at risk . . . just to make itself stronger? If he can do *that*, then I can only guess what he's fully capable of, and I'm not sure if you're going to be able to defeat him, even if I do somehow manage to hack operating powers onto you in Elementia."

Stan felt like the air was being drained from his lungs, and he was forced to conjure a block below himself and sit. It hadn't even occurred to him that he probably wouldn't be able to get operating powers in Elementia at all . . . and that he was more than likely going to have to fight Herobrine without any aid, armed with only an axe. The Elementia Army had no plan to defeat Herobrine—in all their strategy talks, they had treated Herobrine like the elephant in the room. Nobody was willing to bring him up, terrified by the prospect of what he might be able to do. If Stan didn't get operating powers . . . they were all doomed. And even if he did . . .

"But I'll tell you one more thing, noob." Stan turned to face Sally, who was giving him an encouraging smile.

"If I had to pick anybody in Elementia to fight Herobrine, then I'd choose you in a heartbeat."

Stan smiled. For a while, they simply looked at each other. Nothing was said. Nothing was done. They just stared into each other's eyes, taking in the immense respect that they shared. Before long, though, Stan stood up.

"Well, I'd better go now. The tunnelers are probably under the Adorian Village by now, and they'll be getting ready for the attack."

Sally nodded. "Good luck, noob. I may not be sure if you can take down Herobrine, but I have no doubt at all that you'll be able to take back my hometown."

Stan gave a laugh as he nodded in agreement, but then, his face hardened. Stan focused, and once again, the words flashed in his mind.

DISCONNECT FROM SERVER?

"Yes."

"The preparations for the attack are all ready, sir," Sirus reported, standing in full salute and sounding official. "We're directly underneath the main street of the Adorian Village, and we're all ready to, you know, totally blow our way in and take out all the Noctem soldiers by surprise. Haha, they won't know what hit them!"

"Thank you, Sirus," Bob replied, nodding his thanks. "Please go and prepare the troops for the assault. I'll be there in a minute."

Sirus nodded and took off as Bob turned to his brother, who was sitting next to him alongside all the other Elementia leaders in the base of the cave. "Come on, Ben," he said, commanding Ivanhoe to walk away from the circle. "Let's inspect the troops. And get ready, guys, we're gonna launch the assault as soon as Stan gets back."

Bob and Ivanhoe walked away from the circle of players and toward a mass of troops farther down the tunnel. Ben followed them. Leonidas watched them go and looked around.

This cave wasn't a natural mine that had been expanded, like the bunker beneath Element City had been. This was a square-shaped tunnel, carved through the stone block underground by hundreds of miners, desperately digging as fast as possible to avoid the encroaching Wither that was blasting its way in, with Noctem troops not far behind. About twenty troops had stayed behind in the bunker to man the redstone traps that had been set up, and although the Noctems hadn't followed them into the tunnel they had dug out of the cave, they hadn't heard back from the troops either.

Leonidas, lost in his train of thought, suddenly realized that everybody was looking at something. He followed their line of vision and saw that everybody was staring at Sirus, who was conversing with the two police chiefs in his jittery fashion.

"I still can't believe that he's alive," Kat said.

"I still don't completely understand that," Cassandrix said, turning to face Kat. "Could you please explain to me what happened to him? And why everybody finds this so amazing?"

Kat was quite pleased to find that Cassandrix was talking to her in a civil manner. Although Kat tried to be pleasant toward her, Cassandrix only returned the attitude half the time, while reverting to her snappy, unbearable personality the rest of the time. Kat was glad to see that, today at least, she was being agreeable, and answered her question.

"You see, Cassandrix, Sirus was our redstone engineer

during the Battle for Elementia, when we first took down King Kev. That was back before the Mechanist joined us."

Hearing his name, the Mechanist looked up, revealing his tired and stressed face for a moment before returning to the book he was reading.

"Anyway, a lot of players died in that battle, and he was one of them. And even though none of us saw it, one of our friends named Archie said that he saw Sirus get killed in battle. Apparently, it happened right as the battle was ending, right before the castle tower blew up, in fact. We all thought that he was dead, and according to him, he was. Yet somehow, he managed to come back."

"I see," Cassandrix replied, looking mystified. "But . . . do you have any idea how? I mean . . . the server's difficulty is locked on Hardcore, and there's no way to change it unless King Kev himself did it. And even then, he gave up his operating powers! So there's no possible way that Sirus could have gotten back onto the server through simply respawning!"

"Yer guess be as good as any o' ours, lass," Commander Crunch responded solemnly, "but fer now, thar's no way t' know fer certain. More than likely, it had t' do wit' some sort o' glitch, but fer now, we 'ave more important thin's t' worry about."

There was a dark silence around the circle of leaders. They all knew that that was the understatement of the century. Nobody knew what to say. They all knew exactly what they were about to go into, and yet at the same time had no idea.

"I still can't believe that the Noctems managed to find us," muttered Kat.

"Why is that so surprising?" Charlie demanded defensively. "They've been inspecting every block of the city nonstop since they've broken through the wall. It's not *that* surprising that they've managed to find us!"

"Calm down!" exclaimed Kat, shocked by Charlie's aggressive tone. She had no idea what had come over him since they had rescued him from the prison on the Mushroom Islands, but Kat didn't like it one bit. She had expected that by now he would be back to his normal, friendly, soft-spoken self, but if anything he had only gotten worse.

"What I meant," Kat continued cautiously, "was that Ben and Bob have been sending spies out into the city, to see how close the Noctems were to finding us. According to the intelligence they gathered, the Noctems were doing most of their searching in the Merchant's District, on the total opposite end of the city. If that's true, then it makes no sense that they managed to discover us here so quickly."

"Well, however it came about, th' attack couldn't 'ave come at a worse time," Commander Crunch replied darkly. "We 'ave t' act fast, now that th' Noctems know where we be, 'n' we 'ave no time t' put together an actual invasion plan. We be forced t' jus' rush willy-nilly into th' Adorian Village, 'n' hope that this cockamamie assault wit' no thought put into it somehow works."

"You're right," growled Leonidas in disgust. "Why couldn't the Noctems have broken in, like, just two or three days later? That would have made everythin' *so* much easier!"

Suddenly, Charlie leaped to his feet, prompting all to turn toward him. He looked distressed and mortified, and it seemed as if he were on the verge of tears. For a moment, nobody moved as Charlie looked like a deer in the headlights of his friends' concerned looks. Then Charlie turned around and marched away from the circle without a word, a sob escaping his mouth as he limped down the tunnel.

"Wha' be his problem?" Commander Crunch asked incredulously as he turned to look at his comrades, and saw that nobody had the slightest idea what was wrong with him.

"I'll be right back," Leonidas said determinedly and, before anybody could stop him, he stood up and took off down the tunnel after Charlie.

"What do you want?" demanded Charlie as Leonidas caught up to him, weaving around a group of soldiers pulling on diamond armor as he went.

"I wanna know why you're so upset, man," Leonidas said straightly. "You've been totally out of it ever since we met up, and you seem like you're upset with me. Listen, dude, I know I haven't really known you for long, but it's pretty obvious to me that you've got somethin' going on."

"Oh it is, is it?" Charlie spat, looking beyond outraged. "Well, thank you for noticing!"

"Charlie, listen . . . I know that your injury has been bothering you—"

"Shut up!" Charlie bellowed at the top of his lungs, causing all in the vicinity to turn and stare at him. "Just shut up and go away! I don't want you to be here! Just . . . *leave*!"

And Charlie took off, hobbling down the mine as fast as he could, crawling under the nearest outcrop of rock that he could find.

Leonidas took a deep breath. Although he could feel his frustration at Charlie's attitude boiling in his stomach, he knew that in this case, he had to be the bigger man. From what Stan had told him, Charlie was usually calm, collected, and even timid. In other words, miles from what he had just witnessed. Something was very wrong, and Leonidas was going to find out what.

Slowly, he crept over to the edge of the cave, to the outside of the stone-block dimple in the wall. As he peeked into the crack, he was surprised to see that Charlie was actually crawling awkwardly out of the hole. Leonidas stepped back as Charlie grabbed on to the cave wall and pulled himself to his feet, bearing his full body weight on his good leg. He looked up at Leonidas, eyes still slightly red, but a tired, apologetic look on his face.

"Sorry," Charlie mumbled, unable to meet Leonidas's eyes. "Look at me, what I've become . . . screaming, throwing a fit, running away and hiding in a cave . . . pathetic . . ."

"Charlie, I know that ya don't think highly of me," Leonidas said hastily, unwilling to acknowledge that what Charlie had just said was true. "Maybe you're having a hard time forgivin' me for the things I did in the past . . . maybe it's something else I did, I dunno. But trust me, man . . . I'm not just some idiot who's only good for a fight, I've got a brain, too, and I've seen a lotta crap since I've joined Elementia. If you're willing to talk, I wanna do what I can to help ya. So please, Charlie . . . can ya tell me what's wrong?"

Charlie sighed. "I don't have a problem with *you*, Leonidas. . . . Well, I mean, I do, but it's not a real problem. It's totally unfair to you, and I know that. . . ."

"Tell me."

"It's just . . . ever since you joined us, you've been nothing but amazing. You've helped us fight, you've talked with us, you've become a part of our group. Everybody loves you, and I was just really jealous of that—the fact that you've done terrible things in the past, but you're one of our greatest assets now. For me, it's exactly the opposite. I mean, look at me. I can barely walk, let alone fight, and . . . since I was imprisoned, I've really hurt our cause. And now there's nothing I can do to fix it."

"What're you talking about?" exclaimed Leonidas, taken aback. "I mean . . . okay, man, I'm gonna level with you. Since we've met, ya haven't been very helpful to us in the fightin' department, but you've done other stuff! I mean, it was your idea to tunnel under the wall to get into Element City! Where's this idea that you've done more bad for us than good comin' from?"

Charlie looked Leonidas in the face. "Leonidas, can I tell you something? And if I do, do you swear you won't tell anybody else?"

"Sure, man," Leonidas replied, genuinely concerned now. "What is it?"

Charlie took a deep breath. There were tears streaming down his face, and his features expressed more pain and disappointment in himself than Leonidas had ever seen. There was a moment of silence, only broken by the scuffle of troops down the cave preparing for battle, as Charlie prepared to reveal his darkest secret.

"I'm the reason that the Noctem Alliance found this cave. I told Drake where the entrance was when he was torturing me on the Mushroom Islands."

Leonidas's jaw dropped. He looked at Charlie, hardly able

to believe what he had just heard, as Charlie rambled on, sobs interspersed with his choked-up speech now.

"I didn't want to. . . . I held out for as long as I could, trying to endure the pain that those savages put me through in that prison. The last thing I wanted was to give them what they wanted, our secret war plans . . . but then they started on my legs . . . it was unbearable, Leonidas. They forced my legs into a pit full of silverfish and told me that the only way out was to tell them where the secret bunker was . . . the little monsters started to chew at my legs, gnawing away . . . it was too much, I had to make it stop. . . . so I told them.

"I should've held out. I should've died, rather than to tell them where the bunker was. I mean, Crunch held out fine. He just shook it off, the way I couldn't. . . . And now, because of me, we're all in danger. They forced us to move before we were ready, and throw together this half-baked assault that'll cause who knows how many of our fighters to die. And I can't even fight on the battlefield alongside my friends to make up for my mistake."

As Charlie finished, Leonidas stared at him. He was utterly speechless. There was no anger in the stare, no exasperation, not even shock. Only sympathy shone on Leonidas's face as he absorbed everything that Charlie had just told him.

Charlie said nothing. He looked down at the ground

again, gave a heavy sigh, and proceeded to limp away from the crack in the cave wall toward Ben and Bob, leaving Leonidas standing alone.

"Look at them all."

"I'm sorry?" Cassandrix replied, looking up from the iron boots she was pulling on to look over at Kat, who was already armored up with Rex sitting beside her, watching a large group of players load up their own gear. Judging by their mostly leather armor, they were lower-level players. Despite the fact that the army had distributed the armor for the battle, it had somehow occurred that the lower-level players had gotten the weaker armor (not that Kat or anyone else had time to fix this inequity).

"I can't believe that those players are being forced into combat," Kat replied sadly.

"They haven't been forced!" Cassandrix replied vehemently. "Bob and Ben have made it very clear that only the soldiers are required to take part in the invasion. All others are volunteers. Those players wouldn't be part of the invasion if they didn't want to be."

"Yeah, well, they might as well have been forced into it," Kat spat in disgust. "I mean, sure, we didn't outright say that they had to, but what would happen if we lose? What would happen to the lower-level players? What would they have to come back to? Face it, Cassandrix, those players aren't fighting because they want to. They're fighting because they're afraid of what will happen if they don't."

"Honestly, darling," Cassandrix laughed, rolling her eyes. Kat's ears perked up in alarm, as they did whenever Cassandrix used the word *darling*. "You're acting like putting lower-level players into combat is the worst thing in the world . . . as if the little brats shouldn't have to fight, just because they're new and inexperienced. Well, Kat, darling, I have a question for you: If they don't fight, then however are they going to *gain* experience?"

There was a moment of silence as Kat stared at Cassandrix.

"Exactly," Cassandrix continued. "You need to stop holding the hands of the lower-level players, Kat, or they'll never learn anything for themselves. Why, I never had a group of upper-level players looking after me when I first joined Elementia—there *were* no upper-level players! But did that stop me from taking part in the Terramist War? No, of course not! I fought that war, and in doing so, not only did I help to establish the original Kingdom of Elementia, but I also learned the skills of Minecraft by myself!"

Cassandrix looked smugly at Kat, as if positive that there would be nothing that Kat could say that would pass over her insurmountable wall of logic. However, Kat merely returned a knowing smile.

"So, let me get this straight, Cassandrix: You took part in a war when you were a new player, and that's how you learned to fight so well?"

"That is correct, dear."

"Okay, okay. And Cassandrix . . . during that war . . . how many times did you die, and spawn back in your warm, comfortable bed?"

"Well . . . to be honest, there was more than one time that I found myself dead, and respawned."

"And if you were in that same scenario today—if you were a new player, and you took part in a war with no combat experience—what would happen to you if you died?"

There was no reply. They both knew what happened if a player was killed in Elementia today.

"Cassandrix, I have no problem with the way that you learned how to play Minecraft, and I even see where you're coming from," Kat said pointedly, "but the world has changed. The rules of the server are different from when you were a new player. If new players today make one wrong move, they'll be kicked out of Elementia with no second chance, so I don't see the harm in helping them out a bit. Just keep that in mind."

And with that, Kat stood up and walked down the tunnel toward the makeshift armory, Rex following behind her, leaving a speechless Cassandrix in their wake.

All throughout the night, preparations went on for the inva-sion of the Adorian Village. By morning, everyone was ready. All leaders, soldiers, and volunteers were brimming with armor and weaponry. Charlie was staying behind in the cave, to watch over those players who didn't have enough armor, or were too weak from hunger to fight. At the break of dawn (according to the single golden clock that somebody had managed to take into the underground with them), the fighting forces of Elementia congregated around a section of cave wall. This particular wall was covered with ladders leading up to the roof of the cave. The group of players was clustered around one specific ladder, which had been desig-nated the night before.

Before long, a cheer erupted from the crowd. President Stan was climbing the selected ladder, and when he reached the halfway point, he jumped off and onto a nearby ledge of coal ore blocks that was jutting out from the wall. He was wearing a smile ear to ear. In the night, a wonderful, unex-pected surprise had befallen them, which he was happy to share with his citizens who were as of yet unaware.

"My citizens, at long last, the day that we've been await-ing for weeks is finally here. In a few minutes, we will burst into the Adorian Village, swarm the streets, and drive the forces of the Noctem Alliance out, taking a giant leap toward returning control of Elementia to its rightful, elected rulers!"

Another round of applause and shouts of admiration erupted from the crowd.

"I cannot thank you enough for your patience, endurance, and valor, my citizens. I am fully aware of how difficult your lives have been since the Noctem Alliance declared war on Elementia months ago. However, by the end of today, all our pain and toil will finally come to fruition when we raise the colors of Elementia over the Town Hall of the Adorian Village!

"Now, my citizens," Stan continued, the roar of the crowd dying instantly as they realized he had more to say, "I have a very exciting announcement. In the middle of the night, a very special player came to us. He arrived in our cave after trekking for days across the server, avoiding Noctem forces, and taking another few days to find the entrance to our cave. He is a good friend of mine, and a loyal leader of yours. Ladies and gentlemen, please welcome back Councilman Jayden!"

The applause rumbled through the cave as Jayden climbed up the ladder and took his place on the ledge next to Stan. It was amazing, he thought, that so many of the people were happy to see him. Most of them hardly knew who he was, yet they were as excited to see him as Stan, Kat, Charlie, and the others had been the previous night. He supposed that

that was simply an added benefit of being friends with Stan.

"Okay now, everybody be quiet!" Stan commanded, and the crowd immediately complied. "Councilman Jayden has agreed to join our assault as a general, even after his long journey. As such, you are to do what he says and follow his commands the same as you would myself or any of my comrades. Now, prepare to mobilize, troops. When I give the signal, swarm up the ladders, through the ground, and into the streets!"

And with that, Stan climbed up the ladder, Jayden directly below him, ascending higher and higher toward the roof of the cave and leaving the electric energy of the troops below him as he vanished into the dark belfry of the cave.

After Stan had been totally enveloped by the darkness in the upper dome of the cave, it wasn't long until he reached the ceiling above him. He looked upward and aimed a punch at the block directly overhead. The sound of his fist on the wooden block reverberated through the spacious cave, sending the scattered bats that had been nesting in the darkness flying down to where he had just come from.

Stan looked down at Jayden, who was still clinging to the ladder beneath his feet. "Give me the potion," he ordered.

Jayden complied, reaching into his inventory and handing it up to Stan, who pocketed it carefully. Aside from the joy that Jayden's return had brought to Stan and his friends, they were also elated that he had managed to sneak a few potions out of Nocturia. The Potions of Slowness, in particular, were of vital importance to the first part of their plan.

Stan drew out a diamond axe, and for a moment, he allowed himself to relish in the feeling of completion that washed over him as he held his choice weapon back in his hand. DZ's diamond sword (now sitting in a chest in the mine; he had plans for it later) had served him well on his odyssey to return to Elementia, but there was no feeling in the world like having an axe clutched in his hand. Wasting no more time, Stan drew back the axe and shattered the wood block above him in two strokes.

He pulled himself up and through the opening and found himself in the main room of a house. Stan grinned. Charlie's aim had been spot on when he had calculated where to dig the hole. Stan turned around and pulled Jayden out of the hole, and they surveyed the house. It was plain, with hardly any outstanding features, just a cobblestone counter with a dispenser on it, some potted plants, and wood plank–block walls with glass window panes. Outside the windows, Stan could see the streets of the Adorian Village.

This was Stan's first time in the village since it was reopened, and very little had changed in that time. After the Battle for Elementia, Stan had immediately delegated a team to rebuild the burned-down village. It looked largely the same now as it did then—houses similar to those in an NPC village, gravel roadways, and a brick Town Hall in the center. However, there were two major differences that struck Stan as he surveyed the village in the early light of dawn.

The first was the wall. Thinking that it was wise to defend the village against any more attackers, Stan had ordered a cobblestone wall to be built around the village, fortified with the Mechanist's redstone defenses (though not nearly as impenetrable as the Element City wall had been). Stan could see the top of the wall over the houses of the village. Several Noctem troopers were patrolling the top of the barricade, their black armor silhouetted against the sunrise. That was the second change. Even at this early hour, Stan could see Noctem soldiers standing guard at the corners of the stone-block sidewalks, and platoons of troops marching through the streets.

Suddenly, Stan became acutely aware of footsteps over his head. He turned around just as a player burst into the room from up a flight of wooden stairs that he hadn't noticed before. This player was skinned as if she was planning on attending a disco party, with a tie-dye shirt, pink shorts, and rainbow tights. The bright colors bore a sharp contrast to the black tunic on her head.

"Who do you think you—" she started to demand, but was cut off when the bottle of potion Stan had thrown shattered on her face. Slowly, her eyes slid out of focus, and a slurred "intruders" slid out of her mouth before she slumped to the ground, unconscious. Stan was relieved that the potions Jayden had snagged were so strong; they had plenty of time to take her back down into the mine and imprison her until the battle was over.

Stan gestured to Jayden, who hoisted the limp body of the unconscious player over his shoulder and descended back into the mine. Moments later, he reemerged, and a line of other players followed him up the ladder and into the house.

"Charlie's got her in a holding prison, along with all the others we had to knock out," Jayden said to Stan. "Phase one went off without a hitch. We now have troops in houses all over the village, and when you give the signal, we attack."

Stan was beside himself. He couldn't believe that the plan was progressing so flawlessly. He reminded himself to thank Charlie the next time they met up; without his amazing mining prowess, they never would've been able to calculate so precisely where to make the tunnels. Stan's only regret was that they hadn't been able to dig under the Town Hall, which was their primary target—the floor was made of obsidian. However, that was a minor concern. With an ambush this size, Stan was confident that they would be able to overpower the Noctem forces; after all, most of them were still in Element City, according to their spies.

He realized, with a start, that he was being watched; the eyes of all soldiers in the room were fixated on Stan, awaiting his command. Stan took a deep breath and drew his axe. The time had come to take back the Adorian Village.

"Give the word to start the assault!" Stan bellowed down into the hole they had just climbed out of.

"Roger that!" Charlie's voice echoed up out of the mines.

Within seconds, Stan could hear yells and shouts outside, immediately followed by the clash of blades and a series of explosions. With a war cry, the soldiers in his house rushed out the door, Jayden at the helm. With one last deep breath, Stan let out his own battle cry as he charged out into the streets.

It was pandemonium. The Noctem soldiers in the city were totally blindsided, completely unprepared to deal with a wave of over a hundred republic fighters at once. Many drew their weapons to fight, only to instantly be killed by the republic soldiers, whose adrenaline levels had been inflated to the maximum in anticipation of the attack. Most of the Noctems realized that there was no sense in fighting, and instead fell back toward the center of the city, as if the Town Hall was a huge magnet that was drawing them in.

"Don't follow them!" Stan cried out, as his soldiers sprinted back and forth around him as if he were standing in the center of a highway during rush hour. "Spread out and occupy the streets! We need to establish a presence across the entire village if we're going to secure it!"

Stan looked around, and his eyes landed on Kat, who was busy telling her troops where they were to go. He jogged over to meet her.

"Hey!" he panted as he reached her. "So far so good, I'd say."

"Yeah," she agreed as she looked around, surveying the distribution of the republic troops through the streets. "We're lucky this village isn't very big. There aren't that many streets to occupy."

"True," Stan said hastily. "Come on, we've got to hurry. They're all falling back to the Town Hall. That's probably where they're going to mount most of their defenses. We've got to get over there fast, before they dig in their heels too deep."

"Right," Kat nodded. "You grab a group of players and get to the Town Hall. I'll grab everyone else to help you."

"Sounds good!" yelled Stan, already taking off to a mass of troops. They were standing in the middle of the road, weapons drawn, on standby and waiting for orders from the commanders.

"Come on!" Stan cried, and all the fighters turned to look at him. "Follow me to the Town Hall!"

The giant mass of players proceeded to run behind Stan as he hustled down the main road of the Adorian Village. All the houses now appeared to be empty, and the streets were deserted except for Stan and his men as they rushed into battle. Before long, they burst into the town square and laid eyes on the Town Hall.

The brick-block structure stood proudly in the center of the Adorian Village; while not a particularly tall building, it still towered over the other structures in the humble town. Stan watched as the last of the Noctem troops rushed through the iron double doors of the building. When the last of them had entered, the doors slammed shut, and the whir of red-stone mechanics began to hum in Stan's ears. An instant later, the gravel around the base of the brick building sunk down, revealing a moat of lava ten blocks thick that stretched around the entirety of the Town Hall.

Stan was simultaneously impressed and infuriated. The Noctems had clearly been well trained in what to do in case of a surprise attack, and it wouldn't surprise him if the interior of the Town Hall was laced with booby traps, making it extremely difficult to break into.

Suddenly, alarm bells went off in his head as Stan realized that the Noctems were now standing on top of the Town Hall. Bows were drawn, fire charges and potions were held in their hands, and TNT cannons were being aimed down at Stan and his men, loaded and prepared to fire. However, Stan's eye was immediately drawn to the men who were standing with buckets of molten lava. All together, they tipped over their lava buckets, attaching source blocks of lava to the outside of the building. An infinite flow of lava began to rush out of the source blocks, pouring down the side of the Town Hall and eventually into the lava moat below.

The Town Hall now stood surrounded in lava, the molten liquid covering the base in an impenetrable wall of liquid fire. Stan had to give credit where credit was due; this was a superb plan. He certainly wouldn't be able to get in there without the fight of his life.

"Stan! What happened here?"

Stan turned around and saw Kat, Rex, Leonidas, Commander Crunch, Cassandrix, the Mechanist, Ben, and Sirus, with the entire invasion force behind them. All were staring in awe at the giant cube of molten liquid that was the Town Hall.

"I'll tell you what happened," Stan replied gravely. "They've just set up one of the best defenses I've ever seen. I have no idea how we're going to get in there now."

"Aye, leave it t' me, laddies," Commander Crunch growled, a grin on his face and a manic glint in his eye. "I've seen this before. I know how we be gettin' past that wall o' lava."

"You've seen this before?" Ben demanded incredulously.

"Eleven times, as a matter o' fact. Now *charge*!"

And with that, Commander Crunch drew his sword and rushed forward, directly toward the lava moat. A large chunk of the mass of troops broke off and followed after him, charging directly toward the bastille of fire. It wasn't long before arrows and fire charges started to rain down from the roof into the mass of oncoming troops, and the blasts of the TNT cannons started to follow.

"Come on, let's cover him!" Cassandrix cried, and with that, all the remaining troops drew their bows, and started to rain arrows onto the roof of the Town Hall. As they did, the fire from above spread out, now reaching them as well as Commander Crunch's troops. Stan's soldiers found that they had to spread out and encircle the Town Hall, so they could continue with their suppressive fire and not be a massive target.

"This would be so much easier if we could just blow our way in there," the Mechanist said, as he let loose another arrow. He turned to Ben, who was fighting next to him. "I don't suppose anybody has any TNT or redstone on hand?"

"No," Ben said back, harsher than the Mechanist was expecting. "We used it all up while we were making the bunker." He drew another arrow, targeting the operator of one of the TNT cannons on the roof. He fired his bow, only to miss.

"Not that you would know," he grumbled under his breath as he loaded another arrow. Though it was soft, the Mechanist heard this, and gave a great sigh as he loaded another arrow.

Commander Crunch's men were nearly at the wall of the Town Hall now. They had pulled cobblestone blocks out of their inventory and were building a narrow bridge across the lava moat. Each time one of the soldiers was hit by an arrow and knocked into the lava, another would step forward to take his place. Commander Crunch stood at the front, sword drawn, spinning it around like an expert as he deflected the arrows that were flying out of the lava flow and directly at them. Although these arrows made building the bridge very difficult, Commander Crunch was glad that the Noctem Troops were firing at them from within the building. If they weren't, he would never be able to figure out where the doors were, as they were hidden behind the flow of lava.

Finally, the bridge reached the wall. Commander Crunch spun his sword around like a helicopter, deflecting all the arrows that he could, and even then allowing some to glance off his iron chestplate or fly back into the horde of soldiers behind them. This created an opportunity for a soldier behind him to reach up and place two cobblestone blocks on the wall above Commander Crunch's head. Instantly, the lava parted over the two blocks and was diverted to the sides, opening up a gap in the lavafall. Behind the gap were two open iron doors through which the arrows were flying.

The second the doors were no longer covered by lava, a flow of Noctem troops started to flow out to attack Commander Crunch and his men. Sensing that now was the time to help, Stan shouted an order back to his men and sprinted toward the cobblestone bridge. As he ran across the open gravel road, the firestorm of arrows, fire charges, and TNT blocks intensified, but Stan pressed onward, knowing that all they had to do was get inside the building to escape the onslaught from above.

Finally, they reached the bridge, and didn't break pace as they dashed down the two-block-wide cobblestone passage. As they approached the Town Hall, Stan could see the fighting going on inside, but he could also see something that made his heart stop. There, sitting at the end of the bridge alongside the inventories of those who had been killed, lay Commander Crunch, his hand clenched to his stomach and his shattered iron chestplate beside him. Stan gestured for the rest of his men to sprint inside and join the fight, but he knelt down beside Commander Crunch.

"Are you okay?" Stan asked desperately.

"Aye, lad, I'll be fine," Commander Crunch grunted with a grimace. "'Tis jus' a flesh wound . . ."

"Here, let me see it . . ."

Commander Crunch winced as he moved his hands away from his stomach, revealing a gash that appeared to be from a sword slash. Stan's heart started to race; they had no medical supplies on hand to heal him with.

"Stan, go on 'n' fight," Commander Crunch said in a surprisingly hearty voice. "I promise ye, I'll live. I've survived worse than this. I'll jus' stay here till ye can find me some medicine."

Still worried, yet also reassured by Crunch's insanely upbeat demeanor, Stan nodded and took off into the Town Hall, leaving the wounded commander in his wake.

The fighting in the main hallway of the Town Hall was intense. While the Noctem troops were vastly outnumbered, they were also far better equipped. Stan's eyes locked on to one Noctem soldier who let loose a Splash Potion of

Weakness, causing all five republic soldiers he was fighting to wince and fall to their knees.

Right as the soldier was about to finish them off, Stan intervened, catching the soldier off guard and knocking his diamond pickaxe out of his hand, and sinking his diamond axe into his chest in the next swing. Stan's soldiers, still dazed by the potion, looked up at him gratefully. Stan called another soldier from down the hall to defend them until the potion wore off.

Stan looked around, and before long, his eyes caught sight of Kat. She was just making her way into the Town Hall, fighting off an attacking Noctem soldier as she did so. It wasn't long before she stuck her diamond sword in the player's chest and burst into the hall, Jayden right behind her. Stan dodged and weaved through the fights going on around him to meet up with them.

"We're gonna need more soldiers in here if we're gonna overpower them!" Stan cried out.

"We can't get any more in right now!" Kat cried out over an explosion from somewhere above them, as Rex tackled a Noctem soldier who jumped out at her. "They're laying down too much suppressive fire for us to get any more troops into the building!"

"Then we've gotta take out those archers and TNT cannons!" Stan replied, turning around and setting his eyes on a stairway at the end of the main hall. "Come with me! You, too, Jayden!"

Kat and Jayden nodded and followed Stan down the hall. A few Noctem troops tried to attack the three councilmen, but the trio made short work of them. As they reached the staircase, Stan turned around and saw that more and more Noctem troops were pouring out of the side doors in the hallways and joining the battle; the republic troops were getting slaughtered. Stan took a deep breath and, telling himself that shutting down the Noctems on the roof was the only way to save his people, he sprinted up the staircase, Kat, Rex, and Jayden following behind him. He turned a few corners, ignoring the doors that were next to the stairs on the way up, and before long he burst onto the roof. What he saw made his jaw drop in shock as Rex started to whimper.

The roof of the Town Hall was covered with dead players. Fallen bodies were despawning all around, leaving piles of items in their wakes. Bows, arrows, potions, and fire charges were scattered haphazardly around the outside edges of the brick-block floor, and the brick TNT cannons sat unmanned. There were no Noctem troops at all remaining on the roof. Instead, standing in the midst of the carnage were the members of ELM. Arachnia stood staring at Stan with a wild grin on her face, while Creeper Khan and Lord Marrow stood menacingly behind her.

Stan panicked; he hadn't been expecting them to be here, and he knew that the three of them couldn't take down these assassins alone. He turned around, ready to sprint back down the stairs. Just as he took his first step, there was a burst of purple smoke between him and the stairs as Ender-chick appeared, an amused look on her face and a diamond sword raised. The three players and the wolf were trapped on the roof.

Instinctively, Stan, Kat, and Jayden all drew their weapons, and stood back to back, Rex in between them, snarling. Stan was looking at Arachnia.

"What's going on here?" Stan demanded, glaring at Arachnia and trying not to let on how terrified he was of a four-on-three fight against these modded players. "Why are all the Noctem troops dead?"

"Why, we killed them, of course," Arachnia replied with a chuckle, drawing her diamond sword and examining her reflection in it nonchalantly.

"What? Why would you—"

"Because, Stan, we are no longer under the employment of the Noctem Alliance. You've managed to slip out of our grasp enough times that Lord Tenebris dismissed us."

She gave a sly chuckle. "Just think how foolish he's going to feel when we capture you before he does."

"If you want him, you're gonna have to go through us

first!" Kat shouted, brandishing her sword, as Jayden gave a hearty nod of agreement and Rex gave an aggressive bark.

"Well, if you insist!" Creeper Khan exclaimed as he aimed a punch in midair directly at Stan. He recognized this motion from his training with Sally, and he instantly knew what was coming.

"Get down!" he bellowed, tackling Kat and Jayden out of the way as the ground beneath them exploded, leaving a gaping hole in the brick-block roof of the Town Hall, through which people could be seen battling below.

"Stop that!" Arachnia yelled, whipping around to face Creeper Khan. "Stan has to be alive. You've got to be more careful! Leave him to me and Lord Marrow . . . Enderchick, help him take out the other two."

And with that, Enderchick raised her diamond sword and charged at Jayden, the closest target, while Lord Marrow drew an arrow in his bow and fired it at Stan's heart.

Stan leaped forward and deflected the arrow, just as Jayden locked his axe with Enderchick's sword, while Kat and Rex turned to face Creeper Khan. The arrow fell to the ground, and Stan could see that it was smoking. His eyes widened as he realized that the arrow must have been hacked to have the effect of a Potion of Weakness; if one hit him, he would fall unconscious. He knocked another arrow to the side with his axe, then raised it yet again to counter the diamond sword that Arachnia had jabbed at him.

Two blades clashed over and over, but Stan was surprised to see that Arachnia was hardly trying to attack him at all. Rather, she seemed to launch a quick strike, and when Stan blocked it, she would dodge his counterattack and move around until she saw another opening, not even trying to follow up. On one such strike, Stan saw that her sword, too, was trailing gray smoke. Stan was shocked, and suddenly realized that if either Lord Marrow or Arachnia landed one hit on him, he would be knocked unconscious.

And Lord Marrow was continuing to fire at him. It was nearly impossible to block his arrows while fighting Arachnia at the same time, and even with Stan's legendary fighting skills, there were still too many close misses for comfort. Stan knew that it was only a matter of time before one of them got lucky, and he had to find a way to stop it.

A risky idea popped into his head, and, not seeing any alternatives, Stan decided to go for it. The next time Arachnia emerged for a sword strike, Stan countered, but didn't let her go. Instead, he pressed into her blade, trying to overpower her. Arachnia pressed back, clearly having the superior leverage; her blade started to slide slowly down the wood of Stan's axe, toward his hand. From the corner of his eye, Stan saw Lord Marrow about to fire. Right as Arachnia's blade was about to cut into his hand, Stan dropped his weapon, catching the mobhunter off guard as he slammed into her, sending her careening to the side and directly into Lord Marrow's oncoming arrow. His projectile sunk into her shoulder blade, and she instantly slumped to the ground, unconscious.

Stan raised his axe, preparing to finish the job, but suddenly had to hop away from more of Lord Marrow's arrows. He had been trying to shoot Stan while avoiding Arachnia, aiming carefully, but now that Arachnia was down for the count, there was nothing to stop him from firing an almost machine-gun-like stream of arrows at Stan. He raised his axe to defend himself, but still found he had to dash around in unpredictable patterns to avoid getting hit.

Realizing that he was getting nowhere, Lord Marrow went for a different approach. He began to fire different types of arrows, which erupted into fire the moment they touched the ground. Stan found himself cut off by the flames, and with limited space to maneuver, it was only a matter of seconds before a fiery arrow collided with his chestplate. A miniature explosion erupted directly in front of him and knocked him to the edge of the roof, his head slamming into the ground.

In a daze, Stan could barely make out what was around him. He was only aware that his chestplate was still on fire. He could barely make out the form of Lord Marrow walking up to him, notching an arrow that was leaking gray smoke, and taking aim at a kink in his armor. Stan was in too much pain to move or do anything to stop him from firing.

But Lord Marrow didn't fire. Without warning, his eyes slid out of focus, and he fell forward onto the ground, unconscious with a sizable mark on the back of his head. His amazement overpowering his pain, Stan looked up to see who it was who had saved him.

There, silhouetted against the now-rising sun, dirty and torn up, a diamond pickaxe in his hand and a giant smile on his face, stood G. He reached down to help Stan to his feet.

"G . . . ," Stan managed to get out, slurring his words from his pain, "What're . . . you doing here?"

"Oh, I was just in the neighborhood, and I figured I'd help you guys out," G replied, his grin widening. "Well, I mean, I wasn't just passing through . . . I kind of traveled halfway across the server to get to this particular neighborhood. Dude, you're hurt pretty badly. Drink this, I stole it from Nocturia."

G produced a Potion of Healing from his inventory, which Stan graciously drank. Immediately, his head cleared, and he was able to think complete thoughts again. Aware that his chestplate was still on fire, Stan ripped it off, tossing it over the edge of the roof and into the lava moat below.

"G, it's awesome to see you again," Stan said hastily, "but we can catch up in a minute. We've gotta take out those two over there!" He pointed over to Creeper Khan and Enderchick, who appeared to be getting the upper hand on Kat, Rex, and Jayden.

G merely smiled even wider. "Don't worry about it, man . . . my friends'll take care of it." And with that, G put his hand to his mouth and gave a loud whistle.

Within a few seconds, the air above them was filled with Ender Pearls, tossed from the ground below. As they landed, the rooftop was flooded with players, all dressed in tattered Elementia Army uniforms and carrying stone weapons. Stan's heart leaped, but he saved the question of where these soldiers had come from for later. He stepped forward to the center of the mass of players that was now converging around the members of ELM.

Enderchick and Creeper Khan stood in defensive stances, looking wildly at the horde of players, as Arachnia and Lord Marrow lay unconscious behind them. Enderchick looked desperate and panicked, but Creeper Khan's eyes were closed, a pensive look on his face. Then, he opened them, and stepped forward.

"Stand down!" Stan yelled at them, stepping forward and raising his axe. "You're outnumbered, and I know that all of you can't teleport away at the same time!"

"You're right, President Stan," replied Creeper Khan with no emotion whatsoever, and suddenly, he started to glow. A dim red light radiated from his skin, casting a red filter over his Creeper-like face. Enderchick stared at him for a moment, as if trying to figure out what was going on, until suddenly, her mouth fell open in horror.

"*What?*" Enderchick cried. "Khan . . . you . . . you, like, *can't* be serious!"

"My mind's made up," he replied, not even bothering turning around to face her. "Get the others out of here, Enderchick."

Enderchick gave a sniffle, a tear running down her cheeks, as she grabbed the unconscious forms of Lord Marrow and Arachnia. Realizing what they were about to do, Stan yelled, "Shoot her!" and pointed at Enderchick, but it was too late. The trio disappeared in a puff of purple smoke, as the arrows cut through the violet haze and bounced off the brick blocks below.

"What're you doing?" Stan demanded, terrified to see that the red light now radiating from Creeper Khan was growing stronger and stronger. "Stand down right now, and we'll spare your life."

"It doesn't matter now," Creeper Khan said, looking Stan directly in the eye. "I've decided that it's time for us both to die, Stan. There's nothing either of us can do about it now."

"What . . . what does that mean?" Stan demanded.

"I've decided to use my Final Nova," Creeper Khan replied in a monotone. "In twenty seconds, my body is going to explode into the biggest blast that Minecraft has ever seen.

Nothing will be left of this village except a crater. The Elite Legion of Mobhunters may have been unable to take you prisoner and become rich beyond our wildest dreams, Stan, but that won't stop me from destroying you and everything you hold most dear."

"Kill him!" Stan shouted in horror. A barrage of arrows flew from the crowd of people only to bounce off Creeper Khan as if he were wearing armor with Projectile Protection.

"Nice try!" Creeper Khan said loudly, a deranged smile on his face. "Now that I've used my Final Nova, I can't be killed until I explode! There's nothing you can do to stop me!" And with that, he laughed maniacally.

Stan stood in place, totally stunned and unsure what to do. If Khan was telling the truth, then the explosion was less than ten seconds away. The entire Adorian Village would be destroyed. There was nothing that could be done. Stan's mind was frozen. He stood as still as a statue, completely at a loss as he tried to comprehend what was happening.

Suddenly, Stan heard a commotion in the crowd. G stepped forward from amid the throng of people and stood opposite Creeper Khan. He had a determined look on his face, and a tear running down his cheek.

"G!" a cry erupted from the mass of stupefied Elementia soldiers, as Jayden burst into the clearing, Kat right behind him. "What're you doing?"

G closed his eyes, took a deep breath, and opened them again, before saying, "I'm doing what has to be done."

He turned around to face his fellow councilmen, a sad smile on his face opposite the stunned confusion on theirs.

"Jayden," he said, turning to face his best friend, "thank you. For everything."

He turned his head slightly to the left, and his eyes met Kat's. There was a moment of silence, broken only by Creeper Khan's ongoing laughter and the sounds of battle from below them, as the two players held each other's gaze.

"Kat . . . I'm sorry. I hope that you can forgive me for everything I've done."

And then, without waiting for a response, before either Jayden or Kat could ask what G meant, G turned around and drew out his diamond pickaxe. With no hesitation, he took off, sprinting at top speed toward Creeper Khan, who was still laughing like a lunatic. By the time he realized what was about to hit him, it was too late.

G slammed into the mobhunter like a truck, his pickaxe sinking deep into Creeper Khan's chest. The two players tumbled backward, across the roof. G was holding Creeper Khan in a bear hug to prevent his escape, and he made no attempt to stop as the pair of players plunged off the roof and over the waterfall of lava.

"Nooooooo!" Jayden cried, finally freed from his trance as

he rushed over the edge of the bridge as quickly as he could, horror etched into every square inch of his face. He reached the edge just in time to see his best friend vanish into the moat of lava below, still clutching Creeper Khan as if his life depended on it.

Jayden found himself staring without comprehension into the lava pit for a few seconds before the explosion went off. Stan managed to grab Jayden by the back of the neck and pull him away from the edge just before he would have been burned to a crisp by the massive spray of lava that rose up out of the moat.

The noise was deafening, and all the players on the roof found themselves knocked to the ground by the massive magnitude of Creeper Khan's suicide attack. The ground below them shook like an earthquake, and the sounds of screaming could be heard as the supernova explosion rocked the Adorian Village to its core.

Then, just as quickly as it had started, the tumult stopped. Stan was lying on the ground, terrified to move, and only aware of one sound—the sound of sobbing beside him. Stan dared to move his head, only to see Jayden, sprawled out on the ground, crying his eyes out. Slowly, Stan pulled himself to his knees, and then to his feet. He felt shaky, and had to work to keep his balance, but it seemed like there had been no permanent damage to him from the blast.

Stan looked around, still feeling slightly dazed from the explosion and saw, to his amazement, other players getting up around him. Miraculously, it seemed that Creeper Khan's final attack hadn't killed a single player on the rooftop. Stan made his way to the edge of the roof and looked over the side. It wasn't what he saw that made Stan question what appeared before his eyes—it was what he didn't see.

The explosion, which, based on the shockwaves that it had sent through the ground, was the biggest explosion that Stan had ever witnessed in Minecraft, had hardly done any damage at all. The moat of lava was still intact, as was the flow of lava cascading down the side of the Town Hall. The only indication of the blast that he could see were a few dislodged dirt blocks next to the lava moat, into which the lava moat was now spilling over. Slowly but surely, Stan realized that the lava must have cushioned the explosion, and by sending Creeper Khan into the moat, G had just saved all of their lives.

As this thought crossed Stan's mind, it suddenly dawned on him what had happened to G. G was dead.

Stan suddenly felt like a fist of ice was clenching his heart. He hadn't seen G in so long . . . not since he had left for Nocturia all those weeks ago. And now, in a blink of an eye, before Stan had even had a chance to ask him how he'd been . . . G was gone, banished from Elementia. As this fact washed over Stan, it dawned on him that of all the players who had taught him the ins and outs of Minecraft, right here in this village back when his level was in the single digits, Jayden was the only one remaining.

Stan looked over at Jayden. He was still on the ground, beside himself with grief. Stan's heart swelled with sympathy—this player had lost his three closest friends in Minecraft, and was now all alone in the world. Stan couldn't imagine how he felt. It would be like if he lost Kat, or Charlie.

As much as he longed to go over to Jayden and comfort him, he hardened his heart as he realized what had to be done. They were still in the midst of a battle. They had a job to finish. And so, Stan commanded his troops to follow him back down the stairway and into the Town Hall.

Jayden didn't even notice that they were gone. He didn't notice the smoke from the explosion dying down and blowing away. He didn't hear the gasps of disbelief from below him as Stan's troops found that most of the Noctems had been taken out by the explosion. He didn't acknowledge the hoots and cheers going on below them, in celebration of the fact that the Adorian Village now belonged to Stan and the Elementia soldiers. And he didn't notice as Kat climbed back up the staircase and joined him on the roof.

Rex immediately turned his focus to Jayden, offering himself to be pet. Kat didn't comfort Jayden, though; there would be time for that later. Instead, she made her way over to the edge of the Town Hall. For the first time, she looked down at the moat, the damage on the gravel shoreline, and the lava waterfall that she knew was hiding massive internal damage to the Town Hall.

She had come within an inch of death today. They all had. Creeper Khan might have destroyed the entire Adorian Village in the blink of an eye if it weren't for the player who had gone down with him.

As G had turned to Kat, and spoken the last words that he would ever say on the Minecraft server Elementia, she had recognized something in his voice. It was something that she hadn't been ready for, something unexpected, and something amazing. What she had heard was sincerity.

G was sorry for what he had done to her. She had heard it in his voice, had seen it in his eyes. And he had sacrificed himself for the sake of all of them. Kat looked into the settling cloud of smoke that still hung in the air, and a single tear rolled down her cheek, falling from her face and landing silently in the lava moat far below her.

"Thank you," she whispered.

And with that, Kat turned around, took a deep breath, and walked over to Jayden, prepared to comfort him.

I t was an hour before the Adorian Village was under the full control of the citizens of Elementia. The wall around the village perimeter was occupied by Stan's troops, and the few Noctem soldiers that hadn't been killed in the battle were now imprisoned under strict supervision in the hotel. The lava flowing off the Town Hall had been removed, revealing the war-torn skeleton of a brick-block building beneath. Stan didn't really care about the Town Hall, though; he was much more interested in the storehouses.

Since he had last been to the Adorian Village ages ago, several storehouses had been constructed of brick blocks. They stretched across one side of the Adorian Village, stuffed to the brim with food, materials, medicine, weaponry, and everything in between. Materials had been distributed to all the republic fighters within a day of breaking into these warehouses. The soldiers graciously healed their battle wounds with Potions of Healing, and got their first square meal in ages, before passing the food on to the citizens. These starving victims, who had stayed in the mine and were too sickly to fight, were elated to finally eat real food and have real medicine. With the essentials distributed, the warriors finally started to loot the warehouses for high-grade weaponry.

"Sweet!" exclaimed Stan, as he reached into a chest and pulled out a diamond axe, glimmering with the luster of enchantment. Suddenly, he did a double take, not sure that he had recognized the enchantment correctly.

"Sharpness?" he asked in awe. He turned around to face Sirus, who was brandishing a new diamond pickaxe. "How did they make this?" he asked. "Only swords are supposed to have offensive enchantments on them. Did they use hacks?"

"Oh man, you're so behind the times, man," Sirus said in his jittery fashion. "You've been able to mix up enchantments on stuff for a while now, but you don't do it on an enchanting table now, no no, you've gotta do it on an anvil, you know, one of those things that always falls on people's heads in a comedic fashion in cartoons but would probably squash your entire body into a fleshy puddle of goop if it were to happen to you in real life—"

"He's right, Stan! Check this out!" a call came from across the room.

Stan jogged over to the end of the warehouse, where Kat was standing over a large gray block that Stan knew to be an anvil. On the top of the hunk of iron, side by side, were Kat's diamond sword, already glowing brightly with enchantments, and a book, bound with a red leather strap. For some odd reason, Kat was smashing the cover of the book in with a cast-iron hammer, a bead of sweat trickling down her blocky forehead from the effort as Rex looked up at her quizzically.

Stan was about to ask Kat what she was trying to do (he knew that she didn't like reading, but this was taking it a bit too far), but then, on a particularly hard strike, the book vanished into thin air. A cloud of glimmering dust hung in its place for a moment, before drifting through the air, as if carried by an undetectable wind, and wrapping itself around Kat's sword. The dust hung there for a moment yet again, before being drawn onto the sword by some mysterious force, causing the sword to glow even brighter.

"Look at this," Kat breathed, in utter awe of what she was holding in her hands. The sword was shining brighter than any piece of weaponry that Stan had ever seen, and the luster was shifting in hues between red, purple, and blue. "This sword is now enchanted with the highest levels of Knockback, Fire, and Sharpness . . . all at the same time! From now on, I hereby name this diamond sword, 'Gas-Powered Stick.' *Eeeeek*, I'm so excited!"

Kat raised her clenched fists to her mouth and did a little dance, smile wide, like a kid whose parent had just caved in and let her buy the toy that she really wanted. Stan smiled and shook his head as Kat bathed in her own mirth, and then he became aware of Ben walking over to him and, for the first time since the death of his brother, a smile was on his face, too.

"Hello, Ben," Stan said politely, as Kat walked over to join the two of them, returning her newly enchanted diamond sword to her inventory. "How's the occupation holding up?"

"Pretty well, actually," Ben said. "We've got troops on the full perimeter of the wall, and we're ready to go totally underground in a minute in case the Withers attack. Not only that, but thanks to all the extra gear in these warehouses, we have enough to give everyone here diamond armor. Commander Crunch is actually teaching a class of new players in combat as we speak, so we'll have more soldiers on standby."

"Excellent!" Stan replied, as Kat grinned even wider.

"Anyway, that's not the reason that I've come to talk to you, Stan," continued Ben. Stan expected his tone to shift to a more serious note, but to his surprise, Ben continued to be rather cheery as he kept talking. "We've got some news, both good and bad. Which one do you want to hear first?"

"Surprise me," Stan replied with a shrug.

"Well," continued Ben, now struggling to contain a huge smile, "when G came back from Nocturia and had those rescued prisoners with him . . . well, that wasn't all that he brought back."

"Wait, what? What do you mean? Did he bring back more fighters?"

"Well, no, not exactly . . . but I still think you're gonna be pretty happy. Come on in, guys!" Ben yelled.

He turned to face the entrance to the warehouse, and Stan and Kat turned to follow his gaze. Slowly, two forms, one as tall as a player and one half the size, stumbled awkwardly into the warehouse. As Stan realized who they were, his heart lifted.

"Greetings, President Stan!" Mella exclaimed as she made her way toward Stan. Little Stull smiled up at him as he walked next to her.

"Mella! Stull!" Stan cried out in joy as he rushed over to see them, Kat not far behind him, as Ben smiled on. "I'm so glad to see you guys!"

"It is very good to see you as well," she replied, slowly yet kindly, "now we are not Zombies, and therefore we are not going to try to eat you."

Kat laughed. "Yeah, that's probably for the best. So what happened to you guys? How did you get back here?"

"I do not remember very much of what happened," Mella said, clearly thinking hard about it. "I know that I was in the village, when a large explosion took away most of my house. I went to the church, along with Stull and Blerge, and waited with the rest of my people until the sun came up. The Zombies broke through our door, and one of them attacked me. The next thing that I remember is being carried through a tunnel, with a group of kind players, led by a player who called himself Goldman.

"He told us that we were turned into Zombies by bad players, and that he freed us from the bad players and he was taking us to the village with the good players. When we got here, Goldman told us to wait in a hole that he dug near the village until a player would come to get us. We waited there for two days, and today a player returned to us and brought us here.

"And here we are!" Mella exclaimed, raising her arms in the air. It seemed that she was one step away from yelling out "Ta-da!" as Stull tried to imitate her, struggling to raise his stubby little arms into the air.

Stan gave a warm-hearted smile. He would never tire of the innocuous simplicity of the NPC villagers. As he let Mella bask in her own glory for a moment (from the look on her face, she was quite proud that she had remembered every-thing that had happened so she could recount it to him), Kat stepped forward.

"Mella, we're very happy to see you two, and we can't tell you how relieved we are that you're okay," Kat said, managing a smile for a moment, before bearing a pained expression. "But there's something that we have to tell you."

She took a deep breath, and closed her eyes before continuing. "Do you . . . know what happened to the NPC village?"

She opened her eyes, prepared to see a horrified, scared

expression on Mella's face . . . but she didn't. Rather, the villager had begun to wander around the warehouse, weaving in between the players, as if totally unaware that anybody was talking to her. Kat rolled her eyes, grabbed Mella, and pulled her back over to the group, her eyes sliding back into focus.

"We were told what happened to our village," little Stull suddenly piped up, tilting his head backward to see. "Me, my mother, and my brother were the only ones who escaped from the village alive. My father and my future wife are both dead now. This is very sad."

Stan wasn't sure what to say. Obviously, he felt terrible for Mella and Stull; their entire life had been ripped away from them by the Noctem Alliance, and they were, as of now, the only survivors of their village. On the other hand, neither Stull nor Mella, who had refocused and was now reentering the conversation, seemed particularly distraught about it.

"You are surprised that we are not upset," Mella said. Kat and Stan turned to her in surprise. "Do not worry about us. We used to be very sad that many of our friends and family are dead, and we were very sad that we do not have a home. However, there is nothing that we can do about it now. We cannot focus on the fact that our village has been destroyed, or that our family is dead, or that the one who brought us here named Goldman is now dead. We must simply move on."

The mention of G's name hit Stan like a sucker punch to the gut. To be honest, of all his friends, he was probably the least torn up that G was gone. The two of them hadn't been particularly close, and during the rise of the Noctem Alliance they had gone through a period of open hostility, especially when he was acting out toward Kat. However, now that he had died—and he had sacrificed himself for the sake of the entire army—Stan felt like there was a black hole in his chest where G used to be. Although G was flawed, he was still a good guy at heart, and he only ever did what he truly believed was best, even when things got hard.

Despite this, Stan had forced himself not to think about G. Right now, they had to devote all their focus to destroying the Noctem Alliance, and ensuring that nobody would ever be struck down by their tyranny again. Mella was right. They simply had to move on. He knew that it would be easier said than done, however. Kat had seemed slightly more solemn then usual since G's death, although she was slowly becoming more upbeat. Jayden, on the other hand . . . Stan hadn't seen him since his best friend's death. It occurred to him that maybe he should go in search of Jayden. . . .

Stan suddenly realized that he had become lost in his own train of thought. He looked up and saw that Mella and Stull were playing together, carefree and happy, as Ben was in serious discussion with Kat. Realizing that they must be talking about the state of the war, he rushed over to join them.

". . . and the Noctems don't appear to be preparing for any attacks," Ben said, with Kat nodding her head as Stan arrived. "In fact, from what we can see, they appear to be shifting all their efforts to defense. They're drawing in their troops from all across the server, and concentrating them in Element City."

"What do you think that means?" Kat asked.

"It means that Lord Tenebris is ready to end the war, and end it on his terms. He wants to have a battle, all our forces versus all of his, and he wants it to happen in Element City."

Stan nodded solemnly, trying to think through the implications of this. "Do you think that our armies are prepared for an attack on Element City?"

"I think we're as ready as we'll ever be," Ben replied. "Now that we have food and medicine, we've got tons more volunteers. I'd say that, as of now, we have around three hundred fighters in total, and the Noctem Alliance has probably close to four hundred in the city. I know that those odds aren't great, but they're the best that we're going to get."

"I agree," Kat said, nodding with a pensive look on her face. "So are you saying that we should march on Element City as soon as possible and confront them full on?"

"Not quite," Ben answered. "You see, according to the

spies my brother and I have sent out, the Noctems are draw-ing troops from all over the server—from their outposts, from the Nether, from the Mushroom Islands, you name it. And yet, for some reason, they haven't done anything with their troops in Nocturia. Their capital has about another hun-dred troops in it, and the Noctem Alliance hasn't moved any of them—which is kind of odd, when you consider that they seem to be preparing for a final battle. You'd think that they'd move at least a *few* of those troops."

"So . . . what are you saying?" Stan asked, confused. "Are you saying that we should invade Nocturia instead?"

Ben looked up, and Stan was surprised to see a grin on his face.

"Even better," he replied. "Do you remember back when we first declared war on the Noctem Alliance, and you had to leave the meeting because Sally was contacting you?"

"Yeah . . . ," Stan replied, not sure where he was going with this.

"Well, I seem to recall that she told you something rather interesting—something about how the Noctem Alliance was planning to lure you into the Capitol Building in Nocturia, and then detonate it, because they had turned the Capitol Building into a giant bomb."

"Yeah, she did say that . . . ," Stan answered slowly, still unclear as to what he was getting at.

"Well, when you told that to me, I started thinking to myself, *Gee, if they turned that entire building into a bomb, then that seems awfully risky.* I mean, wouldn't it be unfortunate if some unforeseen incident caused said bomb to go off?"

Stan's jaw dropped as he realized what Ben was suggesting. "You don't mean . . ."

"Oh, I *do*, Stan," he continued, his eyes blazing with wild energy. "We're gonna blow up Nocturia."

There was a moment of silence as Stan and Kat tried to comprehend what he had just said. Kat was the first one to speak.

"Okay, Ben . . . As awesomely awesome as that sounds, I'm not sure that it's gonna work. I mean, how do we know that the place is still in danger of blowing up? That seems like a feature that they would've gotten rid of by this point."

"Because our spies heard them talking about it," Ben replied. "Thanks to the Potions of Invisibility that were stored in the warehouse, it's been a lot easier for us to get close to the Noctem leaders and spy on them. Earlier today, Drake ordered that the TNT that was built into the walls of the castle no longer served a purpose now that the war is almost over, and that it should be disarmed within the next three days. We need to get to the Capitol Building before they're done, and use a redstone charge to detonate a block of TNT in the building. That should start a chain reaction that will destroy the entire Nocturia complex, including everybody inside."

A chill of excitement ran down Stan's spine. He imagined that, in one fell swoop, he could take out a hundred Noctem soldiers, crippling the Alliance beyond anything they could imagine. He could hardly believe his ears.

"So what're we waiting for?" Kat demanded. "We have three days to take out a fifth of the Noctem Army all at once. Why haven't we mobilized yet?"

"Because . . . there's a complication," Ben said, looking tired. "While we were listening to the soldiers, Drake let something else slide. Apparently, they're working on building an army of mobs to help with the defense of Element City, and the base of operations is in Nocturia. Which means . . . that Oob is there."

Stan felt like all the air was being sucked out of his lungs. Here, in front of him, was the chance to launch the biggest attack on the Noctem Alliance since the war began. It would no doubt be an invaluable move if they wished to win the war. And yet . . . to blow up Nocturia would also mean to kill Oob.

"Many of my soldiers," said Ben, slowly and carefully, "have told me that they believe it is worth it to lose the life of one Zombie villager in order to take out the second-largest city the Noctem Alliance controls. I'm leaving the decision to you, President Stan."

"Hey!" exclaimed Kat in fury, butting her way in between them. "What about the other council members? Shouldn't we get a say in what to do?"

Ben shook his head. "I'm sorry, Kat, but we don't have time to debate this. It's an incredibly important matter and, given that we only have three days, we can't waste time organizing a vote."

Something clicked in Stan's head. He remembered a long time ago, as Blackraven had stood up at the council table in Element City, and yelled out at them all . . . *I only want what is best for Elementia, and I would like to see action taken against our enemies quickly, without wandering through the political swamp of your bureaucratic elections.*

Blackraven had made the exact same argument for appointing himself to the council that Ben was making now. And yet, now, everybody was agreeing with Ben, whereas half of them had jumped down Blackraven's throat at the idea.

"Stan, you can't do it!"

Stan snapped out of his thoughts and realized that Kat was appealing to him, a look of desperation in her eyes.

"You can't kill Oob, you . . . you just *can't*! I mean, we've known him for so long now . . . he's our friend! His life is no less valuable than any of ours just because he's an NPC villager! There's got to be another way to destroy Nocturia without killing him!"

Stan knew that what she was saying was true. Oob was their friend. They could never just leave him to die. That would be like abandoning Kat or Charlie! He knew that he could never do that. On the other hand, the idea of a hundred Noctem troops sitting out in the tundra suddenly made him far more uneasy than it ever had before as they prepared for the closing phases of the war. And here was an opportunity to take them out forever. Stan thought that . . . just maybe . . .

"What was that?" a voice came from behind Stan. He turned around and saw Mella walking up to him, with little Stull asleep in her arms. "I heard you say the name of Oob, who is my son. Did you say the name of Oob, who is my son?"

As Stan looked back into Mella's quizzical, trusting eyes, all hints of doubt vanished from Stan's mind in an instant.

"Yes, you did, Mella," he replied confidently. "We're breaking into the Noctem Capitol to free your son."

It had taken far too much time to put together the plan for the infiltration of Nocturia, but now that Stan had entered the subzero snowstorm yet again, he was confident that their plan was solid. He looked ahead of him, past Ben, who was shielding his eyes from the snow. Stan's eyes locked on to Jayden, who was at the front of the trio. Even though he couldn't see Jayden's face, Stan knew that he bore a look of grim determination and vengeance.

In the Adorian Village, Stan had found Jayden alone in an abandoned house. He had clearly been crying for the entire day, and Stan totally understood. When Jayden had first met him, he had gotten to know Stan, played practical jokes on him, and taught him, all alongside G, Archie, and Sally. And now, months later, all three of those friends were gone. Jayden was the only one remaining, and all of them had been taken out by the Noctem Alliance (or, in Sally's case, the regime of King Kev, which had led to the Alliance's creation).

When Stan had told Jayden that they were going on a mission to blow the capitol of the Noctem Alliance off the face of the server, he hadn't hesitated to volunteer. Stan was relieved that Jayden was feeling up to coming with them; out of all of them, he had by far the most inside knowledge of the Noctem Capitol Building, having stayed there for weeks on end.

Stan only hoped that they were almost there. They had been traveling for two days through the countryside of Elementia, speckled with abandoned Noctem outposts, and were just now in the midst of the trek through the tundra. Time was running out.

Suddenly, Stan's heart leaped. A few shimmering lights shone out of the darkness of the eternal blizzard and, slowly but surely, the silhouette of the Nocturia complex faded into view. Stan took a deep breath as he realized that, if their mission went according to plan, it would be the last time that they would ever see the magnificent complex from the outside. Jayden raised his hand to indicate a halt, and he turned to face Stan and Ben.

"We're close enough," Jayden said, his voice still gruff and gravelly from his days of woeful mourning and silence. "Use the potions now."

Stan pulled the Potion of Invisibility out of his inventory and drank it along with his two friends. As Stan let the tingling feeling spread from his mouth through the rest of his body, he sincerely hoped that the last of the potion wouldn't go to waste. The Potions of Invisibility in the warehouse had proved invaluable for spying on Element City since they had taken over the Adorian Village, and the three of them had taken some of the last remaining bottles for use on this mission. Stan resolved to make it count.

It wasn't long before the potions had taken effect. All three players stood invisible, without armor on their bodies or weapons in their hands. The only indication of where Stan's comrades stood was a faint shimmering, as if the air was irradiated, that Stan could only sense if he focused as hard as he could. After fumbling about for a moment, Stan found what he was looking for, and grasped Ben's hand, as

Ben did the same to Jayden in front of him. As soon as the chain of the three invisible players was completed, they took off running.

Stan's heart, already racing from the effort, was thumping faster than he was aware was possible as they entered through the stone brick–block wall surrounding the Nocturia complex. It didn't slow as they sprinted straight past the four guards watching over the door framed with quartz blocks. The Potion of Invisibility only lasted for a short time. He could only pray that Jayden managed to locate a safe place in the capitol for them to reappear before that time came.

They were dashing past houses now, dozens and dozens of plain, tiny houses, constructed of cobblestone and wood-plank blocks, the windows on the wood doors revealing darkness inside. Stan supposed that these were the abandoned houses of the players who had made their way to Element City. For a moment, he considered questioning Jayden as to whether one of these houses would be a good place to reappear, but he decided not to. Whatever Jayden was planning, Stan trusted him. Fortunately, they reached the front doors of the Noctem Capitol Building just as a Noctem trooper was walking out, and they managed the slip through the iron doors just before they swung shut.

As the trio entered the main hall and dropped their hands, Stan allowed himself to take a deep breath, finally breathing in air that wasn't below freezing (although the air in the capitol certainly wasn't warm). There was no time to stop, though. Stan saw the other shimmers pressing onward, and he followed.

Stan's anxiety levels were through the roof as he crossed the floor of the Capitol Building rotunda. Guards were stationed around every corner, and there were several lone soldiers passing through the center of the rotunda. Once or twice, as Stan sprinted past a soldier, he did a double take, and Stan's heart stopped. Luckily, nobody pursued them, but Stan still felt like he was about to have a panic attack. The potion was surely close to running out.

Stan ducked behind one of his two friends into a side hallway, not illuminated by the light of glowstone as the rotunda had been. The hallway was made entirely out of stone-brick blocks. Stan followed the shimmering figure around a corner and into another hallway, just as it grew much more substantial. In a matter of seconds, it had finally turned back into the form of Ben. Jayden materialized right beside him, and Stan looked down at himself to see that he had reappeared, too.

"Don't worry," Jayden said quickly, before Stan could voice his alarm, "they won't look down here. This part of the building isn't done. They just built it so that the capitol would be symmetrical, and they haven't actually done anything with the space yet. And best of all, this"—Jayden grinned as he gave three sharp raps on the stone-brick wall across from him—"is the outside wall of the castle."

There was a moment of silence as they all realized what this meant. Then, slowly, Ben drew out a diamond pickaxe. He walked over to the wall and struck a piece of stone brick. As he chipped away at the block, Stan held his breath. Now was the moment of truth. If the TNT had already been removed from this wall, then the first part of their mission would be a total failure. Ben raised the pickaxe and, with all his might, he delivered one final strike to the stone-brick block. It broke, collapsing onto the floor, revealing a block of red sticks, with a white label bearing the black letters TNT.

Ben pumped his fist in excitement, while Jayden smiled a wild smile and Stan sighed in relief.

"Okay, Stan, you know the plan," said Ben as he handed the diamond pickaxe to Stan. "And please—I cannot stress this enough—*do not* blow up the building until we're outside."

"I promise." Stan nodded as he took the tool and started to carve out more of the stone-brick blocks, being careful to leave the TNT blocks in place. "Good luck, you guys. Be out as soon as possible, and don't do anything too reckless."

Jayden and Ben nodded as they pulled black leather armor out of their inventories, slipped it on over their heads, and proceeded to make their way back out into the main part of the building, Jayden leading the way. Stan, meanwhile, turned his attention back to his job.

Stan reached into his inventory to double-check that he had everything that he needed to complete his job. To his relief, it was all there: several stacks of redstone dust, a stack of redstone repeaters, a map, and a lever. He raised the diamond pickaxe and struck the nearest TNT block. It immediately broke off, falling to the ground, and Stan pocketed it. Hastily, he continued to dig into the wall, mining through blocks of stone brick and TNT until eventually he was inside the wall. Wasting no time, Stan picked up some of the stone-brick blocks from the ground and fastened them on to the section of the wall that he had just tunneled through. Now, if anybody were to come across this section of the wall from inside the building, it would appear untouched.

Stan knew that, even though he was concealed, he couldn't slow down. It wouldn't be long before Jayden and Ben had gotten Oob, and he would be shocked if they managed to smuggle the villager out without being discovered by the Noctem troops. If they were to get out safely, Stan would have to be ready well before they left the Nocturia complex. With that knowledge in mind, Stan dug a downward stairway through the furrowed dirt-block ground, stopping when the stone-brick wall was directly above him.

Pulling the redstone dust from his inventory, Stan reached back up through the terraced dirt blocks and laid a trail of redstone down the steps and toward him, starting at the base of one of the TNT blocks and ending at his feet. Stan pulled the map from his inventory and oriented himself so that he was facing toward the front gates of the Nocturia complex. Pulling out his pickaxe again, Stan then proceeded to dig forward, tunneling through dirt and stone blocks alike, and sprinkling redstone dust behind him on the ground.

After Stan had been digging and laying down dust for what he counted as ten steps, he pulled a redstone repeater from his inventory and put it on the ground at the end of the redstone dust. The stone plate of the mechanism had a few buttons and switches on it, but Stan was most interested in the arrow inscribed on the smooth stone base of the contraption, which was pointing in the direction he had just come from. Stan knew that he had to be vigilant in making sure that each and every one of the repeaters was facing toward Nocturia, or else the entire redstone circuit would malfunction.

On and on Stan went, in a pattern: dig further down the tunnel, lay redstone dust behind him, lay a repeater every ten steps. Every once in a while he would check the map to see how close he was to being outside the boundaries of the Nocturia complex.

Finally, after what seemed like an eternity of constant digging, Stan checked the map and saw that he was a good distance outside the outer walls of the Noctem Capitol. He aimed his pickaxe upward, and before long, he broke the frozen topsoil and stumbled into the darkness of the eternal blizzard. Determined to finish the job properly, Stan laid the redstone dust up the hole he had just climbed, and when he got to the top, he placed the lever in his inventory on the ground, careful to ensure that it was connected to the rest of the trail of redstone.

Stan was relieved that his mission had been a success. Nocturia was now one lever pull away from becoming a massive crater in the middle of the tundra. All he had to do was wait for Ben and Jayden to emerge carrying Oob, and then activate the redstone circuit. Stan's mind was racing, and his heart was pounding with excitement as he used the pickaxe to carve a trench in the snowy ground (they had to take shelter from the blast behind something). As he worked, Stan imagined how large the explosion would be. If what Ben had said was true, and all the outer walls were laced with TNT, then Stan couldn't comprehend the size of the blast. More than likely, it would be larger than Creeper Khan's dying attack.

Suddenly, Stan stopped as this thought struck him. The memories of being on the roof of the Town Hall came flooding back to him, as he once again stood before Creeper Khan, sure that the entire Adorian Village was about to be destroyed. The feeling of dread that had washed over him was unlike anything he had felt before, to think that all of his people were about to be wiped out . . . even those who hadn't wanted to fight to begin with. . . .

Stan knew that not everybody in the Noctem Alliance was a terrible person. Obviously, they were all terribly misguided in their beliefs, but not all of them were purely evil minds like King Kev or Caesar. In fact, Stan had trouble believing, based on what he had heard about them, that Tess and Spyro were terrible people by nature. They were just doing what they thought was right, like almost every other player who had followed the path of the Noctem Alliance. Stan realized that there was a possibility, however slim, that any member of the Noctem Alliance might one day repent, and see the error of their ways.

If Stan pulled the lever, then none of the one hundred players in the Nocturia complex would ever get that chance.

As Stan sat in the snow, frozen in conflict, his mind torn two ways, he became aware that he was being watched. Stan whipped his head up, his newly enchanted diamond axe flying into his hand as his eyes fell on a figure standing slightly below him on the hill. The player was standing perfectly still, his cloak billowing in the raging gale. As Stan squinted to make him out more clearly, he realized that the figure was wearing dark pants and shoes, with a black cape and hood that obscured his eyes, revealing only a pale mouth locked into a frown.

Stan's heart skipped a beat. Since he had met up with his friends, they had all told him stories . . . tales of a mysterious player who had appeared to each of them and saved their lives. In fact, Stan had heard that it was because of this mystery player that his friends had accepted Leonidas into their group. While he had largely ignored his friends' stories, being too occupied with the war effort to give them much thought, he remembered them saying that the player never spoke . . . and yet, somehow, they all knew his name.

As Stan looked at this player, he knew the name, too.

The Black Hood stared at Stan, still not moving, still not smiling. Stan miraculously felt no surprise that this mystery player existed. Rather, he only felt a sense of desperation, like a pupil begging a teacher for help. Somehow, he knew that the Black Hood held the answer to his dilemma, although he had no idea how.

"I can't kill them," Stan said aloud, the anxiety evident in his voice as he spoke to this spectral player. "We aren't on a battlefield. Those players are probably lying safe and happy in their beds. They think that the war is nearly over, and that soon they'll get to go home to their families. How am I supposed to take them all out?"

The Black Hood didn't answer. He simply continued to

stare at Stan, not a muscle of his body making even the slightest motion as he stood, stoic, his billowing cape forming a magnificent silhouette against the light of the building that Stan was supposed to destroy. Stan stared back, desperately hoping that, if he stared hard enough, the answer would reveal itself.

"You've always had the answer for all my friends!" Stan cried out over the blizzard, as a tear formed in the corner of his eyes. "You've always done everything you can for them! Is there anything you can do for me?"

Still, there was no response. Instead, a particularly strong gust of wind kicked a spray of snow in front of the Black Hood, obscuring him from view. By the time the snow had blown away, the Black Hood had vanished.

And yet, Stan didn't have time to acknowledge the disappearance of the mysterious player. Rather, his focus shifted to the blast of sound that was echoing up the slopes of the hills. Stan scrambled to the edge of the hill to where the Black Hood had been standing and looked down. There, racing across the tundra toward him, were two players, one of whom appeared to have a third form slung over his back. And far behind them, a giant mass of forms seemed to be swarming around the Nocturia complex like ants, turning into waves that surged toward the exit gate.

"We've got him!" Jayden's voice came out, as his face

came into view next to the form of Ben, who had an unconscious, shaking Oob over his shoulder. "Pull the lever, Stan!"

Stan glanced down at the lever, then out at the massive outpouring of troops that had reached the gates of the outer wall. He wondered how many of those players were only fighting because they felt they couldn't live in Element City under him . . . just like his soldiers back in the Adorian Village were doing now.

"What are you waiting for?" Jayden bellowed. "They'll be out of range soon. Activate the bomb!"

Stan gave his head a blunt shake. He had to do it—he knew that he had to. Without thinking, Stan reached down to the lever, but the second he grabbed it, he halted in his tracks. It was so simple. All he had to do was push the lever forward, and it would all be over. But still, he would never be able to cleanse his hands of those hundred lives.

"Do it! NOW!" Ben bellowed.

Stan acted on instinct. He thrust the lever downward, activating the mechanism with a distinctive click. Instantly, a surge of electric power rushed down the line of redstone dust, pausing for a split second as it hit the first redstone repeater before the revitalized charge continued down the line. For a moment, Stan couldn't hear anything as he rushed back into the trench he had just dug, alongside Jayden, Ben, and the unconscious Oob.

BOOOOOOOOOOM!

The explosion was so loud, so powerful, and so forceful that Stan felt himself slammed backward against the back of the trench, unable to move. He squinted his eyes open against the blinding light to see a giant fireball rupturing the walls of the Capitol Building of Nocturia, reducing the entire building into rubble in a split second. The wave of fire continued from the building, spreading at the speed of sound across the countless shacks, and eventually sending the outer wall flying into the air in a million pieces. The soldiers on the ground turned around in a frenzy to see what had happened, only to be consumed by the blast. Stan forced himself to duck low into the trench to avoid being struck by the massive force. He felt it billow over his head like a train, still supremely powerful even after traveling so far.

The blasts didn't cease there. A series of smaller, yet still massive explosions continued to erupt within the giant fireball, sending loose blocks and items flying through the air like a volcano spewing out magma and stones. Single lit blocks of TNT went sailing through the air, glowing white like shooting stars through the still-raging blizzard. Some burst in midair like fireworks, while others struck the ground in blasts, peppering the snowy ground around what had once been the Nocturia complex with miniature craters the size of Creeper holes. Stan ducked his head down into the trench again for fear of being struck by a stray explosion.

For a long time, Stan didn't move. He couldn't move; his brain wouldn't let him. It wasn't until long after the last remnants of explosions had died that Stan finally dared to peek his head over the top of the bank and look over the field before him.

The Nocturia complex, which had once stood as one of the most ornate, intricate, and well-crafted cities in all of Elementia, now ceased to exist. The crater from the supernova was so large that Stan couldn't make out the bottom. Thousands of blocks wide, the hole stretched down so deep that it simply appeared to be black. Not a single structure remained even partially intact, and there was no sign of life whatsoever.

Stan continued to stare, feeling a hole in his chest that felt as large as the hole that was now the gravesite of hundreds of players before him, all because he had pulled the lever. Then Stan's mind refused to take any more, and he passed out before he hit the snow.

As he stood on the bridge of Element Castle and looked down over the city, General Drake tried to remember an older time, when Element City had been a much more colorful place. After all, he had lived here once, long ago, before he had chosen to leave and join the Noctem Alliance, being fed up with his then-stagnant, dead-end life. The city looked much different now, though—darker, and more foreboding. The eternal gray cloud still hung over the towering buildings of the city, dimming the sunlight as the two Withers patrolled the skies, under the telepathic grip of the one who, at this very moment, was torturing Drake's comrade for his failure.

From such a height, Drake could see every street of Element City, all lined with troops. There were over four hundred Noctem soldiers in all, armed to the teeth with potions and enchanted weapons, prepared for the imminent attack on the city. Stan2012 had taken control of the Adorian Village, and since the admittedly unexpected destruction of Nocturia two days ago, there was only one place for Stan's army to go now.

Drake heard uneven footsteps behind him, and he turned around to see General Spyro limping toward him. His entire body was covered in burns from fire and potions, and from the agonized expression on his face, he was just barely managing to stay upright.

"I'm glad to see that he went easy on you," Drake said coolly.

"Trust me . . . so am I," grunted Spyro as he reached Drake, extracted a wood-plank block from his inventory, placed it on the ground, and wasted no time in sitting down, a sigh heaving from his mouth. "I know that I deserve . . . much, much worse than what I got. I suppose I'm lucky that Lord Tenebris is so . . . merciful . . ."

"Yes, you are. . . . We both are," replied Drake wistfully, remembering the agony that Lord Tenebris had put him through for his failures. "It will all be over soon, though. As soon as we can destroy President Stan's army, life will be easy—and we'll be heroes."

"Yeah, I know. . . . *Augh!*" The shout escaped Spyro's mouth as he moved slightly, causing the pain in a particularly burned part of his arm to flare up. Drake handed a Potion of Healing from his own inventory to Spyro, which he graciously drank.

"Thanks," Spyro said softly as he sighed in relief.

"Don't mention it."

"So, is there any news on the war front?" Spyro asked, his voice slightly stronger now.

Drake took a deep breath and let it out. *So he doesn't know,* he thought. "Actually, there is a rather big development,

Spyro . . . not a good one. Apparently, President Stan knew about the TNT hidden in the walls of Nocturia, and he activated it. The entire city is gone, and they took out over a hundred of our guys . . . including Tess."

There was a moment of silence as Spyro stood there, looking at the ground, trying to absorb what Drake had just said. Finally, he looked up, disbelief in his face.

"You're saying . . . that . . . Tess is dead?"

"Yes."

"And . . . they took out a hundred of our soldiers?"

"Yes, Spyro. President Stan destroyed just over a hundred players in the blink of an eye. That's almost twice as many as we took out in our biggest attack. And from what I heard, it wasn't just any random soldier that did it . . . it was President Stan himself."

"You're kidding."

"No, I'm not," Drake spat in disgust. "I can't believe that he would do something like that. I mean, it wasn't like when we attacked the Spleef Arena, where we had a solid reason to do it. A lot of the players in Nocturia were trainees, not even ready to go into combat. And a lot more weren't even there for combat at all. They were there for construction and mining and such. Even Tess was just there to oversee training. It's not like she was ordering out military operations from Nocturia or anything. But now, it doesn't even matter. They're all gone."

Spyro didn't respond; he didn't have anything to say. Neither did Drake, for that matter. The two remaining generals of the Noctem Alliance stood silently on the bridge, overlooking their troops and reflecting on just how senseless the loss of all those players, including General Tess, truly was.

"I don't believe you," Kat said incredulously, staring at Commander Crunch, eyes wide. "Don't you dare lie to me about something like that!"

"I assure ye, lass, I ain't lyin'," Commander Crunch replied with a proud, toothy grin. "Th' trainin' program really has been goin' that well. All hundred o' th' new players I've been trainin' 'ave been advancin' remarkable smartly, 'n' they'll be able t' march into Element City in battle alongside th' rest o' us when the time comes."

"So . . . ," Cassandrix said, the gears whirring in her head. "If I'm counting correctly . . . then that means that . . ."

"Right ye be, poppet . . . now we 'ave jus' as many fighters as th' Noctems do: four hundred apiece."

"Excellent!" Kat exclaimed, so loudly that Rex looked up at her in concern, and several people nearby glanced at her, but she didn't care. She had been worried sick ever since Ben had told her that they may potentially be going into a fight of three hundred versus five hundred, but now it seemed like they would be much more evenly matched.

"So we're up a hundred fighters . . . ," Cassandrix murmured to herself before looking up at Kat. "And you're certain that Nocturia has been destroyed, correct?"

"Hey, the spies haven't led us wrong yet," replied Kat. "They say they heard the Noctem generals say that Nocturia had been destroyed. If that's the case, then I'd expect Stan, Ben, and Jayden to be back any minute now."

"Aye aye-o, ma'am," Commander Crunch replied with a hearty laugh. "Now, I be gonna brin' me newly graduated students t' th' storehouses 'n' get them suited up fer battle. Could ye two do me a favor 'n' tell Bob th' good news?"

Kat and Cassandrix nodded and immediately began to make their way toward the hotel, Rex on their heels, as Commander Crunch headed toward the Town Hall.

"I'm totally speechless," Cassandrix breathed. "A hundred players, turned into military-grade fighters in just a manner of days . . . I'd never have believed it . . ."

"Well, if anybody can do it, Commander Crunch can. I mean, he may be totally insane, but he knows what he's doing. Not to mention that those players really believe in our cause," Kat answered wisely as they passed the guarded hotel rooms where the Noctem prisoners were being stored. "And they know how desperate the situation is."

"I suppose you're right," Cassandrix sighed. "I suppose

that given the circumstances, just about anybody can rise to the occasion . . . even if they're lower-level players."

Kat stopped in her tracks and whipped around to face Cassandrix, a look of sheer disbelief on her face. There was a moment where neither of them moved before Cassandrix spoke again.

"Relax, darling . . . I was only joking . . ."

Cassandrix continued walking, but Kat still didn't move. Instead, a look of understanding crossed her face as she looked at the player standing beside her. Cassandrix turned around and looked at Kat expectantly, waiting for her to say something.

"Cassandrix," Kat finally said, "have I ever thanked you for everything you've done for us?"

"Well, I hardly see occasion for that, dear. After all, I've done just as much or, to be totally frank, slightly less than you and the other leaders."

"I know that," Kat replied, "but it's just . . . what you said to me, back when we were in prison together on the Mushroom Islands . . . it was really eye opening."

"Oh come on, darling, you're not still on about that, are you? Look, I already told you—"

"What I'm trying to say is that what you said struck me as something somebody in the Noctem Alliance would say."

Suddenly, it was as if the air around them had dropped

twenty degrees. Cassandrix glared back at Kat, making it very obvious that she had entered dangerous waters.

"Yes," Cassandrix said coldly. "You said that as I was talking."

"But . . . you're not a member of the Noctem Alliance. It would have been so easy for you to leave and join them but . . . you didn't. You stayed here with us, and you've risked everything for the sake of the lower-level players."

Cassandrix said nothing. Instead, she opened her mouth, only to close it again, and then looked down at the ground. She then repeated the same motion again, clearly searching for the correct response. Then, she finally talked, and Kat was taken aback by how sincere she sounded.

"Well . . . to be totally frank with you, Kat, I initially refused to join the Noctem Alliance because I didn't approve of their methods, even if I agreed with their ideals. And I only joined the army because I was one of the only high-level players left in the city, and I hadn't been drafted yet because of my role in the Spleef tournament."

"Oh," Kat replied, sounding crestfallen. "Well, in that case—"

"*That being said,*" Cassandrix cut in, causing Kat to look back up at her. "That may have been the reason that I joined the army in the first place, but it's not the reason that I'm fighting now. Spending all this time fighting the Noctem

Alliance, seeing all the trouble that our people of all levels have gone through to take them down, and . . . well, even talking to you . . . It's opened my eyes to quite a few things. I suppose what I'm trying to say is . . . I would fight alongside you in this army if I were to do everything over again."

Cassandrix gave a warm smile, which Kat returned. She found it hard to believe that the big-lipped, pale-faced player standing across from her was the same person who she had hated the most out of everyone in Element City just weeks ago. Kat realized that Cassandrix hadn't said that she agreed with Kat's views on how lower-level players ought to be treated, and to be honest, Kat doubted that she would ever truly feel that way. However, Kat knew in her gut that, from now on, Cassandrix would look at things in more than one light . . . as would she.

The two girls broke eye contact simultaneously, and walked the short distance to the hotel room where Bob was holed up. Kat told Rex to sit, and pushed the wooden door open. She had to do a double take to ensure that she was seeing correctly.

Bob was sitting on Ivanhoe in the middle of the room, as they had expected, but they were not alone. In front of them, sitting on another saddled pig and looking incredibly frustrated, was Charlie. He was holding a fishing rod, on the end of which was a carrot, which his pig was looking at with marked longing. Both players looked up as Kat and Cassandrix entered the room.

"Um . . . are we interrupting something?" Kat asked awkwardly.

"No, of course not!" exclaimed Bob with a grin. Unlike Charlie, he looked quite enthusiastic about whatever it was that was going on. "I've been teaching Charlie how to ride a pig, and I think that we've got this one fully trained. Go on Charlie, demonstrate."

Charlie looked miserable; he took a deep breath, let it out, and then grunted, "Forward, Dr. Pigglesworth."

The pig gave a complacent grunt and began to trot forward. With the humiliated-sounding commands of "Stop, Dr. Pigglesworth" and "Turn, Dr. Pigglesworth" and "Backward, Dr. Pigglesworth," Charlie maneuvered his pig all around the room.

"Um," Kat said slowly, not sure what to say as Charlie and the pig stopped in front of them. "That was . . . very impressive, Charlie."

"Wasn't it?" beamed Bob. He was clearly very proud of all that Charlie had accomplished.

"Honestly," Charlie grunted, looking as though he felt degraded, "it's bad enough that I'm forced to ride this stupid thing, but why did you have to give it a nickname like that?"

"Hey, it's not my decision!" Bob replied defensively. "All

the war pigs are given their names when they're born. And for the record, Dr. Pigglesworth has always been one of my favorites."

"Well, great then!" spat Charlie in disgust. "If that's the case, then why don't we trade? If you're forcing me to act like I'm as crippled as you are, the least you can do is give me a pig that has a cool name like Ivanhoe!"

Bob's jaw dropped and he stared at Charlie, clearly stung deeply by this. Charlie continued to glare back in anger for a moment, before his infuriated look cracked and then broke altogether, revealing embarrassment and shame. Kat and Cassandrix looked on, not wanting to be there, but not positive how to walk away. After a full minute of tense silence, Cassandrix cleared her throat and spoke.

"Eh, hem. Well, Bob, em . . . we thought that it would be pertinent for you to know that Commander Crunch has trained all his lower-level players much faster than we had anticipated. They should all be prepared to fight when we invade Element City, which means that we'll have four hundred fighters in total, the same number of troops as the Noctem Alliance has."

Bob didn't look at them. He gave an absentminded "Thank you for telling me" without moving his gaze away from Charlie. Their job done, Kat and Cassandrix scurried out of the room, slamming the door behind them. Charlie heard Cassandrix let out a muffled "Well that was fun," from behind the closed door in a higher-than-normal voice, and finally, he spoke.

"I'm sorry," Charlie said, his head drooping in shame as Dr. Pigglesworth started curiously sniffing the ground, apparently oblivious to the emotions of the one riding him. "That wasn't fair."

"Thank you for apologizing," Bob replied, stroking Ivanhoe absentmindedly between the ears, which caused the pig's nose to crinkle in pleasure. "You've got to realize, Charlie . . . I know what you're going through."

"Don't say that," Charlie grunted, a note of anger returning to his voice. "You have no idea what I'm going through."

"What are you talking about?" Bob asked incredulously. "How do you think I felt when Caesar cut my leg off? Do you think that I just hopped on Ivanhoe and carried on like nothing happened? Of course not! I was just as depressed as you are now for weeks before I accepted what had happened to me!"

"It's different for you!" cried Charlie. "I mean, look at you! Even without your legs, you're still one of the best archers we've got! You're probably better now than you were before because Ivanhoe's so fast and has so much stamina! You can still be a great archer while riding on a pig. How am I supposed to fight in hand-to-hand combat using a pickaxe if I can't use my legs?"

"Charlie, I know that it's going to be hard to adjust," Bob replied, "and . . . well, I'm gonna level with you, you're probably not going to be as good in a fight as you were before. But if you focus on what you can't do, you're gonna put yourself in a really bad place. You need to focus on what you can do, and how lucky you are."

"Lucky?" laughed Charlie bitterly. "How, in any sense of the word, am I supposed to be lucky?"

"Because you didn't end up like my brother! You're still alive!" shouted Bob.

Charlie felt the response that was about to leave his mouth hit an invisible wall. There was nothing that he could say in response to that. There was another long moment of silence as Bob stared at him, tears welling in his eyes. Finally, a sigh escaped the police chief's mouth, and he spoke.

"Charlie, I'm sorry that you have to ride into the battle for our freedom on the back of a pig, I truly am. But I'll say it again: don't think about the limitations that your condition is causing you. Instead, focus on everything that you can still do! Charlie, do you realize just how useful you've been in helping us plan this attack?"

"Well . . . I mean, I guess . . ."

"Charlie, you've been amazing!" Bob exclaimed. "You've been the driving force behind all our battle plans since we got back to the village! I mean, you've pretty much mapped out everything while Ben and I were getting the troops organized and the people safe. This attack that we're about to pull off wouldn't be half as solid without you, and thanks to your plans, Nocturia is gone! When I was reading your notes for the first time, I was totally blown away. You suggested things that Ben and I never would have thought of!"

"Well," Charlie replied, "I suppose that you're right . . . I guess I have always been better at planning than doing the actual fighting . . ."

"Exactly," Bob replied. "Charlie, your shining moment of glory isn't going to be on the battlefield, like the rest of us. Your moment of glory is going to come when we stand on the bridge of Element Castle, and look over the city that we've won back, and you know that you were the grandmaster who moved all the chess pieces around the board and made it possible."

"That's right," a voice from behind them replied.

Bob and Charlie turned around to see Leonidas standing in the doorway, a smile on his face.

"How long have you been standing there?" Charlie asked.

"Long enough to know that everything that Bob said is true," Leonidas replied, walking into the room and sitting on a wood block to look at the two pig-backed players at eye level. "Your ideas 'n' strategies have already done more for us than ya know."

Charlie smiled. "Thanks, guys. That was just what I needed to hear. I think I'm gonna be okay."

"Good," Bob said kindly. "And if you ever feel down and need to talk, come to me, okay? I've been stuck with this little guy a lot longer than you have, man," he added wearily, patting Ivanhoe on the head, "and I'm pretty used to it by this point. I'm sure I can help you out."

"Will do," Charlie replied. "Thanks for everything, guys. I haven't gotten my gear together yet, so I'm gonna go do that. I'll talk to you later. Let's go, Dr. Pigglesworth."

Charlie nudged forward on his pig's head, and proceeded to exit through the door. Leonidas and Bob watched him go, smiles on their faces, as Leonidas closed the door behind him.

"Charlie's a good guy," Leonidas sighed contentedly. "I'm sure glad that he's finally managin' to shake off the demons that got into his head when the Noctem Alliance tortured him."

"Yeah," agreed Bob. "He's got a good heart, and I know that he'll do anything for our cause. It honestly didn't surprise me that he blamed himself so much when he gave the location of the bunker to the Noctem Alliance."

"How do ya know about that?" Leonidas asked in alarm.

"Our spies have brought quite a lot of information to us, Leonidas," Bob replied wisely. "And honestly, it wasn't too hard to guess. It made a lot of other stuff make sense. I didn't want to tell Charlie I knew because I knew he'd have a hard time facing me. And I don't blame him. People aren't themselves when they go through what the Noctem Alliance put Charlie through."

Leonidas nodded pensively as, without warning, the door slowly creaked open. Both players in the room looked up to see the Mechanist stepping meekly into the room. Instantly, the entire atmosphere changed; Bob glared at the Mechanist with a harsh glint in his eye, causing the Mechanist to recoil as Leonidas looked between the two of them with concern.

"What do you want?" Bob asked coldly. The Mechanist cringed yet again at the harsh tone, and his voice was meek as he responded in his quivery Texas drawl.

"I'm sorry if I'm interrupting anything . . . but I'm a little bit confused, Bob. I was looking over the plans for the invasion that you made with Ben and Charlie, and I saw instructions for all the commanders except for me. What should I be doing during the battle?"

"Well, I thought the plans made it clear," Bob replied. "The instructions for all the commanders are listed. Everyone not listed is going to be serving under the commanders."

"Wait, hold up," the Mechanist replied, as he realized what Bob was saying. "Are you implying that . . . you want me to just be a normal foot soldier during the attack?"

"It wasn't an implication, Mechanist," Bob spat. "It's written on the page, plain as day."

"But . . . but . . . ," the Mechanist sputtered, sounding incredibly hurt. "You don't need me to . . . I don't know . . . set up some redstone booby traps? Or take down their automatic defense grids? Or *anything*?"

"I think that I've made myself very clear!" Bob shouted. Everyone in the room looked on in shock as Bob dismounted Ivanhoe, clutching the wall and pulling himself upright on his good foot so he could look the Mechanist in the eye.

"All players whom my brother and I have dubbed the most experienced—*and the most reliable*—are the commanders. All others are going to serve as ground troops for the invasion. And I suggest that you stop talking back to your superior, soldier! Stand down now, or you're going to be kicked out of this—"

"Enough!" Leonidas bellowed, pushing his way in between the cowering Mechanist and the raging Bob. The Mechanist stumbled backward in a panic, as Bob was shoved off balance and tumbled to the wood plank–block floor with a crash.

"What do you think you're doing?" Bob demanded, glaring at Leonidas as he attempted to get up off the floor.

"I'm puttin' an end to this nonsense!" grunted Leonidas as he grabbed Bob's arm, jerking him to his feet. Bob looked at Leonidas incredulously as he remounted his pig, and his look was mirrored by the Mechanist.

"We're at war," Leonidas said in the manner of a drill sergeant, looking back and forth between the two players with an authoritative expression on his face. "At some point within the next two days, we are gonna march into Element City and fight for our lives to take it back from the Noctem Alliance. It's going to be the hardest thing that any of us've ever done. And if we stand even a tiny chance of winnin', we've all gotta trust each other and work together! That means that both of y'all are gonna have to finally confront the issues you have, and resolve 'em!"

The two players looked at Leonidas, then at each other. They held their gaze for a moment before the Mechanist finally looked away in disgrace as Bob continued to glower at him. Leonidas took a deep breath and addressed the elephant in the room.

"I know that both of y'all think that the Mechanist is responsible for Bill's death."

"I'm sorry!" the Mechanist burst out; Bob's glare did not ease up. "I never should have started drinking that stupid potion again. I knew it was a mistake! Stan was gone, and I felt like I had to fill his shoes. . . . I just got so stressed out, and I cracked!"

"And because you couldn't take the pressure, my brother

is gone," Bob spat bitterly. "He worked hard every minute of every day, even after the Noctem Alliance surrounded the city. He gave his life to save you, and how do you repay him? By moping in a cave, stewing in your own guilt while the people of his city were on the brink of despair and revolution!"

"I know that there's nothing that I can say that will change anything that's happened," the Mechanist whimpered, "but you need to know, Bob . . . I'm never going to forgive myself for what I did to you, and both of your brothers."

"Stop this!" Leonidas cut in before Bob, who was apoplectic with rage, could respond.

"Shut up, Leonidas, this doesn't concern you!" Bob yelled, jabbing his blocky finger at the Mechanist. "I've been holding back my anger toward this useless piece of trash for way too long now. It's about time that I give him a piece of my mind!"

"And what will that prove?" demanded Leonidas. "That you're never gonna forgive him for forcing Bill to sacrifice himself? That he should be stricken with guilt for it? Look at him! He feels so bad about what he did that he can hardly even function anymore! It destroyed him!"

"It really has, Bob," the Mechanist agreed miserably. "You have no idea—"

"Shut up!" Leonidas spat at the Mechanist. "Everythin' that Bob said to you just now was one hundred percent true! If your idea of repaying Bill's sacrifice is to constantly mope over the fact that Bill had to sacrifice himself for you, then it probably would've been better if he'd just let you die and saved himself!"

"I know that!" the Mechanist sobbed, having broken down as Leonidas spoke. "I was . . . I was just so distraught by what happened. . . ."

"And there's the problem in all this," Leonidas replied conclusively, looking back and forth between Bob and the Mechanist. "Both of y'all are so obsessed with Bill's death that it's causin' ya to make stupid decisions! I'm sorry for your loss, but it's in the past now! Ya can't let your entire life be dictated by it. Trust me, I know."

"How dare you!" growled Bob. "You have the nerve to talk about my brother like that . . . you didn't even *know* him! You were too busy leading the Noctem Troops to victory over *our* city! What makes you think that you have *any* right to talk about how I should feel?"

"Because every night that I was a member of the Noctem Alliance, I went to sleep feelin' horrible about what I was doin'!" cried Leonidas, tears welling in his eyes now. "I've never had anythin' against lower-level players, or villagers, or anybody that the Noctem Alliance hates! I only joined King Kev's army to save my family, and he made me do terrible things. I joined the Noctem Alliance because I felt like those terrible things had become a part of who I was, and that killin' and destroyin' were the only things that I could do anymore.

"I let the past define me . . . and it took the death of the family that I had sworn to protect to make me finally realize that I had a choice. I could either live in the shadow of what I had done or let my past go, and do all I could to make up for my mistakes. *That* is the reason I'm here today, and not over in Element City with the Noctem Alliance plottin' to kill y'all."

There was a moment of silence as Leonidas finished his speech. Bob was staring at Leonidas, no longer totally angry, but feeling a mix of anger, confusion, fascination, and sympathy. The Mechanist was staring at Leonidas as well, tears still in his eyes, and looking totally lost for words. Leonidas rubbed his eyes, took a deep breath, and continued to speak.

"I'm not sayin' that ya need to forgive the Mechanist for what he's done right now, Bob. And I'm also not sayin' that ya shouldn't be sorry for what you did, Mechanist. But both of you need to stop lettin' Bill's death cloud your judgment. We're in a war, and we need all the clear minds that we can get, 'specially when they're as brilliant as the ones y'all have.

"Bob," Leonidas said, turning to face the police chief. "You've got the greatest redstone expert in the history of Minecraft at your disposal. Do somethin' with him, will ya?"

Bob sighed, looked up at Leonidas, and gave a begrudging nod.

"And you, Mechanist," continued Leonidas, looking down at the frail old inventory sitting on the floor. "Ya want Bob and Ben to forgive ya, right?"

"More than anything," the Mechanist replied earnestly.

"Then earn it," Leonidas replied simply. With that, he turned to face the wooden door, walked over to it, opened it, and walked out, closing it behind him, leaving Bob and the Mechanist sitting pensively in his wake.

Leonidas gave a deep sigh as he walked out of the room. He had entered to get his assignment for the invasion from the police chiefs, but he realized that it wasn't the right time. And besides, he could worry about that later. There was something else that he had to do before he left for battle, perhaps never to return. It was time to take his own advice.

He exited the front door of the building and walked down the street. As he went, he passed several Elementia soldiers, all of whom gave him a smile or a friendly nod hello, which Leonidas happily returned. All these players . . . they had accepted him, despite all the horrible things that he had done in the past. However, before he could fully accept his past himself, there were three more people he had to speak with. Finally, after walking across the village, Leonidas came across the building—a small structure, constructed just in the past few days, made of cobblestone, wood planks, and glass.

Leonidas took a deep breath and pushed the door open.

All three members of the villager family were locked in a hug, but broke apart when the door opened. As they saw who had come, all three looked slightly confused.

"What are you doing here, Leonidas?" Mella asked.

"I had to see y'all one more time," Leonidas replied, trying to keep his composure despite the feelings of guilt welling within him. "I'm going to war tomorrow, and I might not come back."

"Ah," Mella replied.

"I heard that you three villagers weren't gonna be there at the battle," Leonidas continued awkwardly. "I heard that you were gonna be staying here at the village, along with like thirty other players who weren't goin' into battle."

"This is true."

"And before I leave . . . I just need you to know . . ." There was a catch in his throat, but Leonidas continued.

"I am so, *so* sorry," Leonidas continued, tears beginning to stream down his face. "I am *so* sorry for everything that I did to you. I know that it's my fault that the rest of your village is dead, includin' Blerge. But I promise ya, I never wanted anythin' but the best for ya. You villagers are my family, and when I saw those soldiers takin' advantage of ya, I got so mad that I wasn't thinkin' straight. I don' expect ya to forgive me, but—"

"Leonidas, we know that the players who were in our village to protect us were not treating us kindly."

Leonidas, who was doing all that he could to keep from breaking down, looked up in surprise. "What?"

"At first, we did not realize that we were not being treated kindly," Mella continued. "We knew that the players were sent there by Stan, who was very kind to us, and so we believed that those players that Stan had sent to us were being kind to us, but in a different way. We did not think that Stan would send bad players to us."

"I'm sure he didn't mean to," Leonidas replied quickly, jumping to Stan's defense.

"I know that he did not," Mella said solemnly. "Stan is a good player, and he made a mistake. You are also a good player, Leo-nidas. But I am not sure what you did was a mistake."

"It was," Leonidas replied glumly. "Even if those guys were terrible to you, they still would have fought off the Noctems when they attacked the village. They would've wanted to save their own butts."

"Maybe they would, maybe they would not have," Mella continued. "What is important is that you were not trying to hurt us, Leo-nidas. You were only doing what was best for us . . . or at least, what you thought was best for us. And now my family and me are no longer surrounded by bad players.

We are surrounded by players who are good, and nice to us . . . and you are one of them, Leo-nidas."

Leonidas's heart lifted as Mella gave him a warm smile. Then, Oob stepped forward. He looked Leonidas directly in the eye and spoke.

"When I was a little villager," he spoke slowly, his face screwed up in concentration as if he were trying to meticulously pick every word he said, "I was told by my family about a player named Leo-nidas, who we called the Sacred One. I learned about how, when bad players came to our village, the Sacred One gave himself to them for the sake of protecting us. I always wanted to meet this player, who was so kind, so brave, and so selfless. Now that I am finally meeting you, Leo-nidas, I would just like to say . . . thank you for everything, o Sacred One."

Tears of joy ran like rivers down Leonidas's face. He rushed forward and scooped up the three villagers into a tight embrace, his spirit lifting as the memory of the villagers, the guilt that had been weighing him down for all these weeks finally evaporated. He was with his family once again, and they forgave him. If he died in battle tomorrow, it would now be with no regrets.

Stan opened his eyes and surveyed the area around the spawn point, which had once been a featureless expanse of grass blocks. Now, however, it wasn't anything close to flat; the terrain bore evidence of countless hours of training. The surface of the ground was pockmarked with craters, and half-destroyed structures stood proud and tall, looming against the brilliant pastel colors of the setting sun.

"Sally?" Stan cried out quizzically. He knew that she wanted him here. In the midst of the greetings upon his return to the Adorian Village, Stan had definitely heard her voice ring out from beyond the server. It was different this time, though, very staticky and fragmented, causing Stan to wonder if everything was still okay.

"Coming!" Sally's voice echoed from somewhere Stan couldn't see. He waited for a moment before Sally emerged from behind a tall tower of bedrock blocks with a few holes punched through the center. She levitated toward him until she finally reached him and set her feet firmly on the ground. Stan smiled; it was always nice to see her.

"Thanks for coming, noob."

"No problem, always happy to visit," Stan replied. "Is something wrong? You haven't contacted me for nearly a week now." Even though his training was complete, Stan had found it odd that, after contacting him almost daily since their lessons began, she had been silent since their last meeting before the invasion of the Adorian Village.

"Well . . . there is a bit of news," Sally replied slowly,

causing Stan's heart to sink, "but we'll get to that in a minute. First, tell me how the invasion of the Adorian Village went. Did you manage to take it back?"

Stan nodded, and spent the next ten minutes detailing all that had happened since their last meeting. Through the recounting of the battle, Stan momentarily forgot his worry about Sally, but instead a new uncomfortable feeling took rise within him. When Stan told Sally about the attack on Nocturia, her eyes widened.

"Whoa whoa, back up," she exclaimed, trying to process what he had just told her. "Are you saying that . . . you managed to take out over a hundred Noctem Alliance soldiers, including one of their generals, in one fell swoop?"

"Yes," Stan replied, feeling slightly queasy. "And I've been feeling sick to my stomach ever since."

"Why? That's amazing, noob!" cried Sally, her face totally lit up. "Do you have any idea how much easier it's gonna be for you to take down the Alliance when you have one less general and a hundred less troops to deal with?"

"Yeah, I know, but . . . those troops weren't even in combat. Lord Tenebris . . . ugh . . . *Herobrine*," Stan corrected himself under Sally's glare, "ordered that all troops return to Element City except for them. That means that those troops probably weren't meant for fighting at all."

"You don't know that," scoffed Sally. "He was probably

just keeping them there so that they could sweep through Element City and mop up whatever was left of you after the big battle was over."

"Yeah, I guess . . . ," Stan murmured before another thought occurred to him. "But what if some of those players were actually just upper-level players who didn't want to live under the republic anymore? I mean, Nocturia wasn't a military base. It was the capital of the Noctem Alliance's country. They stopped launching attacks from there as soon as the battles on the Cold Front ended, so doesn't that mean that I technically killed over a hundred citizens? I mean—"

"Stop it, Stan," Sally ordered in such a voice that he immediately ceased talking. "You can't worry about it now, the deed is done. Maybe it was right, maybe it wasn't. All that matters now is that you're going into an even fight, and you have that much better a chance of defeating Herobrine and his army."

"Yeah . . . ," Stan said after a minute. "I guess you're right. . . ." But as hard as he tried, he still couldn't get the image of the crater where Nocturia used to be out of his mind.

"Anyway," he said, eager to change the subject, "you said you had news?"

"Yeah, I do," Sally replied. Stan's stomach clenched; he recognized that tone of voice, and he knew that it was seldom followed by good news.

"What happened?" Stan asked.

"Well . . . ," Sally replied. "Have you wondered why it's taken me so long to get back to you after last time?"

"Well . . . yeah . . . but I just assumed it was because the training was over."

"Oh, come on, Stan," Sally laughed bitterly. "You're my only means of finding out what's going on in Elementia. I'm not just gonna stop contacting you!"

"Your friendship means a lot to me, too," Stan said sarcastically. "So why didn't you contact me?"

Sally sighed. "Security became even tighter somehow. I was really close to figuring out how to hack into the player files and give you operating powers, but then, out of nowhere, new software showed up. My computer didn't even recognize it. It just said that it wasn't possible to even look at the internal mechanisms of the server anymore."

Stan cursed under his breath. "So all the work you've done so far has been for nothing?"

"Pretty much," Sally said sourly. "I'm gonna have to totally restart my efforts to get you operating powers, Stan . . . and that's actually what I want to talk to you about."

"Wait . . . what do you mean?"

"Well, you're planning to invade Element City soon, right?"

"Yes. We were planning on suiting up tonight, and marching out tomorrow."

"Yeah, well . . . I think it might be best if you held off until I got you operating powers."

"Wait . . . what?" Stan demanded, incredulous. "You want us to call off the attack?"

"I think you have to," Sally replied sadly. "I think that you'd have a much, *much* better chance of beating the Alliance if you had them, so I think that it's worth holding off."

"But . . . we have so many advantages right now!" Stan cried. "The Noctem Alliance is still reeling from the attack on Nocturia. They've never been more vulnerable than they are now! And we've just trained a hundred new soldiers that the Noctem Alliance doesn't even know about! It's only a matter of time before they discover that we have them. If we want the element of surprise, then we have to attack tomorrow!"

"But Stan," Sally said fearfully, "they've got Herobrine."

"So?" Stan demanded. "They've got one of him. We've got a hundred soldiers! Are you saying that Herobrine alone is going to be powerful enough to make up for a hundred unexpected fighters, *especially* when the Noctem Alliance is so disorganized right now?"

"That's the thing, Stan . . . *we don't know*," Sally replied darkly. "Nobody has any idea how powerful Herobrine is, and you won't find out until you fight him. You only have one shot at this, Stan, and I think that when you take it, you should be as ready as you possibly can be. From what you've told me, the Noctem Alliance seems to be willing to hold out in a stalemate a little while longer. Why don't you use that to buy time for me to get around this blockage?"

"And how do you know that you're gonna get past it, huh?" Stan demanded, staring at Sally accusatorily. "You've been trying nonstop for months now, and every time that it seems like you're close to cracking it, something else pops up out of left field and makes you start back at square one. You're telling me that I shouldn't strike now while we've got a tiny window of opportunity just so that you *might* be able to get me operating powers, when you've been trying and failing to do it for weeks?"

Sally opened her mouth and raised a blocky finger again, then closed it. She stared at the ground for a moment, in deep thought, then looked back up at Stan.

"Stan, I told you what I think you should do," Sally said calmly. "You're going to return to Elementia, and I'm not going to be there. You're the president, and so it's your choice. Whatever you say, your people are going to go with. So choose wisely, noob."

Stan looked at Sally for a moment, unsure of what to say. Then he nodded and turned his back to the setting sun, away from Sally. He knew that their conversation was over. He took a deep breath, and the words appeared in his head.

DISCONNECT FROM SERVER?

"Stan!"

Just as he was about to leave, Stan turned around to face Sally one more time. She was standing facing him, and as the sun disappeared under the horizon behind her, Stan saw the earnest meaning in her face.

"Please do the right thing," she said.

Stan held her gaze for a moment, nodded again, then turned away. The words reappeared in his head, and as Stan prepared to say the words, the crater in the midst of the tundra where Nocturia had once been flashed in his mind. As the image of the troops being engulfed in a wave of fire resurfaced, Stan knew that he would rather die than have the deaths of those hundred players be for nothing.

"Yes."

Ben, Bob, and Charlie heard a whooshing sound behind them, and they looked up from their schematics, spinning around. Stan had appeared in the other end of the hotel's planning room, right beside the window that showed the sun setting behind the skyline of the trees of the Great Wood over the village wall.

"Hey man," said Charlie, giving Stan a polite nod of the head. "How'd the talk go?"

"Fine," Stan said purposefully. "Guys, I've made my decision about the invasion."

The three players stared at Stan, their eyes wide and their ears perked. They had been waiting for Stan's decision for hours now.

"Go on," Ben said in anticipation.

Stan took a deep breath, and then replied.

"Prepare the troops. We invade Element City tomorrow at the stroke of noon."

Although he was trying to focus on the battle plans that he had propped up on his pig's head, Charlie couldn't help but notice that the farther that they marched down the road toward Element City, the darker the midday sky was becoming. He glanced up and there, not too far away, he could see the dark gray shroud that the Withers were casting over Element City. The march didn't slow down, however. Charlie still walked on, with the sounds of four hundred heavily armed soldiers marching in unison behind him on their way to take back their home.

The preparations for the invasion had been largely silent. There had been no big speech delivered, no final pep talk, no announcements of any kind. All the soldiers now marching down the road knew exactly what they were headed into. Words were not necessary.

At a glance, anybody would find it impossible to believe that many of these players had only been training in combat for the past week. Besides marching perfectly in unison, each and every player was suited in a glistening helmet and chestplate of diamond armor. The same held true for the weapons. Each player was fully equipped with a diamond weapon of their choice, as well as iron backups. To equip every player with such high-tier equipment, however, came at a cost. The storehouses back in the Adorian Village had been totally cleared out. If this invasion were to fail, there were no remaining materials to fall back on.

Charlie returned the plans to his inventory. He didn't need them. He knew them like the back of his hand by now, and looking at them further would only heighten his already overwrought nerves. Charlie had been aware for a while that he would be commanding the assault on Element City, but now that they were on their way, the full realization of what he was about to do struck him like a bolt of lightning. Charlie took a deep breath. He couldn't think too hard about it. He knew what he was doing, and his only job at the moment was to keep his fear at bay. Only with discipline could he lead his people to victory.

Charlie's thoughts drifted to his commanders, and he turned around, glancing over his shoulder into the massive wave of soldiers that was marching behind him. Jayden, Commander Crunch, and Sirus all walked ahead of the troops. All three of them bore the same expression: grim and determined, with no hint of joy in their eyes as they imagined what they would find in Element City. Charlie knew that, somewhere deep within the hundreds of players, Stan, Kat, and all the other commanders marched. They had special missions to do while the other soldiers were fighting, so they took to the center of the assembly to stay inconspicuous.

Charlie imagined that, at this moment, their expressions mirrored those of the commanders out front, including himself.

A crash of thunder sounded from overhead, causing several soldiers in line to raise their heads in alarm. A moment later, a light drizzle of rain began to fall from the sky. Charlie gave an offhanded glance at the sky, wondering how much of the discoloration above was from the thunderclouds and how much was from the Withers.

Charlie squinted through the rain, and there, slowly but surely, the Element City wall came into view. As he approached, the silhouette of the newly repaired structure loomed into sight, rising out of the mist. They didn't check their speed as they advanced closer and closer to the main gate of the city. The forest that they had been marching through started to thin out; more and more trees had chunks ripped out of them, or else were just lowly woodblock stumps.

Finally the forest ended altogether, giving way to the badlands that had been torn into the ground by the weeks of warfare around the outer wall. The giant ditch around the entirety of the outer wall sunk far below ground level; to approach the ditch from within it would be an uphill battle. Charlie raised his hand, ordering a stop. When they reached the edge of the trench, he could finally see the wall clearly. He did a double take. As prepared as he was for the attack, he had not expected what he was now seeing.

A bridge had been built across the open expanse of the badlands. Constructed of wood-plank blocks, it was five blocks wide, and extended from the edge of the forest to the base of the wall. Wood-plank blocks also extended from the top of the bridge all the way down into the base of the trench, concealing the underside of the structure. The other end of the bridge sat at the exact center of a giant rip that had, alarmingly, been left in the center of the wall surrounding the sprawling city, with the Withers hovering far off over the castle. The entire open portion of the wall was totally filled, from end to end, with Noctem soldiers, clad in black leather armor, all of whom had some sort of weapon drawn and ready. And standing directly at the center of this massive wall of Noctem Troops, at the exact center of the bridge's far end, was Drake, his cape billowing in the wind and a leering smile on his face.

The players behind Charlie were dead silent as they stared across the bridge at the soldiers clad in black who would be attempting to kill them within the minute. Charlie heard movement behind him, and he turned around to see Jayden, Crunch, and Sirus glance at each other, the same thoughts in each of their heads.

Charlie was on the same page. He had been anticipating a hard fight through the trench to enter Element City. It didn't make sense that the Noctems would not only leave a giant gaping hole in their wall, but also build a bridge to make their entrance into the city easier. Clearly, something wasn't right here.

There was movement on the Noctem side of the bridge, and Charlie's eyes immediately locked on to Drake. The Noctem general had taken a step forward and was now walking at a strolling pace down the center of the wooden bridge toward Charlie. Immediately there was a bustle in the front lines of the Elementia soldiers as all of them drew their bows and trained them on Drake. The moment they did so, the Noctem archers at the other end of the bridge did the same, aiming at Charlie, who raised his hand to indicate his men hold fire. *Something is very odd about this situation,* he thought to himself. As he did so, Drake continued to walk, finally coming to a stop at the center of the bridge. He gave Charlie a look, as if to indicate that he should walk out to meet Drake halfway.

"Wha' do ye want us t' do, General?" Commander Crunch whispered up to Charlie.

Charlie looked out at Drake. He knew that this must be some kind of ploy. There was no way that Drake would do this with no ill intent. And yet, as Charlie made eye contact with Drake, he immediately got a feeling in his gut that Drake wasn't going to attack him . . . and that, despite all his better judgment, he should go out to meet the Noctem general.

"I'm going out to meet Drake," Charlie whispered back. "Keep on holding. Don't fire unless they do first."

Before anybody could respond to him or Charlie could talk himself out of it, he gave a tug on Dr. Pigglesworth's saddle, and the pig began to trot slowly forward, onto the wooden bridge and toward Drake. As he traveled across the open expanse of the trench, Charlie could feel all eight hundred of the warriors on both sides training their eyes on him. Charlie took a deep breath and shook off the incredible tension that was hampering his breathing as he continued forward. Finally, after several agonizing seconds of walking with bated breath, Charlie stood face to face with General Drake.

"That's a fine-looking pig, Charlie," Drake said with a smirk, looking downward slightly to meet the eye level of the seated Charlie. "It's good to see that you've managed to continue to be useful to your people. Very few have even survived our Silverfish Torture, let alone returned to the battlefield after it."

"Well, I've been a thorn in your side for this long," Charlie replied wittily. "It would be a shame to stop now that we're so close to taking our city back."

"Oh, you think that the city is yours," Drake said, with a

note of pity in his voice, as he shook his head and gave a sad smile. "Oh dear . . . You know, it's going to be a shame to kill you and all your men, Charlie. You're all so clueless that it's nearly pitiful."

Something snapped in Charlie's head as Drake said this, and he growled back, "Don't insult me, Drake. Just tell me why you wanted me to come out and meet you."

"Oh, I just had a few questions for you about the setup you've got going over there," Drake replied conversationally, looking at the wall of Elementia troops, many of whom were still aiming at him with their bows.

"Funny," Charlie said, glancing down at the bridge they were standing on, "I could say the same thing to you."

"So where's your president, anyway?" Drake asked, scanning the rows of soldiers, looking for Stan. "I'd have expected him to be out front."

"That's none of your concern," Charlie replied quicker than he had intended.

"Ah, I see," Drake chuckled. "I suppose that he'll pop up during the battle at some point. I suppose that I'll just have to cross that bridge when I come to it. That ought to be fun."

"Speaking of crossing bridges," Charlie asked suspiciously, "what's the deal with the one we're standing on?"

"Well, it's a manner of courtesy, of course," Drake replied, as if it should be the most obvious thing in the world. "You took all the time to evade us, raise an army, and march all the way to our doorsteps. Lord Tenebris has great respect for you for doing that, Charlie, and as such, he ordered that you should at least have a fighting chance at getting *into* our city before we kill you all. Therefore, the bridge is here for your convenience. You can use it to avoid traversing the trench. I assure you, it's totally safe."

"And why should I believe that?" Charlie demanded.

"Oh, Charlie, would I lie to you?" Drake laughed with a smirk. "I'm a member of the Noctem Alliance, my friend. Although we may not follow your rules, when we set rules for ourselves, we'll play by them to the death. You can trust our word. We're going to destroy you, and don't expect us to play fair for a moment while we're within the city. But I give you my word that the bridge is safe to cross. It's not booby trapped or anything like that. Now, why don't you go back and lead your men across, while I do all in my power to stop you?"

And with that, Drake turned his back to Charlie, and proceeded to march back toward his soldiers. Charlie stood in the light rain in total shock, trying to comprehend what Drake had just said. After a moment, though, he just gave up. Drake was clearly trying to play some sort of mind game with him . . . or else he was just a lunatic. Charlie shook his head; although he knew that the time had finally come to put these psychopaths out of commission, he still felt like this moment hadn't come nearly soon enough. He ordered Dr. Pigglesworth to turn around and make his way back to the Elementia soldiers at the far end of the bridge.

Charlie had a gut feeling that Drake was telling the truth about the bridge. As despicable as the Noctem Alliance had proven themselves, the one honorable thing that they did seem to exemplify was sticking to their word. Charlie remembered the first time he had met Drake in the Nether months before, where Drake had sworn during the interrogation that he would not lie to them. Indeed, in time, everything that Drake had revealed had turned out to be true.

Charlie still had no idea *why* Drake had told them those things. The second that the general had tried to escape, he had done so with ease, but Charlie had better things to do than to try to work it out. He had been trying to decipher the warped, maniacal mindset of the Noctem Alliance for far too long now. The days of fighting with trickery and deceit had finally come to a close. It was time to do the fighting in a language they could both understand perfectly.

"What's the deal with the bridge?" Jayden asked, as Charlie reached the front of his men and turned around to face the wall again.

"It's safe," Charlie replied unemotionally, not taking his eyes off Drake. "Charge when I give the word. Have your archers stay back and cover us from the rear."

"What?" Jayden asked incredulously. "How can you be sure that it's safe?"

"I'm your commanding officer. Don't question me," Charlie replied, a bit more harshly this time, causing Jayden to back down. "I'll stay back with the archers and follow you in a bit. Ready your weapons."

"Ready your weapons!" Jayden, Crunch, and Sirus replied in unison. Instantly, hundreds of bows and diamond tools emerged into the hands in the army, and readied themselves for an attack.

"Ready!" cried Charlie. "And . . . *charge*!"

Charlie waved his hand forward and watched as hundreds of diamond-clad warriors rushed ahead, parting around him like a rock in a raging river as they ran toward the bridge. Charlie heard a cry ring out from the Noctem end, and a shower of hundreds of arrows flew into the sky, soaring through the air and crashing down like a meteor storm into the tide of players now surging across the bridge and into the city.

"Cut to the sides!" Charlie bellowed as his soldiers started to fall to the rain of projectiles.

Jayden, Crunch, and Sirus at the head of the charge exchanged a quick glance and nodded to each other. Just as the mass of troops barreling across the bridge was about to hit the wall of Noctem soldiers, now drawing their closer-quarters weapons, Jayden and Sirus leaped off the bridge on both sides, landing firmly in the trench below. The streams of troops followed their three leaders like a diamond snake dividing in three, pouring off the bridge and swarming through the trench, leaving only Commander Crunch's troops to fight the soldiers blocking the main entrance to the city.

As Crunch and his men collided with the black wall of Noctem troops and engaged them in swordplay, the Noctem troops appeared to be disoriented as they tried to branch into sections to break off the three-pronged assault of Crunch, Jayden, and Sirus. It was too late, though. By the time the Noctem troops had made their way into the trench to combat Jayden and Sirus's soldiers, the republic soldiers had already drawn Ender Pearls from their inventories and were teleporting to the top of the Element City wall in an ever-growing cloud of purple smoke.

Charlie looked on with a smile at the battle going on before them. He still had no idea why Drake had let them into the city so easily, but whatever the reason was, it had given Charlie's invasion force an upper hand in the first phase of their invasion plan. The Noctem Alliance was now falling back from the city wall as Commander Crunch pushed his soldiers through the gates and into the city. Meanwhile, Jayden and Sirus had both managed to get nearly all their troops over the Element City wall using their Ender Pearls, and Charlie could see that some of them had even stayed on top and were now firing arrows down into the city.

Charlie glanced down at the bridge and saw the bodies of about five Elementia soldiers vanish into nothing, leaving a floating pool of items in their place. His heart clenched as he saw this, but loosened slightly as he saw hundreds of items spilled at the gateway where the Noctem Alliance had been standing guard. He took a deep breath and reminded himself that many of his people were about to die, and he would just have to accept this. With a heavy heart and a mindset that was trying as hard as it could to be optimistic, Charlie dug his heels into his pig and made his way down the bridge and into the city.

As he sprinted through the streets of his city, Stan couldn't believe the scale of the war breaking out all around him as the rain continued to fall. All throughout the streets, hundreds of soldiers were engaged in armed combat, fighting as hard as they could to destroy each other as sparks flew from their connecting blades. Arrows flew across the sky like deadly sparrows, some flying a bit too close to him for comfort. The scents and hues of dozens of noxious potion gases clouded the air, only getting stronger by the second. The bangs and whizzes of the fire charge dispensers and

TNT cannons rang through the air, creating a deafening din that almost drowned out the battle cries of the eight hundred combatants spread across Element City. Every so often, the side of a building would explode as a TNT cannon missed its mark, sending dust, blocks, and various debris flying.

Stan felt extremely vulnerable as he sprinted through this metropolitan battlefield, completely devoid of armor and without his diamond axe in hand. He knew that it would render the Invisibility Potion moot if he were carrying anything visible, but the fact that he was so defenseless made him feel jittery and panicked as he ran. And he couldn't have those feelings now . . . not with what he was about to do.

Finally, after running across hundreds of blocks of streets and buildings within the battle zone, the rendezvous point came into sight. Stan hastily made his way into the dilapidated remains of the old Spleef Arena, and wasted no time in ducking into the base of a fountain that still stood in the central plaza. Though the building itself hadn't been used in years, and it had been picked apart by vandals, the remaining structure of the arena still maintained the regal splendor it had in its heyday. The old arena and the flat expanse of overgrown grass surrounding it was calm, but Stan could still hear the sounds of warfare as they spread farther and farther across Element City. Stan's heart raced; there was nothing to do but wait for his friends and hope that they made it without incident.

As soon as he thought this, Stan heard footsteps above him and, without thinking, crouched to the ground, ready to draw his axe at a moment's notice. The footsteps halted, and after a few seconds of silence, the visible form of Kat leaped up over the side of the fountain and dropped down beside Stan, landing in the stone basin.

"Hello? Is anyone here?" Kat whispered tentatively, her sword drawn and tightly clutched in her hand.

"Yeah, I'm here," Stan replied, and as soon as he said it, he realized that his hand was starting to fade back into visibility. Kat looked at him and gave a sigh of relief, the tension in her body lessening slightly.

"Glad to see you made it here okay," Kat said as she sat with her back to the fountain wall. "You have any trouble?"

"No, it was pretty smooth," Stan replied as he sat down next to her. "How about you?"

"Same," she replied, looking at the ground as she absent-mindedly chiseled into the stone with the tip of her diamond sword. "I wish that I didn't have to leave Rex back in the village, though . . . I felt so exposed without him."

"Well, you know it was for the best," Stan replied solemnly. "He won't be any help to us on the mission, and the last thing we want is for something to happen to him."

Kat said nothing in response. Stan hadn't expected her

to. There was nothing to say. They were about to charge into Element Castle to try to take down Lord Tenebris once and for all. To talk about it would only rekindle the fear that the two of them were barely suppressing.

"I wonder where the others are," Stan said after a little while.

"Oh man . . . I hope they're okay," Kat said nervously. She glanced up out of the fountain and toward the gray sky above, from which rain was still falling, occasionally accented by a clap of thunder. Stan looked at her in concern, his heart feeling as if it were being wrung out like a sponge. As he stared at Kat, the rain drizzling down over her and a light mist hanging above them, it truly hit him for the first time that there was a high possibility that some of them—or all of them—would not live to see the end of the day.

"Kat?" he whispered.

"Yeah?" she replied, in equally hushed tones.

"Well . . . it's just that . . . I want you to know that . . . if we don't make it back . . ."

"Don't say that!" Kat hissed, her eyes flaring with anger as she glared at Stan; he immediately backed off. "We're going to kill Lord Tenebris and all walk out of here alive!"

Stan stared downward at the basin as Kat continued to glare at him. He didn't dare question her. And yet, from the corner of his eye, Stan saw that Kat, too, was looking forward.

She stared intently at the cobblestone-block wall across from her, as if trying to extract some hidden message from it.

"We're all going to be just fine . . . ," she murmured to herself, still staring, as if entranced, at the wall.

There were footsteps above, and without thinking, Stan and Kat immediately drew their bows and aimed them up, lest they be discovered by Noctem Agents. But they soon returned their weapons to their inventories. Leonidas's head came into the well, saw both of them, and smiled.

"Excellent, y'all are here!" he exclaimed. "Warp up outta there. We've gotta get a move on. Yo, Cassandrix, they're both down there!"

Stan and Kat both drew Ender Pearls from their inventories and pitched them up out of the well. Stan closed his eyes as he warped onto the solid brick ground above. Brushing off the slight sting in his knees, Stan saw Leonidas and Cassandrix, both clad in full armor glowing with enchantments.

"You're late." Stan snickered as Kat appeared beside him in a puff of smoke that was instantly dissipated by the strengthening rainfall.

"Be that as it may," Cassandrix replied with an arrogant snicker, "at least the two of us are fully armored and ready for the assault."

Stan looked down at himself and realized, to his embarrassment, that Cassandrix was right. Both he and Kat hadn't put on their diamond armor after the Invisibility Potion had worn off. Hastily, Stan tossed the armor out of his inventory to the ground and began to put it on, Kat doing the same as Cassandrix and Leonidas chuckled to themselves.

Finally, Stan secured the diamond helmet on his head. His entire body was covered in glowing diamond, from his head to his feet to the axe clutched in his right hand. Kat looked equally menacing. The radiant luster of the armor shone through the rain, particularly from the three-pronged enchantment on Kat's sword.

Stan took a deep breath and looked at his three friends, who were no longer laughing, but clutching their weapons in their hands and looking deadly serious. It was time to end the war once and for all.

"Are you ready?" Stan asked.

"Yes, sir!" all three players replied in unison, shouting to be heard over the now raging storm.

"All right," replied Stan, his eyes glinting with fury as a flash of lightning illuminated the sky behind him, accompanied by a crash of thunder.

"Let's do this."

Charlie's eyes widened as he realized that a block of TNT was soaring out of the raging rain and right for him. He yanked the reins of his pig to the right as hard as he could, swerving away just before the flying projectile would have made contact. The TNT hit the ground in a massive burst behind Charlie, leaving a sizable hole in the center of the street. As Charlie felt the shockwave from the explosion crash over him, he scratched Dr. Pigglesworth behind the ears in thanks.

Although the war between the eight hundred players was now spreading throughout the city, the majority of the combat was still confined to the Merchant's District, which bordered the outer wall near the entrance. Charlie had been on his way to the front lines to command the troops, but he could now see that the combat along the main roads was too thick. He instead fell back behind a half-destroyed building, where he found Ben looking at the battle plans laid out on a crafting table, his eyes skimming the pages so fast they nearly appeared as blurs.

"How're we looking back here?" Charlie asked, parking his pig next to Ben's table as the police chief looked up at him.

"Pretty good so far," Ben replied quickly. "We've broken their first line of defense and they're being driven back into the city. At this rate we should make it to the castle within a couple hours."

Charlie sighed at the idea of fighting an uphill battle for the next two hours, especially considering that the longer the combat raged, the more casualties there would be. This thought reminded him to ask Ben about the deaths on both sides so far.

"Well, it's kind of hard to get a certain read," Ben said matter-of-factly, "but based on what I've seen, I'd estimate about fifty dead on each side so far."

Charlie's stomach contracted as if all the air had been sucked out. In the short time that they'd been fighting, both sides had already lost an eighth of their soldiers! Would there be anybody left to fight on either side by the time they got to the castle?

"Calm down," Ben said sternly, sensing Charlie's panic. "It's not surprising that we lost so many during the initial strike. I'm sure the rate of casualties will only go down from here . . . at least, until they make their last stand at the castle, that is."

"Great," replied Charlie miserably.

"Don't mope, Charlie!" Ben ordered, the drill sergeant in him showing itself in full now. "The invasion so far has been a fantastic success, you have nothing to complain about! Now go out there and lead your people."

"Yes, sir," Charlie replied unwaveringly, and he commanded the pig back out into the open. The street was nearly deserted now, as the fighting had moved up the street and deeper into the merchant's district. Charlie knew that he couldn't just march up the street. He'd be taken out by snipers or TNT cannons if he rode up the street alone. Charlie glanced around and noticed an alleyway branching out from the main plaza. It looked like it went in the general direction of the combat, and it appeared totally unoccupied. Drawing his pickaxe, Charlie urged Dr. Pigglesworth forward across the clearing, ducking into the narrow side street.

The two-block-wide path was paved with dirt, unlike the rest of the city, and walls of solid brick rose skyward on either side of Charlie. In fact, the alleyway bore a striking resemblance to the one in which Charlie, Stan, and Kat had stayed upon their first-ever entrance into Element City. Another clap of thunder burst from overhead as the rain continued to crash down from the sky in sheets. Charlie edged slowly onward, pickaxe drawn, and eyes and ears on the ready to detect the slightest hint that somebody might . . .

It all happened at once. Charlie heard the sound of teleportation behind him, and at the same instant felt the tip of a sword wedged into a chink in his diamond armor, one thrust away from killing him. He froze like a deer in the headlights, pulling back on the saddle to bring Dr. Pigglesworth to a halt along with him.

"Move a single block further and you're dead," the voice of Arachnia hissed from behind him.

Charlie was unable to move. He was unable to breathe. He was unable to process anything other than the shock that ELM had not yet given up their hunt . . . and they now had him.

"It's good to see you, Charlie," Arachnia said with a sly smile as she walked around to face him. Charlie heard the stretch of a bowstring behind him and knew that Lord Marrow had an arrow aimed at his head. "Although I know that the same isn't true for you. You probably thought that we had given up on capturing the president after the episode at the Adorian Village."

Charlie said nothing.

"No matter," Arachnia continued with a faint chuckle. "You will be very useful to us. Enderchick, bring him back to the hideout."

"Should I bring the guh-*ross* pig, too?"

There was a pause before Arachnia replied. "Yes, I think so. I'm sure we'll find a use for it . . . around dinnertime, that is."

Charlie's stomach flipped, and he felt a blocky hand on his shoulder. Before he knew what was happening, everyone in the alleyway vanished in a puff of purple smoke, leaving the ominous corridor deserted once more.

As Charlie reappeared, he couldn't see an inch in front of his face. Although the city outside certainly hadn't been bright in the midst of the rainfall and haze of potions in the air, Charlie's eyes were not ready to instantaneously adjust to the darkness of wherever Enderchick had warped them. He was just beginning to make out the light of a row of windows when a fist slammed into the side of his head. The last thing Charlie heard was the squeal of Dr. Pigglesworth as Charlie saw stars and was knocked out cold.

The eeriest thing about Element Castle was . . . how quiet it was. As Stan walked down the stone brick–block corridors of his castle, tailed by his three friends, the sounds of their footsteps echoed, casting the sharp tapping sounds upward to bounce through the arched ceilings of the main hall. Their Potions of Swiftness had cut the travel time to Element Castle from the old Spleef Arena in half, and they had still encountered no soldiers of either allegiance, even as they had crossed the castle grounds.

Although Stan's friends may have been surprised, he wasn't. He had had a gut feeling that Lord Tenebris would want to enter this duel unaided—the best of the Noctem Alliance versus the best of the republic.

In utter silence, the four players began to ascend the stone-brick staircase. They hadn't spoken a word to each other since they had left the Spleef Arena, and they knew it was no time for conversation. They were now inside the castle, the point of no return left in the dust far behind them. Five players would enter the council room, but without question, at least one of the five would not come out. But if any member of Stan's team was going to go down today, it wouldn't be without a fight.

Cassandrix carried two diamond swords, one at

each hip, both glowing with Sharpness. She was the only one of the four players not to wear diamond armor, instead opting for her white-leather Spleef armor. Much like DZ, she preferred the increased mobility of the lighter, thinner armor. She also opted not to use a bow and arrow, and instead carried numerous Splash potions tucked safely into her inventory.

Leonidas was fully armored in a diamond helmet and chestplate, as were Kat and Stan. He had two bows, glowing with Power and Fire enchantments respectively, slung across his back. However, his prized bow, which he had named Hornet, was clutched in his hand, radiant with enchantments of Fire, Power, and Infinity. A single arrow was notched in this bow, with dozens of others at one hip and an unenhanced diamond sword on the other.

Kat clutched her fully enchanted diamond sword (Gas-Powered Stick) in her right hand. One sword with a Fire enchantment hung at one hip, and a blade with Knockback was on the other. Slung across her back was Ol' Reliable, a bow with a simple Infinity enchantment. This was widely believed to be the oldest surviving weapon in the entire army. It was the very same bow that Kat had enchanted in the Apothecary's cabin, which she had continuously repaired on an anvil over time.

Stan was equipped exactly the same as he had been the

day that he had fought against King Kev. A diamond axe with Sharpness was held firmly in both hands, with two iron axes swung over his back. A Power bow hung at one hip, and the arrows at the other. Stan had worn this same set of armor the last time that he had dispatched a tyrant; he figured that if it wasn't broken, it wasn't worth fixing.

Finally, after what seemed like a full hour of walking, they were there. Stan, Kat, Leonidas, and Cassandrix stood at the iron door to the council chamber. All four players stared at the door. They knew what was on the other side, and they knew that there would never be a better time to face it.

Stan reached out a trembling hand and pressed the stone button on the wall. The redstone mechanism roared to life and the entire team watched with bated breath as the iron door slowly swung open.

Charlie's eyes fluttered, struggling against what felt like some sort of invisible energy that was forcing them shut. Finally, he wrenched his eyes open, and after a moment, they adjusted to the dark. He was lying on a stone brick–block floor, and a very uncomfortable one at that. Not moving his head at all, fearing what might happen, Charlie looked around.

He was lying in a circular room that he recognized as the inside of one of Element Castle's towers, specifically, the one that had to be rebuilt after King Kev had blown it up. Battlements were opened all around the circular room, allowing a segmented aerial view of Element City. Although he could see the city, it was still dark as night within the tower. Charlie was shocked that no monsters were spawning. Leaning against the far wall were Arachnia and Lord Marrow, each holding their weapons, eyes trained on the floor with impatient looks on their faces.

Charlie's stomach filled with acid as he pondered what to do. Every moment that he lay in the middle of this floor, the republic troops were out on the battlefield without a commander. He had to get back down to the battle as quickly as possible. But he had no idea how he was going to do that without Dr. Pigglesworth's help and, as he performed an immobile search of his inventory, he realized with a jolt that his pickaxe had been taken from him. He was totally defenseless.

"Hey!" Arachnia bellowed.

This is it, Charlie thought, his heart racing. *She knows I'm awake. What are they gonna do?*

"How much longer until you can warp again?"

"Omigosh, Arachnia, just give me, like, two seconds . . ."

"Do I really have to spell this out for you?" Arachnia said, clearly agitated with Enderchick, whose voice Charlie could hear from directly behind him. "You've got to get out there and find Stan as soon as possible! We can't hold Charlie in this tower forever, and he's probably the only person who Stan will turn himself in for!"

"But I'm, like, still kinda confused. Will Stan know that we have, ya know, the real Charlie?"

"You've got his pickaxe, don't you?"

"Yeah," Enderchick replied lazily, and Charlie's heart leaped as he heard the sound of something clattering to the ground. His pickaxe was now on the floor directly behind him.

"That's all you need. Stan will recognize it, and he'll turn himself in. Then we turn Stan in to Drake and finally call this mission a success."

"But still, like, how will Stan recognize Charlie's pickaxe?"

Enderchick and Arachnia continued to argue as Lord Marrow stared at the ground in stoic silence, but the gears in Charlie's head were whirring. They were planning on trading him for Stan. Arachnia was right, even if she was probably just guessing. Stan definitely would turn himself into them in exchange for Charlie's safety, and Charlie knew that, for the sake of the republic, he couldn't let that happen.

"It's all your fault. If I hadn't brought you, I'd have enough energy to warp again right now!"

A smacking sound echoed throughout the chamber, followed immediately by a squeal of pain. Charlie's stomach clenched. Dr. Pigglesworth's sound of anguish had echoed from behind him, and he could hear his pig breathing heavily.

Charlie's mind kicked into overdrive. For whatever reason, the members of ELM hadn't killed his pig yet, and Enderchick had been careless enough to toss his pickaxe to the ground directly behind him. He had everything that he needed to facilitate an escape and return to the battlefield.

There was only one problem. Charlie knew that he had no chance of taking on the three remaining members of ELM by himself. It would take him a few seconds to even mount Dr. Pigglesworth from the ground. In the time that took him, Lord Marrow would have already shot a tranquilizing arrow into his forearm. It was only a matter of time before Enderchick felt up to warping again. Charlie had no idea how he was going to escape, but he knew that he would have to act soon.

The light of the council room's torches flickered over Stan and his friends as they stood in a row of four inside the council-room door, weapons drawn. From the windows in the stone brick–block walls, Stan could see the sprawling metropolis of Element City beneath the gray skies. This was the first time that Stan had returned to his council room in weeks, and though it was nearly unchanged, there was one difference that struck a chord of deep discontent within Stan.

The council table had been removed. The block-high platform of stone bricks where Stan and his friends had drawn up the constitution of Elementia and made every law since then was gone. A flat expanse of stone-brick blocks now lay between Stan and the elevated throne on which a single player now sat. Stan found himself unable to move as, for the first time in his life, he laid his eyes on Lord Tenebris.

The leader of the Noctem Alliance was sitting cross-legged on the throne, his blocky hands pressed together and a devious leer on his face. Stan had heard that Lord Tenebris, or Herobrine, had nearly the same skin as him, but he was still surprised to see that, in fact, their skins were exactly identical in every way except one. And like the missing council table, this one subtle difference made Stan's skin crawl with uncanny anxiety as he stared into Lord Tenebris's empty, white eyes.

And, yet, as Stan looked his greatest adversary in the face for the first time, he couldn't help but feel something odd. The emptiness of his eyes bore into Stan's own, forcing him to devote all his willpower to maintaining the bond of contact, but Stan still could have sworn that, deep within the empty sockets, something was familiar.

The sensation lasted only for a few seconds, however, before Stan couldn't help but look away. It had been like trying to stare into the sun. Stan's entire face felt like it was burning up. And after all, it didn't matter what Stan might have sensed in those eyes. All that mattered was that it was finally time to kill the leader of the Noctem Alliance. Stan clutched his axe tightly and looked back up at Lord Tenebris.

"Ah, if it isn't the leaders of the Republic of Elementia," Lord Tenebris said with a chuckle. His voice was deep and calm, yet also menacing beyond compare. Just hearing him speak gave Stan the impression that Lord Tenebris could tell exactly what he was thinking.

"Stand down," Stan announced, sounding much braver then he felt as he stared at Lord Tenebris. "There are four of us and only one of you. There's no use in fighting."

"Oh, Stan, Stan, Stan," Lord Tenebris chuckled, closing his eyes as he shook his head and clicked his tongue. "Let's not be hasty. We're going to have a lot of fun, so why rush? Let me at least greet you before we begin. Let's start with you, Cassandrix."

Cassandrix, who was standing at the opposite end of the line as Stan with her diamond sword drawn, gasped, clearly shocked. "How do you know my name?" she demanded.

"Why, everybody knows your name, Cassandrix," Lord Tenebris replied, almost conversationally. "After all, you are one of the greatest Spleef players in the history of Element City . . . or, at least, you were, until you started to become overshadowed by the new players."

"What?" Cassandrix gasped, blindsided. "What are you talking about? How do you know that?"

"I know all that has ever happened on this server." Lord Tenebris chuckled. "And I know what you've been through, Cassandrix. It *is* a tragic tale . . . always the best player in the Spleef League, but never appreciated, always held back by your mediocre teammates. Then finally, after years of obscurity, Spleef returns to Elementia, and you see your chance to gain the glory you always deserved . . . only to realize that you're outdated and useless in comparison to the new players on the scene."

"Shut up!" Cassandrix growled, but Lord Tenebris continued.

"Why, then, Cassandrix, have you joined their side? You of all people must realize that lower-level players are nothing but verminous scum, infesting our server and taking opportunities from hard-working players like you, who have lived in Elementia since before they even knew what Minecraft was. So why do you defy me, when I, for all intents and purposes, am working for your benefit?"

"I'd rather die than join you!" Cassandrix screamed in rage, glaring at Lord Tenebris with tears in her eyes. "Regardless of whatever you might think of the lower-level players, they're still players, and no player deserves the things that you've been doing to them!"

Lord Tenebris chuckled again. "Very well, Cassandrix," he replied, still keeping his voice very casual. "If you would like to try to fight me, to fight to create a world where the lower-level players have everything gift-wrapped for them at the expense of older players like you, so be it."

"What beef do ya have against lower-levels, anyway?" Leonidas shouted, as Cassandrix stared at the ground, her eyes wide and a horrified expression on her face. "What did they ever do to you?"

Lord Tenebris slowly turned his head and fixed his gaze on Leonidas, who abruptly glanced sideways to avoid eye contact.

"Well, well, well, if it isn't General Leonidas," Lord Tenebris said, the level tone of his voice more unnerving than if he had been shouting at them. "It's so . . . interesting to see you here. I must admit that your treachery surprised me. I pride myself on my foresight, but I did not anticipate that you would ever stand alongside the president of Elementia, with an arrow notched in your bow and trained on me."

"Answer my question," Leonidas hissed, pulling the string of his bow even more taut.

Lord Tenebris laughed. "Leonidas, my friend, you misunderstand. I'm far more than a simple player who was wronged by the new players. Surely, by now, you must have worked it out!"

And with that, Lord Tenebris stood up from his chair, and stretched out his hand. Stan tried to raise his axe to block whatever was about to happen but, to his horror, he found that he was totally unable to move. He felt the horribly familiar sensation of being held in place by Sally's operating powers as he stood, totally immobile, in the psychic grip of Lord Tenebris. Stan's eyes flicked to the side as he realized with an awful jolt that all his friends were frozen as well, as if they were living statues. His heart beating out of his chest with panic, Stan turned to face Lord Tenebris, and his heart-beat stopped.

Lord Tenebris's eyes were open wide, and a gust of wind had started to blow through the open windows of the council room. The rush of air grew stronger and stronger by the second, and within a few moments a hurricane-force gale was ripping through the council room. The air seemed to spiral around Lord Tenebris as he slowly began to levitate into the air, his hand outstretched. His face was no longer jovial and conversational, but intense and twisted, radiating power. A primal rush of fear shot through Stan's body as Lord Tenebris opened his mouth and began to speak.

"**I HAVE EXISTED SINCE THE BEGINNING, AND I AM THE GREATEST BEING IN ALL OF MINECRAFT!**" Lord Tenebris's voice sounded over the raging storm, amplified now to sound as if thousands of voices were speaking from directly within Stan's head. His ears felt like they were about to burst. "**MY POWER IS SECOND TO NONE, AND I AM FAR GREATER THAN ANY PLAYER, THAN ANY**

OPERATOR COULD EVER DREAM! AFTER THE DEATH OF KING KEV, ELEMENTIA, THE GREATEST MINECRAFT SERVER IN ALL OF HISTORY, HAD FALLEN INTO THE HANDS OF PARASITES, AND I KNEW THAT, AFTER YEARS OF SLUMBER, IT WAS TIME TO RISE AGAIN! I CAME TO ELEMENTIA OUT OF NECESSITY, TO LEAD THE DISGRACED SOLDIERS OF BIRTHRIGHT TO VICTORY OVER THE ROACHES THAT HAD INFESTED THE LAND! AND TODAY . . . TODAY IS THE DAY THAT I WILL FINISH WHAT THE GREAT MARTYR HAS STARTED! I AM THE UNIVERSAL EMBODIMENT OF THE SPIRIT OF THE TRUE KING OF ELEMENTIA! I . . . AM . . . HEROBRINE!"

Lord Tenebris's mouth gaped open, and his eyes seemed to pop out of their sockets, as he let out an animal roar that pierced even the slicing winds of the storm. Outside the council-room windows, Stan could see dozens of lightning strikes, illuminating the now-blackened sky and filling the vortex of space around Element Castle with an awful amalgamation of light and dark. The scene was too much for Stan's senses to comprehend. It was far beyond anything that his worst nightmares could have possibly fabricated for themselves. Stan was now positive where all the power being diverted from Elementia's core was going—more raw power was radiating from Lord Tenebris than Stan had ever sensed before in his life.

Then, all at once, the lightning stopped. The pitch-black sky outside the windows brightened, returning to the murky gray cloud of the Withers. The cyclone of wind spiraling around the levitating Lord Tenebris quickly died down, and he himself took a deep breath, letting it out as he sunk downward, touching down on the stone-brick floor. He was no longer on the elevated platform on which the throne sat, but instead stood with his back to the stone brick–block wall, on the same level as Stan and his friends. With a start, Stan realized that he could move again, and instantly raised his axe into a block, the weapon shaking uncontrollably in his now trembling hands.

Lord Tenebris's face was tranquil once again, no longer smiling, but not showing any other emotion either. He raised his hand again, and before Stan could even realize what had happened, he felt an intense heat well up behind him. He jumped forward as fast as his legs could carry him, desperate to avoid the fire that had sprung up behind him. As he landed on the floor, next to his equally disoriented cohorts, Stan glanced around the room. The entire council room perimeter had been ignited into a blaze, fire ringing the room and blocking the door. Within the ring of fire was the flat expanse of stone-brick blocks where Lord Tenebris and the four players stood.

"I, like the Alliance that I lead, hold the principle of honor very close to my heart," Lord Tenebris said, as if presenting a business proposal. "Therefore, I am going to give you a choice as to your fate."

Stan was too terrified to respond. Never in a thousand years could he have possibly prepared for what Lord Tenebris was capable of. He had just displayed a show of power far greater than any player, even one with operating powers, could ever achieve.

"Your first option," Lord Tenebris continued, "is to come with me to the battlefield. There, in front of all the citizens of Elementia, you will surrender to me, and declare the war over. I will then proceed to execute each of you, as well as the rest of your commanders. It will be swift, it will be painless, and all the rest of your citizens will be allowed to live in peace under the rule of the Noctem Alliance.

"Your other option," Lord Tenebris said, after a brief pause to let his offer sink in, "would be to remain here, and fight me, four on one. I will not hold back on you, I will show no mercy, and I shall draw it out for as long as I possibly can. Once I am finished, I will go to the battlefield and assist my soldiers in wiping out all who serve you.

"This is not something that I wish to do. The war is over, and I do not wish to kill civilians unless absolutely necessary. However, the choice is yours."

There was a moment of silence, with only the sound of the light breeze blowing through the council room and the crackling fire all around them. Stan was too stunned even to think properly. Only one single thought permeated all his thoughts: *I am about to die.*

He had no choice but to obey Lord Tenebris. There was no way that any of them could possibly escape from the council room with their lives, and even if they did, Lord Tenebris would find them. To fight Lord Tenebris would be torture. Stan remembered during the fight with King Kev, when his opponent had set him on fire and repeatedly tossed him into the air. Stan had never felt any greater agony in his life, but he knew that it would surely be child's play in comparison to what Lord Tenebris would put them through if they refused to submit to him. And that was only what he would do to *them*. If they tried to fight Lord Tenebris, their fate would be shared with all who had ever followed Stan.

But on the other hand, if they did choose to be executed and end the war . . . then what? The citizens of Elementia would live on under the rule of the Noctem Alliance. Was that fate really so much better than a torturous death? Most of Stan's followers were lower-level players. They would be banished from Element City and sent to fend for themselves in the wild. Even with the skills that they had learned in training under Commander Crunch, it would be difficult to survive. The Noctem Alliance probably wouldn't leave them alone, either. Wherever the new players started their civilization, Stan was sure that upper-level players would go out of their way to harass and abuse them. If Stan surrendered, then his people might live on, but so would the hatred.

"I'm waiting," Lord Tenebris said, sounding slightly irritated now. "I don't know about you, but I'd prefer to stop this fighting as soon as possible to preserve as many of my followers as I can. If a decision is not made soon, then perhaps I briefly forget about my honor and go through with the option that I would find most fun."

Stan's throat felt as though it were being squeezed shut as his mind raced, trying to decide the lesser of the two evils. Somehow, the fact that he was going to die no matter what he chose barely even registered to him. All he could think about was which choice would result in less despair for his subjects, who had given their all to fight the Noctem Alliance and deserved as little pain as possible when the chips fell where they may.

Suddenly, Stan became aware of a new sound in the voiceless room—the sound of footsteps. Stan looked up and saw Kat stepping forward. Her hands were empty, and from where he was standing, Stan couldn't see her face, only the back of her diamond armor. He watched, transfixed, as Kat walked directly in front of Lord Tenebris, knelt down, and sunk into a deep bow.

Lord Tenebris smiled as Stan found himself unable to even process what he was seeing. "So, Kat . . . you're willing to speak for your president and your country, and surrender to me?"

Kat said nothing. Instead, in one motion, she let out a ferocious war cry as she sprung upright, her enchanted diamond sword in her hand, and headed directly for Lord Tenebris's unprotected stomach.

Lord Tenebris acted just as quickly as Kat. He knocked the point of the sword away with his left hand, and instantly stretched his right hand out toward Kat.

Kat froze. She was still frozen in the midst of recovering from her attack. At the same moment, Stan felt the telepathic grip of Lord Tenebris lock him in place, and once again he felt the utter helplessness of having no control over his own body. Lord Tenebris no longer looked smug or arrogant. Instead, his face showed nothing but shock, which slowly morphed into rage, a burning hatred that contorted his features into an ugly ball of resentment.

"Wrong choice," he hissed dangerously.

A blast of thunder rang from directly outside the battlements, and Charlie had to use all his willpower to keep from moving. With no warning, a hurricane-force gale had begun to rip through the tower, and Charlie could see an electric storm outside, sending slashes of light and energy across the black sky. Charlie knew that this couldn't be a natural storm, and with a start he realized that Stan and the others had probably started to battle Lord Tenebris. They were probably right below him in the council room.

Charlie didn't allow himself to think about his friends, though. Right now, he had to focus on saving himself, for the sake of his troops. His mind raced, trying to conceive a way in which he could hop on his pig and ride out of the tower before ELM cut him down. Try as he might, though, he couldn't think of any way to make it work.

"I'm almost ready to go, Arachnia!" Enderchick chortled from behind him.

"Well, get a move on, then," Arachnia replied darkly, speaking at a normal volume as the winds died down just as suddenly as they had started. "I don't know what caused that storm, but I do know that I want to get off this tower as soon as possible. I don't like being so close to Lord Tenebris."

Charlie's heart skipped a beat. They were getting ready to put their plan into motion! The instant that Enderchick disappeared with his pickaxe, Charlie knew that there was no way he could possibly escape—the tool was the only thing that he had to fight off Arachnia and Lord Marrow. Charlie desperately tried to picture his surroundings. He had lived in this castle for months, and he knew it like the back of his hand. There had to be something around him that he could use to facilitate an escape. . . .

Then, suddenly, Charlie heard it. It was faint, and he could barely make it out over the light breeze, the drizzling rain, and the sound of distant warfare . . . but he could still unmistakably hear it. A breathing—deeply pained, horrifically raspy, almost metallic—a sound that vacuumed all hope and warmth from the air.

Without really thinking, Charlie turned his head to peer outside the battlements. It didn't matter if he was seen; he had to know if he was hearing correctly. Sure enough, there it was, flying not too far outside the walls of the tower, pure darkness seeping out of its body and floating into the sky, its three skeletal heads looking out over the city. Charlie had no idea what the Wither was doing there, but he wondered if perhaps he could use it to his advantage.

In the space of a second, an insane plan flooded Charlie's head. He knew that there was next to no chance that it could possibly work. He had never before come up with a plan where so many things could go wrong. In the next second, Charlie heard the sound of Enderchick, right behind him, standing up, and giving a yawn. Charlie imagined she was probably stretching out, feeling refreshed after her long rest. It was do-or-die time.

Okay, Charlie, you got this, he said to himself, trying not to think too hard. *Just act. One . . . two . . . THREE!*

Charlie leaped onto his knees and grabbed the handle of

his pickaxe on the ground, right as Enderchick grabbed the diamond pick. Before she had even realized what happened, Charlie wrenched the weapon from her hand, took aim, and threw the weapon as hard as he could. As all three members of ELM leaped to their feet and trained their weapons on Charlie, the diamond pickaxe spiraled out one of the open battlements, through the rainy sky, and directly into the back of the Wither's center head.

The effect was immediate; the boss mob let out a horrifying roar. Before they could attack him, the three members of ELM spun around, glaring out the window to see what had made the noise. What they saw made their eyes widen, and they dived out of the way to avoid the massive explosions as the blasts from the Wither tore the wall of the tower to shreds. In the midst of the recoil from the blast and the flying rubble, Charlie reached to the floor and, with two hands and his good leg, propelled himself upright, hopping to the side and landing on top of Dr. Pigglesworth. He gave the pig a sharp kick with his heels, and the two of them sprinted across the floor of the tower toward the door that led to the castle bridge.

"Get him! He's escaping!" Arachnia's strangled cry erupted from the tumult within the tower. "Enderchick!"

Charlie glanced behind him and saw Enderchick standing in the center of the tower, her eyes trained directly on him. So focused was she on Charlie and his pig riding away from her at a breakneck pace that she didn't even notice the Wither, which had floated into the room and was now aiming all three of its heads directly at her. Before she could even make a move, all three of the black skulls struck her, sending her flying through the air, a trail of dropped items leaving her body as she went.

Charlie couldn't help himself. He ordered Dr. Pigglesworth to stop in the middle of the castle bridge, and he turned back around to watch the tower. Through the lingering smoke from the explosions, Charlie could see the two silhouettes of Arachnia and Lord Marrow. Though they initially tried to dodge the blasts of the undead demon, the explosions engulfed the room, tearing through the walls and eventually obscuring them from view.

Charlie stared, transfixed, as the entire tower ruptured from the inside out, in a constant barrage of blasts that continued for a full minute until, finally, the Wither flew over an expanse of stone-brick blocks, pockmarked by the dents from the explosions. In the midst of the dust and still-falling rubble, Charlie could make out three bodies lying on the still-intact floor, items levitating on the blocks around them.

There was no time for Charlie to react. He couldn't think about the three players that he had just killed. He couldn't even be relieved that the bounty hunters who had been hired to capture his best friend were now eradicated. All Charlie saw was the Wither, levitating above the bombed-out tower, its six eyes trained on him.

Charlie turned his pig around and kicked it into high gear just as the first black skull left the Wither's mouth. It exploded behind him, and Charlie immediately regretted stopping to watch the destruction of the tower. He raced forward on Dr. Pigglesworth's back as countless black skulls rained down right on his heels, destroying the flat expanse of stone brick on which King Kev and Stan had fought many months ago.

The other tower, Charlie thought desperately to himself, fixing his eyes on the tower at the other end of the bridge. *There's a staircase into the castle in there . . . if I can just get into the other tower . . .*

A massive blast erupted right in front of Charlie. He grabbed Dr. Pigglesworth's reins and yanked backward on them, causing the pig to squeal and screech to a stop less than a block away from plummeting into the abyss below. He glanced around wildly, looking for an escape route, but there was none. The hole in front of him blocked his route into the castle, and the entire castle bridge behind him had been completely blown apart, leaving nothing but a sheer drop to the rotunda floor hundreds of blocks below.

The Wither was levitating directly above the hole it had just blasted into the ground. The beast took in a raspy breath, and in a burst of light, a skull shot out of its mouth. This projectile wasn't black like the others. It was light blue and traveled much more slowly—headed for Charlie.

He had nowhere to run. All he could do was steer Dr. Pigglesworth out of the direct path of the slow-moving blue Wither Skull before it struck the single, tiny remaining piece of ground he was standing on and exploded.

Stan devoted all his willpower to moving the arm that was holding his diamond axe, but it was no use. Lord Tenebris's supernatural grip on him was too powerful. He glanced over at Cassandrix and Leonidas, and saw that they had given up fighting, recognizing the futility. They were only focused on Kat.

Kat stood in front of Lord Tenebris, her diamond armor shimmering in the glowing orange light of the fire. Although her arm was still in position from her deflected attack on the Noctem leader and she, too, was totally immobile, she glared at Lord Tenebris with a defiant look on her face.

"So," Lord Tenebris whispered, his white eyes staring deeply into hers. "You thought you could trick me."

Kat said nothing. She just continued to stare unwaveringly into the empty white sockets of Lord Tenebris's eyes, almost radiating her hatred of him and the Alliance he commanded.

"Perhaps you didn't understand me, Kat," Lord Tenebris continued in a soft voice that sent chills down Stan's spine. "If you care for your people in the slightest, I believe that it would be in your best interest to bow down to me."

"Never," Kat growled, speaking for the first time since entering the council-room chamber. Her face was contorted with grit and determination, and no fear showed in her eyes as she stared down her opponent, her resolve blazing as brightly as the fire that surrounded her.

Lord Tenebris's eyes widened. Within an instant, all sense of restraint and subtlety went right out the window. His face twisted, his features accentuated by the fire, and he seemed to be the embodiment of a demon as he stared back at this player who defied him.

"I said . . . **BOW!**"

Kat sank to her knees. Her hands were forced down onto her thighs, and slowly, she began to lean forward, her head moving closer and closer to the floor. She was shaking like mad, streams of sweat trailed down her face, veins popped in her head, and her teeth gnashed together as she did all she could to battle Lord Tenebris's telekinetic grip. Despite all her efforts, her head continued to sink. Right as her forehead was about to press into the stone-block ground, she spoke.

"No . . . you . . . *don't*!"

It was as if Stan was watching in slow motion. Kat's head

snapped upward, her body flying up out of the kneeling position, arching backward as she broke free of Lord Tenebris's hold. As the force of her motion carried Kat upward and back onto her feet, she let the arrow notched in the bow in her hand fly forward, directly into Lord Tenebris's unguarded chest.

Lord Tenebris glanced down at the projectile protruding from his heart. He didn't look pained, or angry, or even surprised. He merely looked confused, as if he had no idea where it had come from. Stan could only see the expression for a split second, however, before Kat's sword struck Lord Tenebris across the forehead.

Lord Tenebris stumbled backward, dazed and unprepared as Kat let loose another blow, this time across his stomach. The Knockback and Fire enchantments on the sword took effect as the supreme leader of the Noctem Alliance burst into flames. Kat didn't stop. She was like a machine, rushing forward and delivering strike after strike after strike to Lord Tenebris, sending him flying farther and farther backward across the council-room floor.

Stan felt himself released from Lord Tenebris's psychic grasp, but he was still unable to move. He could only watch as Kat dominated Lord Tenebris, the foe that they had been fighting against for months.

Within seconds, Lord Tenebris had been pushed all the

way across the floor. He slammed into the elevated platform on which his throne was perched with a dull smack. He slumped down, his back against the wall, and his arms, legs, and head limp as he sat in the midst of the ring of fire, flames engulfing his entire body.

Despite her rush of adrenaline, Kat took a moment to catch her breath, never taking her eyes off Lord Tenebris. As she stood in the center of the chamber, the eyes of her three friends locked on her with awe and utter disbelief, Kat came to an alarming realization. Lord Tenebris was still alive! If he had died, she would have seen the telltale burst of items around him—even in the fire they would linger for an instant before being burned into oblivion.

She had delivered sword blows to all of Lord Tenebris's vital points, and he was sitting in a vortex of fire. Kat knew that if he was still alive, he wouldn't last much longer. She could very easily just stand by and let the fire finish him off. But . . . no. Kat knew that she couldn't do that. After all that this demon had put her and her friends through in the past months, she wouldn't be satisfied with anything less than delivering the killing blow herself.

Kat grasped the hilt of the diamond sword firmly in her hand. She glared at the unconscious form of Lord Tenebris. Her eyes flashed, and she let out a savage cry as she rushed forward, her sword trailing behind her, and when she was just a few blocks away from Lord Tenebris, she leaped into the air, soaring through the flames and bringing the blade down with all her might.

The diamond sword halted in place when it was just pixels away from the crown of Lord Tenebris's head. Kat had frozen in midair.

Lord Tenebris was still lying in a slouch against the throne platform, limp and unconscious . . . limp, that is, except for his hand. His blocky right hand was raised, clenched into a fist, and suspended directly in front of Kat's face. All at once, Stan felt Lord Tenebris's grip tighten again. He was totally unable to move, leaving him, Leonidas, Cassandrix, and Kat to watch as Lord Tenebris opened his eyes.

The Noctem ruler stood up straight. Detestation was ripe in every line of his still-burning face as he inhaled deeply, then let it out. In an instant, all the wounds that Kat's sword had inflicted upon him vanished. The arrow popped out of his chest and fell into the fire, to be consumed by the inferno. The fire erupting from his body extinguished, and he was totally unaffected by the flames all around him as he began to fly upward, his hand still outstretched toward Kat, who levitated slowly upward with him.

The two players, one standing upright, the other still in the final stage of a killing blow, continued to float upward, until finally, they were level with the platform on which the throne sat. Lord Tenebris looked up at Kat. He was looking at her differently now, as if he was just realizing what she was, and that something was horrifying and detestable.

"Why, Kat?" Lord Tenebris asked, sounding disgusted. "Why do you fight me? Why do you continue to fight when you know you cannot win?"

"Because I used to be like you."

Kat was no longer angry or shocked. She spoke with a passion, a drive that outshone anything that her anger could ever produce.

"I was violent, I was arrogant, I wasn't afraid to step all over others for my own good. I thought that others were lower than me, even when they were kind to me and showed me mercy. I realize now that kindness and mercy made them higher than I could ever hope to be.

"Lord Tenebris, I will never stop fighting you. As long as you're still brainwashing the misguided players of Elementia, manipulating their hatred instead of curing it, I will *always* be there to stop you. You can do whatever you want to me. You can torture me. You can terrorize me. You can kill me. But no matter what you do, I will never break!"

Lord Tenebris said nothing. There was a long silence, during which he just stared at Kat, an inquisitive look on his face. Then, without warning, he jerked his right hand hard to the left.

Kat was flung through the air across the room and hit the left wall of the council room with a smack. Lord Tenebris then quickly moved his hand to the right, fist still clenched, as Kat followed, hurtling through the air at breakneck speed as she hit the opposite wall with a smack. Over and over, Lord Tenebris jerked his hand in every which way, sending Kat bouncing from wall to wall, accented by a pronounced smack, and an occasional crunch.

Finally, Lord Tenebris slowly lowered his hand, and Kat hovered near the ground. She was unconscious, her limbs sprawled out around her and various wounds covering her entire body, but her sword still tightly gripped in her hand. Lord Tenebris took a deep breath, flipped his hand upward, and then unclenched his fist.

Kat was launched into the air. No longer held rigid in place by Lord Tenebris's mind, she spiraled through the air, spinning ungracefully like a top about to fall over. She continued to fly upward, losing momentum until finally she peaked, and she began to fall back to the floor, rapidly gaining speed.

She never reached it.

Lord Tenebris glared at the falling girl with empty, unfeeling white eyes. Closing one eye, he took aim, drew back his fist and, when he had a clear shot, pushed his hand forward, an invisible pulse of energy leaving him and heading directly for Kat.

The explosion rocked the council room.

Ordinarily, Stan would have panicked at being unable to raise his diamond axe to block the attack. Ordinarily, he would have had to grit his teeth as the shockwave from the explosion crashed over him, sending ripples through his body as if it were made of gelatin. Ordinarily, he would still be in shock, trying wildly to figure out how Lord Tenebris had survived the assault he had just endured.

But Stan didn't think any of that.

Instead, all he could do was stare, seeing but not believing, not feeling, not comprehending, at the body of Kat, lying in the center of the council-room floor. She was sprawled out face-down on the ground, her limbs crooked, as the perfect ring of items sat on the floor around her. A slight distance from her hand, her diamond sword lay on the ground, having left her hand for the last time, still glowing with many marvelous hues from its various enchantments.

HEROBRINE'S MESSAGE

tan had been in Elementia for over half a year now. In that time, he had made many friends, a good number of whom had been struck down in the battles against King Kev, and then the Noctem Alliance. He had seen terrible things, but after he had gotten through the death of DZ, more than a month ago, he thought that he could handle anything.

And yet, as Stan found himself unable to remove his eyes from the center of the council-room floor, where Kat's body had vanished, leaving only her sword and other items in her inventory remaining, Stan found himself completely and utterly floored with disbelief. This wasn't just another one of his friends, this was Kat . . . *Kat*, who had been with him through thick and thin since he had first joined Elementia, who was his closest friend other than Charlie, who had come so far, changing from a girl who leaped out of the woods to ambush unarmed players into a brave warrior who would give her all to defend those she cared about.

Was that player . . . was Kat . . . one of his closest friends . . . really gone?

A shriek of anguish sounded to Stan's right, and he whipped his head to the side to look at Cassandrix. She had completely lost it; her eyes were wild, her face was twisted with insane fury, and although her teeth were gritted, a wild cry of hatred still radiated from her mouth as she rushed toward Lord Tenebris. Stan found this the most odd—he was still unable to move.

Lord Tenebris stared at her in surprise before leveling his right hand directly at her. She froze in place for a moment, bending forward from the weight of Lord Tenebris's invisible grip, but with an animal cry she snapped back upright again. Stan watched, thoughts and emotions exploding within him like fireworks, as Cassandrix slowly struggled forward. Somehow, she was managing to fight through Lord Tenebris's psychic hold, her eyes nearly dripping contempt as she advanced on the flabbergasted demon. He seemed nearly unable to move as he watched in incredulity as Cassandrix stood in front of him and drew her sword, raising it over her head.

"**ENOUGH!**" Lord Tenebris bellowed. In two rapid motions, Lord Tenebris stretched out his arms to either side of him, fists clenched, before sending them slamming together directly in front of Cassandrix's face.

The white-clad Spleef player found herself flying backward across the council room, unable to resist the sheer power of this blast. At the same time, Leonidas, who had been standing beside Stan with his mouth hanging open, totally nonplussed by what he was seeing, shot forward, as if he had been hit by an equally powerful energy blast from behind. The two players flew across the room at nearly the speed of sound. In the exact center they collided, their heads bashing together and bouncing off each other with a loud crack. Stan watched, his heart plummeting, as Cassandrix and Leonidas fell lifeless to the floor in a crumpled heap.

Stan glared at them intently, refusing to accept what he had just seen, refusing to imagine what Lord Tenebris had possibly just done to his friends. Stan's heart gave a tiny jump as both of the players let out tiny moans of pain. They weren't dead. They were just unconscious.

Suddenly, Stan became aware that somebody was standing directly in front of him. He allowed his gaze to move away from his two comrades, and slowly looked forward to stare into the blank, callous eyes of Lord Tenebris.

"Ah, President Stan," Lord Tenebris said with an evil smile, no trace of sympathy or regret on his face. "You have no idea how long I've waited to be in this position. Just you and I . . . face to face."

As much as he wanted to look away, Stan didn't let himself. He had no idea what Lord Tenebris was about to do to him. All that mattered was that he did all he could to spite this demon. Stan refused to give Lord Tenebris the satisfaction of seeing him back down and submit to him. And so, he forced himself to look Lord Tenebris directly in the eyes as he spoke.

"You know, Stan, I could have destroyed you a long time ago if I had wanted to," Lord Tenebris continued. "It would have been so easy for me to just teleport into Element Castle and kill you in your sleep from the start. However, I didn't. You are the player who killed King Kev, and went on to create the most disgusting regime in the history of Elementia. I figured that it would be best to let you think that you had a sporting chance before I crushed you. After all, it's like they say . . . the higher you are, the harder you fall."

Stan still didn't break his gaze. Staring into the eyes of Lord Tenebris was one of the most difficult things that Stan had ever done—the two empty voids of whiteness seemed to project some sort of dark sorcery that made Stan feel as if his soul were being withered away the longer he stared. It was only Stan's desperation to deny Lord Tenebris his satisfaction, and the knowledge that he was about to die anyway, that empowered Stan to keep looking.

"But oh, Stan," Lord Tenebris replied, sounding wild and manic as he licked his lips. "Your fall has scarcely begun."

Lord Tenebris drew back his right hand, and Stan tried to brace himself for the blast, forgetting that he was still bound rigidly in place. Instead of firing at Stan, however, Lord Tenebris punched upward, and a second later, the roof of the council room exploded. Lord Tenebris bent his legs and leaped into the air, rocketing into the sky. Stan felt his insides squish into the lower half of his body as he accelerated to match Lord Tenebris's pace in the space of a split second. He could only close his eyes as he flew upward toward the open sky above, falling debris and rain battering his face like a barrage of bullets.

Within seconds, Stan had burst through the hole in the council-room roof. He looked down and realized with a start that he was flying nearly fifty blocks over the castle. His stomach clenched as he stared down at the castle and the city far below him, terrified to think of what Lord Tenebris was planning to do to him up here. Refusing to look down any longer, Stan turned his gaze out over the sprawling metropolis and saw the smoke rising from the distant battle zones.

"Don't worry, Stan, I'm not going to drop you," Lord Tenebris said smoothly. Stan looked above him and saw Lord Tenebris staring down, wearing a sadistic leer. "I just figured that up here would be the best place to enjoy the show."

Stan barely had time to question what he meant by that before he felt a light-speed rushing sensation, not unlike when he used an Ender Pearl, which lasted for the blink of an eye before he felt normal again. Jolted by the unexpected teleportation, Stan opened his eyes, and repositioned himself. He glanced up at Lord Tenebris, who was looking down with an ecstatic expression. Stan followed his gaze to the ground. What he saw made his heart nearly stop.

Below him was the Avery Memorial Courthouse, in front of which the entirety of both armies, close to seven hundred total players, had congregated. However, they weren't fighting, and as Stan focused, he realized with a horrified jolt that all his men had been totally surrounded. Less than half the troops wore diamond armor, and they were all huddled together in a cluster, unarmed with their hands above their heads, looking nervously at the ring of armed black-armored troops that surrounded them.

Lord Tenebris cackled above him. "Honestly, Stan . . . did you really think your army stood a chance? The Noctem Freedom Fighters are the highest-level players on the server, fighting with the highest tier of weaponry, fueled by the blazing convictions of their belief in their superiority. Did you think for even a second that you could train your pathetic, spoiled lower-level subjects enough to match them . . . and in just *one week*, no less?"

Stan didn't care how Lord Tenebris knew that they had been training for only a week. He barely even heard him at all. All he could do was look down into the diamond mass that, based on the cloud of gray smoke rising from the ground, had just been sprayed with a cloud of knockout gas. His fear for his friends' safety coursed through his veins as he thought of Charlie, Jayden, Ben, Bob, the Mechanist, Commander Crunch, and so many others who were down there, and now totally at the mercy of Drake and Spyro.

"Don't worry, Stan, my generals aren't going to hurt them now that they've stopped fighting," Lord Tenebris said, as if he could read Stan's mind. "They won't do anything without the go-ahead from me, and we still have some business to attend to before we can address those traitors."

Stan barely had time to ponder what he was talking about before they were again hurtling through space at the speed of light, then coming to rest in midair. Stan opened his eyes, still dazed from the teleportation but wondering where they were, and what Lord Tenebris was going to unleash on him next.

Stan looked up, and immediately, something felt wrong. The sky above him was dark, and he could see countless stars, and the white rectangle that was the moon. And if he could see the sky, that meant that there were no more Withers around, which meant . . . they weren't over Element City anymore. Stan looked down, and his racing heart stopped dead.

Below them sat the Adorian Village, surrounded by forests and illuminated with torchlight. The wall still stood strong, but there were no guards in sight.

"I have to say, Stan, there was one thing in particular you did that impressed me. I was very surprised that you managed to take this village from me," Lord Tenebris said slowly.

His face was stagnant, and Stan couldn't read his emotions. "Of course, from what I've heard, the assassins whom Drake hired ended up helping you indirectly, so perhaps I shouldn't give you too much credit. Nonetheless, you did manage to catch me off guard, which is not something that is easily done.

"And what a perfect place for you to set up your base of operations! I mean, the Adorian Village was founded out of the belief that new players ought to be treated like toddlers who need their pathetic little hands held as long as they're playing the game. I suppose that you could call the Adorian Village a symbol of all that you stand for, Stan."

Lord Tenebris's lips curled upward into a wily smile. Suddenly, Stan realized with a horrible lurch of his stomach what Lord Tenebris was implying.

"No, please don't," Stan stammered.

"Do you know what I need to do, Stan?" Lord Tenebris asked in a mockingly playful voice. "I need to do something big, something grandiose. It must be something that will last, and serve as a reminder to the posterity of the power I possess, and what happens to those who are foolish enough to fight back against the most righteous ideals of the Noctem Alliance—"

"Lord Tenebris, I'm begging you!" Stan pleaded, and before he could stop himself, he blurted out, "There are civilians down there! Dozens of players who are too weak or too wounded to fight are in that village right now! And there are NPC villagers, too!" Tears were gushing from Stan's eyes, as he desperately tried to appeal to the heartless monster who possessed him, willing to do anything to save Oob, Mella, Stull, and the rest of his players.

Lord Tenebris's eyebrows raised for a moment, but then, without warning, he looked enraged. "Do you mean to tell me," he growled, "that you have more soldiers down there? And they abandoned you because they were too terrified to face my men?"

"No!" Stan bellowed. "They're just civilians. They couldn't fight even if they wanted to! You said that you wouldn't attack civilians! Please, at the very least, bring them back to Element City, with the rest of my people! Your soldiers are there, too!" Stan cried, suddenly remembering. "The troops we captured in battle are imprisoned in the village! Are you really going to kill your own men?"

But Lord Tenebris paid no attention. The gale-force winds from the council room had returned, kicking up from nowhere and swirling around Lord Tenebris like a cyclone. The clear night sky above them was rapidly being overrun by looming gray storm clouds. Far below, Stan could see players swarming out of the houses, gazing up at the sky and trying to figure out what was going on.

Lord Tenebris took a deep breath and closed his eyes. Then slowly, he stretched his right hand out over the city, and opened them again.

Instantly, every single house in the village burst into flames. Even if Stan wasn't being held still by Lord Tenebris, he still would have been frozen, in body and mind. The people below screamed in horror as their dwellings were engulfed in the blaze. Stan saw several players pointing up to the sky at them. He, too, looked up at Lord Tenebris, waiting to see what else this fiend could possibly do, and saw that his hand was glowing with a radiant light. Without warning, the light intensified, shining so brightly that Stan was forced to look away. Back down in the village, the winds were blowing even harder now, and Stan could see his people struggling just to stand upright.

There was a crack of thunder, and a bolt of lightning struck the roof of the Town Hall, causing a chunk of it to be blown away in the static discharge. In the split second after the strike, everything was silent, and Stan felt as if the air were alive, as if all the energy around him was evaporating. Then, in an instant, the dark night sky was filled with light, sound, and power as thousands of thunderbolts rained from the heavens, covering the Adorian Village in blinding light. Stan closed his eyes, but the radiance was so bright that it scorched Stan's retinas even through his eyelids, sending his senses into overdrive with the cyclone winds and sounds of explosions below.

Slowly but surely, Stan's eyes adjusted, and he even found himself able to open his eyes a little. Looking down at the Adorian Village was still like looking into the sun, but Stan managed to glance up at Lord Tenebris, whose glowing hand seemed nearly dull in comparison to the flashes below them. As he looked up at the face of his captor, Stan's already crippled heart felt like it took another ice-cold stab as he saw the twisted features, illuminated and shadowed to look infernally cruel and evil in the light.

Then, as suddenly as it had started, all of it stopped. The winds stopped blowing, Lord Tenebris's hand stopped shining, and the lightning strikes stopped. Such a drastic shift in light left Stan blinded, and it was about half a minute before his eyes had fully adjusted. As Stan saw more and more of what was below him, he felt the air drain from his lungs. Eventually, when his sight had completely returned, Stan felt as if he were about to pass out from the sheer magnitude of horror that lay below him.

The Adorian Village, which had just this morning stood proud and strong in the midst of the Great Wood, had been totally razed. Not one single building was still standing. The site where the wooden motel had been was now as featureless as if players had never been there before. The tiny wooden hut where Oob and his family were staying was nowhere to be seen. The brick Town Hall had been torn to shreds, and despite that it was the most complete remaining building in the village. Only two brick-block wall segments, connected at a right angle, remained upright.

There was not a single player in sight.

Stan barely had time to take in what he was seeing when, in a blink of teleportation, he suddenly found himself in the midst of it. The psychic grip released him, and he fell to the ground on top of one of the only sections of gravel road that had not been torn apart by the lightning. Stan raised his head, and though his body was shaking, he managed to look around.

The village was far worse from this level. The ground had been torn into an uneven, cratered landscape, not unlike the war-torn trench outside Element City. The fires seemed far more numerous, and the smoke and heat spiraling around him threatened to choke Stan, but not nearly as much as the items. Now that he was at ground level, he could see the dropped inventories of countless fallen players, scattered across the barren landscape.

As Stan's mind attempted to make sense of all that was around him, he felt as though his brain was full of fuzz, and not able to totally process what he was seeing. Stan realized that somebody was watching him. Slowly, he turned his head to look directly ahead of him, where Lord Tenebris stood at the other end of the patch of gravel. He was looking down at Stan, totally emotionless. Stan stared back. He felt nothing toward Lord Tenebris. No anger, no hatred, not even fear. Stan's mind was too overwhelmed to feel anything, and so he just stared blankly up at Lord Tenebris, like a child processing the world around himself for the first time.

"You knew that this would happen, Stan," Lord Tenebris said in a deadpan. "Perhaps you tried to convince yourself otherwise, perhaps you lied to yourself and believed that you somehow had the upper hand in this war, but you never did. In fact, even calling this a war is giving you far too much credit. After all, in a war, there must be at least two sides."

Stan said nothing.

"Why, Stan? If your fight was so futile, then why did you bother to put up one at all? Did you really think that you could overthrow the Noctem Alliance through tactful and honest methods, the same way you did to King Kev and his kingdom? I refuse to believe that you didn't know who I was before you challenged me today, Stan. And the moment you found that out, you should have given up the fight, right then and there. You must have known that, regardless of what you did against the Alliance I command, you could never beat me."

Stan remained silent.

"And now look at you. Your pitiful resistance has been crushed, your troops have been captured, and your leaders are being lined up for the firing squad as we speak, awaiting my command to finish the job. You have no backup, you have no contingency plan, and your best friend is dead. You're pathetic and weak, totally at my mercy. If I wanted to kill you now, I could do it without raising a finger. But . . . I won't."

Stan, who had been staring up vacantly at Lord Tenebris, now looked down to the gravel below him, failing to imagine what Lord Tenebris could possibly do to bring him lower.

Lord Tenebris took no notice of Stan's movement. Instead, he focused intently on both his hands. In his right hand appeared a golden apple, shimmering with a brilliant luster, brighter in the darkness than any golden apple that had ever been seen in Elementia. In the other hand, a glass bottle appeared, filled to the brim with bloodred potion.

"I will say this, Stan. As pathetic as you are, I still find that I have a great deal of respect for you. Your ideals may be selfish and misguided, and your arrogance and pride may well be admired by your followers. However, I cannot deny that your devotion to your people is admirable, and that, while it may have been pointless in the long run, you did manage to evade my grasp for far longer than I had anticipated. Therefore, out of respect for you as an adversary, I only see fit to give you one final choice."

Lord Tenebris reached down and placed the golden apple and the potion side by side on the block in front of Stan. He looked up from the ground, and stared at the two items.

"These two items are very special, Stan," Lord Tenebris explained. "The apple is not just any golden apple. This is an enchanted golden apple. It is the best healing item in all of Minecraft. If you eat it, you will find yourself totally reinvigorated, and more ready to fight than you have ever been in your life. The potion, on the other hand, is one that you should recognize—the Potion of Harming. This particular potion is from my personal collection. It is brewed to Level Three, which is much more potent than any potion regularly available. It is strong enough to kill you the moment it touches your lips."

Stan felt as though a black hole were opening in his chest as he realized where Lord Tenebris was going with this.

"Here is your choice, Stan. You may choose to eat the golden apple, and return to Element City to challenge me. There, we will have an honorable duel to the death in front of all our people, and the winner shall be crowned the new ruler of Elementia.

"Alternatively, you may choose to drink the Potion of Harming and save yourself the humiliation. It will be quick, painless, and instantaneous."

Lord Tenebris was quiet for a moment to let his offer sink

in. Stan continued to stare at the two items, still with almost no comprehension, for a full minute before Lord Tenebris spoke again.

"You have until sunrise to make your choice. I will be waiting back at Element City for you to challenge me. If you choose the second option, I will know. If you adhere to my deadline, then regardless of your decision, none of your people will be punished for their actions under your command, with the exception of your leaders and closest friends. I would tell you not to run away, but I know that you aren't going to."

And with that, Lord Tenebris turned his back on Stan, walking slowly into the cloud of smoke that was descending over the blazing ruins of the city until he had totally faded from view.

For the longest time, Stan remained still. Within the past ten minutes, so much had happened. Stan needed ample time to process it all. It was only after the last bit of information had been realized that the depression came crashing over him.

Stan had failed himself, and he had failed his people. He should have known that Lord Tenebris would be far too powerful for him and his friends to handle. And that fiend was right about him—how could he have possibly expected an army of anything less than the most talented, skillful, and experienced players to take down a force of four hundred

Noctem fighters? They should have trained longer, and with that thought, Stan remembered with a horrible jolt what Sally had said. If they had waited just a little bit longer . . . Stan might have had operating powers, and all this could have been avoided. . . .

Stan realized, though, that this thought was moronic. Even if he had somehow managed to get operating powers, there was no way that he ever could have taken down Lord Tenebris. Summoning gale-force winds on a whim, sending down a storm of thousands of lightning strikes—these were things that he had never seen before, far greater than anything a normal operator could achieve. Whatever Lord Tenebris had done to himself, Stan knew that he was far beyond anything that he could ever . . .

Suddenly, something else that Sally had said struck Stan like a rock thrown at his head. Stan teetered over and fell to the ground, his heart stopping dead as he remembered. Lord Tenebris was siphoning energy from the server itself. He was drawing in more and more power from Elementia to make himself stronger. Eventually, the lack of power would corrupt Elementia, creating a game-breaking glitch that would throw the server into chaos. And that glitch could travel across the internet as a virus, infecting countless other servers until multiplayer Minecraft ceased to exist.

That meant that . . . by failing to defeat Lord Tenebris . . .

Stan had condemned all of Minecraft to be destroyed. This game, which had meant so much to him, his friends, and so many others across the world, this game that had enabled people to play in their own world, to do what they wanted, and to have the freedom to build, explore, and fight at the pace they wanted—it was all going to be gone.

Stan glanced down at the two items on the ground in front of him. The golden apple was truly a thing of beauty, shimmering in marvelous hues of gold even in the darkness of the smoldering city. The Potion of Harming looked innocuous, sitting on the gravel with its deep red contents, but Stan knew better.

Stan wondered if there was any point in returning to Element City and challenging Lord Tenebris. What would it accomplish? He would show up, and Lord Tenebris would wipe the floor with him, putting him through excruciating pain and humiliation before finally ending his life. In terms of his people, it didn't matter. Stan believed that Lord Tenebris would allow most of his people to live on, but Stan could do nothing to stop the execution of his friends. If he went back, his friends' last memories in Elementia would be of their leader being mutilated and destroyed. What's more, Stan found that he hardly even cared that he and his friends were on the verge of death. He was already too dead inside to feel anything.

Stan reached down to the ground and clasped the bottle of bloodred potion. Slowly, he raised the potion bottle and looked at it intently. In his reflection, slightly warped in the reddened globe of glass, Stan saw a player who looked damaged, pathetic, and utterly defeated. A sigh of apathy escaped his mouth. There was no hope anymore.

Stan put the glass of the bottle to his mouth, and slowly began to tilt it backward.

"Arf!"

Right as the potion was about to enter his mouth, the noise startled Stan. He looked around wildly, trying to see what made the noise, and when he looked behind him, he saw it. There, standing in the middle of the torn-up road, panting slightly with his blocky tongue hanging out of his mouth, sat a wolf. Miraculously, despite being in the center of the razed city, this wolf was totally unharmed, and hadn't even gotten dirty.

"Hey, Rex," Stan breathed.

At the sound of his name, Rex's tail began to wag, and he bounded over to Stan, leaping up on his hind legs and beginning to lick Stan's face. Somewhere within his deadened soul, Stan felt a slight warmth begin to ignite within him as he returned Rex's affection, scratching him behind the ears and beneath the collar as the wolf tapped his foot in pleasure. For a while, Stan just sat there, playing with the wolf, and he began to feel a little bit of joy.

"How did you manage to survive, boy?" Stan asked, still baffled.

Rex lowered himself down onto all fours again, and he tilted his head to the side in confusion. Stan wondered just how much the wolf could understand. He had never owned a dog himself, and he had never talked to Kat about . . .

At that moment, for the first time since Lord Tenebris had blasted him out of the council room, the realization of what had happened washed over Stan yet again, threatening to crush him like a steamroller. Stan had endured so much since the battle had begun, so much had been destroyed and so much lost, that he had barely had time to comprehend any of it fully. But now, in the midst of the ruined Adorian Village, for the first time, the realization truly hit Stan that one of his best friends was gone from Elementia forever.

"You're looking for Kat, aren't you," Stan said quietly, as tears started to well in his eyes.

At the sound of his master's name, Rex's ears perked up, and his eyes widened with joy. The wolf looked around, as if expecting to see Kat appear at any moment. Stan struggled to choke back sobs as the wolf began to pace the ground around Stan, sniffing everywhere, and looking so hopeful. When nothing was found, Rex looked inquisitively up at Stan, his head curiously cocked to one side.

"Well, you can forget about it," Stan managed to get out. "Kat's dead."

Rex was silent and immobile for a moment. Then, he tilted his head to the other side and let out an inquiring yip, as if he didn't understand what Stan was trying to tell him.

"Didn't you hear me?" Stan moaned, his voice shaky and uneven. "Kat is dead, Rex. She's not coming back for you."

Rex looked extremely confused, staring at Stan intently, as if trying to read him. The wolf realized that Stan was on the verge of breaking down in tears, and he began to mirror Stan, his eyes widening in sorrow as he began to let out soft whimpers. Suddenly, without warning, Stan felt an intense surge of anger at Rex for being so empty-minded, so uncomprehending.

"Don't you get it, you stupid animal!" Stan bellowed, his face contorted with agony and tears gushing down his face like rapids now. *"Your master is dead! She's never coming back for you! You will never . . . see . . . her . . . ever . . ."*

And with that, Stan broke down. He let out a wailing cry of *"aga-aain!"* as he burst out into unapologetic sobs, collapsing onto the ground and burying his face into Rex's neck. He hugged the wolf tightly around the neck, desperate for anybody to share in his grief and heartache. Stan felt as though a giant piece of himself was being torn out and digested in acid. Rex sat tall and strong, letting out his own whimpers of grief, but not moving in the slightest as he let Stan, one of the first players that he had ever trusted, cry into him as Stan's body shook with spasms of unquenchable pain.

For the longest time, the player and the wolf sat in the middle of the bombed-out graveyard that was the Adorian Village. Stan's sadness showed no signs of slowing as he remembered everything that he and Kat had been through together—their first meeting in the woods, their training with Sally and her friends, their quest to take down King Kev, their time on the council, rebuilding Elementia, their war against the Noctem Alliance, their journey to return home to their city, and the last stand, which felt as though it had happened a thousand lifetimes ago.

Suddenly, time stopped. Everything around Stan ground to a halt. His world seemed to pause, as he was hit by a massive realization. He remembered when he had stared into the eyes of Lord Tenebris . . . those empty, white eyes, which pained him to even look at. He had had a feeling that he had seen those eyes somewhere before, although, for the life of him, he couldn't remember where . . .

Not anymore. Stan remembered who the eyes belonged to.

He remembered what seemed like an eternity ago. Adrenaline coursing through his veins and with his entire world on the line, Stan had pitched an Ender Pearl up the wall of Element Castle, and landed on the bridge. He had turned to look at his adversary, and there stood King Kev, leering at him, his sword drawn and pointed at Stan in a clear challenge. Stan had only had a split second to look into his eyes—eyes, of course, that were unique, different from all other players in Minecraft—before the fight had commenced.

Earlier that night, as Stan had challenged Lord Tenebris, he had been forced to look away. The eyes of Lord Tenebris possessed some sort of demonic power, radiating from deep within them, and making it impossible to hold contact with them. And yet, through all the evil and all the power, Stan had recognized something in those eyes—the same indescribable, unique quality that he had seen in the brief seconds before he had charged King Kev, intent on wiping the dictator off the face of the server. Stan felt as though everything that he knew to be true in the world now hung in the balance as he realized what this meant.

Lord Tenebris . . . and King Kev . . . could they possibly be . . .

Questions erupted in Stan's head like fireworks, as he thought of all the reasons that this couldn't possibly be true. And . . . yet . . . he was so sure. Despite everything that Stan knew to be true that contradicted it, he knew what he had seen. The eyes were the only true way to tell one Minecraft player apart from another, for although skins could be changed, eyes stayed the same regardless of what a player looked like, even remaining the same across different accounts. But . . . how? Even as Stan's mind kicked into overdrive at the thought that Lord Tenebris and King Kev could possibly be one and the same, he knew that this couldn't be possible. King Kev was dead. Stan had fought him, and he had watched the king die. Furthermore, King Kev had given up his operating powers long before Stan joined the server. If he had them, he surely would have used them when Stan and the Apothecary had threatened his life. And even if, by some crazy stretch of the imagination, King Kev had returned to Elementia with his operating powers intact, Lord Tenebris—or rather, Herobrine—clearly was not a player. He had demonstrated skills and abilities far more than an operator was capable of. Last but not least, there was no way that he possibly could have hacked his way back in because of the Modelock Mod. If what Sally had told him about the mod was true, there was no way that King Kev could have tampered with the code of his own server. Clearly, only Herobrine, a glitch, would be able to bypass the code of Elementia and attain such unbelievable power.

Stan tried to convince himself that it couldn't be true. He had no idea what Herobrine was capable of. It was more than possible that he had somehow changed his own eyes to mirror King Kev's just for the sake of unnerving Stan. Or maybe what Stan recognized in both of them was their equally sinister nature. Or maybe . . .

Stan was snapped out of his thoughts by the faint crunching of four-legged footsteps on gravel, growing softer and softer. Stan looked up and saw Rex dashing across the uneven street.

"Hey!" Stan called out. "Rex! Where are you going?"

At the sound of Stan's voice, the wolf stopped in his tracks. Slowly, he turned his head to the side and looked up at Stan, his eyes showing an almost humanlike level of importance and determination. Rex raised his front right leg, still looking at Stan, and gave two upward swipes, a clear gesture for Stan to follow him, before turning back around and continuing on.

Stan was floored. His head felt like it was about to explode as he tried to process everything. So many different thoughts, feelings, and emotions were welling in Stan that he felt as if he were about to blow a gasket and pass out in the street. Then, all of a sudden, he decided to stop. Everything that was running through Stan's head stopped. He took a deep breath and stored the thoughts in the back of his mind for later. He stood up from the ground and pocketed the Potion of Harming and the enchanted golden apple. His mind was clear, and he began to follow Rex.

As the wolf led him through the streets of the Adorian Village, Stan pondered what he was doing. He was following Rex through the bombed-out village . . . but why? Where was he going? He realized that he might be going crazy, but it wasn't his lunatic thoughts that were driving him to follow Kat's pet—it was his instincts. A feeling of anticipation washed over him and he felt as though there was something mysterious somewhere in this village, which he would find if he just kept following Rex.

After leading Stan down countless ruined streets, past destroyed houses, Rex finally arrived at the outer wall of the Adorian Village. Although the village had been blown sky high, the wall remained largely intact, except for a crater that had been blasted into the wall, leaving a hole in the base just wide enough to walk through. Rex made his way into the crater and up the other side, walking through the hole with Stan right on his tail.

Now, they were in the Great Wood, which stretched right up to the wall of the Adorian Village. Stan made his way through the trees, having to jog so that he didn't lose sight of Rex. As he made his way through the floor of the forest, weaving through blocky tree trunks as the moonlight cast ominous shadows onto the forest floor, Stan looked around nervously. He clutched his axe, prepared for hostile mobs to sneak out from around the corner of a tree at any moment. And yet, the farther they went, Stan didn't even *see* any mobs as he glanced through the darkness. He had seen monsters lurking in the shadows of the Great Wood even in broad daylight . . . why weren't there any now?

Rex continued to walk forward, and as Stan followed, he realized that the wolf wasn't just ambling around randomly. He had determination, and he knew where he was going. The longer they walked, and the farther that they traveled from the Adorian Village, the more Stan felt a curious sensation that they were approaching something. He had no idea what, but Stan knew that they were getting closer and closer to something.

Finally, after walking for many minutes, Rex emerged from the trees and into a clearing. The clearing was a totally flat circle of grass blocks, not large enough to hold an NPC villager's house. A light fog swirled around the ground as Stan stepped into the clearing, something that he had never seen before in Minecraft. Rex's ears perked up, and his tail wagged as he bounded across the clearing, plopping down loyally at the feet of the player who was standing on the other side.

Stan's heart began to race as he stared at the player. He knew this player. While the stories and rumors had circulated among Stan's friends since their reunion, Stan himself had only seen the player once before. Just days ago, Stan had stood outside the Nocturia complex, debating whether to pull the lever that would detonate the entire city, when the player had appeared in a gust of snow and ice. His black cape and hood that covered the upper half of his face, his deep blue pants and brown shoes . . . Stan had seen them all before.

"Please," Stan whispered to the Black Hood. "I'm in my most desperate hour. My army has been captured, the Adorian Village is gone, the Noctem Alliance has taken Element City, and one of my best friends is dead. Can you help me?"

For a moment, the Black Hood said nothing, standing perfectly still as the fog danced quietly around his feet. The faint moonlight still came down from the sky, radiantly illuminating the Black Hood. A half-frown was plastered onto his face as he looked back at Stan.

"Please," Stan repeated, his voice ripe with desperation. "You must have brought me here for a reason."

"That I did, Stan2012."

Stan gaped at the Black Hood, his eyes wide and his jaw hanging half open. The Black Hood had just spoken to him—something that had never happened to him, or any of his friends. He had what sounded like a Swedish accent. Stan was about to ask him what the reason was when something happened that made the question die in his mouth.

The Black Hood raised his right hand and grabbed the top of his hood. In one single motion, he pulled the head covering backward, revealing his whole face. As he put his hand back by his side, Stan could see that his hair was brown, and that the Black Hood looked nearly identical to himself. Except, that was, for the eyes.

The eyes of the Black Hood were as white as snow, and shined as radiantly as the moonlight above. For a split second, Stan panicked, fearing that Lord Tenebris had materialized in front of him, before he realized that this was clearly not the case. Where Lord Tenebris's eyes were unnatural and sinister, and caused physical pain when looked into, the eyes of the Black Hood were the polar opposite. They were warm, inviting, and Stan found himself drawn into them like a moth to a light. As he stared into the eyes of the Black Hood, he felt that all was right in the world, despite his bitter knowledge that this was as far from true as possible.

"Who . . . who . . . who are you?" Stan managed to get out.

The Black Hood stared directly back at Stan, and, for the first time since he'd shared a glance with Leonidas all those weeks ago, he smiled.

"They call me Herobrine," he replied.

The Black Hood watched, slightly amused, as Stan stood at the far end of the clearing, clearly flabbergasted. He had expected such a reaction when he finally revealed himself to Stan. He chuckled inwardly. This was the first time that he had fully revealed himself to a player in many years, and the reaction was just as priceless as he remembered. The brief moment of humor was bittersweet, though. The Black Hood knew that by revealing himself to Stan, he had driven the nail firmly into his own coffin—he undoubtedly had only hours to live now.

Although the Black Hood let out a sigh of resignation at this thought, he knew it was worth it. Stan needed him. Elementia needed him. Minecraft needed him.

"But . . . what . . . how the . . . who . . . I thought . . . ," Stan sputtered, his eyes darting around wildly as he tried to comprehend the impossible.

"I realize what you must be thinking, Stan2012," the Black Hood said wryly. "Just minutes ago, your life was completely uprooted by a player bearing my name and likeness."

"So . . . you're really . . . Herobrine?" Stan replied weakly.

"Yes," the Black Hood replied plainly.

"But . . . I thought . . . I thought Herobrine was

evil!" Stan cried. "So you . . . you can't be Herobrine! You've been helping my friends and me for weeks now!"

The Black Hood looked at him sadly. "Stan2012, the popular belief that I am a violent, demonic glitch is no longer true. To be frank, the majority of the atrocities committed in my name since the days of Minecraft Alpha, including everything that Lord Tenebris has done, were in fact not my doing. I still fully blame myself for them, but I was not the culprit . . . not directly, anyway."

Stan stared at the Black Hood, as if trying to detect any hint that he was lying. When Stan saw none, he closed his eyes and pressed his hand to his head.

"Okay . . . let's say I give you the benefit of the doubt, and believe that you really are Herobrine. If so, then . . . what . . . are you?"

The Black Hood was silent for a moment before responding.

"To tell you the truth, Stan2012, I'm not sure. I don't know where I come from, how long I have existed, or anything regarding my nature or what I am. However, Stan2012, you needn't tell me that this is your most desperate hour . . . although I have the power to see all that has ever happened in Elementia, I don't need to use this power to see that you need me."

"Oh, I see," Stan spat bitterly. "So you're like, I don't

know, my omnipresent spirit mentor who knows *all who once was, and all that will be*, and is now coming to show me what my future will be like if—"

"Do not ridicule me, Stan2012," the Black Hood cut in, a frown returning to his face. "I have information that you desperately need if you are to save yourself and your country, but if you want it, then I demand that you take me seriously."

Stan's eyes widened. As skeptical as he was about all the Black Hood was saying, for some reason, Stan felt compelled to believe the Black Hood, although he had no idea why. Perhaps it was because of the truth that seemed to shine from his eyes, perhaps it was because this being had clearly defended his friends in the past. Whatever the reason, Stan trusted him.

"Our time here is short," the Black Hood continued, as if he could sense that Stan had opened up and was ready to listen to him. "Lord Tenebris intends to hold his deadline for you, and will begin to execute your friends if you do not return by sunrise."

"Hold up . . . back up," Stan said slowly, as he realized what the Black Hood being Herobrine meant. "If . . . *you're* Herobrine . . . then what is Lord Tenebris? How did he manage to get powers even stronger than an operator if he isn't Herobrine?"

The Black Hood sighed again. "Because, Stan2012, Lord

Tenebris *is* an operator. He's been an operator of Elementia since the day the server was first created, and since then, he's only grown stronger and stronger through his own twisted experiments."

"But . . . how is that possible? In the history of this server, there have only been two operators, Avery007 and King Kev, who're both dead!"

"It's possible because Lord Tenebris and King Kev are the same player, Stan."

The Black Hood allowed Stan a moment to process this. The Black Hood knew that Stan had guessed at this while he was grieving in the Adorian Village, but it didn't make the information any less difficult to comprehend. He watched as Stan struggled to process the claim. The Black Hood could almost see Stan making a mental list of every single reason why that couldn't be possible, before turning to face him.

"I don't believe you," Stan said bluntly, though he still sounded is if he were trying to convince himself more than anything. "That's not possible."

"Well, Stan2012, why don't you tell me why you think that, so that I can explain to you why it is," the Black Hood replied kindly.

"Ha!" Stan scoffed. "How would you know anything about Lord Tenebris or King Kev? How do you know anything about this server?"

"You're forgetting who you're talking to, Stan2012," replied the Black Hood with a smile. He pointed his hand down at Rex, who was still curled up at his feet. The wolf began to levitate into the air and looked around wildly before his tail began to wag. Rex started to fly through the air on his own, paddling his legs as if swimming, as Lord Tenebris continued to talk, absentmindedly keeping his hand pointed at Rex.

"I am the one true Herobrine, Stan2012. I have access to the history of every Minecraft server in the world, including this one. In fact, I first came here because I sensed a great disturbance in the balance of this particular world. I have since familiarized myself with all that has happened in Elementia since its creation, and I will be more than happy to answer any questions that you have."

The Black Hood guided Rex downward, and the wolf touched down on the ground, returning to his sitting position, as Stan stared in wonder. After a moment of stunned silence, Stan finally gathered his thoughts and replied.

"Okay, fine. First of all, King Kev is dead! I watched him stab himself in the chest with his own sword, and then get blown to bits as the tower exploded. Can you explain to me *how* he survived that?"

"King Kev didn't survive the Battle for Elementia, Stan2012. He died in the tower, just like you thought that he did."

Stan did a double take. "But . . . then . . . how . . ."

"Tell me something," the Black Hood said. "What did King Kev look like right before he died?"

As wildly as his head was spinning, Stan tried to think back to that day all those months ago. "Well . . . I knocked him into the tower against the wall . . . and I hesitated to stab him for a few seconds . . ."

"And what did he look like during those last seconds of his life?" the Black Hood pressed on.

Stan stared at the Black Hood incredulously. "What does that have to do with anything?"

"Answer the question, Stan2012," the Black Hood replied, a bit more sternly this time.

Baffled as to why the Black Hood was so focused on this minute detail, Stan pictured the fight in his head once again. "Well, King Kev got knocked to the ground, he was really weak from our attacks . . . he got slammed into the wall, and accidentally opened all the windows . . . and then I wasn't sure if I could bring myself to kill him, he looked so pathetic . . . his face was screwed up in anticipation, just waiting for me to finish him off . . ."

"That wasn't anticipation, Stan2012," the Black Hood replied. "While you were debating whether or not to kill King Kev, he was quickly setting himself up for the greatest escape in the history of Minecraft."

"What does that mean?" Stan demanded.

"As King Kev lay with his back to the wall, he knew that he couldn't win the fight," the Black Hood explained. "Between fighting Avery007, Apothecary1, and you, Stan2012, King Kev had been weakened to the point where fighting was futile. He knew that he had failed, and that his only chance to maintain power in Elementia was to start over again and build a new empire from the ground up: The Noctem Alliance."

"But that still doesn't explain how he escaped!"

"He escaped by changing the game mode of Elementia," the Black Hood replied. "As he sat against the wall, he changed the difficulty setting of Elementia from Hardcore PVP to Normal PVP as quickly as he could. This meant that players who died could respawn. As soon as he did so, he killed himself, respawning at Spawnpoint Hill and immediately proceeding to change the difficulty setting back to Hardcore PVP, so that, once again, any players who died would be banned from Elementia."

Again, the Black Hood stood quietly for a moment, as Stan tried to digest what was being explained to him. Moments later, Stan replied. "There's no way that that happened."

"And why not, Stan2012?" the Black Hood replied patiently, as he prepared to rebut each of the arguments that Stan was about to throw at him.

"Well, first off, you need operating powers to change the

game mode of the server!" Stan said. "And King Kev gave up his operating powers a long time ago."

The Black Hood chuckled. "King Kev *said* that he gave up his operating powers a long time ago, you mean. Think about it, Stan2012 . . . did you ever once see or hear of any evidence that King Kev truly gave up his operating powers, beyond the fact that he never used them?"

Stan opened his mouth to respond, but the retort died in his mouth when he realized that the Black Hood was right. Throughout his time in Elementia, Stan had been told that King Kev was once an operator but had given up his powers in order to keep his people happy. However, he had never once heard of *how* King Kev had given up his operating powers, or, in fact, seen any proof that he had, beyond the fact that he had never used them.

"But . . . then . . . okay," Stan continued, collecting his thoughts. "If King Kev had operating powers this entire time, then why didn't he use them when he was fighting me on the bridge? I mean, I understand why he didn't go using them all the time if he was pretending that he had given them up, but I think he probably would have been okay with using them if his life was in danger!"

"And therein lies King Kev's fatal flaw," the Black Hood replied sadly. "He is arrogant, and he thinks very highly of himself. He was too overconfident to use his operating powers to finish you off quickly. He wanted to toy with you first before destroying you. This trait, and also this fatal flaw, have carried over into King Kev's new identity as Lord Tenebris. Even when Avery007 challenged him, King Kev was far too proud to use his operating powers. If he didn't beat Avery007 fairly, in equal combat, his pride would have been hurt.

"And besides," the Black Hood continued before Stan could respond, "even if King Kev hadn't been too full of himself to use his powers, he wouldn't have anyway, on the off chance that somebody might find out. If the upper-level players discovered that King Kev was deceiving them, their faith in him as a ruler would have vanished."

The Black Hood paused yet again to let Stan absorb what he had just said. Stan looked desperate, grasping at straws to try to find another reason why King Kev's return was impossible. Finally, he spoke.

"Okay, let's say by some crazy stretch of the imagination, what you're saying is true. King Kev kept his operating powers this entire time; he changed the difficulty setting of the server, which allowed him to respawn; then he immediately changed it back. Well, if the server was changed off Hardcore PVP mode, even for a few seconds, then shouldn't at least one other player have respawned? I mean, we were in the middle of a huge battle. Players were dying all over the place.

Shouldn't somebody have died and then respawned in those few seconds that King Kev changed the difficulty setting of the server back to Normal PVP?"

The Black Hood smiled. "Can you think of nobody who somehow managed to respawn in Elementia without explanation, Stan2012?"

As soon as he said this, the memory returned to Stan in a flash. He remembered when he and his friends were tunneling back into Element City and had been ambushed by ELM underground. They were about to be overwhelmed when a giant mass of prisoners barreled through the tunnel, driving the bounty hunters away. Leading the charge was a player with a wild glint in his eyes . . . a player that Stan knew to be dead . . .

"Sirus," Stan breathed.

"Yes," the Black Hood replied. "Sirus666 was killed during the battle of Elementia at the exact moment that King Kev changed the difficulty setting of the server to Normal, and thus, he was able to respawn along with King Kev. They both returned to Spawnpoint Hill at nearly the same time. Of course, King Kev hid, terrified of being seen, but Sirus666 had been hit by a hallucinogenic potion at the time, so even though he saw King Kev duck into the woods, he didn't recognize him."

Stan's head was spinning as all the information came

together. He had been expecting to be able to punch dozens of holes in the Black Hood's argument, but yet . . . somehow . . . Stan found that it all made sense.

"So . . . ," Stan whispered weakly, "it's . . . true? Lord Tenebris and King Kev . . . really are the same player?"

"Yes," the Black Hood replied.

Stan sank to his knees and put his head into his hands. The Black Hood gave a sad sigh as he watched Stan try to comprehend this horrible truth. For the longest time, Stan had believed that King Kev and Lord Tenebris were two different entities, one of whom had built off the back of the other, and had fought independently of each other to take him down. But only now did Stan see that it was all the work of a single player, who had defied death itself to return to Elementia and do all that he could to destroy Stan and his friends.

"I . . . have another question," Stan managed to get out, even though he felt as if all the air had been vacuumed from his lungs.

"I will do my best to answer it," the Black Hood replied.

"Well . . . it's just . . . *why*? Why did King Kev go through all this trouble to return to Elementia? I mean, why didn't he just cut his losses and start another server after he died?"

The Black Hood took a deep breath. The answer to this question was long and complex, yet it held great truths that

Stan must learn if he were to have any chance of vanquishing King Kev for good. The Black Hood knew that he had to express himself correctly.

"The answer to that is quite simple, Stan2012. King Kev still had unfinished business in Elementia."

"Do you mean the lower-level players?" Stan asked, outraged. "Did he really care about getting rid of them *that much*?"

"Getting rid of the lower-level players never really mattered to King Kev, Stan2012."

"*What?*" Stan shouted, causing Rex to bark in surprise. "Are you crazy? I've lost everything trying to take down two different dictatorships created by this guy, and the main reason that both of them existed was that he hated lower-level players!"

"I'm sorry, Stan2012," the Black Hood replied. "I didn't mean that. Of course getting rid of lower-level players mattered to King Kev. However, it did not matter to him nearly as much as it mattered to the other members of the Noctem Alliance. Do you know the reason why, all those months ago, King Kev made the proclamation that started your journey?"

"Well, I assume it was because he hated the lower-level players," Stan said slowly. He thought that this was obvious.

"King Kev did take issue with the lower-level players, but that's not why he passed that law. He passed the law because

Caesar and Charlemagne asked him to. The only purpose of the law was to keep the upper-level players, the ones with the most power, happy and on his side. This is because all that King Kev has ever wanted in Elementia is power, complete dominance over the server. This is the driving force behind everything that he has done to you, both as the head of the Kingdom of Elementia and as the head of the Noctem Alliance."

"But . . . that makes no sense!" Stan exclaimed. "If he had operating powers the entire time, then why would it matter that he keep the upper-level players happy? He could just force them to do whatever he wanted!"

"Indeed, in the early days of King Kev's rule, that is exactly what he did. After Avery007 was defeated, and King Kev stood as the only remaining operator in Elementia, the server lived in an era of fear. All who stood up against the King were silenced, and many high-level officials were killed for suspected treason. Mecha11, Apothecary1, Bill33, Ben33, and Bob33 were all banished into the wilds. Nobody was happy, not even the upper-level players. Fear spread through the countryside like a pack of wolves, and it soon manifested itself in revolt.

"Many players determined that freedom was worth dying for, and they attempted to take down King Kev, much like what you did, Stan2012. With his operating powers, King

Kev crushed rebellion after rebellion, most of which were led by upper-level players. However, King Kev also realized that Elementia had become a hateful, ugly place. This was not the type of server that he wanted to rule. Therefore, he vowed to turn over a new leaf, and make Elementia a better place. Not many believed that he was capable of it, but when he claimed to give up his operating powers, turning him into a normal player, just as powerful and mortal as any other player, people rallied around him, believing that he truly had changed, and Elementia entered a new age of prosperity."

"But he didn't give up his operating powers. He lied to everybody!" Stan retorted.

"Yes he did, but he was also careful never to use his operating powers again. The only reason he kept them was as an absolute last resort . . . such as when you were moments away from killing him."

"But . . . I still don't understand," Stan replied, perplexed. "If everybody in Elementia was happy after the King said he gave up his operating powers, then how did stuff get so bad for the lower-level players?"

"That, Stan2012, is because King Kev was very clever and manipulative. He knew that if he was going to be benevolent and kind toward his people, he needed the most powerful players to become loyal to him. That way, if a rebellion ever did occur again, he would have a strong group to stand by him through thick and thin. Because of this, while he tried to be kind to everybody, King Kev gave special privileges to the upper-level players who had been in Elementia the longest, and acquired the most resources for themselves. He established a governing council, the Council of Operators, which he filled with upper-level players. Because of this special treatment, the upper-level players loved King Kev, and were willing to do anything to keep him in power.

"At first, the lower-level players weren't oppressed at all. Although they missed out on the special privileges of the upper-level players, they were still able to live in peace. Then, as the prestige of Elementia grew, more and more new players joined Elementia. The upper-level players became scared of the growing majority of new players. They asked King Kev to pass the Law of One Death, which would change the mode of the server to Hardcore PVP, and stop the new players from respawning if they died. Desperate to keep the new players happy, King Kev agreed.

"However, the upper-level players were still scared. The new players outnumbered them. The upper-level players realized that the Law of One Death didn't just apply to the new players—it applied to them, too. Therefore, the upper-level players asked King Kev to banish all new players from Element City. I believe, Stan2012, that you are well aware of what happened from there."

"But after King Kev died, he didn't have any power anymore!" Stan pointed out. "His whole plan to use the upper-level players to stay in power fell apart when the kingdom fell, so why did he come back to Elementia as Lord Tenebris?"

"You're right, Stan2012, that after the kingdom had fallen, King Kev couldn't use the upper-level players in the same way. However, when you took over Elementia, he saw an opportunity to use the upper-level players in a new way.

"King Kev knew that many upper-class players had lost their leader and their special privileges when you won the Battle for Elementia. He saw that most upper-level players hated you and the lower-level players that you protected. Therefore, he took on the new identity of Lord Tenebris, and told the upper-level players that their hatred of the lower-level players was justified. He rallied the upper-level players around him, uniting them under the banner of their hatred and spite toward the lower-level players.

"At first, the upper-level players only joined the Noctem Alliance to take revenge on lower-level players, and take back what was lost in the revolution. Now, however, they have become unwaveringly loyal to Lord Tenebris, eternally grateful that he has restored them to their former glory, and they will follow him no matter what he says . . . the same way that they became loyal to King Kev.

"Back in the old days of the server, it took King Kev years

to unite his people under him, under the banner of trust and camaraderie. It only took *Lord Tenebris* four months to unite his people under fear and hatred. By founding the Noctem Alliance, Lord Tenebris gave the upper-level players what they were looking for: a new leader to rally around, a chance to win back their dominance over the server, and a group that they could blame for everything that had happened to them. That group, of course, was you and your followers.

"This is how the worst tyrants of history form their empires, Stan2012. Desperate people unite under ruthless leaders, often under the banner of hatred of another group. It is a swift and effective way to gain control, but that amount of power given to such a hateful cause will inevitably lead to a permanent scar on the face of the world."

As he finished his speech, the Black Hood watched as Stan pondered what he had just told him. The Black Hood was quite impressed by Stan. He had been through so much in the past day, and yet somehow he was still able to process the information that he was being provided.

"Okay," Stan said when he finally stopped looking as if he were about to pass out from sheer exhaustion. "I have one more question for you."

"Yes?"

"Well . . . it's just . . . ," Stan said awkwardly. The Black Hood could tell that, whatever he was about to ask, Stan was trying not to offend him. "Well . . . if you've known all this the entire time . . . then why didn't you say anything to me or my friends before now? I mean, all my friends have told me how you've protected them a bunch of different times . . . and you appeared to me outside Nocturia. . . . so why didn't you tell me this before?"

The Black Hood gave a sad sigh. He knew that Stan was bound to ask this question sooner or later, and he didn't want to answer. Even as he stood here now, the Black Hood felt himself getting weaker and weaker, and the more information he gave to Stan, the faster his demise would be. However, the Black Hood knew that his own death was inevitable. Hopefully, he would be able to provide Stan with all that he needed before then.

"Stan2012, how much do you know about the history of Herobrine . . . about *my* history?"

The realization washed over Stan yet again that he was talking to Herobrine, the mythical Minecraft being who so many had called a demon, yet who had been working tirelessly to keep Stan and his friends safe for weeks. It only lasted for a moment, though. Stan knew that his time was running out, and Lord Tenebris's deadline would be on him before long. He couldn't shake the innate sense that, if he continued to talk to the Black Hood, the answer to his problems would somehow find him. "Um . . . I know that everybody thinks that you're some sort of glitchy demon that lives in Minecraft and haunts people . . . and that's about it."

The Black Hood chuckled again. "Indeed, Stan2012, that is true, and there is a reason that so many think of me that way. It's because . . . for the longest time . . . I *was* a force of destruction and chaos in Minecraft."

"What?" Stan asked, surprised. "But . . . you've been so helpful to me and my friends! You've done nothing but good in Elementia."

"This is also true," the Black Hood replied. "But that is not how it started. As I have told you before, I honestly do not recall where I came from, and my earliest memories are jumbled and foggy. All I remember for sure is that I came into being during the Alpha days of Minecraft, and soon found that I had access to all the powers that were possible for a player to have in vanilla Minecraft.

"At first, I saw no need to destroy or corrupt worlds. I saw Minecraft as a beautiful place, a place of wonder and splendor. I was particularly fascinated by the players, these beings from a realm outside of Minecraft, who could manipulate the natural world in much the same way that I could, and used this ability to create fantastic structures in a way that I could never hope to. I made a habit of watching the players work from a distance, enchanted by the various things that they built. I never let myself be seen, fearing that if they noticed me, they would stop the work that I found so fascinating.

"However, one day, a player did see me, captured me in a screenshot, and posted it online. I didn't think much of it at the time. . . . People posted fake pictures of player-like glitches all the time. I assumed that nothing would come of it. However, before long, I was shocked to find that the Mojang team released a patch of the game that banished me from entering any Minecraft world ever again.

"I was confused and angry. I hadn't been harming anybody, I had just been watching the other players! Why would Mojang want me to be removed from the game? In any case, I found that it hardly mattered . . . after all, I am a glitch who is capable of adapting, and I soon found that the banishment was not too hard to get around. Before long, I was back in Minecraft, determined to never be spotted again, lest Mojang try to kick me out again.

"Alas, my attempts to be inconspicuous were in vain. Mojang soon released another patch, which banished me yet again, this time making it even harder for me to reenter. Now I was beyond angry; I was furious. Why was I being kicked out of the game? Because of my odd appearance? Whatever the reason was, I didn't care. I was more determined to reenter the game than ever, but now I no longer wished to watch the players. Rather, I wanted to attack, haunt, and frighten the players, to get back at the game that had arbitrarily decided that I had no place in it.

"I learned that the one who had captured me in a screen-shot had fabricated a story about me, saying that I interfered with the world by creating pyramids and tunnels, that I was the spirit of Notch's deceased brother, and that my name was Herobrine. I adopted the persona and the name, and terrorized players all throughout Alpha and into the early stages of Beta. Although Mojang constantly tried to remove me, I found ways around their defenses, always reentering Minecraft to terrorize more players, growing stronger and stronger as more new abilities were added into the game for me to mimic.

"As the official release of Minecraft approached, I knew that the Mojang team was trying to iron out as many glitches as possible in preparation for the new game engine of the Adventure Update. However, I never could have predicted what they put into the game to counter me."

"What did they put in?" Stan asked with bated breath.

The Black Hood closed his eyes. "To this day, I'm not sure exactly what it is. All I know is, whatever they coded into the game, it's not just a patch meant to keep me out. Whatever it is, it's alive, sentient, and capable of adapting, just like I am. I don't know what it is, but I've named it . . . The Voice in the Sky."

As soon as the Black Hood said the name, a crash of

thunder sounded from overhead. Stan whipped his head skyward. The rainstorm had stopped a while ago, and the sky above them was clear.

"That was him, Stan2012," the Black Hood replied quietly. "He lives in the sky, watching me."

"Wha . . . what does he do?" Stan asked meekly.

"I'm . . . not sure," the Black Hood replied frankly. "I don't know who he is, what he is, or what he does. All I know is that, whenever I enter a Minecraft server and interact with the blocks, the mobs, the players, or anything else, the Voice in the Sky tells me to stop. Then . . . if I do not stop . . . my energy begins to rapidly drain."

The Black Hood paused for a moment to catch his breath. As he spoke about the energy draining from his body, it was happening to him. Revealing his face to Stan had given the Black Hood an adrenaline boost, as he was excited to finally be talking to a player again. However, now, the fatigue caught up to him, and he felt his life force draining the longer that he engaged in this forbidden activity.

"To avoid withering out of existence," the Black Hood continued after a moment, "I stayed out of Minecraft servers, forever condemned to hang in the void of cyberspace between thousands of Minecraft worlds. I could watch the worlds from a distance, but I could never enter them, interact with them, or wreak havoc in them again without the

Voice in the Sky catching me.

"And . . . yet . . . as I watched these hundreds of thousands of Minecraft worlds from afar, I no longer felt the need to destroy them. I watched the players working together, building together, and creating amazing structures and worlds together. The amazement with Minecraft that I had felt upon first entering the game returned to me, and I realized how wrong I had been. Minecraft is a beautiful game . . . more than a game, really—it's a beautiful world. It allows people to have a place where they can do anything they want, where the only limit is their imagination. I realized that I had been foolish for wanting to corrupt such a marvelous universe.

"However, the damage was done. The Voice in the Sky was still watching me, and every time that I entered a Minecraft world, I could feel my life force fading more and more by the second. The only time I was ever safe was when I floated in limbo between the Minecraft worlds, watching longingly from far away.

"What I saw shocked me. Even though the players in the worlds had nothing holding them back, nothing trying to keep them out, many still found the need to antagonize others. While I saw many players building together in harmony, I also saw countless Griefers, going out of their way to make the Minecraft experience miserable for others. As I watched these players fight, I couldn't help but feel responsible. I was the original Griefer, the one who introduced the concept to Minecraft. Because of me, Minecraft was no longer a world solely of creativity and wonder, but a world where you had to constantly watch your back, lest you be destroyed.

"Stricken with guilt, I knew that I had to make up for it somehow. I swore to myself, right then and there, that if anything were to ever threaten Minecraft on a large scale, I would do everything in my power to stop it. My opportunity came fairly recently, when my attention was drawn to your Minecraft server, Stan2012."

"Let me guess," Stan said with a dark grimace. "You sensed King Kev pulling energy out of other servers to make himself stronger, and realized that it might create a glitch that could destroy Minecraft."

"Precisely," the Black Hood replied darkly. "I realized that, if King Kev was not stopped, then his unquenchable lust for power may lead him to unwittingly create a glitch that would destroy his beloved server, and countless others along with it. I knew that, regardless of what happened, I had to stop it.

"And yet, I knew that I couldn't. I was well aware that, if I were to try to tell King Kev what he was doing, the Voice in the Sky would intervene. He would destroy me before I could even reach the head of the Noctem Alliance.

"Therefore, I looked into the history of the server of

Elementia, to try to see if there was some other way that I could possibly prevent this ghastly fate. And that, Stan2012, is where I first learned of your story—the most remarkable story in the history of Minecraft."

"What?" Stan exclaimed. "How is my story so remarkable? I've hardly done anything!" He thought glumly about how true his words were as he spoke on. "I led a rebellion against King Kev but didn't even have the guts to finish him off, letting him cheat his way back onto the server. If I had stabbed him the second I had a chance, he wouldn't have been able to change the difficulty setting! Then, when I tried to take him down again, he totally wiped the floor with me!"

"You're right, Stan2012," the Black Hood replied. Stan stared at him in surprise. He had expected the Black Hood to contradict something that he had said, and tell him just how spectacular he really was.

"Hardly anything that you've done matters in the long run," the Black Hood continued. "You were held back by your own mercy in the tower of Element Castle that day, and that did allow King Kev to escape and found the Noctem Alliance. And the moment King Kev turned into Lord Tenebris, and was no longer afraid to use his operating powers, you never stood a chance against him. However, Stan2012, there is one thing that you aren't giving yourself enough credit for."

"And what's that?" Stan spat bitterly.

"You never stopped fighting," the Black Hood replied. Stan was floored to hear the incredible passion in his voice. "So deeply did you believe that the lower-level players of this server did not deserve to be oppressed that you never gave up, and you never surrendered, even when you had impossible odds stacked against you."

"But none of it worked!" Stan cried. "So what does it matter that I tried if I didn't succeed?"

"Stan2012, you must realize what you managed to do," the Black Hood continued, his voice still enriched with passion. "You managed to rally an entire country around you during your fight to take down King Kev, and even if you failed to destroy the King himself, you succeeded in taking down his kingdom. For the first time in years, Elementia was a place where people of all levels could live together in harmony.

"Do you think that your people are ever going to forget what it feels like to live in a country of happiness and equality? Do you think that, now that they've experienced what true freedom is, they will ever stop fighting to get it back? Of course not! And all because *you*, Stan2012, were brave enough to take a stand against the injustice you saw around you. It takes a special kind of person to take a stand when injustice is the law, and you, Stan2012, are one special person."

Stan hesitated for a moment before responding.

"Okay, let's say you're right. Let's say that I'm so special and that long after I'm gone, people keep fighting back against King Kev. It's not like they're going to win! King Kev is the only operator on the server. He's never going to be taken down! My people will just keep on fighting back until they're all dead!"

"And then King Kev will be right back to square one," the Black Hood replied triumphantly. "He'll be in charge of an empire of misery and despair, just like he was when he first defeated Avery007. Remember that all King Kev really wants is power. He doesn't care who he has to step on to get it. And through your example, Stan2012, your people will let King Kev know that they won't be stepped on without a fight."

For a while, neither Stan nor the Black Hood said anything. They simply stood in the clearing as the fog swirled around their feet, becoming lighter and lighter as the sun began to rise.

"Stan2012, I would like to thank you," the Black Hood said, and Stan was shocked to see a tear streaming out of his radiant white eye and down his face. "For the longest time, I believed that I had ruined Minecraft. I thought that, through my chaos and destruction, I had set an example for Griefers and tyrants all across the countless servers of the game. Your story showed me, though, that however bad things may get, there will always be those who are willing to stand up for what's right.

"I guess what I'm trying to say is . . . thank you, Stan2012, for doing the right thing, no matter how hard it was," the Black Hood replied, as he gave Stan a gracious smile.

Stan took a deep breath and let it out. He knew that the Black Hood was right. He had never failed to do what he thought was best for Elementia, and he couldn't stop now. Stan clutched his axe tightly in his sweaty palms and looked at the sky. The celestial lights of the sky were beginning to fade, and a light pink glow was starting to illuminate the eastern sky.

"I've got to go back there, don't I?" Stan said gravely, as he turned to look northward, toward Element City.

"Yes," the Black Hood replied. "Element City needs their president now more than ever."

Stan reached into his inventory and pulled out the enchanted golden apple and the Potion of Harming. It seemed like eons ago that Lord Tenebris had stood before him in the wreckage of the Adorian Village, offering both of the items to him. Stan looked down at the two items in his hand, and in both the shiny gold curve of the apple and the red-tinted face of the potion bottle, he saw his reflection. He saw the face of a brave, proud player who had never once turned his back on his country, and would fight to the death to defend it and the ones he loved.

He raised the golden apple to his mouth and swallowed it in three bites. Instantly, a surge of energy shot through Stan's body, coursing from his head through his core and spreading to his limbs. He felt as though he were under the effect of ten Potions of Swiftness at the same time. Stan glared hatefully at the Potion of Harming in his other hand and, in one motion, he pitched the toxic potion as hard as he could into the woods. Seconds later, in the far distance, he heard the shattering of glass.

Stan clutched his axe as the rising sun illuminated the right side of his face. He took yet another breath and let it out in a determined grunt. Stan knew that, within the hour, he was going to be dead. Lord Tenebris was going to do horrible, horrible things to him before destroying him in front of his people, along with the rest of his closest friends. However, Stan knew that none of the people who had followed him would ever forget their sacrifice, and although he might die, his spirit of rebellion never would.

Stan turned back to face the Black Hood one last time. The glitch player's eyes still shone brightly in the rising daylight as he looked proudly on Stan, the player who had given so much to Elementia, and was prepared to give more than could ever be repaid. The Black Hood sighed and looked Stan in the eye.

"Stan2012, I have tried to do all that I could to help your cause without jeopardizing my own existence," the Black Hood said carefully. "I have helped each of your friends in numerous ways, but I have still failed to do anything to help you."

"That's not true," Stan replied with a bittersweet smile. "You helped me realize what I can do to save my people, and you risked your life to do so. I can never thank you enough."

"Still . . . ," the Black Hood continued slowly. "I feel that I owe it to you to do something for you that might help you . . . in a different way."

"That's okay," Stan said darkly. "Where I'm going, I won't need any help."

"It wasn't a recommendation," the Black Hood said simply, and with that he reached out his hand toward Stan.

Instantly, Stan felt himself being pulled forward toward the Black Hood and being forced to his knees. Stan recognized the horribly familiar sensation of being held in Lord Tenebris's psychic grip. Stan was just about to let out a shout of terror when the Black Hood reached out with his free hand and put it to Stan's head.

Suddenly, Stan wasn't terrified anymore. The power from the golden apple coursing through his veins seemed to amplify, expanding further and further until finally, Stan felt as though he were exuding energy from every pore of his body. The power continued to grow and grow, until finally, the energy reached its peak. Stan fell to the ground in a crumpled heap, shaking as he tried to contain the sheer power that he now felt inside himself.

"What . . . what did you do to me?" Stan managed to get out as his entire body twitched with spasms.

"You'll see in a moment," the Black Hood replied as Rex began to wag his tail beside him.

"Stan! Stan, answer me right now!"

Stan looked up with a jolt. Of all the things that he might have anticipated at that moment, Sally's voice, ringing out of the ether with no static, clear as crystal, was not one of them.

"I'm here, Sal," Stan replied, looking at the ground as he tried to focus on her voice. "Can you hear me?"

"Yes, I can hear you!" Sally replied. Stan was amazed at how clearly she was coming in. "Stan, did you just do something to Elementia's code?"

"What? No!" Stan exclaimed. "Why? What's happening, Sally?"

"I'm not sure," she replied. She sounded excited. "All I know is that somehow, I have no idea how, a hole opened up in the defenses of Elementia's coding."

Stan's heart skipped a beat. "Wait . . . really?"

"Yes," Sally replied. She paused for a moment. Then . . .

"Stan . . . I think that I might have just given you operating powers."

Stan said nothing in reply. His heart was racing as he dropped his diamond axe to the ground and held out his right hand. He took a deep breath and, not believing that it was possible, he focused as hard as he could on the hand, imagining a diamond helmet.

There was a faint pop, and a diamond helmet appeared in his hand.

Stan's mouth hung open, and widened further and further into a smile as he spawned in more items—bowls of mushroom soup, flint and steel, jungle-wood blocks, gravel, end stone—the pile of random items on the ground below him grew larger and larger. Stan drew back his fist and, taking aim at a nearby tree, he fired off a punch. Instantly, the tree exploded as the invisible burst of energy hit it. Laughing wildly now, Stan took a deep breath, jumped into the air . . . and floated in place, held aloft by his newly acquired operating powers.

"Did it work?" Sally's voice called out of nowhere.

"Yes!" Stan exclaimed, pumping his fist as he soared into the air, doing a loop before touching back down on the ground.

"Fantastic!" Sally cried. Stan could almost see the smirk on her face. "Now go on, noob, don't waste any more time . . .

go kick Herobrine's butt! Tell me how it went when it's over."

And before Stan could respond, Sally's voice vanished with a slight static crackle.

Stan was beside himself with glee. He had operating powers now! He wasn't going to have to just hand himself over to Lord Tenebris to die. He had a fighting chance. There was a possibility that he might actually be able to destroy Lord Tenebris and the Noctem Alliance.

All at once, Stan realized what must have happened. He realized why the hole in the defenses had opened up. He realized that he now had the powers of an operator. Slowly Stan turned around to face the Black Hood . . . only to find that he had vanished. Stan looked around the clearing, perplexed, but there was no sign of the glitchy, white-eyed player—or Rex, for that matter.

Stan remembered what the Black Hood had said—the more that he interacted with the players, the weaker he would become. Stan realized that was the reason the Black Hood had only appeared to his friends when they were in very real danger. He also imagined that, just by talking to Stan, the Black Hood had taken a huge risk, jeopardizing his very existence. Was it possible that, by enabling Sally to access the code of Elementia, the Black Hood had . . .

Stan heard an explosion from somewhere far in the distance, and he snapped out of his train of thought. There was no time to ponder what had happened to the Black Hood now. There would be plenty of time for that later. For now, Stan knew what he had to do.

As Stan stood in the clearing, his face illuminated by the light of the rising sun, Lord Tenebris was surely lining up his friends for the firing squad. If Stan didn't show himself soon, they would all be killed. Stan knew that Lord Tenebris's operating powers had been boosted by the power he had stolen from the server, but there was one thing that Stan had that he didn't: the element of surprise. Lord Tenebris had no idea that Stan now had operating powers, and if he played his cards right, then he just might be able to overpower the leader of the Noctem Alliance and finally end this war.

Regardless of what his odds were, though, Stan knew that he at least had to try. As long as there was even the tiniest glimmer of hope left, Stan knew that he always had to try.

And so with a deep breath, Stan picked up his diamond axe, focused as hard as he could on the Avery Memorial Courthouse, and in an instant, he vanished into thin air, leaving the clearing full of swirling mist totally vacant.

Leonidas winced as a bright light shone over his eyes. He grunted as he forced his eyes open to find that he was staring directly into the rising sun. He glanced down at the ground to avoid looking into the rays, and shook the cobwebs out of his head. He was standing on wood-plank blocks, and he could see a gravel street a few blocks below his feet. Leonidas realized that he was standing upright, his back was to a wall of wood-plank blocks, and his arms were propped up on levers that had been attached to the wall.

Leonidas's temple was throbbing at the place where he and Cassandrix had cracked heads. He soon became aware that the air around him was filled with noise, and his head began to pulse with even more pain. Slowly, Leonidas opened his eyes. The sun was indeed shining directly into his eyes, but it was darker than he had expected, as it was shining through the thick veil of clouds cast over the city by the Withers hovering in the air above him.

As his ears and eyes slid back into full focus, Leonidas could see a crowd of soldiers surrounding the platform he was standing on, their heads nearly level with the two-block-high wood-plank platform. The Noctem Army was still wearing their black armor, and were erupting with jeers and taunts at those on the platform. Leonidas realized that he wasn't alone. He looked to his right and left, and saw that all the leaders of Stan's army were propped up on the wall. They were all standing upright, their arms raised up on levers, as still as statues.

Leonidas's heart skipped a beat as he realized what this was—a firing squad.

Leonidas did a quick check and realized to his dismay that his inventory had been totally emptied. He had lost his best bow, Hornet, back at Element Castle, and his other two bows and his sword were now gone as well. Not that it mattered. He knew that if he even tried to lift a finger, let alone arm himself, he would be killed in a matter of seconds.

Out of morbid curiosity, Leonidas looked down the line to see who was there. They were all about to die anyway. He might as well get a good idea of who was about to bite the dust with him.

There was only one player to the left of him before the row stopped, and that was Jayden. His eye was black and he had a sizable gash on his forehead, but he looked more exhausted than pained. Glancing to his right, Leonidas recognized Ben, who looked utterly defeated, and Bob, who was sitting on Ivanhoe, a sick look on his face. Leonidas wondered with a horrible lurch of his stomach if the pig would be executed as well.

Beyond those two were the Mechanist, who appeared to be in deep thought; Sirus, who was glancing around in a twitchy and nervous manner; and Cassandrix, whose face was contorted into a furious, twisted rage. And at the end of the line stood Commander Crunch, who was yelling something that Leonidas couldn't make out into the sea of heckling Noctem soldiers, occasionally interspersed with a hearty seaman's laugh.

Leonidas did a quick headcount: There were eight of them, including him. He went through a mental checklist to see who was missing, and came up with only three.

He wasn't surprised at all that Stan was missing. As the leader of the republic, Leonidas imagined that Lord Tenebris probably had special plans to deal with him. He most likely was still alive and would make an appearance at some point, during which Lord Tenebris would surely make an example out of him.

As for Kat . . . Leonidas didn't think that the image of Kat begin flung around that council room like a rag doll would leave him. Leonidas and Kat hadn't talked much since he had joined their army, but he still knew that she was a tough player with a keen eye for justice who wouldn't take crap from anybody. The image of such a strong-willed and powerful player rendered totally helpless was haunting. Although he knew that the others in the army would be grief-stricken when they found out that Kat had been killed, Leonidas, who had hardly gotten to know her, found her death far more terrifying and unsettling than anything else.

And that left the last missing player. While he hadn't gotten to know Kat all that well, Leonidas had gotten to know Charlie. Charlie had gone from hating Leonidas to accepting him as an ally and friend. The thought that now, after they had finally became friends, Charlie might be gone made Leonidas's stomach clench with dread. He tried to convince himself that there was a possibility otherwise. That maybe, somehow, he had escaped, and he wasn't actually dead. After all, Leonidas had nothing to go on. There was no evidence that Charlie was gone.

But then, all at once, Leonidas stopped thinking about it. It was as if somebody had turned off his ability to care. After all, what was the point? They were in front of a Noctem Alliance firing squad. They were all about to die anyway.

Almost immediately after he thought this, a figure appeared on the wood plank–block platform in front of the lined-up players with a loud crack. This player was skinned identically to Stan, but although Leonidas could only see him from the back, he knew better. He was a little bit surprised that Lord Tenebris was revealing himself to his people. From what he understood, nobody, besides him, had ever seen Lord Tenebris's face and lived. Then again, this was a special occasion.

All at once, the taunts and boos emanating from the rowdy crowd of Noctem Soldiers ceased. For the first time ever, they were beholding the face of their leader. Leonidas watched as the entire crowd stood transfixed and speechless for a moment before turning away uncomfortably, as they found it impossible to hold Lord Tenebris's gaze for more than a second.

"Greetings, my loyal subjects," Lord Tenebris said, his voice deep and booming, carrying across the silent plaza of the Avery Memorial Courthouse without effort. "Today is a historic day in Elementia. Not only is this the day that I first reveal my face to you, but it is also the day that we celebrate our victory over the forces of Stan2012's Republic of Elementia! Viva la Noctem!"

"VIVA LA NOCTEM!" the crowd rang out. It was the most passionate chant that Leonidas had ever heard the people of the Noctem Alliance let out.

"Standing here before you, totally at my mercy, are the leaders of the Republic of Elementia," Lord Tenebris said, turning around to face them and gesturing with his hand. As the crowd proceeded to continue their booing and heckling, Leonidas heard several of his friends pinned to the wall give gasps of horror as they viewed Lord Tenebris's face for the first time and found themselves unable to look into his eyes.

"These players marched into our city yesterday at high noon," Lord Tenebris continued, his followers instantly going silent as he turned to look over the crowd yet again, "with the intention of taking it away from us. They believe that Element City should welcome all players with open arms, regardless of whether or not they've earned their place here. In fact, a good percentage of their invasion force was composed of lower-level players. That's right. Such is the arrogance of these players standing before you that they believed that, after a single week of training, their lower-level friends were equal in skill to you, the Noctem Freedom Fighters, who have lived in Elementia for years."

Shouts of outrage erupted from the crowd, followed by a fresh round of heckling. Lord Tenebris did nothing to stop this, and Leonidas could almost picture the sadistic grin on his face.

"I would like to thank you, my citizens," Lord Tenebris continued, quelling the ruckus yet again. "I would like to thank you for tolerating the feeble attempts of the republic to fight back for so long now. For months, the Noctem Alliance has gained strength, preparing for the day that we would take back what is rightfully ours. And yet, wherever we went, the forces of the Republic of Elementia were there to make our jobs ever so slightly more annoying, like a fly buzzing around our heads that was nearly impossible to swat.

"But today," Lord Tenebris continued, "today, the fly has finally been squashed. On this day, I claim the Minecraft server Elementia in the name of the Noctem Alliance! Viva la Noctem!"

"VIVA LA NOCTEM!" the crowd echoed back to him.

"And now, we shall all witness the death of the republic, and we shall witness it the same way that we started—together. May I draw your attention to the remaining fighting forces of the Republic of Elementia."

Leonidas's head snapped upright, and he followed the gaze of the hundreds of players around him in the center of the crowd, where there was a large, fenced-off area devoid of players that Leonidas hadn't noticed before. There, with a great roaring of redstone mechanisms, the ground rose until it was several blocks off the ground. Standing on top of this massive elevated platform were close to a hundred and fifty players, all the survivors of the attack. They had been stripped of their diamond armor, and they were huddled together like cattle, looking absolutely petrified.

"I suggest that you step back from the platform," Lord Tenebris said over the insults and verbal abuse being thrown at the players. "The platform is rigged with TNT blocks, and it will be detonated immediately if any of them try anything funny."

The mass of three hundred soldiers in black leather

armor expanded away from the platform, but the foul language and name calling didn't slow down until Lord Tenebris spoke again.

"The players on the platform will be spared, provided that they cooperate with me," Lord Tenebris continued. Leonidas's eyebrows shot up, as did many in the crowd.

"These players have had their minds poisoned by their leaders, standing on the platform before you. They will serve time in Brimstone Prison for their crimes. As soon as they are transferred to the prison, the remainder of the citizens of this city, who are presently locked in the prison, will be released. These terms are in accordance with an agreement that I made with President Stan."

The crowd had been waiting since the speech began to hear the name of the most wanted player in the Noctem Alliance, and now they were so quiet that a pin drop could be heard. Lord Tenebris paused for a moment and glanced at the square sun, which had now risen in full above the horizon.

"President Stan was supposed to be here by now. The agreement was that if he had not come here to duel me by sunrise, I would begin to execute his friends. Tell me, does anybody here see President Stan2012 around?"

Several shouts of "NO!" erupted from the crowd as the Noctem soldiers laughed. Leonidas just looked at the ground bitterly. He knew that Lord Tenebris couldn't possibly be telling the truth. Stan definitely would have turned up if he had agreed to it. More likely, Lord Tenebris had killed or crippled Stan, and was just trying to make Stan look bad for entertainment. Leonidas shook his head. He didn't even care anymore. He was just ready for it all to be over.

"However, before the show begins," Lord Tenebris said as the laughter died down, "I must ask if any players who are about to die would wish to say any final words."

There was a pause as Leonidas tried to think of something to say. However, he couldn't think of anything. And even if he could, he really didn't want to say it. The Noctem Alliance had won.

Lord Tenebris looked back at them and gave a snide little smirk. "Well then, if that's the case . . ." But then, Lord Tenebris's remark was cut off by a lone pair of footsteps. Leonidas glanced up and saw the Mechanist, not looking beaten but rather determined, as he made his way to the edge of the platform.

"Well, well, well," Lord Tenebris chortled as the Mechanist walked up beside him. "If it isn't the great Mecha11, redstone architect of most of this city and the inventor of the TNT cannon. I must admit, it's a shame to kill such a brilliant player . . . almost. Come now, share one last bit of wisdom with us from that radiant mind of yours."

Despite the mean laughs erupting from the crowd, the Mechanist looked unfazed. Rather, he took a deep breath and began to speak.

"I have a few things that I would like to say both to my fellow commanders and also to the brave warriors standing out on the platform in the crowd. First of all, I . . ."

Leonidas was surprised to hear that the Mechanist's voice sounded rather shaky, almost as if he were on the verge of tears. The redstone genius then took a deep breath, composed himself, and continued.

"First of all, I want to apologize to all of you. During my time as your leader, I did not serve my country well. I let the pressures of leading go to my head, and I tried to escape it in ways that"—the Mechanist halted with a catch in his throat before he continued on—"that resulted in the loss of a friend. I then let my grief and guilt overtake me, and I ignored the needs of my people because of it. I take full responsibility for all the misery that you had to go through while you were down in the mine.

"But none of that matters now."

Leonidas, who had been cringing as he anticipated a long, self-deprecating speech about how everything that had gone wrong was the Mechanist's fault, raised his head, his ears perked up.

"I'll tell you what does matter . . . *you*." He pointed out at the players who were standing on the platform and staring at him, intently absorbing every word he said.

"My friends and I are going to die today. There is nothing that we can do to stop that. But you are all going to live on to see another day. It will be difficult for you during your imprisonment in Brimstone, but you'll all survive. And even though we weren't able to overcome those who put us where we are now, I implore you to never forget what it felt like to be a citizen of the Republic of Elementia.

"Remember your freedom. Remember how it felt to walk down the streets and feel safe. Remember how it felt to know that your families and your friends were just a monorail ride away. There may be nothing more that I, or any of my friends, can do to help you. But if you cling tightly to those memories, then one day, I guarantee that you'll be able to help yourselves, and turn Elementia back into the place that you remember so fondly—a place of justice and equality for all."

The Mechanist finished talking. He took a deep breath, let it out, and began to walk backward. As he did, the crowd of Noctem soldiers let out sniggers and snide remarks. Leonidas, on the other hand, stared at the Mechanist in amazement as he reached the wall and put his hands back up over the levers that held them up.

Leonidas looked from the Mechanist to the soldiers

elevated on a platform above the crowds. All of them wore a nearly identical expression: pensive and determined. Leonidas knew that the Mechanist's speech had connected with them. They would never forget it—and the Mechanist was right. One day, however far in the future it may be, those players would return to Elementia. And maybe they'd be able to turn it back into the place that Stan and his friends had worked so hard to create and defend.

Leonidas's heart leaped as he realized that the Mechanist had redeemed himself. He very well may have just inspired the future of Elementia for the better.

"That was very touching, Mecha11," Lord Tenebris replied nonchalantly. He turned to look down the line. "Would anybody else like to say something?"

"I have something to say."

Leonidas's ears perked up. He recognized that voice. His head turned to the right, along with all the other heads in the congregation, to where the voice had come from. There, entering the plaza from the side street, his clothes tattered and worn, was Stan2012, his hands empty and his face knit into a leer as he stared down Lord Tenebris.

Immediately, the crowd erupted. The Noctem soldiers let loose their loudest, harshest round of jeers yet, which just barely drowned out the cheers and applause that burst out from Stan's allies spread across the two elevated platforms.

As Stan made his way up the stairs of the firing-squad platform, standing directly opposite Lord Tenebris, the noise had gotten so loud that Leonidas could barely hear himself think.

"SILENCE!" Lord Tenebris boomed. Leonidas recognized the awful sensation of Lord Tenebris seemingly yelling from directly within his head, making his ears ache. Immediately, all noise stopped.

Slowly but surely, all players from both sides looked up to see Stan2012 and Lord Tenebris staring each other down from both ends of the platform. The two rulers held each other's gaze in the dim sunlight that shone from under the gray veil of the Withers. Leonidas stared at Stan in amazement. How was he holding Lord Tenebris's gaze for so long without breaking it?

"You're late," Lord Tenebris said.

"I apologize," Stan said with a smirk. "I met an old friend, and we had some catching up to do."

Lord Tenebris returned the smirk. "Well, I sure hope that your meeting was worth it. I was seconds away from executing your friends, you know."

"Trust me," Stan said. "It was well worth my time."

Suddenly, Leonidas felt something strange wash over him. It was a sensation that he hadn't felt before. It lasted for only a few seconds.

"I assume that you remember the terms of our deal," Stan said evenly.

"Indeed I do," Lord Tenebris replied. "The winner of this duel is the rightful ruler of Elementia."

As the crowd of Noctem soldiers snickered, Leonidas suddenly became aware that his inventory was no longer empty. He checked the contents as inconspicuously as he could and found, to his utter bafflement, that his inventory now contained an unenhanced bow and two stacks of arrows.

Leonidas heard a soft gasp beside him, and as he looked down the line, he saw that all his friends were wearing equal expressions of amazement. Was it possible that *all of them* had mysteriously gotten weapons?

"Well then," Stan said after the sarcastic laughter died down. "How about we stop wasting time and begin?"

"With pleasure," Lord Tenebris replied. He took a deep breath, and a diamond sword materialized in his left hand, glimmering with various enchantments.

Stan didn't move. He merely stood there unarmed, as he smiled at Lord Tenebris. "Go ahead," he taunted. "Make the first move."

Leonidas stared at Stan with confusion. Why didn't he have a weapon drawn? What was he playing at?

Lord Tenebris stretched out his empty right hand at Stan, took a deep breath, and then grunted. As he did, an arrow materialized from his fingertips, flying directly at Stan. Stan stood totally still, not even bothering to defend himself. Leonidas's eyes widened, and he flinched right as the arrow was about to enter Stan's chest. . . .

But it didn't. Right as the arrow was upon Stan, it changed trajectory, curving left and flying past Stan's left arm.

A collective gasp rose from the crowd on both sides as Lord Tenebris raised an eyebrow. He lifted his hand again, and sent three more arrows flying directly at Stan. All three times, the same thing happened—right as the arrows were about to hit Stan, they suddenly changed course, flying in three different directions.

The crowd was now totally silent, and Leonidas's jaw was dropped. What was he watching?

Lord Tenebris's mouth opened slightly, and his eyes grew wider as he tried to comprehend what was going on. He raised his right hand again, throwing a punch that produced a fireball. The fireball flew just as fast as the arrows had, directly at Stan.

Without even batting an eye, Stan raised his right hand. As the fireball made contact with his hand, he caught it, stopping it dead in its tracks. Lord Tenebris watched in bewilderment as Stan held the fireball up, then proceeded to clench his fist, crushing it. When he opened his hand again, nothing was left but a few light gray wisps of smoke, which were quickly carried away by the wind.

Lord Tenebris didn't look confused anymore—he looked angry. He drew back his fist, took a deep breath, and launched it as hard as he could at Stan. It appeared that nothing had left Lord Tenebris's hand, but Stan knew better, as he sensed the pulse of explosive energy heading toward him. Stan reached out his right hand and caught the pulse of energy, using the force to spin around and release it, sending it flying right back at Lord Tenebris.

The Noctem leader let out a faint shout of surprise as he sensed the blast coming, and he crossed his arms over his face as the blast hit. The explosion knocked Lord Tenebris backward toward the edge of the platform. He lowered his arms, still smoking from the explosion, and stared at Stan, who was standing perfectly still. Disbelief was etched on every pixel of the Noctem ruler's face.

"What did you . . . how did you . . . ," Lord Tenebris managed to get out. "What are you doing?"

Stan stared at him for a moment, total confidence on his face, and taking in every moment of Lord Tenebris's shock before responding.

"Taking back my country," he said with a determined grin, before shouting, "Armies of Elementia! *Charge!*"

Immediately, Leonidas raced forward and attacked the Noctem soldiers on the ground. He allowed his instincts to carry him forward, rushing past Stan, off the platform and into the crowd, drawing his bow as he did so. He looked at the other commanders of Stan's army in amazement. On one side of him Jayden was pulling out a diamond axe, while on the other side Bob drew out a bow and charged on Ivanhoe over the side of the platform and into the crowd of stupefied Noctem soldiers.

Lord Tenebris looked around wildly, trying to figure out what was happening. His eyes landed on the platform where the imprisoned republic fighters were stationed. To his utter surprise and dismay, these players, too, were pouring over the sides of the platforms, diamond weapons drawn. *How is this possible?* he thought to himself. *Their inventories were empty! Well, I suppose it doesn't matter . . . they're all about to die anyway!*

"DETONATE THE PLATFORM!" Lord Tenebris cried out, desperately hoping that his soldier manning the lever that detonated the platform would pull it. And yet the soldiers still continued to pour over the edges, into the crowd of baffled troops.

Lord Tenebris repeated his shout two more times, but to no avail. The platform remained solid and intact. By now, nearly half the players on the platform had jumped off and were engaging the Noctem Forces, who were totally caught off guard, in battle. Lord Tenebris was beside himself with fury. *Why isn't anyone pulling that lever?*

"Looking for this?"

Slowly, Lord Tenebris turned around to face Stan. He was still standing calmly at the far end of the platform, and in his outstretched hand was a lever, the redstone dust falling to the ground indicating that it had been freshly yanked off a circuit. Stan released the lever, and it dropped to the ground with a clang.

For a moment, Lord Tenebris just stared at Stan. He was totally unable to process what had happened. *How had Stan suddenly gained these miraculous abilities?* Stan didn't let him ponder it for long, though. He jumped into the air and began to float just above the ground as a glowing diamond axe materialized in his hand. Lord Tenebris's mouth opened slightly, but then he closed it as a savage sneer crossed his face.

Fine, he thought to himself, *have it your way, Stan.*

He switched his enchanted diamond sword to his right hand, held it in front of him, and leaped into the air, rocketing at top speed toward Stan, who mirrored him and flew directly at Lord Tenebris. It was only a matter of seconds before the two players, flying directly at each other, met in the center of the wood plank–block platform. Their blades clashed together, sending a shower of sparks down to the ground below them as the two operators teleported away.

As Jayden looked around, he realized that most of the Noctem soldiers had managed to get over their shock and were beginning to fight back. Indeed, Jayden still had absolutely no idea how a diamond axe had appeared in his inventory, nor how the same thing had happened to all his friends and allies.

All he knew was that, whatever was happening, it was because of Stan, whom Jayden had seen fly toward Lord Tenebris and warp into the sky. Stan had clearly gotten operating powers somehow, and was now using them to fight Lord Tenebris. As soon as that fight finished, Jayden was sure that Stan would help them subdue the Noctem armies. Until then, though, Jayden knew that they had to buy Stan as much time as they could.

"Well, well, well . . . look who we have here," a voice with a Welsh accent spoke from behind him.

Jayden spun around and saw three players staring at him with contempt. He realized with a jolt that one of them was Zingster, the harsh corporal who had overseen Jayden's training in Nocturia. The other was LemonKipper, who had the skin of a mermaid and was a stuck-up member of Jayden's class. He didn't recognize the third player, who had no face. His or her skin (Jayden couldn't tell) was totally black, except for a giant number 4 that stretched from the player's head to their toes.

"Hey guys," Jayden said, raising his axe and dropping

into a fighting stance, "long time no see." He had seen Zingster and Kipper fight, and he knew that he could take both of them.

"Don't sound so chipper," Kipper snarled at him. "We're gonna make you pay for what you did to Nocturia, Councilman Jayden."

"Wait . . . that's right," Jayden said, realizing that Kipper and Zingster should probably be dead. "How did you three escape Nocturia?"

"I got caught swiping some QPo," Kipper said, no hint of guilt in his voice, "and Zingster decided to take me out into the tundra to teach me a lesson. When the bomb went off, we decided to head over here."

"I let him get away with the theft," Zingster grunted. "Because we've got bigger fish to fry!"

Zingster drew out his pickaxe and rushed into Jayden as Kipper did the same with his sword. Jayden knocked the pickaxe out of the way and locked the blade of his axe into the sword. The two players struggled to overpower each other for a moment before Zingster recovered and attacked again, forcing Jayden to feint away from Kipper and dodge.

Well, they've both gotten better, Jayden thought to himself as he swung his axe at Zingster's hand. The Noctem corporal dodged and used the opening to body check Jayden, sending him to the ground with a thud. Immediately, he rolled to the side to avoid a stab of Kipper's sword, and rolled several more times to avoid the sword that repeatedly plunged into the gravel. All of a sudden, Jayden felt his axe fly out of his hand, and looked up in time to see Zingster raising his pick-axe for another strike, just as Kipper did the same.

Jayden rolled to the side while swinging his feet around, dodging the sword strike while sweeping his legs behind Zingster's knees, sending him tumbling down, his pickaxe flying into the air. Jayden used the momentum to leap to his feet, catching Zingster's pickaxe while using it to counter Kipper's sword strike. Once again, the two players pressed into each other's blades, sending sparks flying, until Jayden finally started to win. He came closer and closer to overpow-ering Kipper, and was about to overtake him when he sensed something flying at him from the corner of his eye.

Instinctively, Jayden ducked, and the flying potion hit Kipper squarely in the face. The impact knocked him to the ground, right on top of the recovering Zingster. The cloud of gray smoke from the bottle wafted to the ground, surround-ing the two players and knocking them unconscious.

Jayden had gotten slightly sprayed by the gas, too, and he felt a little woozy. He turned to face the thrower, and found the player skinned with the 4. Without another word, the player produced another potion bottle from nowhere, and tossed it at Jayden with a grunt.

The good news was that, from the grunt, Jayden could tell that this player was female. The bad news was the barrage of Potions of Slowness flying from her hands directly at him. Still armed with Zingster's pickaxe, Jayden didn't have enough reach to block the potions without getting hit, so he was forced to dodge, duck, and weave between the bottles. The fumes of the potions began to rise, and Jayden felt himself becoming more and more affected by the vapors.

Before long, Jayden decided to call it quits and sprint away from the player. As fast as he tried to run, though, the potion weighed down on him, making him feel as if his legs were just blocks of lead. He knew it was futile as he heard the player approaching him from behind, but he kept running until the player body checked him, sending him careening forward. He landed at the base of the Avery Memorial Courthouse, slamming his head on the bottom step and sprawling out on the ground, knocked out cold.

The player with the 4 on her body smiled and drew a Potion of Harming out of her inventory. She walked over to Jayden and held the Potion of Harming over Jayden's face. She was about to let it go when—

"Hey!"

The player looked up, and there, at the top of the steps of the courthouse, stood another player. He was wearing a light tan leather tunic and pants. His clothes were covered in burn marks, but he still sat tall and strong atop the pig he was riding. The player was aiming a bow at the girl.

"Get away from him," Charlie growled as he let the arrow fly.

His aim was dead on, and the potion bottle shattered in her hand. The cloud of red toxins enveloped her arm and she gave a screech of agony before looking up at Charlie contemptuously, drawing two more Potions of Harming as she set her sights on him.

Charlie stood still, and gave a smile. He knew that he wasn't good enough with a bow to repeat that shot, so instead, he raised his hand and gestured forward.

The player with the 4 looked slightly confused, but then her eyes widened in horror as a massive wave of players began to pour out of the courthouse directly toward her. She turned and sprinted as fast as she could onto the battlefield, desperate to avoid the massive wall of thousands of players who were dashing down the stairs. All of them were unarmored but were holding up various weapons of different materials, chanting, "Down with the Alliance!" and "Long live President Stan!" as they charged into the plaza to fight the Noctem forces.

After a few minutes, all the thousands of players had left the courthouse and were joining the battlefield. Looking out at the plaza, Charlie gave a satisfied grin as the players he had just led from the courthouse joined the fight. He glanced down the stairs and noticed that Jayden was still lying there, and he was starting to stir.

Charlie ordered Dr. Pigglesworth down the stairs and pulled up next to Jayden. He extracted a bucket of milk from his inventory and poured it into Jayden's mouth. Instantly, the effects of the potion vanished, and Jayden sat up straight, rubbing his head where he had fallen on the stairs. He looked around in a daze, and when his eyes landed on Charlie, they widened.

"Charlie?" he asked in awe.

"Yeah, it's me," he replied with a smile.

"But . . . how did you get here?" Jayden asked as Charlie helped him to his feet. "And . . . *where* did you get that many players to help us?"

"Well, it's kind of a long story," Charlie said as Jayden extracted a Potion of Healing from his inventory.

"Give me the short version," Jayden requested as he started to drink the potion.

"Well, basically, ELM captured me and warped me up to the tower, and I got the attention of one of the Withers to help me escape," Charlie said. "It did manage to kill them, but it also blasted me off the tower."

"Yikes!" Jayden exclaimed. "How'd you get out of that one?"

"The same way that Stan did," Charlie replied. "I had a Potion of Fire Resistance on hand. Well, it wasn't totally the same," he said as he scratched his pig between the ears. "I gave mine to Dr. Pigglesworth as we were falling, and he kind of acted like a fireproof life raft and swam me out of the lava moat after we landed. I got a little burned," he said, gesturing to the scorch marks all over his clothes, "but I shook it off."

"Okay," Jayden said with a nod, "but that still doesn't explain where you got thousands of players to come and fight for us!"

"Well, being in all that lava got me thinking," Charlie replied, "and I realized that with all the fighting going on in Element City, there was probably nobody guarding Brimstone besides the Wither Skeletons. I had been away from the battlefield for so long that it probably wouldn't have made a huge difference if I went back or not, and I realized what we could probably use most were reinforcements. So after we got out of the lava, I snuck back into the castle and went to the Nether."

"And you freed everyone who was locked up in Brimstone?" Jayden asked, amazed.

"Yep. Actually, to be honest, I have this little guy here to thank," said Charlie, smiling as he pet his pig on the head again. "I was able to use the bridge to get from the castle's Nether Portal to the prison, but I still had the Wither Skeletons to deal with, and I didn't have a weapon. Dr. Pigglesworth was able to dodge all the Skeletons' attacks, and I was able to free all the soldiers and citizens who the Noctem Alliance locked up in there . . . which, I had forgotten, was the entire population of the city."

"And they all joined the battle?"

"Yep," Charlie said. "I told everybody that our final battle against the Noctem Alliance was going on, and everybody said that they wanted to help out. They looted the storehouse at the prison, scraped together any weapons they could, and followed me to the portal in the courthouse. So that means that, as of right now, the entire population of Element City, citizens and soldiers alike, is out there fighting the Noctems."

The two players turned to look out on the battlefield again. Indeed, now that the citizens from Brimstone were out on the battlefield, the Noctem forces were outnumbered ten to one. Jayden and Charlie both knew that, despite the massive advantage in quantity, the Noctem soldiers were still skilled fighters, and the two Withers were still raining their skulls of death down into the battlefield. They still had a long way to go before the battle was won.

Bob!"

Ben looked up from the map he'd pulled off a dead Noctem soldier and saw his brother riding Ivanhoe toward the abandoned store that he was concealed within. As Bob rode through the doorless frame, Ben was relieved. The map had showed him some very odd things that he needed to ask about.

"Hey, bro," Ben replied as Bob reached him. "What's going on out there? Because either this map is malfunctioning or about a thousand new players just entered the battlefield."

"That's no malfunction," Bob replied, and Ben was shocked to see that his face was lit up with joy. "Charlie just came back, and he brought everybody who was locked away in Brimstone with him."

"Really?" Ben said. "That's fantastic! And all of them are fighting?"

"Yes, but that's not entirely a good thing," Bob replied solemnly. "On the one hand, we now outnumber the Noctems by a ton. But on the other hand, we still have to worry about *that*."

Bob pointed out the window, and Ben followed his finger until his gaze locked on one of the Withers. The giant skeletal mob, which had been harmlessly floating in the sky, was now firing indiscriminately into the crowd. A rapid-fire barrage of black skulls flew from the three mouths of the monster, creating a blitz of explosions that was spreading through the crowd.

"Now that there are so many republic fighters in the crowd, the Wither isn't afraid to hold back anymore," Bob explained, an urgent note in his voice. "It realizes that, regardless of who it fires at, it will probably hit more of our soldiers than theirs. We've got to take that thing down, and fast."

Ben was blown away by the notion that any mob in the game would have the reasoning skills to think like that. Then again, Lord Tenebris's psychic grip on this particular Wither had probably bent its mind in odd and unexplainable ways. Anyway, it didn't matter. Ben knew that his brother was right, and their top priority had to be taking down the Withers.

"All right," Ben replied. "Let's go."

Ben yanked a Potion of Swiftness out of his inventory, guzzled it down, and immediately felt a surge of energy course through his veins. He took a deep breath and ran out of the building and onto the battlefield, Bob right behind him. Ivanhoe was fast enough to keep up with the potion-enhanced Ben, so it was side by side that the two brothers raced across the outskirts of the plaza and toward the Wither.

As they ran, Ben looked at the fighting players and saw, to his delight, that the Noctem forces were starting to be overwhelmed. He saw various throngs of black-clad players all fighting back to back as they were swarmed by the sheer number of republic players who were now on the battlefield. His stomach lurched with disgust when he saw a republic fighter fall to the ground, items flying about him in a falling halo, and it only encouraged him to sprint faster.

After dashing as fast as they could, the two police chiefs were finally close enough to the Wither that they could hear the screams of its victims as it continued to fire its life-draining projectiles into the crowd. Ben looked at his brother, who pointed to a brick-block building at the corner of the plaza, the bottom floor of which had been partially torn apart by TNT blasts. Ben nodded, and the two of them sprinted into the building. He hardly noticed the dilapidated remains of a store on the ground floor. His eyes immediately locked onto a staircase. He didn't break his pace as he raced up the stairs, his brother on piggyback right behind him.

They burst onto the roof and looked out over the Avery Memorial Courthouse plaza, where thousands of players were now fighting. Not too far away from them, the Wither was hovering high over the battlefield, still bombarding the field with skulls. Although the explosions were tearing rifts in the groups of Noctem and republic players alike, nobody made any attempts to stop the monster; they were all too busy fighting one another.

"How are we gonna take that thing down?" Bob asked,

desperation in his voice. He looked at his brother, who appeared to be in deep thought. "Do you have any ideas, bro?"

"Well . . . I do have one. . . ."

"Spit it out!" Bob cried.

"Well . . . ," Ben said, pausing for a moment, as if unsure that he wanted to suggest it, then finally replying, "We could try Operation Hook, Line, and Sinker."

Bob stared at his brother for a moment, mulling over this insane idea.

"But . . . that operation was designed to take down Ghasts! That thing probably has twenty times the firepower of a Ghast!" Bob said, sounding overwhelmed. "And also, in order for that to work, we'd need Bill."

"Well, I'm sorry, do you have a better idea?" Ben demanded as a particularly large blast sounded in the middle of the battlefield, accompanied by another morbid chorus of screams. "At the very least, we'll be able to distract it for a little while, and hopefully we can hold it at bay until Stan's ready to come down here and finish it off!"

"Might we be able t' help ye?" a voice came from behind them, cutting off Bob's reply. The two brothers looked behind them and saw Sirus and Commander Crunch walking across the top of the roof, bows and arrows in their hands and enthusiastic smiles on their faces.

"Yeah, you can!" Ben shouted with glee, happy with any backup they could possibly get.

"How did you guys know we were up here?" Bob asked.

"Oh, we were just over on the roof of that building over there"—Sirus pointed over to the building next door—"and it was pretty funny 'cause, at first, we ran in there to avoid the Wither, but then we saw it was an anvil store, so we've been dropping anvils off the roof onto the heads of the bad guys ever since then!"

"Uh . . . guys?" Ben said slowly. He looked back and forth between the two players as if they were insane. "You . . . both have bows and arrows in your hand. Why didn't you just use those?"

"Oh, I be sorry, Mister Reason 'n' Practicality," Commander Crunch spat sarcastically. "Pardon me if, in th' midst o' all o' this ghastly warfare, we felt th' need t' inject a wee bit o' classic cartoon-style comedy into the mix."

Ben and Bob stared at him for a moment, now absolutely positive he was insane, before realizing that it didn't matter. Sirus and Crunch were here, and they were both competent with a bow and arrow—that was all that really mattered.

"Okay, here's the plan," Ben explained, as Sirus and Commander Crunch listened intently. "You three shoot at it from behind me. I'll have my sword out, and I'll block all its attacks."

The three other players nodded and, wasting no time, they stood side by side behind Ben, notching arrows in their bows and training them on the Wither. Ben dropped into a fighting stance, his sword raised and ready to deflect.

"Ready . . . aim . . . FIRE!"

On Ben's command, three arrows flew over his head, over the crowd of warring players, and directly into the backs of each of the Wither's three heads. The giant boss mob shrieked in agony before spinning around and setting its sights on the rooftop where the four players stood. Bob, Commander Crunch, and Sirus didn't stop, continuing to send arrows flying into the Wither's body as the monster let loose its first flurry of attacks.

Ben leaped into action, swinging his sword through the air and cutting all the Wither Skulls in two, creating small gray explosions that just barely grazed his skin. The Wither and the players continued to fire at each other. As more and more arrows sunk into the scattered pieces of black flesh hanging from the beast's skeletal rib cage, Ben spun his sword around, deflecting countless explosions, the Knockback Enchantment on the sword keeping the blasts far enough away that he hardly took any damage from them.

Before long, the Wither started to tire. It was clearly taking heavy damage from the barrage of arrows, and its rate of fire was beginning to drop.

"Come on guys, keep going!" Ben shouted as he knocked two more skulls out of midair in a double explosion. "It's almost dead!"

As the three players continued to send arrows into the giant mob, the Wither stopped firing for a moment. Ben was confused and a little disturbed. Why would the Wither cease its barrage? He watched the boss mob open its mouth and, as if in slow motion, it fired a single projectile out of its center mouth.

As Ben raised his sword to deflect the blast, he realized that it wasn't in slow motion. A single skull had shot out of the Wither's mouth and was moving toward him at a crawl. Unlike the other projectiles, which were black and charred like the heads of the monster, this one was a cerulean shade of blue. Ben hardly had time to question what this was before the slow-moving blue skull was upon him. He raised his sword to block the attack, cutting through the air in front of the skull and sending a Knockback shockwave slicing into the skull.

As soon as the wave of energy made contact with a skull, it ruptured into a massive black explosion, which knocked Ben off his feet and sent him flying backward. Bob, Commander Crunch, and Sirus had no time to react as Ben slammed into them, sending them all falling to the ground in a crumpled heap.

Ben felt as though he was covered in some sort of corrosive sludge as he lay there on top of his friends. He had taken the full brunt of the blast from the blue skull, and he felt his energy draining as he tried to force himself to get up. It was futile, though. He felt as though he suddenly weighed several tons, and was unable to move. He watched in dismay as black smoke began to rise out of his body and drift toward the Wither floating above them. Upon reaching the Wither's body, the dozens of arrows sticking out of its rib cage began to pop out, falling to the rooftop with a clatter.

Ben was stupefied, and found himself unable to move as his brother, his friends, and Ivanhoe struggled to push him off them. The Wither was floating closer and closer to them. It was all he could do to watch, his heart stopped in place, as the monster's three mouths opened and began to glow. Ben heard three collective gasps from behind him as he closed his eyes, his face screwed in anticipation of what was to come. . . .

"Hey!"

The shout came from Ben's left, and he opened his eyes just in time to see a diamond pickaxe flying through the air and lodging itself into the right head of the Wither. As the head let out a ghastly wail and rolled limply to the side, the tool still sticking out of its skull, the Wither turned to face the noise, letting out a wail of outrage. Ben turned as well, as did his three fellow fighters, and he had to do a double take to ensure that he was seeing correctly.

There, on top of the house immediately to their left, standing next to a loaded TNT cannon made out of cobblestone, was the Mechanist. Another diamond pickaxe was clutched in his right hand, and his left hand held a lever on the side of the cannon. He was staring at the Wither with daggers in his eyes and a glower on his face.

"Try this on for size," he said as he yanked down on the lever.

There was a hissing sound from within the mechanism next to him, and a second later, a muted explosion rang out as a lit block of TNT came soaring through the air on a collision course with the Wither. The ignited explosive struck the Wither in a massive burst of light and sound, and the skeletal demon proceeded to let out a ghastly wail of agony as it slowly sank down to the ground.

Ben watched, awestruck, as the Mechanist sprinted as fast as he could toward the edge of the building. He leaped over the gap between the two buildings, touching down as the Wither reached the ground, still dazed from the blast as an odd white force field seemed to envelop it. What the energy field surrounding the Wither did, Ben never found out, as the Mechanist jumped into the air, delivering a flying kick that knocked the monster to the ground. Without missing a beat, the Mechanist raised his pickaxe and drove it as hard as he could into the skeletal chest of the monster.

All at once, a horrible, high-pitched screech rang out from within the Wither, causing all in the vicinity to cover their ears. The Wither's eyes and mouths flew open in agony, glowing with a radiant white light as the skulls began to crumble, turning into a fine black dust that was immediately blown away by the soft wind. The Wither began to shake, and the ear-piercing screech continued as all the bones and flesh that composed the monster began to vanish, turning into dust on the wind.

Then, without warning, a white light flashed from within the Wither. The daze was so bright, and so unexpected, that Ben, the Mechanist, and all the others on the rooftop were momentarily blinded. It only lasted for a few seconds, though, and by the time their vision returned, all that remained of the Wither was a stain of black dust on the roof of the building.

The Mechanist took no time to reflect over his kill. Instead, his eyes were immediately drawn to the limp body of Ben, still lying sprawled out on the ground as the others attempted to untangle themselves from the pile on the ground. The Mechanist pulled out a red potion that he had gotten from a dead soldier, just as Bob realized what had happened to his brother.

"No," he said, his voice uneven as he awkwardly pulled

himself over to Ben. He shook his head back and forth as he clutched Ben by the shoulders. "No . . . you're okay, bro . . . you've *gotta* be okay. . . ."

"He's fine," the Mechanist replied, gently pushing Bob out of the way before he could object. He poured the potion down Ben's throat.

"What . . . what happened to him?" Bob asked, still staring at his brother as Sirus and Commander Crunch pulled him up and helped him remount Ivanhoe.

"The blast range of the blue skulls is bigger than that of the black ones, and more powerful, too. The blue ones can blast through anything except bedrock," the Mechanist said almost robotically as he put his hand to Ben's head. "He got hit by the blast and inflicted with the Wither effect. It's a worse kind of poisoning that can be fatal if left untreated."

"So . . . is he gonna . . . ," Bob stammered, his face as white as a ghost.

The Mechanist turned to face him and smiled. "Your brother will be fine, Bob. The potion I just gave him will give him enough strength to survive until the Wither effect wears off."

"Mechanist . . ."

The Mechanist looked down at the source of the feeble voice and saw Ben looking up at him, his eyes fluttering open. Bob's face broke out in relief, but Ben only looked up to the old redstone mechanic with the wild white hair. He looked exhausted, yet still a smile crept to the corner of his mouth as he spoke.

"Thank you. And . . . I'm sorry."

"You don't have to be," the Mechanist replied, returning Ben's slight yet earnest smile.

Ben opened his mouth as if he were about to reply, but then shut it and gave a sigh of contentedness as his eyes closed, his head rolled to the side, and he passed out.

Leonidas emerged from the rabble of brawling players, and he took a deep breath. The fighting that had now spread across the entire plaza was intense, and he had just sprinted right through the thick of it. Everywhere he looked, the glut of republic soldiers and citizens were teaming up to bear down on the Noctem soldiers with full force, and the black-clad forces were fighting back just as hard. Twice, Leonidas had halted his run through the crowds, taken aim, and sent an arrow into a Noctem soldier, thus preserving the life of a citizen the soldier was about to overpower.

He might have stopped more than twice, but he had a job to do.

As he was fighting, he had seen Bob run with his brother into an old run-down store, above which one of the Withers floated, firing its deadly blasts down into the crowds.

Leonidas knew that, with the only archer as good as he was occupied fighting the boss mob, there was a very important task he had to do.

Even if it wasn't his job, he still would have sought the task out anyway. This was personal.

Leonidas walked slowly around the outer ring of the battle-field, and the further away from the courthouse he went, the higher the number of Noctem soldiers in the crowd. The soldiers of Lord Tenebris were truly giving it their all, charging into the battle with weapons blazing and fire in their eyes, but Leonidas could also see another trait present, written all over their faces: fear. For the first time, as the Noctem soldiers gave it their all against the thousands of republic players, a pit opened in their stomachs as they considered the possibility that they might not win this battle.

Leonidas was nearly back at the execution platform, and he saw that this was the only place on the entire battlefield where the majority of the players wore the black colors of the Noctem Alliance. This was where the Noctem Alliance was digging in their heels and fighting most ferociously. Even as he watched for just the space of a few seconds, Leonidas saw nearly ten Elementia players try to fight their way into the mass of black leather and get cut down in the process.

Leonidas's heart gave an unpleasant jolt as he saw these players die, but it confirmed what he had guessed. The execution platform was where the Noctem Alliance was fighting their hardest, and this would be by far the most difficult area for the republic forces to take. If his target was going to be anywhere, it was here.

Trying to avoid attracting attention from the Noctem forces, Leonidas covered his face as he stealthily slipped into the decrepit house closest to the execution platform. Judging by the weathered sign Leonidas saw above the door, it used to be part of the Apothecary's chain of potioneers. Indeed, as he made his way through the ground floor, he saw empty cauldrons and brewing stands strewn haphazardly about, shattered glass bottles covering the floor and making it appear to shimmer. Leonidas was careful to avoid making a sound as he scaled the stairs to the second floor.

This floor was totally barren; Leonidas assumed it used to be someone's living space, but not a single item remained on the flat wood-plank floor. He made his way across the floor to the window. From there, he could see all the way across the sprawling plaza in front of the Avery Memorial Courthouse, filled to the bursting point with players that Leonidas was sure, for better or for worse, were fighting the final battle of the war.

Leonidas knew that the biggest thing he could do to ensure the republic's victory in the war was to eliminate the opposing leaders, so he drew his bow. Notching an arrow in it and pulling the string taut, he looked out the window, scanning the cluster of black forms right below him. He scanned every single face that he could see, desperate to find one of the two players that he was looking for. His heart started to race as he searched. Leonidas knew that the longer he stood looking out this window, the better the chance that . . .

"Looking for me?" a voice called out from behind Leonidas.

Slowly, Leonidas turned around, his bow still raised, until he was facing Spyro. The Noctem general stood at the top of the stairs, his glowing diamond sword shining an eerie light on his black leather armor as he dropped into a fighting stance, a wicked grin on his face.

For a moment, the two players stared at each other. Leonidas remembered, long ago, when Spyro had been a mere private, helping him to construct Nocturia. Back then, he had been so innocent, so curious, and so open-minded, even going so far as to question if the Alliance he had joined was doing the right thing. Now, though, Leonidas stood across from a savage killer, twisted by months of leading an organization of hate and intolerance. He knew that he had no choice but to destroy the Noctem general . . . but he also knew he had to at least try to avoid the conflict.

"Stand down," Leonidas said in a monotone, his bow still trained on Spyro's forehead. "I don't want to hurt ya, Spyro.

You're not a bad person . . . you're just lost. The Noctem Alliance is gonna fall today. Please, don't fall with it."

"That's funny," Spyro replied, raising an eyebrow. "The great General Leonidas who trained me would never try to negotiate a surrender. He would just start the fight as fast as possible, and end it even faster."

"The General Leonidas *you* know is dead," Leonidas replied proudly. "I ain't never pickin' a fight again unless I have to, and I don't want to do it today. Please, Spyro . . . I'm beggin' ya . . . stand down. Stop this."

For a moment, Spyro's mouth hung open, and his eyes were wide, as if he were in deep thought. Then, all of a sudden, his eyebrows creased, his eyes grew bloodshot, and his face contorted into an ugly mess of rage as he gave out a battle cry, sending a Splash Potion of Harming directly toward his former master.

Leonidas didn't even flinch. He may have promised himself to never start a fight again, but he would never hesitate to finish one. Within an instant, an arrow had shot the potion out of the air in midflight, and Leonidas had sent a flurry of arrows flying from his bow, directly at Spyro. Despite Spyro's best effort to deflect the attacks with his sword, the arrows came too many, and too fast. It was only a matter of seconds before one of the arrows found a chink in Spyro's armor, and he slouched down to the ground as five more arrows sunk into the weak points.

As Spyro lay on the ground, six arrows sticking out of him, struggling to stay alive, Leonidas advanced on him, one final arrow in his bow. He stood over the Noctem general, staring down at him with pity, while Spyro returned a glare of utter loathing.

"Do ya have any last words?" Leonidas asked sadly as he pulled the arrow back, aiming directly for Spyro's temple.

Spyro said nothing. Instead, in a surprisingly swift motion for somebody who was teetering on the verge of death, he raised his hand to his mouth and let out a long, high-pitched whistle.

Leonidas had no time to comprehend what he was doing. Seconds after he started to whistle, the wall behind Leonidas exploded, showering him with dust and debris and knocking him to the ground, sending his bow and the arrow notched within it flying out of his grasp. Leonidas squinted his eyes through the dust, and as he looked out the massive hole where the wall used to be, his heart stopped dead. There it was, floating directly above him, its raspy, metallic breath wheezing through its charred black rib cage as the six eyes of the Wither trained on Leonidas.

"There!" Spyro coughed, and Leonidas tore his horrified eyes off the giant skeletal mob to see Spyro pointing over at Leonidas's bow, which was still sitting in the corner of the room. As he saw his weapon lying on the wood plank–block floor, for the first time, it hit him like a stack of bricks that he was unarmed, and totally defenseless. No sooner had he begun to move toward the corner of the room, desperate to retrieve his bow, than he heard the sound of the Wither firing another attack from behind him. Leonidas barely had time to raise his arms over his face before the skull connected with the bow lying on the floor. The force of the explosion slammed into Leonidas, sending him tumbling back to the ground, now with black wisps of smoke rising from his arms.

In horror, Leonidas looked over at where the patch of floor had been, only to see that the entire corner of the house had been totally blown to bits. His weapon was gone.

Leonidas's heart rate, already racing from the Wither's attack, now skyrocketed to dangerous levels as he realized that he was totally defenseless. He still had a glut of arrows in his inventory, but nothing to fire them with. He had no way of fighting back against the Wither, which was now aiming for him again.

It was all Leonidas could do to dive-roll to the side, desperately trying to avoid the onslaught of explosions tearing the ground around him to shreds. Leonidas's head whipped around wildly and saw that nearly the entire floor had been blasted apart by the Wither's attacks. Only a few wood-plank blocks remained levitating over the ground floor of the shop below. Leonidas looked above him and saw a window. Without thinking, acting on pure survival instinct, Leonidas launched himself off the floor, flying out the window before the Wither could blow him to bits.

Leonidas felt himself falling through the air for a moment before landing with a crunch on the dirt blocks below him. He let out a shout as pain seared in his legs, and he allowed himself a second to lay still to let the pain die down. In that second, he looked around him. He had landed in a narrow alleyway, about four blocks wide. The building on one side of the alley Leonidas recognized as the seafood restaurant next to the Avery Memorial Courthouse. The other side of the alley was the Apothecary store, or rather, what was left of the store. The Wither's explosive attacks had blasted off huge chunks of the second floor, so the only things remaining that Leonidas could see were a few fragments of brick-block wall.

A raspy breathing registered in Leonidas's ears, and he knew that his brief respite from the fight was over. Although his legs still felt as though they were blazing with flames, he forced himself to stand, just as the Wither floated out from around the side of the house. All six of its beady white eyes trained on Leonidas, who was trembling as he imagined how he was going to fight this thing with no bow.

All of a sudden, an Ender Pearl flew down from the

second floor of the Apothecary store, and landed just below the Wither. Leonidas's jaw dropped in disbelief as out of the cloud of purple smoke walked General Spyro. He was no longer full of arrows and clinging to life by the skin of his teeth, but he looked totally happy, healthy, and sadistic. As Leonidas stared at him, he noticed that the Noctem general was smoking with the red fumes of a Potion of Healing as he looked up at the Wither and pointed toward Leonidas.

"Finish him off," Spyro ordered with a cruel smile.

The Wither took another breath in and fired three skulls directly at Leonidas. Despite the colossal strain on his legs, Leonidas still found the strength to hop backward, dodging the explosions that blasted giant holes in the ground.

As Leonidas caught his breath, trying to keep his will to continue fighting alive, he realized with a start that the holes the Wither had blasted in the dirt-block ground of the alleyway had not made a crater. Instead, they had opened up a hole that revealed a drop of more than ten blocks down into a cave. It dawned on Leonidas that they must be over one of the abandoned mines underneath the city. He saw a bright light shining up from the cave, but he hardly cared what it was. All he knew was that he had already sustained a lot of damage, and he didn't have enough health to survive a more than ten-block fall. If the Wither's blasts knocked him down there, he would be killed on impact with the ground.

The Wither fired a steady stream of projectiles at Leonidas, not giving him a moment of rest as he dodged the stream of explosions by mere inches. It wasn't long before Leonidas realized that it was futile to dodge the blasts that were ripping the alley apart, revealing more and more of the old mine below them. Desperately hoping that he could outrun the Wither's attacks before one managed to connect, Leonidas turned around and began to sprint down the alley as quickly as he could.

What he didn't expect was to run headfirst into a brick wall.

Leonidas fell to the ground in a daze, looking up and realizing, with a horrified lurch of the stomach, that the alley was a dead end. Instantly, the adrenaline kicked in as Leonidas leaped to his feet, desperately looking for a way out. But there was none. And there, hovering over the torn-up dirt floor of the alleyway, floating closer and closer to him, was the Wither.

Leonidas was just about to break down, losing all self-control in the midst of this horrific turn of events, but instead he let out a sigh. He took a deep breath, and realized that there was nothing that he could do about it. His time had simply come. He had defied death one too many times, and now, it was all over for him. He closed his eyes, reflecting on how content he was to have made up for all the mistakes in his past, as he readied himself to be blown to smithereens by the Wither.

"Arraaaughh!"

Leonidas winced as a grating, high-pitched wail rang out from the other end of the alleyway. He opened his eyes and followed the gazes of Spyro and the three heads of the Wither to see what had made such an ear-splitting noise. What he saw made him question whether or not the Wither effect that was poisoning his body had affected his brain in any way. He couldn't possibly be seeing correctly.

There, at the other end of the alley, standing in the opening between the two brick buildings, stood Oob, Mella, and Stull. The three villagers were shrieking and wailing while looking up at the Wither, as if they were giving some sort of ghastly singing performance. The Wither, meanwhile, turned and surveyed the three villagers quizzically.

While Spyro just looked stunned, Leonidas's heart had dropped into his stomach. *What're the villagers doing here?* he thought to himself desperately. *Why aren't they in the Adorian Village? It's way too dangerous for them here!*

Spyro finally seemed to snap back to his senses, and he glanced up at the Wither, who was now staring intently at the villagers, as if it were absorbing every single wail that they let out.

"What are you doing, you stupid monster?" Spyro

demanded, glaring up at the Wither indignantly. "Destroy those impudent villagers, and then destroy Leonidas!"

The Wither didn't shoot the villagers. Instead, it turned around and glared down at Spyro, rage ripe in all six of its eyes. Spyro's jaw dropped, and he cowered as the Wither let out a deadly, hollow roar. Its three mouths aimed at Spyro, and he cringed in preparation for the blast that never came. The three heads just kept pointing, white mouths glowing menacingly.

"It is okay, Leo-nidas!" Mella called across the ravaged alleyway to Leonidas, who was still staring at the renegade Wither, refusing to believe his eyes. "The big black boss skeleton monster thingy is on our side now. It will not attack you any more than it has already attacked you."

"But . . . but . . . what did ya do?" Leonidas sputtered, trying to comprehend what had just happened. "And what're y'all doin' here?"

"We told the big black boss skeleton monster thingy to stop attacking you!" Oob said, sounding as though this should be obvious. "And we are here because we were bored of staying in the Adorian Village and wanted to come help you. It is a good thing, too, because we heard a large boom right after we—"

"But . . . then . . . why did it listen to ya and stop attackin' me?" Leonidas cut in.

"The big black boss skeleton monster thingy listened to us because we spoke to it in its native language. We remember how to speak in that language because we learned how to speak it by getting turned into Zombies. Getting turned into Zombies was bad, because we wanted to eat players, but it was good because we learned how to talk to the big black boss skeleton monster thingy!"

"Wait, hold up . . . you guys still remember how to talk in the language of the Wither? And ya just told it to stop attackin' me?"

"Is that not what we just said to you, Leo-nidas?" Mella said in exasperation. "The . . . um, how do you say it . . . Wither . . . will always listen to something that talks in its own language before it will listen to something that talks in the language of players and villagers."

"But . . . if ya could stop the Withers all along . . . then how come y'all waited till now to do it?" Leonidas sputtered.

"The reason that we waited until now to talk to the Wither is because we did not think of talking to the Wither until now. Um . . ." Oob looked to the ground and blushed before he continued talking to Leonidas. "Well . . . please do not tell this to the other players, Leo-nidas . . . but I have realized that when compared to players, we villagers are not very smart."

Leonidas rolled his eyes and chuckled. He was about to

thank them for saving him when something caught his eye. A figure emerging behind the villagers, sword in his hand. . . .

"Look out behind you!" Leonidas bellowed, but it was too late; Drake had already plunged his sword into Mella's back and pulled it out, sending her falling face-down to the ground. Before her sons could react, Drake grabbed Stull by the scruff of his brown collar with one hand and raised his glowing diamond sword to the front of the baby villager's neck with the other.

Leonidas gave a holler of fury, and was about to yell out at Drake when he felt a horrible lurch in his stomach. He looked down at his skin and saw black smoke rising from it. He realized with a jolt that, in his elation over being saved by the villagers, he hadn't even noticed the deadly poison from the Wither's attack getting stronger and stronger. He attempted to get out one final word, but the toxins overwhelmed him, and he slumped to the ground, unconscious.

Oob looked wildly back and forth between his mother, his brother, and the Noctem General. Mella lay on the ground, totally immobile, and making no sounds. Oob couldn't tell if she were dead or alive. Stull looked petrified, afraid to make even the slightest movement as he stood still as a statue, a horrified expression on his face and a sword held to his throat. Drake looked absolutely sinister, holding the sword totally still and calmly glancing over to see Spyro still cowering under the threefold glare of the Wither. He looked back at Oob.

"If you don't want this little one to end up like her," he said slowly, jerking his head toward Mella, still lying on the ground, "you'll tell that Wither that from now on, it is no longer allowed to take commands from villagers. Only from members of the Noctem Alliance."

Oob's mind was racing. His concern for the limp form of his mother barely registered as he looked at his brother. Oob was torn. On the one hand, he knew that if he gave the Wither back to the Noctem Alliance, they would use it to do bad things . . . *very* bad things. But on the other hand . . . if he didn't . . . they would kill Stull.

Drake chuckled as his lips curled upward into a smile, amused by Oob's inner conflict that showed on his face. "Don't feel bad, little guy," Drake growled maliciously as he raised his sword closer to the baby villager's neck. "This would be a hard choice for a *player* to make, and you . . . you are far, *far* less than a player. You're nothing but a simple-minded, ignorant, useless little—*Aaaauggh*!"

Drake let out a cry as the arrow sunk into his right hand. The sword fell to the ground with a clang as his left hand flew out wildly to the side. He involuntarily released Stull, sending him flying through the air and crashing into his older brother. Cringing, Drake ripped the arrow out of his hand, and spun around to see another player standing at the end of the alley-way, lowering her bow. Her leather armor was pure white, stained with the marks of warfare, and he hardly noticed her giant, red lips next to the outraged scowl on her face.

"Don't you *dare* touch them," Cassandrix hissed.

Desperately, Drake snatched his sword off the ground and raised it over the two villagers, who were still lying in a heap on the ground next to their mother. *Fine,* he sneered to himself. *If I can't have the Wither . . . no one can.* Drake plunged his sword downward, and it was about to enter Oob's back when a massive force collided with Drake. Cassandrix slammed shoulder-first into Drake, sending him tumbling across the ground, coming to a stop at the very edge of a hole the Wither had blasted into the ground.

Within seconds, Cassandrix was upon him. Before Drake had a chance to even regain his footing, her diamond sword had sliced through his black leather armor, sending him tumbling backward. Down he plummeted into the old mine, but not before reaching up and grabbing Cassandrix's foot, pulling her down with him.

The two players fell for a few seconds, tumbling through space, before hitting the dirt-block ground below them with a thud. They rolled in opposite directions from the impact for a few blocks before coming to a stop. Cassandrix opened her eyes and winced. The fall had dealt quite a lot of damage to her, and it felt as though a few of her insides had been displaced. From behind her, she heard a moan, and instantly she felt wide awake. Drake was damaged, too—this was her opportunity to finish him off. Cassandrix forced herself to a standing position and, as fast as her damaged legs could carry her, she made her way over to Drake, who was still struggling to get to his feet.

As she walked, she noticed something peculiar. The sound on the dirt blocks below her feet seemed different than usual, yet somehow familiar. Cassandrix looked around the cave and saw several holes in the ground, through which a bright light was shining. One of them was right next to her. Cassandrix peered down into the hole, and her heart skipped a beat as she saw a massive lake of lava nearly twenty blocks below them. As she examined the hole further, she realized with a jolt that the entire expanse of dirt that she and Drake had landed on was only one block thick.

All at once, she was hit by a rush of comprehension as she realized what this was—an expanse of dirt blocks, forming a one-block-thick platform over a lake of liquid. As she stood across from her opponent, who was just tossing an empty potion bottle to the side, fumes of red smoke started to rise off him.

All right, Cassandrix, she thought to herself. *Time to earn the title of Elementia's greatest Spleef player.*

Cassandrix raised her sword as Drake raised his, but stood still as he began to charge at her. *I'll have to play defensively,* she thought. *I've taken a lot of damage, and he's all healed up from his potion, so I'll have to let him tire himself out.*

Drake was nearly upon her now, and he raised his sword to strike. Just as the blow was about to fall, Cassandrix sidestepped the slash, spinning around and sweeping her feet underneath Drake. As he toppled to the ground, Cassandrix raised her own sword, and she knew that Drake would expect her to stab him and roll out of the way, and that's exactly what she let him do. As he rolled backward, Cassandrix drove her sword into the dirt block, gripped it tightly, and twisted. Instantly, the frail dirt block was destroyed, falling down into the lava below and disappearing into a puff of smoke.

Drake was back on his feet, and he reared up to deliver another strike. Cassandrix felt the pain of the fall searing through her legs and knew what she had to do. As Drake charged in, she sidestepped yet again, lessening the impact as Drake brought his blade down on her, only to be countered by her own diamond weapon. For a moment, the two players pressed their weapons into each other, sending sparks onto the dirt-block ground every time they slid across each other. Bolstered by the potion, Drake began to overpower Cassandrix, and she took a deep breath and drove her sword downward, still locked onto Drake's. The two swords tore through the dirt-block ground, cutting a crescent-shaped hole into the ground, revealing the lava below.

Drake hardly noticed the molten liquid below. He was more interested in Cassandrix, who proceeded, with a calm and calculated air around her, to sidestep every attack that Drake threw at her. More often than not, Drake's sword stabbed deep into the dirt, and once the sword was free, the block broke with a crunch, falling into the lava pit below.

After a minute of fighting like this and not landing a hit, Cassandrix could tell that Drake was starting to get frustrated. His eyes were wild and manic, and his sword strikes were getting more powerful and less precise, now destroying a bit of the floor with every single strike. Cassandrix kept a level head, continuing to move around Drake in a circle, dodging blow after blow as he stood in place, wrecking the floor around him. The floor was now so thin that she had to hop between single blocks that were floating over the now-exposed lava moat, but Drake's attacks were so wild in his aggravation that she was able to dodge them effortlessly.

After a few minutes had passed, Cassandrix stepped away from Drake after a particularly fierce sword strike and looked at him with a smile on her face.

"It's over, Drake," she said.

"What are you talking about?" Drake demanded, spit flying from his mouth in rage. "Neither of us have landed one single attack!"

"Yes," Cassandrix replied smugly, gesturing to the floor around Drake, "*you* have."

Drake looked down at the floor, and his mouth dropped open in shock. He was standing on a tiny island of blocks that was floating in the middle of a ring of emptiness that stretched all the way down to the lava. Drake looked around in desperation, hoping to find some way to escape this island, but then he saw, to his horror, that Cassandrix was reaching her sword out into the pitfall, destroying all the remaining blocks that Drake might have had any hope of jumping onto.

When she finished, she looked up at Drake. His eyes widened, and his pupils shrank down to tiny dots as he watched Cassandrix draw out her bow.

"No! No, please!" Drake begged, dropping to his knees. "I beg of you . . . have mercy!"

"I might, Drake," Cassandrix replied as she pulled back the string, hatred etched into her face. "If *anybody* else had stabbed an innocent villager and threatened to murder a child, then perhaps, if he pleaded insanity, I might've let him live. But you forget, Drake . . . you're nothing but a simple-minded, ignorant, useless little Noctem."

And with that, Cassandrix let the arrow fly.

Drake whipped out his sword as fast as possible, deflecting the arrow, but two more were already on their way. Drake tried to block the stream of arrows flying from Cassandrix's bow, and at first, he was successful. However, it only took one misstep for an arrow to sink into Drake's hand yet again, causing him to howl in pain and drop his sword into the pit of molten lava below him.

From there, it was all over. One more arrow to the chest was all that it took to send Drake tumbling off his little island, down into the molten pit below.

Cassandrix raced over to the hole and trained her bow on Drake's falling body, lest he have a Potion of Fire Resistance and survive the impact. But alas, she didn't have anything to worry about. The second that Drake made contact with the lava, his items burst out around him in a ring and were instantly burned to a crisp as his body slowly descended into the lava and ceased to exist.

Cassandrix took a deep breath and let it out. She still hurt badly from the fall down into the cave, and there was nothing she wanted more than to sit for a moment, allowing herself to heal before returning to the battlefield. But Cassandrix knew that she couldn't do that. Despite eliminating one of the three remaining leaders of the Noctem Alliance, she knew that she hadn't earned the luxury of a break. She needed to get Mella and Leonidas some medical attention before it was too late, and then she had to figure out what to do with Spyro.

Cassandrix reached into her inventory and pulled out an Ender Pearl that she had looted from a dead soldier on the battlefield. Not looking forward to the additional pain in her legs the pearl would cause, Cassandrix took a deep breath and pitched the turquoise sphere toward the fractured street floating above. The pearl flew through one of the craters and landed on the street, causing Cassandrix to disappear in a puff of purple smoke, leaving the oozing pit of lava that had just consumed one of the generals of the Noctem Alliance bubbling beneath her.

As soon as he felt the rush of teleportation ending, Stan pushed off Lord Tenebris's sword, as his adversary did the same. The two players tumbled through the air away from each other, and came to a stop about ten blocks apart. They were surrounded by the gray, cloudlike mist that the Withers had cast into the sky; it wasn't thick enough to obscure their vision, but it did give both players a dark tint to their skins. Not too far away, Stan saw the peaks of the tallest skyscrapers in the city rising to about their same height. In the distance, Stan could see Element Castle, which rose even farther into the sky. Hundreds of blocks below them, Stan saw the two warring factions spread throughout the plaza of the Avery Memorial Courthouse, which would surely be the last battlefield of this war.

He had no time to focus on these details, however, as he dedicated all of his focus to the white-eyed doppelganger floating across from him.

Lord Tenebris didn't look shocked by the fact that Stan now had operating powers. Rather, he appeared to be in deep thought as he stared at Stan. It was as if he were trying to gaze through Stan, as though if he focused hard enough, he would be able to read Stan like a book and determine where he had gotten his new abilities.

"I must admit, Stan, that you managed to catch me off guard," Lord Tenebris said after a moment of silence. "This is something that no player has ever been able to do before."

"I'll take that as a compliment," Stan replied snarkily.

"However, it doesn't matter to me how you attained these powers, Stan," Lord Tenebris said, his eyes looking more sinister by the moment as a rumble of thunder sounded in the distance. "Your strength still pales in comparison to the might of I, the great and powerful Lord—"

"You can drop the act now that we're up here," Stan cut in bitterly. "I know who you really are, Kev."

Lord Tenebris opened his mouth for a moment, looking outraged, and Stan was sure that he was about to burst into some sort of tirade. But then, as quickly as his anger had risen, it ceased. He had heard something in Stan's voice that he had, again, not been expecting: certainty. Stan was not simply making an unfounded claim to get under his skin—Lord Tenebris was floating across from a player who unquestionably knew the truth about him.

"So . . . you finally figured it out," Lord Tenebris said, looking at Stan in a calculating manner.

"Yep," Stan replied, looking at Lord Tenebris and shaking his head. "I always had trouble believing that two egomaniacal dictators would be able to gain total control on the same Minecraft server in the span of just six months. At least it makes a bit more sense now that I know it was you all along."

"I must ask, Stan," Lord Tenebris said evenly, his eye twitching at Stan's comment as he tried not to show any cracks in his self-assured persona, "what tipped you off? I thought that I hid my trail quite well."

"Well, let's just say that I had a run-in with a friend who was able to help me put together the pieces of the puzzle," Stan said audaciously. "As a matter of fact, it was the same friend who helped me get the powers that are letting me float up here and talk to you now."

Lord Tenebris's eyes widened, and then his face contorted into an ugly sneer.

"It was that mongrel Sally, wasn't it?" Lord Tenebris snarled at Stan. "She's been a thorn in my side for months now, never ceasing her attempts to break through my defenses, to peel back the layers of protection that I installed to protect my beloved server. . . . She finally succeeded in getting in. . . ."

"Well, Sally did help me quite a bit," Stan replied, his cheery, conversational tone of voice making Lord Tenebris's rage build. The Noctem leader was used to every player whom he spoke to cowering in fear, not treating him like a joke. "But she wasn't the one I was referring to."

"And I suppose that you're not going to tell me who did," Lord Tenebris scoffed.

"Well, I might," Stan replied, his steely gaze equaling Lord Tenebris's as he clutched his axe tightly in both hands, "if we didn't have more important business to attend to."

"Indeed we do, Stan, indeed we do," Lord Tenebris said softly, raising his sword in front of his hollow, white eyes as his face twisted into a sick smile. "The time has come to end this once and for all. It's time for the showdown that was always meant to be. You and I, Stan, one on one, with no armies, no traps, and no tricks.

"Oh, and don't forget, Stan . . . I'm a man of my word," Lord Tenebris simpered, bowing his head. "The terms of our duel remain unchanged. Whoever wins this fight shall be proclaimed the rightful ruler of the Minecraft server Elementia."

"I wouldn't look so cocky if I were you, Kev," Stan shot back, as he returned his axe to his inventory and raised both of his hands in front of him. "I beat you once before. . . . and I'll do it again."

"Oh, that's cute. You're right, Stan, you did beat me once." Lord Tenebris laughed as he, too, pocketed his sword and mirrored the position of Stan's hands. "But you forget— up here in the sky, you don't have Avery or the Apothecary to die for you. The only one that you have to rely on is yourself."

"And that's exactly who I'm counting on," Stan replied as he took a deep breath, drew back his fist, and sent a pulse of explosive energy flying through the air at Lord Tenebris.

Dropping into a fighting stance, Lord Tenebris teleported out of the way of the blast, reappearing a few blocks away, where Stan immediately aimed another blast at him. The two of them repeated this six more times, each time Lord Tenebris reappearing closer and closer to Stan. After the sixth blast, Lord Tenebris was within close range of Stan, and a sword appeared in his hand as he stabbed it at Stan's stomach. In turn, Stan conjured an axe in his own hand, knocking the sword to one side and, in one motion, summoning a globe of dozens of Blazes around himself and Lord Tenebris while warping away.

Stan reappeared ten blocks overhead and looked down to see countless flashes of fire as all the Blazes in the globe opened fire on Lord Tenebris. Then, without warning, all the tiny flashes were totally overpowered by a massive blast of light and sound as Lord Tenebris created an explosion around himself, destroying all the mobs in one fell swoop and sending a shower of Blaze rods falling to the ground far below. Lord Tenebris skyrocketed up to Stan's level and, from ten blocks away, raised his hand and fired a salvo of hundreds of arrows at Stan.

Stan knew that he couldn't redirect all those arrows with his mind at once, and so he raised his hand, summoning a cow to appear in front of him in a puff of smoke. As the arrows all pierced the hide of the animal, killing it instantly as it plummeted down to earth alongside two raw pieces of meat and a leather skin, Stan focused with all his might on the air above Lord Tenebris. Instantly, in a series of pops, dozens of blocks of gravel appeared in midair over his head and began to fall down around Lord Tenebris's head.

The Noctem leader was preparing another attack as he got clobbered in the head with the first block, knocking him out of his focus and sending him tumbling down, directly into the path of the next falling block. Lord Tenebris looked up and realized that he was in a storm of falling gravel and, with a deep breath, he aimed a skyward punch. The invisible pulse of energy connected with one of the blocks, creating an explosion that wiped all the other gravel from existence. Lord Tenebris then aimed a punch directly at Stan, who was still recovering from the effort of creating blocks in midair.

By the time he sensed it coming, it was too late for Stan to block the explosive pulse of energy. It was all he could do to catch the invisible sphere of deadly energy in his outstretched hands. The invisible force powered toward Stan's core, but he found to his utter amazement that, with all his focus, he was actually able to keep it from reaching him and blowing up. Also, the more that Stan focused on keeping the pulse away from him, the stronger it became, and the harder it fought to come toward him. The pulse grew and grew as

Stan tried to keep it at bay, holding the energy pulse between his hands. When he felt as though he couldn't hold it any longer, he pushed both of his hands forward, sending the powered-up blast back at Lord Tenebris.

He felt the enhanced blast long before it reached him, and Lord Tenebris knew that, whatever Stan had done to the invisible shot of energy, it was far more powerful than anything that he had ever created. He doubted that he would be able to survive this explosive blast, or even deflect it if he tried. Lord Tenebris raised his arms in front of him and devoted all of his focus to creating a three-by-three-block barrier of obsidian in front of himself. As the explosion hit the three blocks and ruptured with massive force while Lord Tenebris remained completely safe behind it, he knew that he had just made a huge mistake.

Indeed, at almost the exact moment that the three blocks appeared in midair in front of Lord Tenebris, Stan stretched his hand out toward the shield of obsidian. Before Lord Tenebris could even muster the will to teleport away, the blocks of obsidian expanded off the shield, occupying the same space as Lord Tenebris and continuing to grow until he was totally smothered by the black rock.

Stan looked at the five-by-five cube of obsidian with satisfaction. Lord Tenebris had been totally encased. He would be unable to move, and would soon die from suffocation.

Stan didn't want to take any chances, though. He didn't trust anything or anyone besides his own hand to finish off Lord Tenebris. Stan willed a diamond sword to appear in his right hand, and he stretched it out in front of him as he rocketed directly toward the obsidian prison.

As Stan flew at the giant cube of black rock, he could hear a faint rumbling inside and picked up his pace, desperate to spear Lord Tenebris with his sword before he could try anything funny.

Just as Stan's sword was about to puncture the tip of the obsidian prison, it exploded into a million tiny pieces. Stan screeched to a halt in midair, and even then, he had to warp backward to avoid the hundreds of diamond pickaxes that were whirling in the air around Lord Tenebris. The pickaxes were rotating around him as if in orbit, spinning at a dangerous velocity as Lord Tenebris floated in the center, a devious smile on his face and his white eyes locked on to Stan.

Man, thought Stan to himself as his heart crawled to a stop. *I don't know what he did to give himself so much power, but I sure wish that I . . .*

Suddenly, Stan realized with a jolt that he had made a horrible mistake. He had been so intent on showing off his new powers, on leaving Lord Tenebris completely and totally stunned, that he had nearly forgotten the peril that this server and all of Minecraft was in. And if Lord Tenebris was using new abilities like this by drawing power from the server . . . then that meant . . .

"Kev! Stop!" Stan desperately shouted into the tornado of spiraling pickaxes. "You have to stop using . . ."

But it was too late. Lord Tenebris had already stretched his hand out toward Stan, willing the globe of pickaxes to break from their orbit and come spiraling directly at him. Stan was afraid to teleport for fear of appearing in the path of a flying pickaxe, so he dropped his diamond sword and willed an axe to appear in its place. The pickaxes came flying full force at Stan, and he spun and twirled his axe around. Each time a flying pickaxe struck the blade of his axe, it bounced off in a shower of sparks with a clang and began to fall to the ground far below.

As the globe of spinning diamond pickaxes started to thin out, Lord Tenebris took a deep breath and stretched both of his hands out toward Stan. In one motion, all the pickaxes flew directly at Stan. There were too many of them for him to block all at once. Although he spun his axe as fast as he could, desperate to deflect all of them, one pickaxe slipped through a crack in Stan's defenses and struck him cleanly between the eyes.

Luckily, Stan was hit by the blunt part of the blade and not the point or he would have been impaled through the head. Still, the force of the blow was enough to send him tumbling down, and he dropped his axe as he clutched his face in agony. After falling for dozens of blocks, Stan righted himself and opened his eyes, only to realize that he couldn't see a thing. Taking a deep breath, he focused all his energy on healing, and restoring the health that he had lost. Instantly, Stan felt better, and his eyesight returned to normal—just in time to see Lord Tenebris flying at him at maximum speed, sword outstretched and pointed directly at him.

Stan didn't have time to conjure a new axe and block the attack. All he had time to do was will an enchanted diamond chestplate onto his body before the point of the sword drove into Stan's stomach. He felt a massive crack shatter through the center of the armor, but it didn't go through. However, in the split second after the sword made contact, Stan saw the sword glowing with all three kinds of enchantments. The effects of the Knockback and Fire took effect, as Stan burst into flames and was hit with the blunt shockwave of the sword.

Stan plummeted through the air, far faster than he was aware an entity could travel in Minecraft. He was totally dazed, and barely able to think properly. When his thoughts returned to him, the first thing he noticed were the flames erupting from his body, leaving a trail of gray smoke behind him as he rocketed through space. He willed himself to be protected, and he felt the tickling sensation of Fire Resistance.

As hard as it was to do while shooting forward at such a high speed, Stan forced himself to look where he was going, and saw to his dismay that he was about fifty blocks away from crashing into a skyscraper. It was all he could do to shed his chestplate and encase himself in a new set of head-to-toe enchanted diamond armor right before he made impact with the side of the building.

Stan's body had the same effect as a wrecking ball as he barreled straight through the core of the skyscraper, tearing countless blocks away as he did. As hundreds of blocks were ripped from their place by Stan's body-turned-projectile, he went into a sort of trance, where his senses nearly shut off. He simply turned into a living meteor as he ripped through the core of the building, burst out the other side, and slammed into the stone-block street below. Stan felt himself propelled deep into the ground with a sickly crunch before finally slowing to a halt.

For quite a long time, Stan lay there in his crater on one of the many roads that crisscrossed through the buildings of Element City's Skyscraper District. Slowly but surely, Stan's senses returned, and he came to the realization that he was still alive. He wasn't entirely sure how—even with full enchanted diamond armor and his enhanced level of durability as an operator, he was sure that he should have died from such a huge impact.

Stan opened his eye just the tiniest crack, and his heart jumped as he saw the form of Lord Tenebris, descending from the gray sky to where he now lay. Stan knew that he had to get out of there. As much as he wanted to lie there forever, there was far too much on the line to risk anything now. With a single deep breath, Stan once again felt a wave of healing wash over him, just as Lord Tenebris touched down beside him. He raised his diamond sword over Stan, preparing to finish the job.

Just as the sword fell, Stan vanished, reappearing in the middle of the street directly behind Lord Tenebris. The sword plunged into the stone at the bottom of the crater with a clang, and Lord Tenebris cursed loudly before whipping around, realizing that Stan was there, and meeting his eye.

"I need to talk to you, Kev," Stan said authoritatively. "If you don't stop using—"

He was cut off as a bombardment of dozens of fireballs shot out of Lord Tenebris's hands, directly at Stan. He warped out of the way just in time, and the fireballs flew behind him and collided with the nearest skyscraper in a wave of heat. Instantly, the base of the colossal building burst into flames, and even as Stan watched, the flames began to climb higher and higher up the walls, threatening to engulf the entire tower within minutes.

Stan barely had time to register this, though. He was

too busy dodging the mixed flurry of fireballs and explosive blasts that Lord Tenebris was firing at him like a machine gun, punching back and forth between his hands. Each new burst was accompanied by a grunt from Lord Tenebris, whose face bore a look of insanity.

Stan warped side to side, each time just barely missing the attacks, and each time condemning another building to burst into flames, or be torn apart by an explosion as the missed attacks flew off into the city. Stan tried to speak to Lord Tenebris for just a moment, to beg him to stop for his own sake at least, but every time he reappeared, a new blast of fire and volatile energy was upon him.

Before long, Stan began to tire; having to constantly warp around was really wearing him out. Thus, after one particularly close call, Stan didn't warp again, but instead took off, leaping into the air and flying through the city like a rocket. Behind him, he heard the sound of another player taking flight, and he glanced back to see that Lord Tenebris had taken chase, gaining on him while continuing his barrage of fire from his outstretched hand.

Stan felt the heat as the fireballs gained on him, and rolled to the side, leaving the fireballs to crash into the side of a cobblestone building. Stan cut a sharp turn to dodge another flurry of fireballs, and then began to fly straight up before swerving around the edge of a skyscraper. Behind him, he saw the top of the skyscraper he had just turned around explode with massive force as Lord Tenebris's missed attack connected with it.

Stan continued to fly, weaving in between the mile-high buildings as fast as he could, desperate to come up with some sort of plan to stop Lord Tenebris and speak to him before it was too late. Stan felt a series of explosive bursts coming up on him fast, and he did a barrel roll to dodge them. On and on Stan flew through the city, just barely managing to evade the rapid-fire string of explosions that were shooting from Lord Tenebris's hand. Stan glanced behind him and saw that the buildings in the city were being torn to shreds by what seemed like a straight line of explosions, slashing the buildings like a machete that drew closer and closer to Stan.

Then, all at once, the blasts just stopped. Stan continued to rocket forward through the city, but the line of explosions slashing across the facades of the buildings had totally ceased. His heart skipped a beat as he realized what had happened, and he looked forward again and there, sure enough was Lord Tenebris, floating directly in front of him and aiming his fist directly at Stan.

Finally, Stan thought to himself.

In one motion, Stan summoned an axe in his hand and cut in front of himself, hitting the explosion midflight as it went off in his face. Barely noticing as the blast tore off his remaining diamond armor, leaving him unscathed, Stan let go of his axe, allowing it to fly down to the ground below, as he stretched both of his hands out toward Lord Tenebris, just as the Noctem leader did the same to him.

Instantly, Stan's entire body went rigid, and he found himself nearly unable to move as he was locked into Lord Tenebris's psychic grip. He looked up in shock and saw that Lord Tenebris, too, had gone as stiff as a board, unable to move as he held his hands out toward Stan. The two operators floated, still locked into each other's telekinetic grips and totally immobile. When Stan realized he could talk, he knew that his chance had come.

"Kev, for your own good," Stan implored to Lord Tenebris. "Please listen to . . . *aaugh*!"

All of a sudden, Stan felt the invisible grip that was holding him intensify tenfold. As hard as he tried to fight it, Stan felt his arm moving backward. He glanced up in desperation and saw Lord Tenebris radiating some sort of blue energy from his body, rising off his skin like flames as he stared intently at Stan.

As it moved of its own volition, Stan felt his arm twist awkwardly behind his back. He let out a scream of agony. The more he tried to fight it, the harder Lord Tenebris's power bent his body, twisting it in odd and unnatural ways. Stan's back arched inwardly, far further than it would normally go, and he felt his legs splay apart and begin to travel toward his head. He felt as though his entire body were being compressed in a trash compactor, and he was about to suffocate under the sheer unnaturalness of how he was being contorted by Lord Tenebris.

A ringing cackle filled Stan's ears, and he looked up to see Lord Tenebris laughing. Even as he was trapped in Stan's psychic hold, Lord Tenebris was laughing maniacally as he used his mind to torture Stan.

The more he listened to this evil, sadistic monster laugh, the more it occurred to Stan just who was doing this to him. He was being tortured by King Kev—and by Lord Tenebris. This was the player who had attempted to force all lower-level players to leave his city. This was the player who had destroyed the Adorian Village—twice. This was the player who had ordered the abuse, attack, and murder of the NPC villagers just for his own personal gain. This was the player who had tortured Charlie to the brink of insanity. This was the player who had killed so many of Stan's friends— Adoria, the Apothecary, Sally, DZ . . . and Kat . . .

Suddenly, Stan looked at Lord Tenebris and saw the player that he hated most in all of Elementia, who had done so many cruel and heinous acts, both directly and through his followers, that he was far beyond redemption or remorse. Stan knew that there was no way he could allow himself to be humiliated and tormented by this monster. Stan felt a great power building up inside of him, fueled by his rage and hatred of the one who floated across from him, contorting Stan's body into unnatural shapes as he laughed with pleasure. The power built and built, and when it finally reached its breaking point, Stan released it.

"ENOUGH!" Stan bellowed, his voice booming from directly inside Lord Tenebris's head with the volume of a thousand TNT blasts. Lord Tenebris's hands flew to his ears in shock as Stan uncurled himself into a standing position and thrust his arms and legs, creating a massive explosion around himself. The shock wave crashed over Lord Tenebris, pushing him away from Stan as he continued to speak.

"KING KEV, YOUR TAMPERINGS WITH THE INNER MECHANISMS OF ELEMENTIA HAVE PUT YOUR SERVER AND ALL OF MINECRAFT IN GREAT DANGER!" Stan shouted, a bolt of lightning striking behind him as he continued to bellow as loud as he could at his arch nemesis. "STOP WITH YOUR UNNATURAL AND SORCERER'S WAYS RIGHT NOW, OR YOU RISK DESTROYING ELEMENTIA AND EVERYTHING THAT YOU HAVE WORKED SO HARD TO CREATE!"

Stan felt his fury building up inside him, threatening to erupt out of him as Lord Tenebris stood watching him break down, totally stunned. Then, as suddenly as his outburst had started, Stan stopped. The thunder clouds that had begun to gather over his head parted, and Stan took a deep breath, opening his eyes and looking at Lord Tenebris. He knew that he had to stay calm if he were to win this fight.

"What . . . what are you talking about?" Lord Tenebris asked incredulously.

"While Sally was digging through the code of Elementia, trying to give me operating powers, she found evidence that you were drawing power from the server itself to try to bolster your own strength."

"And so what if I was?" scoffed Lord Tenebris. "This is warfare, Stan. Nothing is off limits."

"What she found," Stan continued calmly as if he hadn't been interrupted, "is that by drawing power from the server, you were weakening it. The more that you used abilities that were beyond the scope of your normal operating powers, the closer you came to creating a glitch that could corrupt Elementia, causing this world that you have worked for so many years to create to be lost forever. And from there, the glitch could travel over the internet, corrupting every other Minecraft server it comes into contact with."

Lord Tenebris stared at Stan. As much as he hated to believe it, he knew that Stan was telling the truth. He had guessed that there might be some side effects to strengthening himself in such a way, but he never imagined that the consequences could be so severe.

"You and I are very different people, Kev," Stan continued evenly. "We have very different philosophies, and very different methods of leadership. I will not deny that I despise you, and will never rest until you're dead. However, there is one thing that I believe the two of us have in common, and that's our love of this server, Elementia."

Lord Tenebris stared at Stan for a moment. Then he looked down for a moment before looking up at Stan again, and giving a begrudging nod.

"Both of us have fought long and hard for this server, each trying to impress our own vision of justice and liberty on it. And yet, look at what we've done to the place we both love so much!" Stan exclaimed.

Lord Tenebris followed Stan's finger, and his gaze landed on the Skyscraper District. Several buildings had been torn to shreds by their explosive battle, and some skyscrapers, including a few of the tallest ones, had been totally engulfed in flames. Black smoke rose thick and pungent from within the district, and in the distance both players could see more black smoke rising from other districts in which the fighting, both between them and their people, had taken place.

"We've been so set on destroying each other that we've nearly destroyed the very thing we've been fighting for," Stan said earnestly. "We have to stop this madness now. If we don't, then there isn't going to be anything worth fighting for anymore."

"Ha, what are you suggesting?" Lord Tenebris scoffed. "That we broker some sort of peace treaty, and live side by side from now until you realize just how ignorant you've been, and come crawling back to me?"

"I never said that," Stan said slowly, although a fascinating idea sprung up in his head as Lord Tenebris said this. He pocketed the idea in the back of his mind, sure that he would have use for it later.

"I said it before, and I'll say it again: I despise you, Kev, and I won't rest until you're dead. I'm just as ready for this war to be over as you are, and I would never want to live in a server that had you in it. I'm sure that you feel the same way about me. However, I think that there are ways to settle our differences without so much collateral damage and risk to our server."

Lord Tenebris looked at Stan pensively. "What are you suggesting, Stan?" he said slowly.

Stan took a deep breath and responded confidently.

"Kev, I challenge you to a duel. A *traditional* duel, just like the one we had on the bridge of Element Castle all those months ago. No operating powers. No flight. No drawing any energy from the server. No healing or enhancements of any kind. Just you and me, armed with only our weapons and our wits, fighting to the death as if we were just normal players.

The terms of the duel remain unchanged from before—whoever walks away is the true and rightful ruler of Elementia."

Lord Tenebris raised an eyebrow, chuckled for a moment, and then replied, "Stan, I accept your challenge."

Stan smiled. He knew exactly what Lord Tenebris was thinking. The last time they had fought, he had outclassed Stan by such a large margin that Stan was foolish to ask that they replicate it now. But Stan knew better. He had only gotten stronger and stronger by the day since the Battle for Elementia, while Lord Tenebris had sat up in Fungarus ordering troops around, doing no fighting of any kind. The Noctem leader was out of practice, while Stan was at the top of his game.

Stan looked below him and focused as hard as he could. With a pop, a single block of bedrock appeared in midair, floating high above the burning Skyscraper District. With a deep breath, Stan willed more blocks to appear, and in the space of a second, a twenty-by-twenty-block square of bedrock materialized. Stan and Lord Tenebris both floated down to opposite ends of the bedrock, totally empty-handed. They kept their eyes locked, glaring at each other until their feet simultaneously touched down on the platform.

The two players took a deep breath, and instantly, enchanted diamond chestplates and helmets appeared on their bodies. Two enchanted diamond axes latched themselves onto Stan's back, while a diamond sword enchanted with Knockback appeared at Lord Tenebris's hip. A bow and a quiver of arrows appeared on Lord Tenebris's other hip, while the same appeared on Stan's. Last but not least, each player's weapon appeared in his hand. Stan's axe had been enchanted with Sharpness, and the purple luster shimmered under the dark cloud cover. Lord Tenebris's sword glowed red and purple, and he grasped the hilt firmly in his hand.

For a moment, the two rulers of their two governments looked at each other. No words were spoken. They both saw the great irony in the situation. After months of fighting, of power struggles, of attempting to get the upper hand on each other, here they were, back at square one. So much had changed since then, and yet, so much had remained the same. As the two players looked at each other, they knew that the time had come to end their conflict once and for all.

With no verbal cue, the two players took off at the exact same time. Stan trailed his axe behind him the same as he had the first day that he had ever picked up an axe in the Adorian Village, while Lord Tenebris had his sword pointed directly toward Stan, the same as he had on the bridge of Element Castle when they had first crossed weapons. In the exact center of the platform, the two operators collided and began to duel.

As the weapons spun and collided with loud clangs, sending sparks falling to the bedrock beneath their feet, Lord Tenebris was immediately struck by how much Stan had improved since their last fight. No longer was he a budding axe fighter who was vastly outclassed by the master swordsman with whom he was in combat. Stan's axe moved fluidly up and down across Lord Tenebris's body, finding countless openings that were just barely blocked by Lord Tenebris's sword, and in turn deflecting his counterstrikes almost effortlessly. He was fighting at the level of a true axe master.

As the duel continued on, the weapons nearly invisible for how fast they were moving, Stan slowly started to press his offensive. He drew back his axe and started to spin it around himself, the blade slashing back and forth in front of him in a spiraling X pattern. Lord Tenebris stepped away from him, further and further toward the edge of the floating platform, but he wasn't worried. Rather, he grinned. Stan had made his first mistake.

Right as Stan's axe was about to cut across him again, Lord Tenebris stepped in close and brought his sword up against the handle of Stan's axe, shoving it down until it met his hand. Stan let go just in time, sending the axe clattering backward across the bedrock platform as Lord Tenebris brought his sword back down and slashed across the front of Stan's diamond chestplate, leaving a trail of fire blazing across it as Stan tumbled backward.

Lord Tenebris rushed forward, hoping to capitalize on Stan's vulnerability while on the ground. However, just as the sword plunged, Stan rolled backward and, reaching behind him, sent one of the diamond axes on his back flying through the air, right at Lord Tenebris. The flying diamond axe struck Lord Tenebris right across the top of the head, sending him to the ground and causing his enchanted diamond helmet to fly off, hurtling through space and off the edge of the bedrock platform into the city below.

Stan picked up the axe that Lord Tenebris had knocked from his hands and charged back toward the Noctem ruler as he got back to his feet, shaking his head out of the daze caused by the impact of the axe. Lord Tenebris's immediate thought was to generate a new diamond helmet for himself, but he caught himself at the last moment. He had sworn that he wouldn't use his operating powers, and he wasn't going to start now. Instead, he raised his diamond sword to counter the axe that Stan had swung at him.

The two weapons collided in a shower of sparks, and the two masters continued to duel. They were very close to the edge of the platform now, the fighting angled parallel to the edge. Stan tried to force Lord Tenebris to feint to the side, take a misstep, and go over—after all, if either of them went over, they were honor-bound not to fly and would fall to their death. Lord Tenebris realized what Stan was trying to do and in one motion he lowered his sword.

The momentum that Stan had been pushing with carried him forward, and he careened precariously close to the edge. As Stan kept himself from falling over the side, he sensed something coming fast from behind him, and knew that Lord Tenebris was about to knock him over. As quickly as he could, Stan ducked under the attack, feeling the rush of the diamond blade travel over his head as he rolled backward. Lord Tenebris recovered from the powerful frenzied sword slash and looked at Stan, just in time to see Stan's other spare axe flying directly out toward him.

It was by a few pixels that Lord Tenebris managed to dodge the axe, and by an equally narrow margin that he managed to dodge the follow-up swing of Stan's single remaining axe that would have knocked him over the edge.

Lord Tenebris started to panic. He was being pushed back quickly now, overwhelmed by the sheer speed, strength, and ferocity of Stan's axe swipes. In his desperation, Lord Tenebris's blocks and counterstrikes were becoming more and more wild and frenzied, while Stan's attacks, though still powerful, were much more controlled and deliberate. Lord Tenebris didn't manage to land a single hit on Stan, but every few strokes of the axe, Stan made contact with Lord Tenebris's chestplate, sending him staggering back and struggling to block the next strike.

Lord Tenebris found that he was being pushed back faster and faster. In one moment, Lord Tenebris looked below him and realized with a start that he had been driven all the way across the bedrock platform and was now standing at one of the corners, just a few blocks away from the edge. Then, without warning, Lord Tenebris felt a sharp pain in his hand, and he cried out. Stan's axe had cut into the Noctem leader's hand, sending his sword flying into the air and off the platform.

Lord Tenebris fell to the ground with a thud, clutching his hand in agony as he slid across the bedrock platform, coming to a stop right where the two sides of the square platform met. His hand was in agony as his head dangled off the platform, the rest of his body sprawled out over the corner. He forced himself to look up and saw Stan advancing on him. Stan raised the axe high over his head and swung it down as hard as he could at Lord Tenebris's head.

The attack never connected. Lord Tenebris's fist shot forward, sending an invisible pulse of energy squarely into Stan's chest.

Stan's axe flew out of his hand and over the edge as he caught the energy pulse with two hands, once again giving all his energy to keep the pulse from touching him. As he winced with focus, Stan looked up, trying to comprehend what happened, only to see Lord Tenebris levitating back up on to the platform, taking a deep breath as red smoke started to seep from his pores.

A shot of rage coursed through Stan as he struggled to hold back the explosive blast in his hands. Lord Tenebris had cheated and used his operating powers.

As he filled with rage, Stan felt the pulse of energy in his hands growing stronger and stronger, until he could barely contain it. Finally, when Stan could hold it no longer, he forced his hands forward, sending the explosive energy blast right back to where it came from.

Lord Tenebris sensed the energy coming and gave Stan a look of undiluted hatred as he took a deep breath and, once again, erupted into some sort of blue aura. Stan's heart skipped a beat as Lord Tenebris stretched out his hands to catch the energy pulse. He was drawing power from the server again.

The invisible pulse hit Lord Tenebris like a truck, and he slid back toward the edge that he had just been hanging over, his face screwed up with the effort of containing such a massive power. For a second that seemed like an eternity, Lord Tenebris held the pulse in his hands and, even from a distance, Stan could feel it growing stronger and stronger. Then, with a mighty roar, Lord Tenebris pushed the pulse of energy forward, sending it back toward Stan.

Stan could feel the energy coming. He could even see a slight shimmering in the air now, like heat rising off pavement, as the pulse traveled toward him. Stan nearly began to panic as he wondered if this super-powered explosive blast was going to overwhelm him the moment he touched it. He was already drained from the last time he sent it back to Lord Tenebris. Then, all of a sudden, Stan's brow knitted, he dug in his heels, and he stretched out his hands in determination. It didn't matter if he would be able to send it back or not—he was too tired to warp. He had to try.

Never before had Stan even imagined the sheer intensity of the energy pulse that he caught in his hands now, sending him sliding ten blocks backward across the bedrock. Although the pulse was now little more than a block in size, it felt as though Stan were struggling to keep a planet from crushing him as he held the ball of undiluted power in his hands. Stan tried to push the pulse off him, but it was as if he were trying to stop earth itself from moving. Slowly but surely, despite all his best efforts, the pulse of energy pushed into him . . . crushing him . . . threatening to overwhelm him . . . until finally . . .

Stan, an eerie, familiar voice called from inside his head. *Don't let the power dominate you . . . fight back, Stan, you must . . .*

"I . . . can't . . . ," Stan got out as his breathing became shallow in the midst of his monumental struggle. "It's . . . too . . . much. . . ."

Remember why you fight, Stan, the voice echoed into his head yet again. *You fight in the name of justice. . . . You fight for those who cannot help themselves. . . . You fight in the name of those who have fallen. . . . You fight for the protection of the game of Minecraft and the server that you love. . . .*

Stan's eyes flew open. He had to overcome this. If he didn't, then not only would Elementia be destroyed, but Minecraft, the world that he and so many others had come to love nearly as much as their own, would be destroyed. He couldn't let that happen. And if he gave up a part of himself to save it . . . then so be it.

Stan let out a savage cry as he straightened his back, standing upright for the first time as he held the ball of energy tightly to his stomach. As the shout continued, Stan poured all his energy into the blast that he was holding before him—all his love for his people, his server, and his game— and, slowly but surely, it grew larger and larger. Before long, Stan knew that he could give no more. Despite his newfound resolve, the intensity of the energy was beginning to force him to the ground yet again. With one great motion, Stan dug in his heels and forced the ball of energy out of his hands and back at Lord Tenebris.

Stan collapsed to the ground. He couldn't stand, and he

could hardly move. He had given all of himself to this one final attack. If it didn't destroy Lord Tenebris, even with all his extra stolen power, nothing would. And there was no way that it wouldn't . . . there was no way that even an operator could return an explosive blast of that magnitude. Stan imagined that he would be lucky if he himself were not wiped out by the sheer force of the blast when it hit. Slowly, he forced himself to look up, to see the impact.

What he saw, he couldn't believe.

Lord Tenebris stood in place, still radiating with a cerulean aura. His eyes were closed, and he hadn't even bothered to hold up his hands to catch the pulse. Instead, he had only one hand outstretched, clutching a diamond sword that was pointed directly at the enormous energy blast. Stan watched as the explosive pulse made contact with the sword and seemed to travel down the blade and into Lord Tenebris, as if the diamond weapon were some sort of lightning rod absorbing the sheer power behind the attack. The energy engulfed Lord Tenebris, causing the aura around him to glow brighter and brighter until it was nearly pure white, and a split second later, a flash emitted from the Noctem leader, so intense that Stan felt as though his eyes were being fried.

For a moment, everything was white. Stan's head fell to the ground, and he could not see a thing. He was totally blinded in the aftermath of the burst of light, and too exhausted from his final effort to kill Lord Tenebris to move even a single muscle in his body. All he could do was lie on the bedrock surface like a rag doll, praying that his plan had worked, desperately hoping that whatever Lord Tenebris was doing had backfired, and that he had disintegrated in the dazzling light.

But as Stan's vision finally started to return, and he found himself looking upward at the gray sky, his heart stopped with dread as he realized that a dark figure was standing directly above him. As his eyes shifted back into focus, Stan could see that Lord Tenebris actually wasn't dark at all; the light blue aura that had engulfed his body before absorbing the blast had now changed color to a royal gold, and tiny little sparks of electricity danced around his body.

Despite feeling as though he were made from rubber, Stan forced himself to raise his head. He was acting purely on instinct. His mind was too deadened from energy loss to form any cohesive plan. As Lord Tenebris looked down at him like a hawk eyeing a wounded mouse, Stan took aim and shot a punch at Lord Tenebris. Not even a tiny explosive attack flew from Stan's hand, and he flopped to the ground yet again, too exhausted to hear Lord Tenebris chuckling at the feeble attempt.

"Thank you, Stan," Lord Tenebris simpered, as he looked down at the pathetic shell of a player that was Stan, lying on the ground. "Thank you for so generously handing me everything that you had. I now have the strength of two fully-fledged operators infused into my body. And now that I know not to draw power from this server, I will draw from all the other servers instead, and destroy them. Elementia will reign supreme as the sole remaining Minecraft server, and I shall be its undisputed and unstoppable ruler."

Stan said nothing. He could hardly comprehend what Lord Tenebris was saying. He had no energy left for thought.

"But for you, Stan . . . ," Lord Tenebris said, holding up the sword that had conducted all of Stan's energy into its owner's body and running his finger across its length lovingly as if it were the most precious object in the world.

" . . . it is over."

Lord Tenebris raised the sword high above his head. Stan didn't realize what was going on. He was lying unconscious on the ground, not a care in the world, and finally happy that, after everything that he had been through since he had first joined Elementia, he was finally resting.

The sword plunged down.

At the exact moment that the sword shattered the back of Stan's diamond chestplate, there was a rush of light and sound, followed by a metallic clang. Lord Tenebris was knocked back with fantastic force, tumbling along the ground as his golden aura trailed behind him like the flame of an Olympic torch, his sword spiraling high into the air and landing with a clatter right next to Stan's unconscious form.

Lord Tenebris skidded to a stop yet again at the edge of the bedrock platform. Grunting with shock, he looked up and saw a figure standing in front of Stan. His vision was a little hazy due to the shock, but as he squinted, he could make out a blue-greenish body with a black cape billowing behind him in the wind.

Lord Tenebris rubbed his eyes as he pulled himself to his feet, sure that he wasn't seeing correctly. Once he was standing upright, he opened his eyes to take another look . . . only to find himself staring into a pair of white eyes, glowing as radiantly as the moon, standing a single block away from him.

His mouth dropped open, and his own white eyes widened as he stared into this mirror image of himself with a black cape, hood, and shawl wrapped around his upper body. Lord Tenebris began to shudder with pure, undiluted fear as he stared into the face with the glowing eyes, the face that was looking more and more furious and disgusted by the second. This being that he was looking at . . . he didn't exist . . . Lord Tenebris *knew* that he didn't exist . . . he was dressed up as this demon to elicit fear in the eyes of the gullible idiots who believed that it was real. . . .

Panic overtaking all else within Lord Tenebris's mind, he

willed himself to vanish and reappear on his throne, only to find that he was locked in place by an unseen force, totally unable to warp, or even move. He was forced to stare straight ahead, into the white eyes of the demon, which seemed to be staring directly into his soul with contempt and hatred. Lord Tenebris began to hyperventilate, totally scared witless over his possession by this demon that was staring him down.

Lord Tenebris struggled, trying to use all his willpower to move, to attack, to do anything to get out of this situation. However, what happened instead elevated his panic to incredible heights. The golden aura, which had been radiating out of his body the entire time, suddenly turned cerulean blue once again, and then faded into nothingness entirely. At the same moment, Lord Tenebris felt a huge amount of energy drain out of his body.

"What . . . are you . . . doing . . . to me?" he stammered weakly as he began to shake violently.

The demon didn't respond. He simply continued to stare through Lord Tenebris, who was forced to stand immobile in front of the white-eyed monster as he started to unhinge.

More than a dozen blocks away, Stan's eyes flew open. He had no recollection of what had happened after he had let his explosive blast, imbued with all his energy, fly at Lord Tenebris. Suddenly, though, he felt wide awake, and as he looked down at his arm he saw, to his utter amazement, that a dazzling blue aura was radiating around him, identical to that which had blazed around Lord Tenebris when he had drawn energy from the server. Stan barely had time to comprehend what this meant before another surge of energy coursed through his body, and the blaze around him changed from cerulean to a brilliant gold.

As Stan pulled himself to his feet, quivering at the sheer amount of power that had somehow been injected into his body, he looked down to the other end of the bedrock platform. There, right at the edge, he could see Lord Tenebris, looking weak, drained, and totally petrified as he stared into the face of another figure, whose back was to Stan, and whose head was obscured by a black hood. As soon as he realized who it was, a blue glint caught the corner of Stan's eye. He turned to look, and there, sitting on the ground, was Lord Tenebris's sword, which he had used to absorb Stan's dying attack.

All at once, Stan was struck by a thought. Actually, it wasn't really a thought as much as it was a fact. Stan knew what he had to do, and as he reached down to pick up the sword of the Noctem ruler, Stan felt as though it had been his purpose to carry out this plan since the very beginning.

Stan took a deep breath and, clutching the diamond sword glowing with the luster of enchantments, he began to run toward the two figures at the far end of the bedrock platform. As he reached his top speed, he found himself able to run even faster, as if he were under the influence of QPO. Before long, Stan found that he was moving too fast for his legs to keep up with, and so he leaped into the air, accelerating even faster as he flew forward, skimming over the surface of the bedrock, directly at the two players.

Right as he was about to make contact with the Black Hood, Stan's instincts kicked in, and he stabbed the sword out in front of him. To his amazement, the Black Hood stretched his right hand out, too, mirroring Stan's position perfectly. He kept rocketing forward, not checking his speed in the slightest as the diamond sword pierced through the back of the Black Hood. In an instant, the Black Hood vanished into thin air in a cloud of purple smoke, leaving Stan to look directly into the face of Lord Tenebris, who stared back at Stan with a total lack of comprehension.

Stan couldn't have stopped if he wanted to. He was moving far too fast. Although Lord Tenebris had been released from the psychic grip of the Black Hood, he had no time to react before his own diamond sword, held outstretched, struck the center of his chestplate. The diamond armor shattered into a thousand tiny fragments, reflecting the brilliant dazzling of the enchanted sword as it entered Lord Tenebris's heart.

Stan's eyes locked onto the eyes of his greatest adversary,

and time seemed to stop as they shared their final gaze. Defeat was ripe in every single inch of Lord Tenebris's face, as he exchanged one final, sad look with Stan. Then, right as the ring of items began to burst out from his stomach, Lord Tenebris took one final breath, closed his eyes, and faded out of existence.

For a brief moment, as Stan plowed through the ring of items, scattering them wildly through the air, he was struck with a note of panic. *What if he changed the game mode again?* Stan thought to himself. *What if he finds some other way back in?*

Then, all at once, Stan found himself struck by an overwhelming, calming sense of peace. A voice sounded out, clear as day in Stan's head, as a bright light appeared at the exact location where Lord Tenebris had disappeared.

Do not fret, Stan, the Black Hood's voice said calmly, as the light expanded, soon engulfing Stan in a giant supernova of light and sound. *He will not come back. It is over.*

nstantly, all fighting stopped. The hundred or so remaining members of the Noctem Alliance, who had been pushed back onto the execution platform, and the leaders of Stan's army, who made up the border between the two factions, all looked up, along with every other player in the plaza. The explosion was massive, illuminating the sky and sending a blast of sound crashing down over all the players whose faces were lit by the white light shining down from the sky. Every single player knew in their gut that, for better or for worse, the clash of the two leaders was over.

As the sky returned to its previous dull, washed-out gray color, the players all continued to look up. It was as if they had forgotten that their opponents existed, that they were even fighting at all. Slowly, each and every soldier, citizen, and villager in the plaza could see a square of blocks floating high in the sky, as if it were some sort of platform. And next to this platform, a single, almost imperceptible dot could be seen, slowly growing larger and larger as it sunk downward, and taking on the form of a player.

Slowly, this player descended from the sky, glowing sword clutched in his hand. His eyes were closed, so there was no way of telling which of the two great leaders it was. However, all the Noctem fighters felt their hearts lift, as all the citizens of Element City and republic fighters felt theirs plummet. After all, the figure was holding an enchanted sword . . . and when was the last time that Stan had ever used a sword in battle?

Charlie, Jayden, Leonidas, Ben, Bob, the Mechanist, Sirus, Cassandrix, Commander Crunch, and the villagers all stared intently at the figure as they stepped back, creating an empty space in the midst of the crowd for the descending player to land. Even at such a close distance, they couldn't tell if this player was their best friend or their greatest enemy, who was skinned identically, save the eyes, which were still closed.

For a moment, the player just stood there, a solemn expression on his face. He took a deep breath. Then, he opened his eyes, revealing the blue pupils of Stan2012, looking victorious, yet also exhausted and, somehow, wiser than he had been.

Immediately, the entire plaza burst out into uproarious applause, with hoots and hollers abounding, ringing through the sky. Elation shone like sunlight out of the faces of every citizen of Element City who was packed into the courtyard, as they realized that their long nightmare was finally over, and that their beloved president had vanquished the harbinger of darkness and pain for good.

Charlie leaped off Dr. Pigglesworth, limping as fast as he could toward Stan, tears streaming down his face as he threw himself at his friend, wrapping his arms around him in a tight hug. Leonidas nearly knocked the two of them over as he joined in, embracing his friend closely as he realized that Stan had destroyed the leader of the organization that had almost claimed his own life. Next to come was Cassandrix, whooping with joyous laughter. Oob and Mella followed, red smoke still spewing from the wound in her stomach, latching on to the group hug as Stull sat on his mother's shoulders shouting out "Victory! We have attained victory!"

Then Jayden, the Mechanist, Commander Crunch, Ben, Bob, Sirus, and all the others joined together in a massive group hug, as the group of players, who had been through so much together, who had given everything to their fight for justice and peace, had finally succeeded in their valiant struggle.

In the midst of the massive group hug, as he heard the joyous sobs and shouts of thankfulness for his safety and his victory, Stan allowed himself a small smile, as he realized that they were right to celebrate. After so long—after so much hatred, violence, and bloodshed—they had accomplished their goals. Elementia was free, and they had now, for the first time since Stan had been in the server, reached the true dawning of a new age.

It was only as Stan realized just what ushering in a new era would entail that his smile vanished, to be replaced again by a look of sad solemnity.

Slowly but surely, the celebrations died down. Although the people of Element City still looked almost joyous enough to brighten the sky that was still dark and gray, they all realized something. The citizens of Elementia all looked at the cluster of leaders that held their adored president in the center and realized that, since he had landed, he hadn't said a word. Within a minute, the entire plaza had returned to being as silent as moments before, as they had watched Stan descend from the sky.

In due time, Stan's friends also realized that they were expecting him to say something. They all began to shrink away from him, giving him some space. As Charlie hopped back to Dr. Pigglesworth on one foot, Stan took a deep breath and let it out. Little did his friends know that he was thinking long and hard about what he was about to say; without a doubt, what he said here, on this day, would shape the future of the server of Elementia for years to come.

"Stan?" Leonidas asked, looking concerned as Stan looked more and more downcast the deeper into thought he went. "Are ya okay?"

Stan looked at Leonidas, his eyes wide and meaningful. He said nothing. There would be time to talk to his friends later, time to thank his followers for their selflessness and devotion to their cause. But now was not that time. Stan had a more important matter to attend to, a matter of historical importance.

Stan took a deep breath, closed his eyes, and began to float into the sky. He heard countless audible gasps from the crowd at this display of his operating powers, but as Stan looked down into the crowd, he heard a commotion. The higher up he floated, the more black-adorned players within the crowd dashed away from the mass of other players. Stan was satisfied—this was the reaction that he was hoping for.

As he watched from above, it looked as though ink were trickling out of clear water as the few remaining Noctem soldiers scattered among the thousands of republic soldiers in diamond armor. As if drawn by magnetism, the Noctems made their way onto the execution platform. There, Stan looked to see General Spyro, standing as still as if he were a statue, his gaze skyward. Stan turned his head, following the stare of the petrified Noctem general. Floating in the sky next to him, pointing all three of its heads at Spyro, was the Wither.

Stan floated up to the Wither and hovered directly in front of its middle head. The skeletal boss mob looked confused, as if perplexed as to why a player was flying in the same way that it could. Stan turned around so that his back was facing the Wither, and stretched out his hand, concentrating hard on the air in front of him.

In an instant, a ring of obsidian blocks appeared hovering in front of Stan, and a split second later, the center of the ring erupted into a vibrant purple flash, which receded into the glowing purple haze of the Nether Portal. There were more gasps and even a few shouts of surprise from below at the sudden appearance of these blocks, but Stan was only focused on the Wither. Its white eyes widened as it felt the presence of the portal, almost as if some unseen force were calling it to enter the Nether.

Slowly, the Wither floated forward through the air, as if entranced, and into the purple mist. There was a flash of purple light as the Wither disappeared, having returned to the dimension that it knew as home. Stan then proceeded to raise both hands toward the portal, and at once, it vanished, disappearing into thin air as dozens of black particles rained to the ground two dozen blocks below him. Stan lowered his hands in front of him and closed his eyes.

"Go in peace," he whispered, as the dark clouds evaporated from the sky, allowing the square block of the sun to shine down freely once more.

After a moment of silence, Stan opened his eyes and started to sink down yet again. Below him, the faces of all his friends lit up, as they assumed that he was finally going to address them. However, to their bewilderment, Stan didn't float toward them. Rather, he sunk down lower and lower, and floated forward, toward the execution platform.

The platform was tightly packed. Every single remaining member of the Noctem Alliance had managed to fit onto the elevated wood-plank stage, which by no means was designed to fit a hundred players. As Stan approached them, still airborne, the ripple of fear that had been bubbling among them since Stan had first appeared now escalated into all-out panic. Although Stan's face still looked grave, with no hint of aggression in it, the fighting forces of the Noctem Alliance let out shouts and cries of alarm as this all-powerful player came closer and closer to them. They were afraid to move, afraid to address Stan. Even now, though, in the face of complete and utter defeat and disgrace, they still stood united as a team, a giant mass of black ready to stand together to the end.

As Stan finally landed on the edge of the platform, there was a shuffling in the crowd. Somebody was pushing their way forward. After a moment, Spyro burst out of the front of the crowd. He had a diamond sword held in his hand and wasted no time in pointing it at Stan, although he had a hard time keeping it pointed that way, his hands were shaking so hard. His face showed a mixture of loathing, grief, and terror. For a few moments, the two highest-ranking members of the two warring factions stood still, staring at each other. Then . . .

"You came down here to force us to join your side, didn't

you?" Spyro said in a rasp, his voice as shaky as his hands.

Stan said nothing. He simply looked back at the Noctem general sadly.

"Well let me tell you right now, Stan . . . it will *never* happen!" Spyro bellowed at the top of his lungs, his sobs of grief and fear threatening to overpower his voice as he shouted at the operator standing before him. "Not one single member of the Noctem Alliance will ever join your despicable republic! We will never stop fighting for justice in the land of Elementia for as long as we're alive! No matter how many times you beat us down, no matter how low you drag us, we will never stop coming back to fight you! You killed Lord Tenebris . . . the greatest being in all of Minecraft . . ." Spyro's sobs nearly overcame him by this point, and he was echoed by the hundred members of the Alliance behind him, before his anguish morphed into rage a moment later.

" . . . and, Stan, for this, we will *never* forgive you! Long live the Noctem Alliance! VIVA LA NOCTEM!"

"VIVA LA NOCTEM!" the crowd of Noctem soldiers echoed from behind him, and from the tone of their voice, Stan knew that they believed in every single word that Spyro had said. That they truly would rather die before they cooperated with the republic.

Therefore, once again, Stan offered no response. Instead, he reached into his inventory and extracted an enchanted diamond sword, leveling it at Spyro.

Although several Noctem soldiers totally lost it at the sight of the weapon, breaking down into sobs or screams, Spyro stood firm, his body shaking as much as ever, but his eyes showed determination as he prepared to become the next in a never-ending line of martyrs for the radical upper-level players of Element City. Closer and closer, Stan walked toward Spyro, until he was standing within striking distance of the Noctem general. Not backing down, Spyro closed his eyes, preparing for the blow to fall. . . .

"Take it."

Spyro opened his eyes and stared at the diamond sword that Stan was holding in his outstretched hand. He wasn't holding it out in an attack stance; rather, he was holding it out in a gesture, as if he were offering it to Spyro.

"What . . . what are you talking about?" Spyro demanded.

"Take the sword," Stan said softly to him, speaking so that only those on the platform could hear them. "This sword belongs to your leader. He used it in the last battle that he ever fought. I want you to have it. Do whatever you want with it. Build a memorial to him and incorporate the sword into it somehow, if you'd like. Just do whatever you have to and commemorate Lord Tenebris as you see fit."

Spyro stared at Stan, uncomprehendingly. Slowly, he reached out, grabbed the handle of the sword, glowing with enchantments of Fire, Sharpness, and Knockback, and took it from Stan. For a moment, he looked at the diamond weapon in reverence, as if it were the most priceless treasure conceivable. Then, in a swift, sneaky motion, he pocketed the sword, and looked up to Stan contentiously.

"What are you playing at?" Spyro hissed.

Stan took a deep breath and looked directly at Spyro, causing him to recoil slightly in intimidation. This effect was accidental and, not wanting to send the wrong message, Stan smiled a tiny smile. When he spoke again, it was loud enough so that even those on the ground could hear him.

"General Spyro of the Noctem Alliance, I hereby declare that you, and every member of the organization that you now command, will be allowed to live, and will not be imprisoned for your crimes against Elementia."

A collective gasp washed through the crowd before it exploded into pandemonium. The citizens of the republic erupted into shouts of outrage and accusations of conspiracy, while the hundred Noctem troopers standing on the execution platform looked dazed and confused. All of Stan's friends looked at him as if he had lost his mind, as did Spyro. Out of the corner of his eye, Stan saw a white form burst out of the crowd, and he turned to see Cassandrix standing at the base of the platform, looking totally flabbergasted.

"Stan, what are you doing?" she demanded as Stan

looked down at her. "Do you not remember what the people of this organization have done? Do you not remember the last three months of war and suffering? Do you not remember that these are the people who . . . who killed Kat?"

At the sound of the name, a wave of anguish rippled up Stan's spine, affecting his heart, stomach, and finally his head as they all contracted in pain and he realized, once again, that one of his best friends was gone for all time. He turned around to look again at the stunned Spyro, who had done so much evil, who had caused so much pain. For a moment, as his stomach blazed with the fires of revenge, he considered retracting his statement and blasting Spyro to dust, along with every other member of the Noctem Alliance that stood behind him.

Then, once again, as suddenly as the fury had flared up, it vanished. Stan took a deep breath as he realized that he was an operator now. He was by far the most powerful player in Elementia, and he could kill anybody that he wanted to effortlessly. The citizens, who were still jeering at him from the crowd from his announcement, believed that, as their leader, Stan would help them to enforce their will on all who disagreed with them. But Stan knew that if he were to fulfill his promise to himself, and truly turn Elementia into the place that King Kev had intended for it in the server's founding, he must not make the same mistakes that King Kev had made. History was one step away from repeating itself, and Stan knew that now was the time for branching off to create his own path.

"Quiet, please," Stan spoke, willing all who stood in the plaza to hear him. While he had not shouted like Lord Tenebris had, the voice still projected itself into the heads of each and every player in the plaza. Instantly, the riots ceased, as Stan turned around and, catching Cassandrix's eye, began to speak yet again.

"I stand by my judgment that General Spyro and the Noctem Alliance will not be punished for their crimes. I would like to emphasize, quite clearly, that this does not mean I believe that their crimes are any less heinous. They still robbed, tortured, and murdered countless players, and committed acts of terrorism that turned our beloved Elementia into a cesspool of darkness and hatred. However . . . I believe that we have far more important things to focus on than dealing retribution."

Stan paused for a moment as the citizens of Elementia murmured among themselves, while the Noctem soldiers continued to look at Stan, trying to figure out what he was trying to do.

Stan had a decision that he had to make. If he wanted to, now would be the most opportune time to reveal the identity of Lord Tenebris to the public. Now that he was dead, there was nothing to stop Stan from spreading the truth. However, as he thought about it, he decided against it. Not only would it weaken the argument that he was about to make, but it would also lead to more outrage and hatred toward the Noctem Alliance, who would surely deny his claims. Stan decided that he would continue to refer to Lord Tenebris and King Kev as separate entities. For now, at least.

"Nobody knew exactly what Lord Tenebris was," Stan said simply. "Some believe that he was a glitch, others believe him to be the reincarnation of King Kev's spirit. But regardless of what he was, he had powers nearly equivalent to those of an operator. He attempted to use those powers to enforce his own will, and his own beliefs, over the people of Elementia. What resulted was three months of the worst war that has ever plagued our server, which has resulted in scores of dead players and an atmosphere of hatred and animosity that has lingered over the countryside.

"Now . . . ," Stan continued, carefully thinking, picking and choosing his words before speaking, "Lord Tenebris is dead. I am the sole remaining operator of Elementia. As such, it would be extremely easy for me to argue that, since the Noctem Alliance has lost this war, their ideals were wrong. Therefore, I could argue that because their ideals were wrong, *my* ideals are one hundred percent correct, and then I could go on to use my powers to enforce my own beliefs over the people of Elementia. However . . . I'm not going to do that."

Stan allowed a moment of silence for this message to sink in. His friends were staring at him, no longer thinking that he was crazy, but instead wondering where he was going with this. Stan continued.

"It is true that I believe that all players, regardless of their level, should have a chance to live in Elementia, even if that means that the upper-level players occasionally must lose out on some of their hard-earned possessions for the sake of the lower-level players. However, if you do not agree with me, I won't hold it against you. I might disagree with you, and at one point I might explain my point of view to you in the hopes that you might change your mind, but I will still be able to coexist with you, provided that you respect my opinions and beliefs as much as I respect yours.

"The reason that I went to war with the Noctem Alliance," Stan said, turning back to face the black-clad soldiers, "is because they did not respect my opinions. Rather than attempting to peacefully coexist, they declared war on my ideals, which are shared by many other players on this server. I was forced to fight back, for the sake of protecting my people.

"But it doesn't matter now," Stan said quickly, as the Noctem troops leered at him aggressively, and boos and shouts toward the Noctem Alliance started to slowly rise from the crowd. "I'm not here to point the finger of blame. The war is in the past now. The time has come to look to the future. While we must never forget the past, we can't let it define us either. Now is the time to let the past go and see the world around us for how it is, not how we want it to be. Because, if you take the time to look, you'll find that that world contains plenty of fantastic opportunities for all players—young and old alike."

Stan took a deep breath. He knew that, in a few moments, he would be announcing something that would shock every single player in Elementia. Regardless of how unpopular this announcement might be, Stan knew that he had no choice but to go through with it if he was going to create his own path.

"For the past three months," Stan continued, "the players of this server have been divided and warring with each other over their beliefs. Due to our fighting, the server of Elementia lies in ruins."

Stan raised his hand out over the skyline of Element City. The eyes of all players in the vicinity looked around, scanning the countless clouds of black smoke rising from the various districts of the city, the blazing fires, and the skyscrapers with massive chunks torn from them.

"Despite having different ideas of what was best for Elementia," Stan went on, "both factions only wanted just that: the best for Elementia. And yet, through our ignorant stubbornness and refusal to coexist, and work to seek out a compromise, we have torn Elementia apart, ravaging it, and creating a giant mess that will only be repaired with the combined efforts of all of us. As we all stand here in this plaza today, the war finally over, we're presented with a new opportunity."

Stan's heart was racing so fast that it felt like it were about to burst. Here it was: the proclamation that would change Elementia forever. Stan took a deep breath and let it out.

"As the operator of this server," Stan said confidently, "I, Stan2012, hereby announce that both the Grand Republic of Elementia and the Nation of the Noctem Alliance are both disbanded. As of today, neither exist anymore."

It was as if everybody in the crowd had been slapped in the face as they stared up at Stan, trying to comprehend that he had just announced that he was getting rid of both of their countries, which they had worked so long and hard to raise and defend.

"Both of these countries were founded out of warfare with each other, and if they stay intact, I doubt that the wounds will ever fully heal. Now especially, the wounds are still fresh. Therefore, I don't believe that the people of the former republic, or of the former Nation of the Noctem Alliance, will be able to live together peacefully. From now on, there shall be two cities in Elementia," Stan said, a small smile on his face as he revealed the plan that he had formulated for the future of his server. "In one of these cities, the law of the Noctem Alliance shall remain supreme. Only older players will be allowed in, and they will have full control over what they have earned, not being forced to share with anybody. In the other city, players of all levels will be allowed in. The older players will help the new players learn and thrive, and the newer players will pay it forward by helping the new players when they themselves become upper-level players.

"But before you get too anxious, my friends, don't think for a moment that I would ever leave you to build a new city from the ground up!" Stan exclaimed. "With my operating powers, I will help both groups build their cities. I shall favor neither over the other, and before long, every player shall have a city of their own to call home.

"I honestly hope that, in the future, the people of Elementia will be able to live as one," Stan said, a slight element of sadness returning to his voice. "I hope that, as time goes by, the people of Elementia will be able to put their differences aside and coexist. However, in the wake of this war, now is not the time. That work will be done in the future. For now, I invite members of Elementia to clap if they are in favor of the idea of the creation of the two cities."

For a moment, the plaza remained silent. Stan wasn't

surprised. After all, he was suggesting a radical idea that would change Elementia forever and require work and cooperation on everyone's part. Stan only hoped that they could see what he saw: two groups divided not only by ideals but by hatred, who needed time to heal before they could ever be united. And besides, Stan would be surprised if both sides didn't find the idea of their own city, without the other side, appealing.

Before long, Stan heard a single pair of hands clapping. He looked down into the crowd and saw Leonidas in the front row, clapping slowly. No sooner had Stan noticed him than Charlie, sitting next to Leonidas on the back of Dr. Pigglesworth, began to clap as well. The clapping soon spread through all of Stan's friends, and then over the rest of the crowd, evolving from cheers into hoots, whistles, and full-blown applause at Stan's proposition. He smiled as he looked out over the crowd, before turning around to face the members of the Noctem Alliance on the platform behind him.

All the members were standing still as statues, not clapping, staring forward at their leader, alone at the front of the group. Spyro was looking at the ground as he mulled over Stan's proposition. As he sensed Stan's gaze on him, Spyro looked up and met his eye. The two leaders exchanged glances.

"I promise you, Spyro," Stan whispered so that only he

could hear, "I'm not trying to take advantage of you. I just want what's best for *all* members of this server."

Spyro continued to stare at Stan, who couldn't read his face as he tried to determine whether or not to trust him. Then, slowly, he raised his hands in front of him and began to clap. As soon as their leader began to clap, the other members of the Noctem Alliance clapped without hesitation.

Stan was overjoyed that the citizens of Elementia were willing to follow his plans. Now that the entire plaza was cheering, thrilled at the idea of living in a brand-new city free of conflict, Stan knew that there was one more matter that had to be resolved before the rebuilding could begin.

"Thank you, everybody, for your support," Stan said with a smile as the applause died down. "I'm sure that, with my help, you will be able to build the greatest cities in the history of Minecraft. However, there is one more matter that must be settled: If we are going to live as two people, in two cities, we still have to decide what will become of the city we already have."

A tense murmuring erupted throughout the crowd as they realized what Stan was talking about. Both sides had given countless lives, and endured awful hardships throughout this war, for the prize of Element City. Now that the war was over and they were dividing . . . what would become of this place?

"I think," Stan continued, "that it would be foolish to create two totally new cities, when we already have one. True, Element City may have sustained heavy damages throughout the fighting, which may take months to fully repair, but it's easier to repair it than to build a completely new city from the ground up. And, in the great spirit of democracy, I believe that the only way that we can truly decide who takes Element City is through a vote."

As the murmurs in the crowd intensified, Stan glanced over at Spyro, who, like the other members of the Noctem Alliance, was eyeing Stan with contemptuous disbelief. After all, there were thousands of members of Element City, and only a hundred members of the Noctem Alliance. If a vote was taken, they were sure to lose.

Indeed, Stan knew that it would probably be the easiest, and the most fair, to simply give Element City to the citizens of the former republic without question. After all, they did outnumber the Noctem soldiers fifteen to one, and it would be far easier to just keep the majority of them happy (especially considering that Stan agreed with their ideals). However, Stan knew that he couldn't do that. If he was going to lead the server of Elementia to a brighter future as an operator, he had to be impartial. He had to give both sides a fair chance, and he knew how to do it.

"However," Stan said slowly, causing the whispering in

the crowd to cease, "not every citizen in the server is going to have a vote on this matter. This is because, although I do not believe that they are superior by default, I do believe that the older players have accumulated more wisdom than the younger players. They have lived in Elementia the longest, and therefore, they will decide what is best for the server that they have called their home for so long. Therefore, only those players who have played in Elementia for a year or longer may vote."

Spyro's eyes widened as shouts of outrage erupted from the crowd. The sea of thousands of players looked angry and betrayed, as they realized that their votes wouldn't count in making this monumental decision. Even Stan's friends, who had appeared pensive while they mulled over Stan's idea of the two cities, now looked at him as if he had lost his mind. Charlie came forward out of the line and glanced up at Stan.

"Stan, what're you doing?" he demanded. "How can you let the older players decide? All the Noctem soldiers are older players!"

"Charlie, I've put a lot of thought into this," Stan replied, his voice calm and patient. "I have a plan that will benefit everybody, and this is part of it."

"But you . . ."

"Charlie, do you trust me?"

Charlie raised his eyebrows, his mouth hanging open

from his retort as Stan cut him off. For a moment, the two friends held each other's gaze. For so long now, they had had each other's backs, fighting off countless dangers and depending on each other to live to see the next day. And now here was Stan, asking Charlie if he trusted him to reform the server that they had worked so hard to win.

Charlie took a deep breath and, his gaze never wavering from Stan's eyes, nodded.

"Thank you," Stan said, and with that, he stood up straight, looked over the furious crowd, and said in his booming, penetrating voice, "Silence, please."

Once again, his voice seemed to have some mysterious influence over the players in the plaza, and their voices faded to silence.

"I would like to assure you all that I have put a lot of thought into what I'm asking you to do right now," Stan said, a slight authoritative note to his voice. "I only want what is best for Elementia, and all who reside here. And to those of you who think that I might give you the short end of the stick because I disagree with your beliefs, you are mistaken. From this day on, I am loyal to no faction, but rather to the entire server, and all its players. I will do what I must to restore balance and order to this server, and I will only take action against a group if they threaten that balance.

"And so I repeat, once again: Only those who have been

playing in Elementia for a year or longer will be permitted to vote to see which group gains control over Element City."

Stan raised his hand toward the execution platform and took a deep breath. A few Noctem soldiers cringed, imagining that he was about to attack them. Instead, the platform of wood blocks that they were standing on expanded, tripling in size instantaneously. One side of the platform extension was made entirely out of lapis lazuli blocks, while the other was made entirely out of iron blocks. Both expansions were the same size as the wood plank–block platform that they branched off from.

"Members of the Noctem Alliance, we'll start with you," Stan said, looking at Spyro. "If you would like Element City to become a city of upper-level players alone, walk onto the platform of iron. If you would like it to become a city of players of all levels, walk onto the platform of lapis lazuli."

Even before Stan had finished speaking, Spyro had begun to walk across the wooden platform, and by the time Stan had finished, he was already standing on the iron platform. Immediately, the entire group of Noctem soldiers trickled off the wooden stage to join Spyro on the platform of iron. As the players walked, Stan counted them and, with his operating powers, checked to see if they had in fact been in Elementia for a year or longer. Indeed, Stan saw that they all had, and by the time the last Noctem soldier had walked over onto the platform, Stan had counted one hundred and four of them.

"All right," Stan said, not surprised by this number. "Now, I invite all players dispersed among this crowd who have been in Elementia for a year or longer to please step forward and take your side."

The crowd churned a bit as the older players snaked their way through the throng of newer players, finally reaching the front of the crowd and ascending the stairs onto the execution platform.

As Stan watched them pick sides, his heart lifted as a nearly unbroken stream of players banked a sharp right toward the lapis lazuli platform. They spread throughout the blue square of blocks like gas expanding into a container, almost faster than Stan could count. And yet, not all of them went to the right side. Stan counted an additional ten players who broke off from the stream and joined the iron platform that held the Noctem Alliance.

Stan was shocked. If those upper-level players hadn't been in his army, that meant that the Noctem Alliance had imprisoned them in Brimstone. Why would they possibly want to join their city? Then Stan reminded himself that this wasn't a city for just the Noctem Alliance—it was for anybody who agreed with the ideals of the Alliance as well. Stan supposed that there were indeed some players who agreed with the Alliance who still hadn't joined them.

After a minute or so, the stream of older players from the crowd waned into a trickle, and then stopped altogether. Stan had counted one hundred and fourteen on the iron side and one hundred and nine on the lapis lazuli side. The platform that held all the Noctem soldiers was larger. Stan's heart sank. He was about to announce this to the people when he noticed movement in the front row.

Stan looked down and he saw Leonidas, Ben, Bob, the Mechanist, Cassandrix, and Commander Crunch step onto the stairs. Stan imagined that they must have stayed behind to count how many players were on each side, and as he did the math for himself, his heart lifted. If all six of his friends went to the lapis lazuli side, they would outnumber the iron side by one, and they would get to keep Element City.

Stan watched, with a huge smile on his face, as Commander Crunch, Ben, Bob, Leonidas, and the Mechanist all walked proudly to the right and joined the lapis lazuli platform. Stan opened his mouth, and was about to declare that Element City would be open to players of all levels, when he suddenly realized that, according to his count, the two sides were tied. Stan was confused. Had he counted wrong?

Then, Stan looked back at the wooden platform. There, standing directly in the center of the two platforms, was Cassandrix. Rather than following the others directly to the blue platform, she looked back and forth between them, debating which one to join.

Stan's heart skipped a beat. He knew that he had promised himself to be impartial, but he couldn't detach himself from all he had done against the Noctem Alliance and he knew in his heart that he wanted the players on the lapis lazuli platform to win. And while he had expected all his commanders to join that side, he had totally forgotten about Cassandrix. Looking at her now, in deep thought, Stan legitimately had no idea which side she was going to join.

For a long time, the two sides stood there, staring at the big-lipped, white-cloth-wearing player. As far as Stan knew, none of the other players knew how close the vote was, besides his friends, who were looking at Cassandrix with their breath caught in their throats.

Finally, after looking at the ground for several minutes, Cassandrix looked up and opened her eyes. She took a deep breath, looking once more toward the iron side and once more toward the lapis lazuli side before turning toward her friends and walking over to join them on the blue platform.

"The results are in," Stan announced loudly, struggling to keep a neutral face while his friends broke out into huge smiles. "By a margin of a single player, Element City will be open to all players, regardless of their level!"

An explosion of cheers erupted from the lapis lazuli side and the crowd below, so loud that it could probably be heard from Spawnpoint Hill. Stan's friends lunged forward and threw themselves onto Cassandrix in a group hug, which she accepted with a warm smile. Stan looked over at the lapis lazuli platform and, making sure that nobody on the other side could see, he allowed himself a small smile in celebration that after all his effort and hard work, Element City was finally a place of true equality and justice for all players.

This moment of happiness lasted only for a few seconds, however, before Stan turned around to face the platform of iron. Spyro's face matched that of every other player who stood behind him. They had a look of absolute and total shock, in contrast to the smug assurance that the Noctem soldiers had been wearing since Stan had announced that only the older players would be voting. Stan walked across the wooden platform until, yet again, he was face to face with Spyro.

"Don't worry," Stan said, as he stared into the hateful eyes of the Noctem leader with no fear. "I'm going to help you build a new city, and reclaim what you've lost. Also, you should know that you, and anybody on this platform, will always be welcome in Element City."

"As long as there are lower-level players in our city, we will *never* live amongst them," Spyro spat, trying to jam as much scorn and disgust as possible into the sentence.

"Just remember, Spyro," Stan said, struggling to keep his

voice steady as his hatred for the Noctem Alliance welled up yet again, "I'm giving you a second chance, and that's a privilege, not a right. I could very easily have killed all of you for what you've done."

Stan moved even closer to Spyro until their faces were inches apart and, for the first time, he allowed his face to mirror the loathing on Spyro's.

"Don't you even think," Stan hissed, "that for as long as I'm alive, Spyro, I'm going to forget what you did to the NPC village . . . or to the Mushroom Islands. I don't want to fight you anymore, and I'm still going to help you to construct a new city. But never forget, Spyro, I'm going to do what I have to do to keep all citizens of this server safe. If you, or any of your people, try to hurt or threaten new players, or anyone else, my generosity will end very quickly."

As Stan took a step back, Spyro continued to look at him. A wide variety of emotions seemed to be running across his face as he processed what Stan was telling him. Finally, he let out a beaten sigh, and he looked up at Stan.

"Fine," he said softly. "Where do you want us to go?"

"Go back to the bridge at the entrance of the city for now," Stan said. "Bring your people with you, and wait there for me. When I'm done here, I'll set you up with some temporary shelters that you can use until we can find a good plot of land out in the wilds for you to build your city on."

Spyro gave a begrudging nod and shouted back at those clustered on the iron platform to follow him. Immediately, the 114 members on the iron platform followed him across the wooden platform and down the stairs. Stan watched them walk by and caught several dirty looks. He continued to look on as the entire horde of black-clad players, with a few other colors interspersed, stepped down off the platform and followed their one remaining general down one of the side roads.

On and on the mass of players went, tramping through the city streets amid countless buildings that had large chunks torn away by TNT or burned away by fire charges. They continued through the streets, their black uniforms blending into the black billowing smoke rising from over half the buildings. Stan continued to watch, keeping his eyes on them until, finally, the last remaining members of the Noctem Alliance vanished from sight, en route to a new home.

Stan took a deep breath. Again, despite his pledge, he couldn't help but feel a sense of pure satisfaction as he watched the enemies he had been battling for so long vanish into the horizon.

Stan turned around and looked over the citizens who had chosen to remain in the city. Up on the wooden platform, Stan's friends were still reveling in their victory. Hugs were exchanged like gifts as everybody tried to adequately express their joy at the departure of the Noctem Alliance.

Stan saw Charlie and Leonidas hugging it out, while Ben, Bob, and Ivanhoe all danced in celebration (no matter how much he did it, Ivanhoe's moonwalking never got old). The Mechanist appeared to be graciously thanking Cassandrix, who in turn complimented the Mechanist on the speech he had given to rally the citizens for the battle. Commander Crunch, Sirus, and Oob seemed to be partaking in a strange celebration of tossing Stull through the air, playing keep-away from Mella, who was desperately trying to catch her son. From the looks of it, Stull was having the time of his life as he sailed through the air like a football.

Stan smiled. At some point, he would surely join in the celebrations. But now, as he looked out over the sea of thousands of players who were partaking in festivities much like those of his friends, Stan didn't feel like it quite yet.

Stan knew that he may have just made a huge mistake. Not only had he allowed the Noctem Alliance to live on, but he had also given them their own city. He may now have operating powers, but there was still only one of him. Not only that, but he had kept the two factions divided instead of trying to force them together. He knew that there was a very real possibility that, from this division, new hatred would spawn to poison Elementia in the future.

Regardless, though, Stan's fears were just those: fears.

He had done what he believed was right for Elementia. The road ahead of him would be long, hard, and taxing, as he sent his server down a new path. Whether it would be a good path or a bad path, Stan didn't know. But he knew that he would always be there to watch over the server, and as long as that remained true, it was bound to be, at the very least, a better path.

With that, Stan took a deep breath and let it out, allowing all his anxieties to float away like a balloon into the sky above Element City, which, for the first time in weeks, was blue. With one final look toward the place where Spyro and the rest of the Noctem soldiers had disappeared to, Stan turned around and walked across the wooden platform, ready for whatever the future would hold . . . for better or for worse.

A faint breeze swept across the sun-cooked dunes of the Ender Desert. Despite the long day of baking in the heat, the blocks of sand that made up this vast biome were cooling down now that the sun had sunk behind the western horizon. A rectangular sliver of moon sat in the black dome of sky, alongside the thousands of tiny shimmering dots that spoke of distant cosmos. The cacti stood proud and tall against the endless sea of tan blocks, and the mobs were just beginning to spawn, ambling aimlessly about without a care in the world.

The night was beautiful. It was as if the server itself was aware that a great conflict had been resolved, and it could finally be at peace.

As the moon rose higher into the night sky, a figure trekked through the dunes, traveling out of the jungle above which the sun had set. He began his walk through the desert, setting a course for the dead center of the desolate expanse of sand. A few mobs turned their heads toward him as he passed, and were about to attack before an odd feeling swept over them, compelling them to leave this particular player alone.

On and on the player walked over the dunes, weaving through the cacti. The slice of moon shone down on the player, revealing brown hair, a turquoise shirt, blue pants, and blue eyes. Stan2012's face bore a look of determination and solemnity.

As the night went on, the heavens spinning slowly above him, Stan continued to walk. He wasn't sure exactly where he was going, but he knew that he would have the right feeling when he got there. Stan was well aware that he could fly instead of walk, or even warp directly where he wanted to be. However, he opted against it. He was going to complete this journey, and he was going to do it on foot, without using his operating powers.

As he walked, Stan thought back on all that had happened since yesterday, when Stan had defeated Lord Tenebris and disbanded the two nations of Elementia. The celebrations in Element City had lasted all throughout the day, and would have gone all night had Stan not told them to get some rest for the next day's work. Stan, however, had not attended those celebrations. He had spent the evening at the outside wall of the city, providing temporary shelters and a supply of food and gear to Spyro, who had been unanimously elected to be the leader of the people who had gone to the iron side of the platform.

Following a good night's rest, Stan had bore witness to the birth of two new nations in Elementia. Spyro had organized his people into the Ironside Kingdom, while the Mechanist had been voted the temporary leader of the Lazuli Republic.

Stan found it amusing that both countries had named themselves after the sides of the execution platform that they had been arbitrarily assigned to, but it hardly mattered to Stan; he wouldn't be joining either of them.

Stan had helped the new Lazuli Republic begin repairs on their city, delegating supplies from the storehouses of Element City. At the same time, he had ensured that the Ironside Kingdom had all they needed to survive in their temporary shelters until Stan returned from his journey and could help them find a new place to build their city.

Although Stan knew there was much work to be done, he wasn't going to rush this journey. He had made a promise, and he was going to fulfill it.

Stan reached the top of a particularly tall sand dune and realized that it would provide him with an excellent vantage point from which to scout out what he was looking for. He peered through the darkness, and after scanning the horizon for a few seconds, he saw a strange color in the endless hills of sand. He looked closer and realized that it was an oasis, a pool of water surrounded by grass blocks. It was the perfect place for what Stan was going to be doing.

As Stan made his way over to the oasis, he remembered his favorite part of the past day. Right before he had left for the desert, a familiar voice had rung out in his head, clear as day. Stan had taken leave from Elementia for a while, returning to SalAcademy.

For the longest time, Stan told Sally everything that had happened in one long, rambling story, while Sally just sat there and took it all in. She hardly reacted to it in the slightest. All that changed was her smile, growing larger and larger the more that she heard. By the time that Stan was finished, he had one question.

"Sally, do you think it was a mistake—disbanding the countries, separating the people, and starting over?"

For a moment, Sally just stood there, thinking. Finally, she looked him in the eye and replied, "I'm not sure, noob."

Stan stared back. He didn't know what to say. Then, slowly, Sally's smile returned, but now it wasn't the huge smile it had been—now, it was Sally's trademark sarcastic smirk. At that moment, it struck Stan that it didn't matter if it was a mistake or not. What was done was done, and he would just have to go with it. The important thing was that, no matter what, his friends would be there by his side . . . including Sally.

Or, at least, most of them would.

Stan was now upon the oasis, and he forced himself to clear his mind. As much as he wanted to dwell on the sweet sensation of victory, and the thrill of sharing it with Sally and the rest of his friends, he knew that he couldn't. Not now. It wasn't a time for celebration.

The oasis was small. The pool was a square of three-by-three blocks, which had several odd blocks of water jutting off it. Stan reached into his inventory and pulled out a wooden shovel. He had crafted it with wood from the jungle he had just emerged from not long ago. If he was going to do this, he was going to do it manually.

Stan walked away from the oasis and immediately began to dig through the sand until his shovel struck a hard surface. Switching the shovel for a wooden pickaxe, Stan harvested the sandstone block, and a second one beneath it. He continued to dig around in the hole, expanding it as he harvested more and more sandstone blocks. Sand would periodically fall down to where he was attempting to dig, and he would clear it out with his shovel.

After several minutes of digging, Stan had enough sandstone. He placed a sand block down and then jumped on it, repeating the process until he had climbed his way out of the sinkhole. Stan made his way back over to the oasis and, sandstone in hand, he began construction.

First, he built a sandstone pillar, three blocks high, at each corner of the pool of water. This left a cross of water between the pillars. Stan then built a sandstone staircase on the grass, three blocks high, which extended over the water to be level with the tops of the pillars. He filled in the cross pattern on the top block of the pillar until he had a sandstone platform, elevated above the water by the four pillars.

Stan pulled a chest from his inventory and placed it in the center of the platform. He opened it, revealing several vacant compartments. Stan took a deep breath, reached into his inventory yet again, and pulled out a diamond sword, glowing with an enchantment of Knockback.

His eyes teared up as he remembered the time he had spent wielding this sword and, more poignantly, the time that he had spent with its owner.

Stan had never met anybody like DZ before, and he doubted that he ever would again. On the surface, he seemed to be an offbeat, somewhat crazy player who took everything with a grain of salt and never failed to make you smile with his sheer zany charm. While that was still true, upon getting to know DZ better, Stan realized that he was much more than that.

Beyond being a master swordsman, DZ's wild coating was merely a facade, behind which hid a deep, introspective person who was trying to find his place in the world. He was an incredible friend, steadfast and loyal, who had sacrificed his own life so that Stan could escape Mount Fungarus.

Stan had never gotten a chance to thank DZ. And now he never would.

As a tear rolled down Stan's face and he gave a sniffle, he placed the sword carefully into the chest. It lay still, immobile, yet still alive with the blue enchantment that shimmered and glowed like the stars in the heavens above.

Stan reached into his inventory one more time, his hands shaking now. As he struggled not to break down into sobs, he pulled out another diamond sword. This one was glowing even brighter than DZ's, bearing three different enchantments of Sharpness, Fire, and Knockback.

Gas-Powered Stick. Kat's sword.

Even after all this time, Stan could not pinpoint the reason that he had asked Kat to join him on his journey to the Adorian Village when he was learning to play Minecraft for the first time. It was probably a foolish thing to do. After all, she had just burst out of the woods and tried to kill him and Charlie. Yet, for whatever reason, Stan had asked that Kat join them, and she had agreed.

Slowly but surely, throughout the course of their quest to take down the Kingdom of Elementia, and the months succeeding it, the girl who had jumped out of the woods, demanding that he and Charlie give her all that they had, ceased to exist. She had transformed, slowly but surely, into one of Stan's best friends in Elementia. She had lost her reckless abandon and disregard for others, gaining wisdom and compassion while not abandoning her willingness to take risks. She always took care to tell people exactly what they needed to hear, even if they wouldn't like it. Perhaps above all else, she was fiercely loyal to those who deserved it, and was unwilling to take crap from anybody.

As Stan traveled across the server in the race to take down King Kev, and then navigated the republic through the minefield of the Noctem Alliance, and then struggled to take back their server from Lord Tenebris's forces, he had always been amazed to have such amazing friends. Charlie and Kat were the two best companions that he could have ever hoped to have, and Stan had legitimately felt like the three of them could accomplish anything that they wanted to together.

The fact that one of them was now gone forever tore Stan's heart to shreds.

Stan couldn't stop the shaking, nor the sobs escaping his mouth, nor the tears now rolling down his face in waterfalls. All he could do was place Kat's enchanted sword into the chest next to DZ's, propped up against the corner with dignity. Stan took a deep breath and, before he could look at the weapons of his two deceased friends one more time, he closed the chest with a creak and a bang.

Even with the weapons no longer in front of him, the grief of it all spiraled around him, threatening to consume him as if it were all hitting him again for the first time. DZ . . . and Kat . . . two of his closest friends . . . dead . . . and gone forever . . .

Stan took a deep breath and looked up into the sky. If he looked carefully through the blurry lens of his teary eyes, he could see the cosmos moving above him. This server, Elementia . . . it was such a beautiful place. This game, Minecraft, held so much wonder, so much potential, and so much freedom—and, less than two days ago, it was all on the brink of extinction.

And yet, it would survive. And the owners of the two blades now sitting safely in the chest before him were the reason for it.

Kat and DZ had given their lives to the revolution against King Kev. Images of the dozens of things that his friends had done flashed through Stan's head.

Kat leaping out of the lava sea, surrounded by a red aura, stabbing Becca through the back and flinging her into the molten pool. DZ leaping into a pit of Zombies and taking them all out in seconds with two slices of his sword. Kat in The End, fighting off dozens of Endermen all at once. DZ thrusting his sword into the neck of the Ender Dragon, causing it to burst into radiant light. Dozens of other images rolled through Stan's head.

Stan's sobs ceased, but the tears continued to roll. The more he thought about the fact that he would never see either of his friends again, the more it felt as if some sort of dark void had opened within him that threatened to steal his happiness and never return it. And yet, as Stan realized what they had died for, and that the game of Minecraft had been saved because of them, he knew that he would be able to go on with his life. It would be very difficult, and the pain would never go away fully . . . but he would live.

Stan pulled the blocks of sandstone from his inventory and surrounded the chest with a ring of them. He then proceeded to cover the ring with a three-by-three square, hiding the chest from view. Never would anybody guess that two enchanted diamond swords were hidden inside. They would remain there forever. If someone were to climb the stairs to the top of the monument, they would find two signs that Stan had placed on top, side by side. They read:

KITKAT783 "KAT"
AND
DIEZOMBIE97 "DZ"

HEROES OF
ELEMENTIA
R.I.P.

Stan descended the sandstone stairs and surveyed the monument. It expanded upward, out of the oasis, and looked striking against the flat expanse of the desert and the short cacti within it. Any players who saw it would climb the sandstone steps and learn the names of these two marvelous players who had sacrificed everything to save the server they loved.

Stan took a deep breath and, tears still flowing from his eyes, turned his back on the shrine and began to walk out into the desert. He extracted a diamond axe from his inventory and clutched it in his hand. Stan knew that the mobs would notice him, and he would have to fight them off. It was what he wanted. Months ago, DZ had asked him on his deathbed to wander the desert for a week after Stan won the war, remembering him and detaching himself from worldly problems.

Stan would do exactly what his friend had asked of him. His stomach rumbled, and it occurred to him that he would also have to hunt his own food while he was out here. It was as if he were a new player, alone and vulnerable in the world for the first time. With a slight chuckle at the thought, Stan wiped the tears from his eyes and set off to hunt.

As he watched Stan leave the shrine and make his way out into the desert to begin his vision quest, the Black Hood smiled as his cape billowed slightly in the wind. The people of Elementia were in good hands. The Black Hood knew that, whatever happened between the players of the server, Stan would always be there to keep them in balanced order.

The Black Hood chuckled ironically at the thought. Here he was, glad that Stan would be able to use his great powers to protect Elementia . . . when he himself could just as easily do the same thing. And yet, the Black Hood knew that this was a foolish thing to think. By speaking to Stan, and helping him attain his own operating powers, the Black Hood had nailed his own coffin firmly shut. In fact, he was absolutely astounded that he had participated in the battle itself and was still alive at all.

The Black Hood knew that he was dying, however. From the moment he had spoken to Stan, he had felt his energy dimming. When Stan had struck him with his sword, the Black Hood had been totally drained of all power, just barely hanging on to enough consciousness to tell Stan that Lord Tenebris had been defeated for good. Since then, the Black Hood had been biding his energy, and not until now had he managed to take physical form.

The Black Hood heard a roll of thunder crash over the desert. He glanced off and saw sheets of rain bombarding the distant jungle. To any players in the vicinity, including Stan, it would appear to be just another thunderstorm. But the Black Hood knew better. He felt a shift in the energy of the server there, a presence that he hadn't felt in months, since the day that he had first entered Elementia and attempted to use his powers.

The Voice in the Sky had returned.

The Black Hood stood perfectly still on the crest of the hill, his eyes closed. He had helped Stan to defeat Lord Tenebris and save Elementia, along with all other Minecraft servers. He had brought Rex into the woods, removed his collar, and returned him to the family of wolves from whom he had been separated months before. And now, as a last order of business, the Black Hood had seen Stan, building and hunting in a way that he still, to this day, found most fascinating. Now that he had seen it for one last time, all was done. There was nothing left for the Black Hood to do in Elementia . . . or in Minecraft.

YOU HAVE INTERFERED WITH THE AFFAIRS OF PLAYERS FOR THE LAST TIME, the Voice rang out in the Black Hood's mind as another thunderclap sounded overhead. **NOW, AS PUNISHMENT FOR YOUR TAMPERING, YOU SHALL DIE.**

"I accept my punishment," the Black Hood replied aloud.

Another roll of thunder, and the Black Hood felt himself begin to fade. His very existence started to thin out, like threads being pulled one by one from a tapestry.

I may be leaving this world, the Black Hood thought peacefully to himself, as his ability to think began to fade as well, *but at least Minecraft, a game of such wonder and promise that had never been seen in the world before, lives* on . . . *and will live on forever, as long there are others who are willing to build.*

And with that final thought, the Black Hood ceased to exist, never to return to Minecraft again.

THE END

FROM THE AUTHOR

Thank you for reading *Herobrine's Message*. I hope you enjoyed it. If you did enjoy it, please tell your friends and write an online review so that others can enjoy it too.

—SFW

CONNECT WITH SEAN

🌐 : www.sfaywolfe.com

📘 : www.facebook.com/elementiachronicles

🐦 : @sfaywolfe, #ElementiaChronicles

📷 : SeanFayWolfe

Links to buy Sean's paperback and ebooks are on his webpage.
Links to Sean's online games can also be found on his webpage.
Go to www.goodreads.com to rate and/or review this novel.

ACKNOWLEDGMENTS

As the Elementia Chronicles trilogy draws to a close, I find it more bittersweet than anything else. Over the course of writing the series, I truly feel as if Stan, Kat, Charlie, and their friends have become a part of who I am, and it saddens me to see them go. Writing the Elementia Chronicles has been the greatest experience of my life, and there are several people who have helped me to share my story with the world.

I would like to thank the South Kingstown High School Drama Club of 2014–15. It truly was thanks to you guys that high school was not just tolerable, but amazing.

I would like to thank Lindsey Karl, Matt Schweitzer, and Julie Eckstein, my team of promoters at HarperCollins who helped me to get the Elementia Chronicles out into the world.

I would like to thank Pam Bobowicz, my editor, for helping me transform my rough drafts into full-fledged novels.

I would like to thank my brother Eric, who always knows what to say to keep me humble.

I would like to thank my brother Casey, the first megafan of the Elementia Chronicles and the one who convinced me to share my story.

I would like to thank Rick Richter, my agent from Zachary Shuster Harmsworth, for helping me join HarperCollins and for always offering up his expertise and wisdom.

I would like to thank my grandmother, who is not only probably the biggest fan of the Elementia Chronicles, but has also supported me in everything that I do, from writing to beyond.

I would like to thank my dad for being a one-man tech-support team and helping the Elementia Chronicles break into the digital world.

I would like to thank my mom for devoting countless hours to promoting and beta-reading the Elementia Chronicles, and for doing everything in her power and more to help me find success with my work.

And last but not least, I would like to thank all my fans, from those who read *Quest for Justice* when it was first self-published to everybody else. It's your praise, criticism, and support that inspires me to share my stories, and the Elementia Chronicles would not be where it is today without you.